FALLEN

T0006001

ALSO BY L.J. SHEN

Sinners of Saint Series

Vicious
Defy
Ruckus
Scandalous
Bane

All Saints High Series

Pretty Reckless
Broken Knight
Angry God

Boston Belles Series

The Hunter
The Villain
The Monster
The Rake

Cruel Castaways Series

Ruthless Rival

Stand-Alones

Tyed
Sparrow
Blood to Dust
Midnight Blue
Dirty Headlines
The Kiss Thief
In the Unlikely Event
Playing with Fire
The Devil Wears Black
Bad Cruz
Beautiful Graves
Thorne Princess

FALLEN

Foe

L.J. SHEN

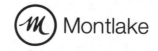
Montlake

This is a work of fiction. Names, characters, organizations, places, events, and incidents are either products of the author's imagination or are used fictitiously. Otherwise, any resemblance to actual persons, living or dead, is purely coincidental.

Text copyright © 2023 by L.J. Shen
All rights reserved.

No part of this book may be reproduced, or stored in a retrieval system, or transmitted in any form or by any means, electronic, mechanical, photocopying, recording, or otherwise, without express written permission of the publisher.

Published by Montlake, Seattle

www.apub.com

Amazon, the Amazon logo, and Montlake are trademarks of Amazon.com, Inc., or its affiliates.

ISBN-13: 9781542036351 (paperback)
ISBN-13: 9781542036344 (digital)

Cover design by Caroline Teagle Johnson
Cover image: © Mark Fearon / ArcAngel; © MirageC / Getty;
© Christophe Lehenaff / Getty; © Brownie Harris / Getty;
© Mark Poprocki / Shutterstock

Printed in the United States of America

To P and A.
I told you we were going to run out of people to
dedicate our books to.
We need to start seeing other people.

I understand that in our work, doesn't matter whether it's acting or writing, what's important isn't fame or glamour, none of the things I used to dream about. It's the ability to endure.
—Anton Chekhov, *The Seagull*

PART ONE

CHAPTER ONE

ARSÈNE

The roofs are different in Portofino.

Flatter, wider, older.

The pastel-colored buildings sprout from the ground, so tightly cramped together you couldn't slide a toothpick between them if you tried. The yachts in the harbor are docked neatly and equally spaced from each other. The Mediterranean Sea glitters under the last persistent sunrays as dusk begins to fall.

I lounge on the balcony of my hotel suite overlooking the Italian Riviera, watching a ladybug spinning backward on its axis, like Venus, on the marble banister.

I flip the ladybug, helping it find its footing, then take a sip of my white wine. Tonight's menu is perched in my lap. The wild boar ragù appears to be the most expensive option, which means I'm bound to order it, just to watch the idiots from accounting sweating into their risotto plates when they realize this conference is going to cost them much more than they planned to spend.

Corporate events are where good ideas go to die. It is a well-known fact any trade secret worth whispering will not be aired during a formal company event. Valuable market information, like a weapon, is traded in the back alleys of the industry.

It isn't my workplace that brought us here. In fact, I have no workplace to speak of. I am a lone wolf. A quantitative trading consultant paid by the hour by hedge fund companies to help them sort through the conglomerate of potential investments. What to invest in, how much, and how to keep up with the annualized returns their clients expect of them. My friends often say I'm like Chandler from *Friends*. That no one has any idea what I actually do. But my job is pretty straightforward—I help rich people get even richer.

"Just trying on this new dress," a feminine voice purrs from behind the balcony door. "Shouldn't be more than ten minutes. Don't drink too much. You're barely civilized for those tux-wearing cookie cutters while sober."

After frisbeeing the menu to a nearby table, I pick up the book next to me and flip to the next page. *Brief Answers to the Big Questions*, by Hawking.

Since we are located on the top floor of the resort, I have a direct view to virtually all the other south-facing balconies overlooking the harbor.

This is how I notice them at first.

A couple, two terraces down from us.

They are the only ones out, soaking in the last rays of the setting sun. Their blond heads bob together. His hair is corn yellow. Hers is titian, a mixture of gold and red, like scorched desert sand.

He is wearing a sharp suit. She, a burgundy dress. Something simple, cheap looking, almost tarty. A call girl? Nah. Wall Street hedge fund tycoons invest in expensive-looking dates. The type with a built-in designer wardrobe, red-soled heels, and private school manners. Pretty Women only exist in fairy tales and Julia Roberts movies. Not a soul in Manhattan values charm, honesty, and quirkiness in women.

No. This is a country bumpkin. Perhaps an ambitious local who found her way into his bed in hopes of earning a large tip.

The couple is sharing a peach and sticky, juicy kisses. The nectar seeps down their lips as he feeds her the fruit. She grins as she nibbles on the fruit's flesh, her gaze holding his. He kisses her hungrily, and she bites on his lower lip—hard—before his mouth rips from hers to murmur something into her ear.

The girl throws her head back and laughs, exposing the pale, long column of her neck. I shift in my seat, my book covering my ever-growing erection. I'm not sure what turns me on more. The peach, the woman, or the fact that I'm officially a voyeur. Likely, all three.

The man dips his head and licks a long trail of the nectar, not letting a good opportunity go to waste. They are leaning against the banister, his body pressed against hers.

Something passes between them. Something that makes the hairs on my neck prickle. Whatever these two are enjoying is something I don't currently have.

I am not a man accustomed to unattainable things.

"Have you tried the white yet?" The glass door whines open. I snap my gaze toward the person the voice belongs to.

"Too much anise and truffle, right?" My date sneers and pulls a pout. She is still in her bathrobe. How many hours does one need to put on a damn dress?

I take a gulp of the wine. "Tastes fine to me. We're going to run late."

"And you care about tardiness since . . . ?" She arches a brow.

"I don't. But I am hungry," I supply flatly.

"Play your cards right, and I might be your dessert." She smiles devilishly, peppering the gesture with a wink.

I swirl the wine in the pristine glass. "No dessert, no date. This is quid pro quo, and I'm not known for my philanthropic notions."

She rolls her eyes. "Can you at least *pretend* to be bearable?"

"Can you pretend to like me?" I shoot back.

She gasps. "*Of course* I like you. Why else would I be with you?"

"I could think of thirty-three million reasons." That is my net worth *before* my impending inheritance.

"Christ, you're crude. My mother was right about you." She slams the glass door in my face.

I place the book on the table, redirecting my attention to the couple on the balcony. They're still at it, making out without a care in the world. He wraps her hair around his fist, tugging, lifting her face, and kisses her hard. Their tongues swirl together erotically. She cups his cheeks and grins, grazing her top teeth over his bottom lip. My cock strains again. She is completely his, I can tell, and that blind conviction she belongs to him, how comfortable she is belonging to another human, makes me want to screw her brains out just to prove a point.

No one is yours, and you belong to no one. We're all just fallen foes trying to survive this universe.

He drags his mouth down her neck, cupping her breasts, pushing the pebbled thing toward his lips. The edge of her pink nipple pokes from her dress. When his mouth reaches the valley between her tits, she remembers herself.

She pushes him away, panting. Maybe she knows they have an audience. If she's waiting for me to be embarrassed, she better get comfortable, because that's not about to happen. They're the ones dry humping in plain sight. I'm just a man enjoying his pretentious glass of wine on a lazy summer day.

The glass door opens again, and Gracelynn Langston reemerges, this time in a black, sequined chiffon dress. An Akris piece I bought her the day after she crawled back into my bed for the thousandth time this decade.

This is Gracelynn's—or as I call her, Grace's—pattern. Fuck me. Dump me. Crawl back to me. It always surprises her to find herself on my threshold, looking pensive, and sometimes drunk, and *always* humiliated.

It never surprises me, though.

I'd come to accept what we are. A dysfunctional, screwed-up couple like our parents were. Minus the physical assault, maybe.

Over the years, I perfected the art of managing my stepsister. Using her explosive nature to my own advantage.

I am now able to detect the precise moment in which Grace is going to leave me. It's always when our relationship starts to feel real and serious. When the salacious shine of fucking your stepbrother wears off, and she is left with the aftermath. With a man she despises. An aloof, taciturn monster. A social pariah, ousted from polite Wall Street society with a two-year supervisory ban for insider trading charges.

And so, like a Swiss clock, the minute she withdraws, I become distant, unavailable; I strategically notice women on the street. The kind of women she doesn't approve of. The ones who wear too much makeup and their secondhand designer bags with all the pride of a hotel heiress.

It works like a charm. Grace always comes back. She cannot stand me. But she cannot stand it even more when I have another woman draped over my arm.

"Zip me up," she demands now, swaying her hips as she saunters to me. She turns around, giving me her back. Each vertebra in her spine is pronounced. She's managed to keep her ballerina body long after she gave up the dream.

I roll the zipper up her back. "How many people will be gracing us with their mediocrity tonight?"

"Too many, as per usual." She speaks with bobby pins in her mouth as she tucks the last of her locks into an updo. "At least they've only invited the top twenty employees and their plus-ones. None of the airheaded PAs, thank God."

Grace does not introduce me as her boyfriend. Rather, as her step-brother, even though our parents have been divorced since we both went to college.

But she introduces me all the same, for I am well known in the stock business. Feared, respected, but rarely liked. She knows my leverage, my pull. I may be the black sheep of the hedge fund world, but I still know how to make money, and people on Wall Street *really* like people who know how to do that. It is their favorite party trick.

My fingers linger when I see the scar on her upper back. The one that reminds me what happened to her. What happened to *me* twenty-four years ago. I run my finger pad over it. Her flesh prickles into goose bumps, and she pulls away like I hit her.

"Is it very visible?" She fusses over a perfectly secured bracelet, clearing her throat.

"No," I lie, tugging the zipper up. I halt. Something comes over me. The need to brush my lips against her scar. Comfort her. I resist the instinct. Instead, I say, "There you go, Venus."

"Venus?"

"The hottest planet on the solar system." I wink, channeling my inner Christian Miller, my friend who somehow managed to perfect the art of enjoying his relationship, as opposed to making it a screwed-up grown-up game like I did.

I can almost *hear* Grace scrunching her nose in disdain. "Thank *Gawd* you're a closeted geek. Could you imagine if other people found out about your astronomy quirk?" She huffs, pushing farther away from me. "Now all I need is a pair of earrings. What do you think, the rose gold diamond studs or the aquamarines?"

The first pair, I bought her for her twenty-eighth birthday, deliberately one-upping her then-boyfriend's gift. She dumped him the same night, horrified with the prospect of ending up with a middle-class Realtor who could only afford to buy her last season's Louboutins. She'd later on waited in my bed wearing nothing but said earrings. The latter pair was a present from me after I ended a three-month affair with Lucinda—yes, her childhood nemesis—when Grace took too long to get back to me after one of our many breakups.

Poor, poor Lucinda. She was in for an unpleasant surprise when she got back from her tour in Paris as a prima ballerina to find Grace scorching up my bed.

My gifts are always laced with intention, purpose, and venom. They're a dirty, violent kiss. A mixture of passion and pain.

"Aquamarines," I drawl.

She leans down, placing a cool kiss on my lips. I want her to move along so I can see if the couple two floors down is now fucking in plain sight. Their brand of kink is better than ours. I glance at their balcony. Grace's gaze follows mine.

Her mouth stretches in a malicious smile. "I see you've met my supervisor. Kind of, anyway."

"You know this tool bag?" I take a sip of my wine.

"Paul Ashcroft? He's Silver Arrow Capital's new COO. I'm sure I've mentioned him."

The company where Grace works as an analyst.

Paul and his companion have their backs to us. They seem to be talking now and keeping their hands to themselves.

"I'm sure you haven't. Not that he seems like a memorable character." I jerk my chin to the woman in red. "He's getting pretty frisky with the help."

Grace lets out a delighted laugh. Nothing brings her more joy than watching another woman being torn apart. "She's a simple creature, isn't she? Believe it or not, he put a ring on it. A pricey one too."

I tsk. "He's a hedge fund manager. Risky bets are where he thrives."

"She's a Juilliard graduate from the Deep South. I'm giving it six months," Grace continues, squinting to get a better look at them.

"Generous of you." I chuckle.

I know men like Paul. Manhattan sharks who glorify soft-spoken southern belles, only to find out that opposites may attract, but they don't make a decent match. It always ends in divorce, a mutual smear campaign, and—if the woman works quickly enough—a fat child support check every month.

"You know me. Kindness is my middle name. I'll go put my earrings on. What, no tie for you?" Grace pouts, looking down at me. I'm wearing a black cashmere sweater and plaid slacks.

"The last thing I want is to make a good impression." I go back to my book.

"You're a rebel without a cause."

"On the contrary." I flip a page. "I have a cause—I want everyone to leave me the fuck alone. So far, it's been going great."

She shakes her head. "You're so lucky to have me."

She disappears into our room, taking her giant attitude and matching ego with her.

I throw one last look at the couple. Paul isn't on the balcony anymore.

But his wife is, and she is staring right back at me.

Intently. With an accusing ferocity. Like she expects me to do something.

Has she noticed me staring?

Confused, I look behind me to make sure it is me she is looking at. No one else is in sight. Her eyes, big and blue and unrelenting, bore harder into mine.

Is this a hostage situation? Unlikely. She looked mighty happy to make out with her husband just a few minutes ago. Is she trying to shame me for watching them? Good luck with that. My conscience was last seen at age ten, leaving a hospital room with a feral growl, punching holes in the walls on its departure.

I meet her gaze head-on, unsure what's happening, but always happy to take part in a hostile confrontation. I arch an eyebrow.

She blinks first. I chuckle softly, shaking my head, about to get back to my book. She wipes her cheek quickly. Wait a minute . . . she is crying.

Crying. On a luxurious vacation in the Italian Riviera. Such fickle creatures, women. Always impossible to please. Poor Paul.

We are locked in that weird stare again. She looks possessed. I should get up and leave. But she looks so deliciously vulnerable, so misplaced, a part of me wants to see what she'll do next.

And since when do I give two shits about what people do?

Coolly, I stand up, grab my hardcover, finish the last of my wine, pivot on my heel, and walk away.

Mrs. Ashcroft might have a problem on her hands.

But it isn't mine to fix.

CHAPTER TWO

ARSÈNE

An hour later, Grace is fluttering between her colleagues on the white-and-gray marbled floor, holding a flute of champagne. She laughs whenever appropriate, frowns in empathy when needed, and diligently introduces me as her stepbrother and finance wiz extraordinaire.

I play along. My end goal has always been making Grace mine for all to see—my father, her mother, my friends. The woman dug her way under my skin. She is permanently inked on each of my bones, and I won't stop until I parade her as my prized possession.

In some ways, I enjoy the way she downplays our relationship. See, the more Grace highlights the fact that we are stepsiblings, the bitterer the pill she'll later have to swallow when we go public.

In my darkest, rawest fantasies, Gracelynn Langston stutters her way into an explanation of how she ended up marrying the person she introduced as her brother for years.

She'll be wearing my ring. Come hell or high water.

The restaurant is bustling with people. Grace and I spend time talking to Chip Breslin, the CEO of the company. He whines about spending the last month slashing high-momentum trades due to tighter Fed policies, glancing in my direction to see if I weigh in on that. I don't hand out free advice. Especially now, when my own trading portfolio is at a standstill due to my new two-year ban.

"Ah, come on, Corbin, throw us a bone or two." Chip chuckles, finally cutting to the chase. "How do you see the next quarter playing out? My pal Jim at Woodstock Trading said you mentioned short-only."

"I'm a professional pessimist." I glance around the room, looking for a distraction. "Regardless, I'm on an imposed hiatus, and not about to break my ban for a chitchat."

"Oh, I wouldn't dream!" He turns red, laughing awkwardly.

"You just asked me flat out, in reality," I respond blandly.

Breslin smiles and says he has to go fetch his wife from the bar. "You know how it is." He winks and elbows me as he makes his exit.

I do not, in fact, know. Grace possesses impeccable self-control in all areas of her life, other than her relationship with me. She is unemotional, calculating, and ruthlessly selfish, like me.

"See, this is exactly why people dislike you." Grace clinks her fingernails—square, polished, nude colored—over her glass. "He tried talking shop with you, and you completely snubbed him."

"There's a handful of people I do not charge for my presence, and I'm currently looking at thirty-three point three percent of them." My gaze dips to her cleavage. I think I'm going to fuck her tits tonight. Grace doesn't like it when I come inside her, even with a condom, but she seems to be down with pretty much anything else my heart (and cock) desires.

"Are you trying to charm my panties off?" She smirks.

"I was hoping you weren't wearing any to begin with."

The room is filling up to a point it's getting too busy and too sweaty, but our spot next to the bar remains empty.

"Everyone's blocking the entryway. What's all this commotion about?" Grace's attention drifts to the entrance.

I turn to see what she is looking at. Paul and his hayseed just walked into the room. Everyone hurries toward them. Including Chip and his wife, the latter zigzagging her way unsteadily, clinging to her husband's arm. The majority of the attention is given to Paul's pretty blonde wife, the party's main source of entertainment. Like an Andy Warhol painting, she is vivid and colorful, bursting at the seams in a room full of people wearing blacks, grays, and nudes. A curious little thing. Her clothes too loud, her smile too big, her eyes wildly exploring every inch of the space she just walked into. I find her adorably infantile.

"Is she handing out free blow jobs over there?" I ask conversationally, knowing my closeted girlfriend is not fond of being ignored, especially for another woman.

"Wouldn't put it past her." Grace bites on her inner cheek, her nostrils flaring. "Winnie's everyone's little lapdog. She sends Paul to work with cowboy cookies—the Laura Bush recipe—and volunteers for kids' charities, and—"

"Her name is Winnie?" I frown down at her.

"*Winnifred.*" She rolls her eyes. "Quaint, right?"

"He married a caricature." I humor her.

The girl is a walking, talking teddy bear. *And* she went to Juilliard, Grace's school of choice back when she still thought she had a chance as a ballerina. I'm surprised she doesn't show more open hostility toward her. Perhaps my stepsister has finally learned how to handle competition.

"I guess we should go say hi." Grace appears like she'd rather vomit in her own mouth than do so.

I don't particularly want to kiss the ring of the Mary Sue who cried on her balcony and gave me the stink eye, but I also don't want Grace to whine about me not being a team player.

We approach the Ashcrofts as much as we can. Women are flocking around Winnifred, demanding her cookie recipe, while Paul possessively wraps his arm around her. Grace shoulders her way into their sphere and air-kisses Paul's cheeks.

"Hello there. How nice to see you two." She moves on to kiss Winnie's cheeks, squeezing her arms. "Why, you look stunning, Winnifred!"

She does not think this woman looks stunning, with her tacky high street dress and the striped heels she probably got on sale at Walmart.

"So do you, Grace." Winnie's smile is genuine and sincere. "You look like you could be in a movie."

Maleficent, maybe.

"This is my stepbrother, Arsène Corbin. We do a lot of business together, so we've grown quite close in recent years." Grace motions to me like I'm an auction piece in a fundraising ceremony. I smirk. The overexplaining always gives her away. If she simply introduced me as her stepbrother, maybe half Manhattan wouldn't be whispering behind her back about my fucking her on the reg.

I reach to shake Paul's hand. He beams. "Your reputation precedes you, Mr. Corbin. How's life outside of the trading world?"

"As unfulfilling as life inside it." I withdraw my dry, rough palm from his sweaty one. "I keep busy, though, investing in more tangible assets."

"Yes. I heard. You purchased a delivery and freight company, didn't you?" Paul strokes his chin. "Very smart, in an era where online shopping is booming."

He looks like the human answer to oatmeal. Privileged, bland, and boring. I've chewed through enough men like Paul in my life to know his aftertaste. He is the kind of guy to cheat on his wife with his secretary as soon as she hits her midthirties. The sort of man who keeps tabs on men like me to see what we're doing, where we're investing, in order to get ideas for himself.

"This is my wife, Winnie." Paul kisses the petite woman's shoulder. She turns her full attention to me, and finally, I can see it. The reason Paul decided she was worth more than a night between the sheets. She is, objectively speaking, radiant. Her skin is rich and glowing, her eyes bright and curious, her smile infectious and reassuring. She is the kind of woman people say lights up the room. Grace, by contrast, is the kind of woman who makes the temperature drop to arctic level anywhere she enters. My heart included.

Fortunately, Winnifred's brand of girl next door doesn't appeal to me.

"Hello!" Winnie flings her arms around me in an inappropriate half hug. Either she doesn't know how to hold a grudge or she doesn't recognize me from the balcony.

I step away from her embrace immediately. Hopefully she is not carrying any cattle diseases.

Paul snickers, obviously finding his wife's lack of formality adorable. "Where're your seats, Langston-Corbins?"

"Says here fifteen and sixteen." Grace holds up our invitation cards.

"We're nineteen and twenty, so I guess you'll have to tolerate us a little longer," Paul says brightly.

Whoopee-fucking-yay.

As the evening develops, so does my suspicion that Winnifred is, in fact, knocked up. She doesn't touch a drop of alcohol, opting for sparkling water all night. She doesn't enjoy the cold meats platter and stays away from those puffing on vapes and cigars. Her frequent trips to the restroom also make me wonder if there's someone cozily napping directly on her bladder.

Grace is busy sticking her tongue in the right people's buttholes. Figuratively speaking, fortunately. She is discussing work with Chip, Paul, and a guy named Pablo, who is a head trader. The three men try to lure me into talking shop, but I dodge politely. As all exotic creatures, I do not particularly want to be poked through the bars of a cage with questions about my insider trading accusations. And I've no doubt everyone here would like to hear about what I did to only get slapped on the wrist.

"Not the bragging type, ah, Corbin?" Paul nods understandably after yet another laconic answer from me about my preferred retail stocks. "Winnie's the same. She doesn't like to speak about her job at *all.*"

"That's because I don't currently have one." Winnie takes a sip of her sparkling water, her cheeks tinting pink.

I turn to face her. A flicker of interest ignites inside me. She does more than play housewife? That's a refresher.

"What do you do, Winnifred?"

"Graduated from Juilliard this year. Now I'm just . . . between auditions, I guess?" She lets out an embarrassed laugh, her southern drawl almost comic. "Can't say I'm busier than a moth in a mitten. It's hard, making it in the Big Apple. What doesn't kill you makes you stronger, right?"

"Or weakens you." I shrug. "Depends on the 'what' factor, really."

She stares at me wide eyed, the simple little thing. "You do have a point there."

"Do you think you have what it takes to succeed in New York?" I ask.

"Would I be there otherwise?" And there's that smile again. The one crammed with all the hope and goodness in the world.

"People come to New York for many reasons. Most of them aren't kosher. How'd you meet Paul?"

With each question, it feels like I'm undressing her. Publicly. Deliberately. And like all naked people in public settings, she is starting to squirm, shifting in her chair now.

"Well." She clears her throat. "I—"

"Waited on his table at Delmonico's?" I take a wild guess. Could be Le Bernardin too. She is a solid eight. Maybe even a nine, in the right dress.

"Actually, I was a fairy at his niece's fourth birthday party." She purses her lips into a thin line, frowning.

"A *what?*" I would splutter my wine if she was worth it. "My apologies, I didn't catch that."

I did, but this is too good not to be repeated. Timeless American entertainment. The textbook version of Poor Girl Meets Moron Rich Guy.

Paul is deep in conversation with Pablo and Grace, oblivious to the fact I'm grilling his wife like she's a prime steak.

Winnifred straightens her spine and looks me in the eye in an attempt to show she isn't scared of me. "I was a fairy character at his niece's birthday party. I glitter-painted his face. He couldn't stop laughing, and was totally on board, even when I drew Tinkerbell on his cheek. I realized he'd make good father material. So I gave him my number."

I bet the fact he probably showed up to that party in a vintage car that's worth more than her family's home didn't hurt his chances either.

"No one else stood a chance after that." Paul, withdrawing himself from Pablo and Grace's conversation, nuzzles his nose into the crook of her neck, giving it an open-mouthed kiss. "She's mine for life now, aren't you, baby doll?"

I bet he thinks this sounded romantic and not like a commercial for a mail-order bride.

"Do I detect a twang, Winnifred?" I ask innocently.

Grace shoots me a stop-it-this-minute look. I've always had the habit of playing with my food; only now, the person I'm chewing is her boss's brain-dead wife.

"I'm from Tennessee." Winnie swallows visibly again. "Just outside Nashville. A town called Mulberry Creek."

"Home of the best apple pie in all fifty states?" I smirk into my wineglass.

"Actually, we're more known for our biscuits. Oh! And inbred tendencies, of course." She gives me a saccharine smile.

So she *does* fight back. Didn't see this one coming.

"C'mon, baby doll. No need to be sarcastic." Paul flicks her chin.

If he calls her baby doll one more time, I am going to break my wineglass and stab his neck with a shard.

"What made you move to New York?" Don't ask me why I keep picking on this woman, because I have no fucking clue. Boredom? Sociopathic tendencies? Your guess is as good as mine.

She looks me dead in the eye and says, "Why, all the big, blinding lights, of course. *Sex and the City* too. I thought, *gee-oh-my*, living there must be just like in them glitzy films. Oh, and don't forget that Alicia Keys song. Huge factor. *Huge.*"

Grace stomps on my foot under the table, hard enough to break a bone. Her knee smashes against the surface, making utensils dance in place. Paul jumps back a little, surprised. Too late. I'm too far gone to care. Winnifred Ashcroft is the only thing remotely entertaining about this event, and feasting on her self-esteem is tastier than eating any other dish served here tonight.

"Winnie's a bit sensitive about being an out-of-towner." Paul pats his wife's head like she's an adorable Chihuahua.

"It *is* like *Sex and the City*, though, isn't it?" I ask her pleasantly, as Grace's heel digs deeper into my loafer in warning, smashing my toes to dust. "You found your Mr. Big."

"Paul's more of a Mr. Medium, if the glimpse in the urinal was any indication," Chip jokes. Everyone laughs. Everyone but Winnie, who stares at me, wondering what she did to deserve this.

You asked me to care. Back on the balcony. Now you'll see just how careless I am with people's feelings.

"Okay, Arsène, time to change the topic." Grace smiles apologetically, yanking at my sleeve. "People are here to have fun, not get interrogated."

I know Grace is not doing this out of the goodness of her heart. She is a savvy woman who wants to get ahead. Right now I'm pissing off her boss and his *baby doll*.

"Actually, I believe it's my turn to ask the questions." Winnie tips her chin up.

I sit back, watching her with open pleasure. She's like that little ladybug spinning on its axis. Adorably desperate. Too bad I'm dead set on Grace, or I'd sample her for a few months. Paul wouldn't even be an obstacle in my way. These type of women go for the highest bidder, and I have the deeper pocket.

"Fire away," I say.

"What do you do?" she asks.

"Jack-of-all-trades."

"Doing what?"

Shrugging, I drawl, "Anything that makes money."

"I'm sure you can be more specific than that. This could mean weapons dealer." She folds her arms over her chest.

Fine. Let's play.

"Equities, corporations, currencies, commodities. Though I'm on a recent ban for insider trading. Two years."

All eyes shift to us. I've yet to address the subject in this room, having inherited from my father the unsavory trait of never giving people what they want.

"Why?" she demands.

"Market manipulation charges." Before she asks what that means, I explain, "They say I misrepresented material to investors, among other misconducts."

"Did you do it?" Winnifred holds my gaze, looking childlike in her innocence.

With the whole room watching, I swipe my tongue over my bottom lip, smirking. "I have one issue, Winnifred."

"Just the one?" She blinks innocently before relenting. "And what's your issue?"

"I never play to lose."

Her eyes, as pretty as bluebonnets, are still on mine. An uncharitable thought crosses my mind. She'd probably look ten times better in Grace's aquamarine earrings. Seeing her in nothing *but* those earrings would bring me a lot of joy. Oh well. Maybe Grace will misbehave and dump me soon, and I'll take up a quick affair with this little thing to remind my stepsister that I'm still a man with needs.

"And people here accept you?" Winnifred looks around us, surprised. "Even though they know you did something bad and undermined their trade?"

"The dog barks and the caravan moves on." I lounge back. "Even people who care stop caring once sentiments translate into action. Humans are notoriously selfish creatures, Winnifred. This is why the Russians invaded Ukraine. Why the Afghans were left to fend for themselves. Why there's a humanitarian crisis in Yemen, Syria, Sudan, and you don't even hear about it. Because people forget. They get mad, and move on."

"I care." She bares her teeth at me like a wounded animal. "I care about all those things, and just because you don't doesn't mean that others are as bad. You're a dangerous man."

"Dangerous!" Grace shrieks, forcing out a laugh. "Oh, no. He's just a kitten. We all are, in the family. Harmless number crunchers." She fans herself, blabbering. "Which I understand isn't as exciting as showbiz. You know, my dad owns a theater. I used to go there all the time as a kid. I found it totally charming."

While it is true that Douglas owns a theater, Grace just pretended to like it growing up to earn his approval. Theater is a low-margin field. Gracelynn only likes things that make money.

The diversion mission is a success. Winnifred averts her attention to Grace and asks her questions about Calypso Hall. Grace answers enthusiastically.

My phone begins to ring. I tug it out of my pocket. The area code says Scarsdale, but I don't recognize the number. I hit decline. Chip tries to ask me something about Nordic Equities.

My phone rings again. Same number. I hit decline.

Get the hint.

Damn scammers and their ability to use numbers in your area code.

The next call arrives from a different number, still in New York. I'm about to turn the thing off when Grace rests a hand over my thigh and says through gritted teeth, while listening to Winnifred gushing about *Hamilton*, "Could be the jeweler. About the necklace you bought me from Botswana. Answer it."

The phone rings a fourth time. Standing up, I excuse myself and amble out of the restaurant's door and to the balcony overlooking the harbor. I swipe the green button.

"*What?*" I spit out.

"Arsène?" a voice asks. It is old, male, and vaguely familiar.

"Unfortunately. Who's this?"

"It's Bernard, your father's assistant."

I check the time on my watch. It is four in the afternoon in New York. What can my father possibly want from me? We rarely talk. I make the trip to Scarsdale a few times a year to show my face and discuss family business—his idea of bonding, I suppose—but other than that, we're virtual strangers. I don't exactly hate him, but I don't like him either. The feeling, or lack of it, I'm sure, is mutual.

"Yes, Bernard?" I ask impatiently, parking my elbows on the railings.

"I don't know how to say this . . ." He trails off.

"Fast and without mincing words would be my preferable method," I suggest. "What is it? Is the old man getting hitched again?"

Ever since divorcing Miranda, my father has been making it a point to have another woman on his arm every couple of years. He doesn't make any promises anymore. Never settles down. An affair with a Langston woman is the fastest cure to believing in the notion of love.

"Arsène . . ." Bernard gulps. "Your father . . . he's dead."

The world continues spinning. People around me are laughing, smoking, drinking, enjoying a perfectly mild Italian summer night. A plane passes in the sky, penetrating a fat white cloud. Humanity is completely unfazed by the news that Douglas Corbin, the fifth-richest man in the USA, has passed away. And why should it be? Mortality is only an insult to rich people. Most accept it with sad resignation.

"Is he, now?" I hear myself say.

"He had a stroke this morning. The housekeeper found him unresponsive at about ten thirty, after knocking on his door several times. I know it's a lot to digest, and I probably should've waited until you got here to tell you—"

"It's fine." I cut him off, running my palm over my face. I'm trying to figure out what I'm feeling right now. But the truth is . . . I don't feel anything at all. Some oddness, yes. The same sensation you get when something you've been used to—a piece of furniture—is suddenly gone, leaving an empty space. But there is no agony, no gut-piercing sorrow. Nothing to indicate I've just lost the only living relative I have in this world.

"I should head back," I hear myself say. "Cut the trip short."

"That would be ideal." Bernard exhales. "I know it's very sudden. Again, I'm sorry."

I put him on speaker and withdraw the phone from my ear, scrolling through the next available flights. There is one two hours from now. I can still make it.

"I'll text you my flight details. Send someone over to pick us up."

"Of course," he says. "Will Miss Langston be joining you?"

"Yes," I say. "She'll want to be there."

She's closer to Dad than I am, the little suck-up. Visits him every other weekend. The fact that Bernard knows that she is with me tells me everything I need to know—Dad knew damn well that I was screwing my stepsister and gossiped about it with the help. Funny, he never mentioned this to me. Then again, the Langston women have been a sore subject for us since he kicked me out to attend boarding school.

I make a pit stop in the unisex restroom before getting into the restaurant. Unzip and take a leak. When I get out of the cubicle, I hear a faint voice coming from behind one of the doors. A bone-chilling, feral cry. Like someone is wounded in there.

Not your problem, I remind myself.

I roll my sleeves up, wash my hands, as the wails grow louder, more erratic.

I can't just leave now. What if someone gave birth to a baby and left it to drown in the toilet? While no one could accuse me of having a conscience, drowning newborns isn't a thing I'm happy to get behind.

I turn off the faucet and make my way back to the cubicle.

"Hello?" I lean a shoulder against it. "Who's there?"

The weeping, which turns into little hiccups, does not subside, but there is no answer either.

"Hey," I try, softer now. "Are you okay? Should I call someone?"

Maybe the police? Or someone else who actually cares?

No answer.

I'm running out of patience, and my nerves are shot as it is. My whole body is reeling with the news about Dad.

"Look, either you answer or I kick down the door."

The cries are harder now. Uncontrollable. I take a step back for momentum and kick the door open. It flies off its hinges, slamming against the large cubicle wall like a casualty in a gory action film.

But I don't find a baby or an injured animal.

Just one Winnifred Ashcroft, curled over the toilet tank in her red dress, makeup smeared all over her face, drinking wine straight from the bottle. Her hair is a mess, and she is shaking like a leaf.

Isn't she pregnant?

Poor Oatmeal Paul. Can't even get himself a sensible trophy wife.

Tears run down her cheeks. She put a good dent on that bottle. It's half-finished. We both stare at one another silently, engaged in some fucked-up contest. Only now, it's clear she doesn't expect me to ask her what's wrong.

"Are you in trouble?" I spit out, asking mainly because it is my civic duty. "Is he hurting you? Abusing you?"

She shakes her head. "You'll never be half the man he is!"

There goes my lifelong mission.

24

I glance around us, waiting for her to pick herself up and evacuate the toilet. She's the most bizarre creature I've ever met.

"My husband is amazing," she stresses, getting riled up, like I'm the one crying into a bottle of alcohol atop a germ colony.

"Your husband is as unremarkable as my least favorite pair of socks, but that's not a conversation I'm interested in having now," I counter. "Now, if there's nothing I can do—"

"Yes, there's nothing. Even if I did need help, I wouldn't turn to you for it. You're stuck up higher than a light pole." She wipes her nose with the back of her arm, sniffling. "Beat it."

"Now, now, Winnifred. I thought all southern belles were sweet and agreeable."

"Go away already!" She jumps to her feet and slams the door in my face, or whatever's left of the unhinged door, anyway.

For a brief moment, I contemplate giving her my number, in case Paul does abuse her. But then I remember my plate is full of my own shit to deal with, including Doug's death, Grace's wishy-washy attitude, my career, and so forth.

I turn around and walk away.

To tell Gracelynn Langston that Stepdaddy Dearest has finally kicked the bucket.

CHAPTER THREE

ARSÈNE

Then

Like all cautionary tales, my story began in a big, sprawling mansion. With stained glass windows, pointed arches, ribbed vaults, and flying buttresses.

Painted murals, hand-carved marble chess pieces, and grand curved staircases.

With an evil stepmother and a snotty stepsister.

The night that changed everything started out normally, as all disasters do.

Dad and Miranda drove into the city to see Chekhov's *The Seagull* premiere in Calypso Hall Theater and left us behind. They did it often. Miranda enjoyed art, and Dad enjoyed Miranda. No one enjoyed us, though, so it was our job to entertain one another.

My stepsister, Gracelynn, and I flattened a cardboard box we'd stolen from the kitchen and took turns sitting on it, sliding down the stairway. We bumped into housekeepers as they rushed between rooms, carrying fluffy warm towels, ingredients for dinner, and dry-cleaned suits. They'd have crushed us like bugs if they could. But they couldn't.

We were Corbins. Entitled, privileged, and powerful. Scarsdale's chosen ones. Destined to squash, not to be squashed.

We slid and we slid down the stairs until our asses were red under our designer garments. My spine felt like Jell-O from all the bumping against the stairs. Neither of us thought to stop. There weren't many things to do in this castle. Video games were forbidden ("They make the mind lazy," Dad said), toys were messy ("And you're too old, anyway," Miranda huffed), and we'd run out of homework to do.

Gracelynn was midair, gliding down the stairway, when the main door flew open. She bumped into my father. Her face pancaked against his shoes, and she let out a comic "*Oomph*."

"What in the . . . Arsène!" my father thundered to the bottom of the stairway, sidestepping her. Fingernail streaks adorned his cheeks. "What is this mess?"

"We just—"

"Decided to get yourselves injured? Do you think I have the time to go to the ER with you?" he spit out. "Go to your room. Now."

"Gracelynn." My stepmother followed briskly, shutting the door behind her. I didn't have to look at her fingernails to know they were caked with my father's blood. When they fought, she always did this. Hurt him. "Go practice your ballet, darling. Daddy and I have grown-up things to discuss."

Daddy.

He wasn't her daddy.

Heck, he wasn't even really *my* daddy.

Douglas Corbin was no fatherly creature.

Yet strangely enough, he didn't hate Gracelynn, another man's child, with the same passion he reserved for me.

"Sorry, Mom."

"It's okay, sweetie."

Gracelynn stood up and dusted off her knees. She ran up the stairs, wrinkly cardboard tucked under her armpit. We shuffled down the darkened hall. We knew the score. Neither of us wanted a front-row seat to Dad and Miranda's arguments.

All Dad and Miranda did was fight and make up. They didn't want us present for either of those things. This was how the games of sliding stairways and tightrope started. Out of boredom because we were always so alone.

"Think they'll punish us?" she asked me now.

I shrugged. "Don't care."

"Yeah . . . me either." Gracelynn shoved her bony elbow in my ribs. "Hey, race you to my room?"

I shook my head. "I'll catch up with you on the roof."

She padded quickly across the golden marble, disappearing into her room.

Whenever they sent us to our rooms, we climbed the fire ladder and hung out on the roof. It was a way to pass the time, and we could talk about anything without the servants eavesdropping and snitching.

I walked into Gracelynn's den, which looked like something Barbie herself had designed. She had a queen-size bed with a pink tulle canopy, a white carved fireplace, and upholstered recliners. Her ballet gear was scattered about.

Gracelynn loved ballet. I didn't know why. Ballet clearly didn't love her back. She made a crappy ballerina. Not because she wasn't pretty—but because she was *only* pretty. She could barely move her feet and, ironically, lacked grace.

The window was open. The wind made the curtains dance. Even they danced better than Gracelynn.

I laced my sneakers before pulling my body out the window. I stomped my way up the rain-drenched iron ladder. I found Gracelynn leaning against one of the chimneys, ankles crossed, exhaling breath vapor like a dragon.

"Ready to *tightrope* it?" She grinned.

The ridge of the roof was edged so narrowly that we had to walk it one foot at a time. For our game, we walked the ridge, chimney to chimney, as fast as we could. We each had our turn. We timed one another, and sometimes—a lot of times—I suspected she was cheating, which was why I never, *ever* let her win.

"You timing me, or what?" Gracelynn lurched her chin toward me.

Nodding, I produced my stopwatch from my pocket. "Ready to eat dust again, *sis?*"

Gracelynn had a problem. Her problem was me. I was smarter than her, scoring higher on tests without even studying. I was more athletic than her—she was a mediocre dancer, while I was the second-best tennis player in my age group in the entire state.

Naturally, I was also much faster than her. I always won. It never occurred to me to let her have a little victory. She was an annoying, entitled brat.

So was I, but let's admit it—I wore my faults better.

"I'm not gonna lose, you . . . you . . . hot dog–water breath!" she choked out, her face turning pink.

I laughed. "Your time starts now, fartface." I raised the timer in the air.

"You know, I'm getting really tired of doing this." She fisted her hair—onyx black, like her eyes—tying it into a painful-looking bun. "Making myself invisible for them. All of my friends' parents—"

"Miranda and Doug aren't parents." I cut her off, squinting up as gray clouds gathered above our heads like schoolyard bullies. It was going to rain soon. "They're just people with kids. There's a difference."

"But it's not fair!" Grace stomped. "Mom punishes *me* whenever your dad annoys her."

This was a good time to point out I was her mother's personal punching bag. Miranda's favorite pastime was lamenting to my father how screwed up I was.

He doesn't laugh. Doesn't cry. Doesn't take an interest in anything but astronomy and math, which—excuse me, Doug—simply isn't normal for a ten-year-old. Maybe there is something wrong with him. We would do him a disservice if we don't run some tests. Oh, and he doesn't yawn when others do! Have you noticed that? That shows a lack of sympathy. He could be a sociopath. A sociopath! Living under our roof.

I couldn't chance Gracelynn running back to her mom with the impression I gave half a crap, so I bit my tongue.

"How do you mean?" I asked.

"Like, I've been wanting this tutu Lucinda's parents bought her from Moscow for ages. It's custom made. Last week Mom told me she'd look into ordering it. But today, before she went with your dad to the theater, she snapped and said it was too expensive all of a sudden, and that I'd grow out of it too quickly. All because he pissed her off!"

"And you care about the stupid dress because . . . ?"

"It's not a dress, Ars. It's a tutu!"

"If you say so."

"I *do* say so! I'll say it all day long!"

"You don't want Lucinda's tutu. You want her talent. And that can't be bought in Russia, or anywhere else," I said matter-of-factly.

Lucinda and Gracelynn were in the grade below me. Lucinda was the girl everyone wanted to be. Beautiful, and nice, and therefore loathed by Grace and her little clones.

"I can't believe you just said that." She balled her hand into a fist, waving it at me. "Mom's right about you, you know."

"Your mom's not right about anything. Now start walking. I haven't got all day," I snapped, starting the stopwatch. "It's on."

"Ugh!" she growled. "I hate you!"

I started counting the seconds out loud, knowing it was gonna freak her out.

"Argh. I'll show you! I'm gonna win!"

She raised her arms in the air and started jogging across the roof quickly. *Too* quickly. Gracelynn was practically hovering over the edge, cutting through the air like a bird of prey. She sliced in and out of the fog like a plane. She wobbled left and right. She was almost at the chimney, but what the hell? She could fall over any second.

"Jesus," I hissed. "Slow down. What are you doi—"

Before I finished my sentence, her right leg missed the needlelike surface. She slipped, swinging herself left to regain balance. Her right leg twisted sharply. She let out a surprised gasp, throwing her arms forward to clutch the chimney. She fell about an inch short.

Gracelynn tumbled down the side of the roof with a feral scream, disappearing out of sight. *Shit.* My lungs closed up, rejecting oxygen. My first thought was, *What was she thinking?* Followed closely by *Dad's going to murder my ass.*

I waited for the thud. Maybe I was a sociopath like Miranda said. Who waited to hear the body of their stepsister hitting the ground from a thirty-foot height?

"Grace?" My voice was drowned out by the rain that began pelting on the roof. "God dammit, Gracelynn!"

"Over here!" she choked out.

Relief washed over me. She wasn't dead. I crouched down to sit on the ridge and slowly slid down the roof until I reached the gutter.

Her fingers were curled around the gutter pipe. Her body dangled in the air.

Should I go get Dad and Miranda? Should I try pulling her up?

Shit, I had no idea. I never thought either of us would be stupid enough to legit *run* across the roof like a maniac.

"Help me," Gracelynn pleaded, tears and raindrops running across her face. "Please!"

I grabbed onto her wrists and leaned backward, starting to pull. Sharp spikes of rain blurred my vision. Her skin was cold, wet, and slippery. Her wrists so delicate I was scared I'd break them. Her fingers

31

clawed into my skin, grasping, as she wiggled, trying to use me as a human ladder. She drew blood, just like her mother had done to my father tonight.

I decided I wasn't going to share Douglas Corbin's fate. I wasn't going to bleed for a Langston woman ever again.

"Pull me harder!" She moaned. "I'm slipping. Can't you see?"

The soles of my feet scorched as I tried to yank her up the roof. The odds were against me. Physics too. I had to climb uphill over the wet shingles while pulling someone my own weight. "You need to hold on to the gutter. I have to call Dad."

"I can't!"

"We're both gonna fall."

"Don't leave me!"

Did she think I wanted to kill her or something? I was about to tip over too.

"Look, I can hold you for a few more seconds and give your arms a rest, but then you gotta hold the gutter for a minute or two until they get here."

She slipped away from my grasp an inch. Wriggled in the air like a worm. "No! Don't leave me! I don't want to die."

"Don't look down," I roared, falling to my knees, pulling harder, with everything I had in me. It felt like my limbs were being ripped from my body. But she was too heavy, too wet. "Just . . . just look at me."

The pressuring, unrelenting weight of her was gone suddenly. My body jerked backward. The back of my head slammed against the shingles. A distant splash assaulted my ears.

She fell.

She *fell*.

Frantic, I crawled along the gutter, squinting down, trying to see past the rain and the mud and the thick bushes. Grace had landed on the canopy covering the empty pool. The belly of it was deep, and there was water all around her.

Gracelynn didn't move. Her legs were in weird angles, and I immediately knew, even before she started screaming, that it was all over for her.

No more fancy tulle costumes, Russian tutus, or dance camps in Zurich.

My stepsister's ballet career was over.

And so was my life as I knew it.

◆ ◆ ◆

The x-rays arrived minutes after Dad and I got to the hospital.

He hadn't looked at me, not even once, the entire journey there. I relayed to him everything that had happened, maybe other than the part where I'd goaded her. No need to be holier than the pope. Besides, she survived, didn't she?

"She's going to be okay, though. Right?" I chased him down the linoleum corridor to her room now. I was so full of adrenaline I couldn't even feel my legs.

"She better be, for your sake," he snarled, staring ahead. "What did you two do up there, anyway?"

"Played a game."

He let out a snort. "You play high stakes. Typical Corbin male."

What did steaks have to do with all this? I'd always been a burger dude, anyway.

"Is that good or bad?" I asked.

"Plainly speaking, it's an incurable condition stemming from too much money, too much ego, and too much time." He plucked his leather gloves by the fingers. "We Corbins tend to be rebels with a cause. Hopefully, yours isn't killing your sister. Rein in on your personality, child."

This was the most he'd spoken to me in months, maybe even years, so I basked in it. It wasn't that he ignored me per se. Dad was good about making sure I got excellent grades, attended my extracurricular activities, stuff like that. He just wasn't about talking all that much.

The verdict came along with the x-rays. Gracelynn was suffering from two broken legs and a minor spinal dislocation that required surgery.

She also suffered from a bad case of being a shit bag.

The latter wasn't a medical diagnosis, but true, nonetheless. As soon as the painkillers kicked in and her legs were cast, she pointed an accusing finger at me, narrowing her tar eyes. "It's him. He did this to me. He *pushed* me, Mommy."

It was the first time I was truly speechless. Pushed her? I'd tried to *save* her, and she damn well knew it.

"Bull crap! You ran on the ledge and fell," I said hotly. "I tried to pull you back up. You almost tore my arms off. Here, I can prove it."

Pushing my sleeves up, I turned to show Dad and Miranda the marks Gracelynn had left on my skin. They were red and deep and raw, already halfway turning into scars.

Gracelynn shook her head adamantly. "You tried to push me, so I fought you. You wanted to get rid of me. You said so yourself. You were tired of sharing Mom and Dad's attention."

This sounded exactly like the kind of thing *she'd* do. I hated getting attention from Dad and Miranda. It was always negative and got me in trouble.

My mouth hung open. "Why're you lying?"

"Why're *you* lying?" She bared her teeth. "You've been caught. Just fess up! You could've killed me."

"Oh, my little dove. What's this monster done to you?" Miranda buried her face in her daughter's neck, throwing her arms around her. She sounded like she was crying, but I bet her eyes were dry.

I looked around the room, waiting for . . . what? Someone to walk through the door and back me up? There was no one in the world who could protect me. I always knew that, but suddenly, the weight of my loneliness was pressing hard against my chest, making it hard to breathe.

"Lying's the cowardly way out, son." Dad's fingers wrapped around my shoulder firmly, warning me not to plead my case. "Come clean and face the consequences like a man."

He didn't believe me.

He was never going to believe me.

He just wanted this to go away for him and for Miranda, so there'd be no more shouting, screaming, and slapping.

Gracelynn, despite lacking everywhere I excelled, was still their favorite child. The *normal* child. The one who laughed, and cried, and yawned when others did.

The painful realization I was truly alone in this world slammed into me.

Staring Gracelynn down, jaw clenched, eyes dead, I shrugged. "Sure. I pushed her. My only regret is I couldn't finish the job. Better luck next time, I guess."

And then it registered to Gracelynn. That this was all real. Not a part of our stupid, made-up games. I could see it in her eyes. The flash of regret, followed by the adrenaline rush. The recognition that whatever she was doing, it was working, at least for now. That she was finally winning against me at something.

But I would never let her win. Not if I still had breath in me.

I turned around and stalked out of the hospital room, leaving behind the poor imitation of what was supposed to be my family.

❖ ❖ ❖

Later that night Miranda returned from the hospital without Gracelynn. Dad and I waited in the dining room, staring at our hands silently.

"Doug, a word," Miranda clipped, summoning my father upstairs. They locked the bedroom door behind them. I pressed my ear to their door, my mouth dry.

". . . too much, for too long. This is sheer neglect. I cannot, in good conscience, allow my daughter to become prey in the hands of your out-of-control son. I've had enough, Doug."

I knew what really bothered Miranda about me, and it had nothing to do with Grace.

I looked exactly like my mother, the late Patrice Chalamet.

I was a constant reminder that she had been alive. That once upon a time, she had stolen Douglas Corbin from her. That if it weren't for Patrice, I would have never been born.

Gracelynn wouldn't have been either.

There was an alternate utopia for Dad and Miranda. A version of reality they'd almost managed to achieve. And it was yours truly who crapped all over it.

The servants talked about it all the time. Whispering as they fluffed pillows, prepared nutritious meals for us, drove Gracelynn and me to our tennis and ballet practices.

As the story goes, Miranda and Dad had been dating on and off throughout college. She overlooked Doug's indiscretions—whatever that word meant—and wouldn't let him out of her sight. When Dad went to a friend's wedding in Paris eleven years ago, Miranda had wanted to join him. But it was a private event, consisting of fifty people, with no plus-one invitations.

That's where he met Patrice. A glamorous wannabe actress from Rennes and the maid of honor. The two had a rendezvous (again, no idea what that meant), after which Dad went back to America.

It never occurred to Doug that Patrice would come knocking on his door two months later with a positive pregnancy test, white as a sheet. Legend says she vomited all over his shoes to prove her point before he even finished asking what she was doing there. And that Miranda was in his apartment at the time, *In a less than decent condition*, one house-keeper had said snidely.

Dad's dad—my grandfather—forced his hand into doing the right thing. So Dad married Patrice, a complete stranger.

The servants always said my grandfather never liked Miranda.

Too high maintenance. Too much of a social climber.

Miranda's answer to the public humiliation had been cold blooded. She fell pregnant with Dad's best friend's child shortly after. A man by the name of Leo Thayer. An Aussie heir to a beef-export empire. So thorough was her counterbetrayal that Gracelynn was born looking so much like Leo that the paternity test Miranda had sent Dad confirming Gracelynn wasn't his hadn't been necessary.

Versions varied about what happened afterward. I heard a few stories from a few servants. But the most popular tale was of how my father and Miranda had rekindled their affair before Gracelynn and I had gone off our wet nurses' milk.

Only now Miranda wasn't the prized girlfriend—she was the mistress. Until Patrice died, and she got promoted to wife.

Miranda, like her daughter, couldn't stand to lose to anyone. Especially a ten-year-old kid.

"I'll talk to him," my father murmured. "Make him understand what he did was wrong."

"That's *not* enough. You think I can sleep at night knowing your son is across the hall from my daughter after what he did to her?"

"We don't know exactly what happened, sweetheart."

It surprised me that Dad stood up for me, but I knew he wasn't going to stand his ground for long. She'd wear him down. She always did. And he, blinded by his own sins, by her beauty, would submit.

"Well, I hate to do this, but it's either him or us."

"And where should I put him?" Dad spit out impatiently. "He's a kid, Miranda. Not a goddamn vase!"

"There's a boarding school not too far from here. Andrew Dexter Academy. Elaine's son goes there. The one who was in that gifted program? I have the brochure . . ." I heard the rustling of paper.

Of course she had the brochure handy.

"You want me to tuck him in a private school on the other side of the state?" he growled. "Jesus, Miranda, listen to yourself."

"Oh, come on, Doug," she said soothingly. "It's a good place. We both know he's being stalled here academically. You'd be doing him a favor. He could be fulfilling his potential, instead of being bored here and getting into all kinds of trouble. We'd love to have him for holidays and summer vacations. He would be so much more manageable."

And so I became *manageable*.

Banished from my own house over a lie my stepsister had told to get rid of me.

Over her jealousy. Her greed.

Gracelynn got her Russian tutu. They put it behind glass, like the Armoury Chamber in the Kremlin. Precious and unattainable. Just like her ballet aspirations.

She also got our parents' full attention.

This was where my obsession with Gracelynn Langston began. The feral hunger to conquer her at all costs.

In the moment of history when she won the one thing that matters—public opinion.

But this was a marathon, not a sprint.

Gracelynn was about to learn her lesson the hard way.

We Corbins always won in the end.

Even if it meant we needed to play dirty.

CHAPTER FOUR

ARSÈNE

"Pull over," Grace instructs after we land in Newark hours later.

The chauffeur flicks his blinker, slows down, and pulls the Cadillac to the shoulder of the road. She pushes the door open, staggers out, and vomits all over the bushes.

She's been crying the entire flight here, talking with her mother on the phone. Not once did Grace ask me how I was coping. Maybe she assumes, like her mother, that I'm a sociopath, incapable of feelings.

Or maybe she simply doesn't care.

What's peculiar is she isn't the emotional type. Falling apart isn't her style.

Stumbling back into her seat, she plasters a hand over her sweaty forehead. "It hurts so much, Arsène. You wouldn't understand."

Wouldn't I?

Her utter selfishness robs me of my breath. She'd had them both growing up. Miranda. Douglas. She never once apologized for what she did to me.

And this is why you want her so bad. Because she's an obsession. An unattainable fantasy. A class of her own.

"He was my father too," I point out flatly.

"But he was closer to me," she whines childishly.

Turning my gaze to the window, I bite my tongue until the metallic taste of blood coats my mouth.

"Look, I'm just exhausted." She shakes her head, more tears spilling from her eyes. I think it's the first time I've seen her cry. Even when she fell from the roof, she was tough about it. "I just want to get there already."

In response, I snap my fingers at the driver. "Floor it."

◆ ◆ ◆

Ten days later, the Corbin mansion is teeming with people. Not in the same way it had been crowded when my father threw his *Great Gatsby*–style epic parties when Grace and I were children.

The memorial service has been elegantly planned and flawlessly executed. Caterers float among guests, carrying platters of finger food and alcohol. A pianist takes requests behind a golden grand piano. Old classics my father used to listen to—"Bohemian Rhapsody," "Imagine," "Your Song."

I stand in the corner of the room with my friends since adolescence—my only friends, really—Christian and Riggs. Christian is a lawyer who owns a white-shoe firm, while Riggs is a professional photographer and possibly the prolific creator of a few new STDs. Christian brought his wife, Arya, along.

"We're so sorry for your loss." Arya gathers me into a hug, refusing to let go. It is more than Grace has done in the past ten days. Then again, Arya is an actual well-rounded human capable of sympathy. Grace is a female version of me. Which makes the ordeal even more peculiar, because she's been all torn up about Doug's death out of nowhere.

"It's fine. We weren't close. Where's the baby?" I pull away from her, looking around. Arya gave birth some months ago to a pink, screaming thing who looks like a bald bookkeeper. Quietly, and only to myself, I can admit I want what Christian has with Arya, perhaps because I know it could never happen.

"The baby has a name." Christian's eyebrows pull together. "It's Louie. And he's home, with the sitter. You thought we'd bring him to a *wake?*"

"I didn't think about him at all," I admit coldly. "I was just making conversation."

Christian eyes me with exasperation. "Mingling is not your forte, buddy. Stick to making money."

"Why weren't you close?" Arya puts an encouraging hand on my arm. "You and your father."

"Good luck with getting a confession out of this guy," Riggs snorts out, raking a hand over his golden hair in slo-mo. "Ars is not the talk-about-it type. I'm gonna go hit the bar. Not that I'm not interested in your sob story, buddy, but . . . oh, wait. That's right. I'm *not* interested in it." He winks and swaggers to the other side of the room.

I wouldn't put it past him to chase tail here. Riggs is shameless in his pursuit of women as if he just found out about their existence last month.

"It's a client." Christian lifts his phone in the air, indicating an incoming call. "And not a happy one. I'll be right back."

"Well?" Arya continues staring at me intently.

I hitch a shoulder up. "My father and I hadn't seen eye to eye."

"Since when?" She tilts her head sideways.

"Conception." I let out a wry laugh. "He made sure I remembered he only married my mother because she was knocked up with me. As if sperm-me escaped from his balls in the dead of the night and found my way between her legs. No personal responsibility taken. When my so-called mother died, he married his ex-girlfriend not even two years later. Supposedly they'd been having an affair throughout his brief marriage. But that's all right, I've been hearing Patrice wasn't anything to write home about in the parenting department either."

I sound as bitter as a pint of Guinness. Truth is, I don't give two shits about my no-show parents. I just want her to do a U-turn from the conversation and stick to safe topics, like the weather.

Arya nods. "Sounds like he was a piece of work. I can relate. Loving someone who doesn't deserve our love is the greatest punishment one could endure."

A sardonic smile touches my lips. "Remind me why we love people by blood connection and not merit?"

Arya considers my question. "Because humanity wouldn't survive otherwise. People are generally not very endearing," she says matter-of-factly. "Look, I know you're not feeling the grief now. Things are too raw, too hot to process. Maybe you never will. And I know we're strangers, for the most part. But as someone who's had a very complex relationship with her father, I just want you to know—if you ever need to talk to someone . . ." She puts a hand on my arm. "That someone could be me. I will understand and never judge."

"I appreciate it." And I do. I would have liked to fall for a woman like Arya. Strongheaded, smart, and compassionate. Someone who is the head of a charity in her spare time. Tragically, I'm in the market only for one egocentric nymph.

"How's the PR business going?" I change the subject.

"Great." Arya smiles. "I'm never out of a job, because people are never out of trouble."

"And the charity you run?" I forgot what it was about. Something with children. Christian doesn't usually ask for favors, which means I am going to need to attend the stupid charity gala she throws every year.

Arya opens her mouth to answer me just as Riggs swaggers his way back with wine, hands Arya and me glasses, and takes a sip from his. "Is the girl talk over? Is Ars ready to purchase his first training bra?"

Arya gives him a playful shove. "Grow up, Riggs."

He makes a face, something between horrified and disgusted. "Not a chance in the world, ma'am."

"Are we taking bets on Arsène growing a heart in this hollow chest of his?" Christian reappears from the veranda, sliding his phone back into his pocket.

"Close." Riggs chugs his wine like it's Gatorade. "Your wife just told me to grow up."

Christian plants a kiss on Arya's forehead. "We'll land on the sun sooner."

"Riggs would probably be the idiot to say yes to going there to take pictures," I point out. Laughter rings in the air.

I'm glad they're here. My core support group. The people I confide in. We grew up together. Fought the odds together. And won together.

From the corner of my eye I spot Alice Gudinski, the spiritual godmother of Christian, Riggs, and me.

"Came all the way from Florida as fast as I could." She breezes toward us and kisses both my cheeks. She is wearing a flowery, colorful dress and looks like an exotic bird, as opposed to someone attending a funeral. She clutches me close, whispering in my ear, "To tell you good riddance. That old fart didn't deserve you as a son. I hope you know that." She pats my back in a gesture more motherly than Miranda ever offered me.

"Hello to you, too, Alice." Christian chuckles beside her. "Forgot your manners?"

She turns to hug and kiss him too. "Outgrew them when I became a widow. Life's too short to be a well-behaved lady."

A-fucking-men.

The pianist begins playing "Friends in Low Places." At my request. Not only is it apt now that Douglas is worm food, but I also know how much my father despised country music. It's my tongue-in-cheek farewell.

"Christian, Riggs, Alice, so nice of you to show your respects." Grace parts the throngs of people, approaching us. She is wearing an off-shoulder black dress and a dramatic eyeliner. She looks impeccable even in grief.

In the ten days since my father passed away, Grace has been acting like a ghost of her former self. She took days off, which I thought she was physically incapable of doing. Most days, she didn't leave bed before noon. I know there's more to her behavior than Douglas, and the only reason I'm not pressing for information is because I'm letting things play out organically to see where her mind's at.

Grace reaches to shake both my friends' hands, then pivots to Arya on her pointy heels.

"Sorry, I didn't catch your name. Christian's new girlfriend, right?"

Arya smiles, letting the intentional insult roll off her back. "You can call me Arya. Or Christian's *wife*. I'm not picky."

"My bad." Grace lets out a throaty chuckle. "Understandably, I'm a bit too preoccupied these days to keep up with your little gang."

I remind myself that this woman is perfect for me. For multiple reasons. All of them practical and hardheaded. We have the same taste, the same values, the same wants. Christian has Arya, and look—they're happy. As happy as his miserable ass can be, I suppose. My stepsister and I can have that too. Or at least a fucked-up version of it.

Yes, Grace can be obnoxious, but so can I. Conquering Grace's heart has always been my end goal. A few vulgar remarks to my friends aren't gonna change that.

"Sorry for your loss," Christian tells Grace in a voice that indicates he couldn't be happier she's suffering. All three of my friends know what Grace did to me when we were kids. None of them have found any redeemable qualities in her current, adult version.

"Thank you. It was so horrible for me." Grace clutches her pearls.

"For Arsène, too, I bet," Arya points out.

"Of course." Grace waves flippantly. "It's just that . . . well, Doug and I had been really close. We had something special, you know?"

"If I had a penny for every time a leggy woman in this room said those words . . ." Riggs chuckles behind his wineglass. "Including your mother, now that I think of it."

Alice lets out a rowdy laugh. Arya joins her.

"Because that's what you need." Arya pins Riggs with a playful glare. "A fatter bank account."

Riggs is a billionaire who needs more money like Grace needs more diamonds. The best part is that despite his wealth, he lives an appallingly modest life. His lack of need to impress drives him to say things no one else in the room would ever think of uttering. Which is why he'd just handed my girlfriend her ass.

"For shame, Riggs. Not everything is a joke." Grace withdraws dramatically.

"Get off your high horse, sweet cheeks." Riggs knocks back his drink. "We both know what drew you to the Corbins, and it's not their character. No offense, Ars."

"None taken, asshole." I raise my drink to him.

"This whole conversation is tasteless and inappropriate." Grace stares Riggs down. She wants an apology, but that's never going to happen.

Riggs inclines his head, feigning grief. "My apologies, Grace. Please, tell me more about appropriateness. There's no one I wish to get a lecture from more than a woman who fucks her stepbrother."

"Hmm." Christian swirls his drink, looking into it. "Definitely been to more traditional funerals in my lifetime, but I prefer this one. Pretty action packed."

Grace's face reddens. She turns to look at me, expecting me to intervene. "Are you just going to stand there and let him talk to me like that?" she demands.

I smooth out my suit. "I can sit down if you prefer."

Arya lets out a strangled giggle, and so does Alice.

"Well, thanks for coming. It is appreciated." Grace turns around, fuming, then stomps her way back to her mother and a cluster of her friends.

Christian elbows me, gesturing with his drink toward her. "Remind me what you see in her again?"

"Beauty. Elegance. Lack of submission."

"You know who also fits this bill?" Alice yawns. "A cheetah, and I wouldn't share a bed with one."

"She puts the ass in nasty." Riggs waxes poetic, plucking another drink from a tray nearby.

I watch Grace's shapely calves as she swaggers off. "That's a feature, buddy. Not a bug."

"I can't believe this is coming from me, but you're going to regret checking that woman's oil." Riggs whistles low.

"No better antidote than the poison itself." I tsk.

"May I remind you she tried to ruin you?" Christian and his poster-ready Clark Kent features darken. "Almost succeeded too. Yet you're obsessed with her."

"And obsession"—Arya sinks her upper teeth into her bottom lip—"is a potent poison. It tastes real sweet and can easily be mistaken for love."

I am well aware that what Grace and I share does not classify as love to most people. But it is big, uninhibited, and everlasting. This is what Christian and Riggs don't understand—Grace and I never have to settle for friendship with sex, the default state of every couple who's been together longer than two or three years.

Our sex is always angry, hot, and hostile. Our animosity infinite.

I traded comfort for passion. Safety for desire. Gracelynn Langston is a risky stock, but I've always played on the dangerous side.

"I'm not obsessed with her," I say, dry amusement in my voice. "I'm obsessed with having her. It's the circumstances that drive this entire operation."

"You're wrong," Arya insists. "The circumstances don't matter. What matters is you'll end up being with someone who doesn't care for you. News flash, Ars—the world is full of people who don't care for you. So, when choosing your partner, you really want to make sure you find someone who'd be in your corner."

Riggs massages his jaw. "Sorry to interrupt your TED Talk, but your heartbroken, grieving stepsister is looking mighty happy right now."

Following Riggs's gaze, I watch Grace standing next to Chip, Paul, and Pablo. Her colleagues came to show their condolences. Grace laughs at something Chip says, smacking his chest playfully, not a care in the world.

Without meaning to—certainly without *wanting* to—I find myself scanning the room for Winnifred. If Paul is here, maybe he brought his wife along.

It isn't that I'm interested in her. I want to see if she is showing a bump. If I was right. I want to see if her blue eyes are still sad and haunted.

As it happens, she isn't here. *Good.* Terrific. More alcohol for me.

"Welp, this is boring," Riggs laments, grabbing an hors d'oeuvre from a floating platter and tossing it into his mouth. "I'm going to try to beat rush hour back to the city."

"With what car?" Christian asks with exaggerated interest. For all his wealth, Riggs does not possess any items of value. No car, no apartment, not even a fucking staple piece of furniture from IKEA. Whenever he is in town, he crashes either at Christian's or at my place.

Riggs throws him a half-dazed look. "Right. I bummed a ride with you. Well, I'll Uber it."

"No need. I rented a car." Alice pats his back. "And anyway, I came here to show my respect to Ars, not his father. Which I did. I'll give you a ride. Corbin, sweetheart, I'll see you soon."

"So long, and thanks for the sashimi." Riggs salutes us.

They trek out of the room. Riggs stops to compliment a few of Grace's attractive friends on their outfits like we're in a fashion show. He gets one number and a lot of inappropriate giggles. The man is as careless as a condom wrapper at a frat party. Though chronologically he is thirty-four years old, based on his behavior alone, I wouldn't give him more than seventeen on a good day. Best of luck to the woman who tries to tame the fucker.

"You need to take care of the Grace situation." Christian turns to look at me as soon as Riggs and Alice are out of sight. "When shit implodes, no one's going to help you tidy up."

"You're right, it *is* my shit to clean. So do me a favor and stay out of it." I clap his back, bowing to his wife. "Lovely seeing you as always, Arya."

"Didn't he want to be cremated?" Grace takes off her earrings in front of my en suite bathroom mirror. I live in a skyscraper on Billionaires' Row. A fourteen-hundred-foot tower overlooking Central Park.

Lounging on the upholstered bench at the foot of my bed, I unlace my loafers. "He did."

"Why'd you decide to bury him, then?" She materializes from the bathroom, lathering her hands in cream.

"*Precisely* for that reason."

I waltz over to my walk-in closet to put my shoes away. Grace falls into bed with a sigh, scrolling through her phone with a bored pout. "You're petty."

"And you fucking love it," I say mildly.

"Do you think he was aware of what was happening to him when he had the stroke?" She sounds pensive.

One could wish.

"Don't know," I say instead, plopping on the other side of the bed. I start undoing my shirt buttons. "Don't care."

"Do you think he thought about us? The few seconds before he died?"

Though I'm unhappy about Douglas passing away—it is never good news when someone in your vicinity pegs out—I don't understand why Grace is trying to humanize the man.

"Maybe." I bristle. "Why does it matter?"

"Oh, no reason. It's just that, you know . . ." She drops her phone on the mattress, whipping her head toward me. "Mom said Doug left something for me in his will."

I still, my fingers pausing around one of the buttons. The air between us crackles with silent competition; I consider my next words, knowing we've started a brand-new mental chess game.

"I hadn't realized Miranda and Douglas were in touch."

She presses against me. Her hands lace over my back, kneading it in a massage.

"They were. They were in talks of reconciliation. Doug had been signaling to her that he was tired of his meaningless girlfriends, and you know how Mom broke things off with Dane not too long ago." She watches me closely for a reaction. Our imaginary swords are still tucked away, our fingers itching to yield them. "But I'm not sure how serious they were."

"That's very convenient." I smirk.

"What are you insinuating?" She rubs at my back.

"Nothing." I push her away, let my shirt slip off my shoulders, and toss it at the foot of the bed. "We'll see if he made some last-minute changes in his will."

I don't care one iota about Douglas's money. I make enough on my own. What I do care about is Miranda getting her claws on something she doesn't deserve. Grace too. They'd been loitering around him for scraps for decades.

"I'm getting a drink." I exit the bedroom and stroll to the living room. I pour myself two fingers of whiskey. Sip it, one shoulder propped on the wall, glowering at the Central Park view.

Douglas fucking me over with a last-minute will before kicking the bucket is a valid possibility. He liked Grace well enough. Hell knows what he felt for Miranda. They'd had their ups and downs. But me? I'd always been a bone in his throat. My indifference toward him, toward his wealth, paired with my financial and mental independence always made him feel emasculated and unimportant.

Then again, I *am* his biological son. Doug always cared about keeping the fortune in the family.

Grace's hands crawl over my chest from behind, splaying over the dark hair.

Her naked body presses against my shirtless frame.

Her tits are hot, her nipples erect. She nibbles on the side of my neck, licking and biting softly. Her breasts feel heavy. Has she finally put on some weight?

"Come to bed, you big grump," she purrs into my ear, nipping on the shell of it.

I stare at the bottom of my glass of whiskey. "Sell it to me, *sis*."

She cups my crotch from behind. I'm hard. She drags her hand higher, pushes it into my pants, and closes her fist around my shaft.

"Jerk you off?"

I put my whiskey down on a nearby table, catch her wrist, and tug her to stand in front of me.

I flip her around like she is a rag doll, bend her over a side table, grab one of her hips, and use my free hand and teeth to rip a condom wrapper. I always have condoms handy in my pocket.

I'm inside her within seconds. She is soaked.

I ride her from behind, closing my eyes, remembering all those times.

When she stabbed me in the back.

When she wronged me.

When she took what was mine and taunted me with it.

So much for having the blissful fucking fairy tale others have.

Grace finishes first. She always does. Nothing turns her on more than knowing she is getting dicked by the man she loathes the most.

I come a few minutes after. Yanking the condom off on my way to the bathroom, I pass by a floor-to-ceiling mirror in the hallway and pause.

I am extremely athletic. I play tennis six times a week. I'm relatively young. Handsome enough, and wealthier than anyone has business to be.

I can find a decent woman. The Arya type. A compassionate, smart, attractive companion whose lifelong wish isn't to see me burn in hell. And yet Christian and Riggs are right. The only woman I have eyes for is my poisonous, fickle stepsister.

"This was good, wasn't it?" she asks when I exit the bathroom.

I nod. "Wanna see a movie?"

I need to decompress after the wake.

"Actually, I'm gonna work on the balcony for a bit." Grace is unplugging her laptop from its charger in my bedroom. "While the weather's still nice and all."

We never share a bed for more than sleep and sex. Never watch movies together. Go to museums, picnics, vacations.

Never do anything that is remotely couple-like.

"It's fine, I have my own projects to tend to." I make my way to my office and close the door.

It is time to call Dad's estate lawyer and see what hell he brewed for me before he died.

CHAPTER FIVE

My taxi stopped in front of the Corbin mansion. I hopped out, a duffel bag dangling from each of my shoulders. I squinted up at the arches of the manor that I used to call home. At the closed door. The empty driveway.

I didn't know why I hoped someone would be waiting for me here. Hadn't I learned anything in my years at Andrew Dexter Academy?

Summer vacation was going to be long, lonely, and full of tension. I should've stayed back.

I dragged my ass to the entrance and raised my fist to knock on the door before remembering, *Fuck it, this place is going to be mine one day.*

I pushed it open all the way. Servants were rushing back and forth. No sign of Dad, Miranda, and Gracelynn.

"Welcome home, Arsène. Your father asked me to tell you that he, your stepsister, and your stepmother went to the country club. There's a golf tournament." Bernard halted in front of me, a manila file under his arm. "They should be back soon. Do you need help settling in? Some refreshments, maybe?"

I shook my head.

I went upstairs to my room and dumped the bags onto the floor. I glanced around, and it didn't take a genius to see what had happened here. Gracelynn had taken over my space. It wasn't pink central or anything, but my closet was open and full of glittery sneakers. The desk was littered with her textbooks, pastel Sharpies, and heart-shaped Post-it Notes. There were scrunchies on my unmade bed.

What the fuck? This place had dozens of rooms. She could've picked any one of them as her second room. But this was not accidental. She was trying to send a message—I was no longer a part of this household.

Defiant, I flung myself on the bed and rubbed my unwashed self over the linen, just to be a dick. Then I stared at the ceiling. The bed still smelled of Gracelynn. Her shampoo and French perfume and expensive nail polish. Why'd she sleep here? It seemed like such a weird thing to do.

The entrance door downstairs opened and shut. Laughter filled the foyer. Dad. Miranda. Gracelynn. They were talking animatedly. My gut twisted with anger.

How fucking lovely: they'd managed to become one happy family the minute I became "manageable."

"He's here," I heard one of the servants announce, and I knew she was talking about me. But as I waited—ten, fifteen, twenty minutes— no one from my so-called family knocked on my door.

This was how it remained for the next few hours. A battle of wills and ego. Who was going to approach who first? Dad or me. Only I was a goddamn fifteen-year-old and he was the grown-ass man who chose his wife over his son.

Skipping dinner was a no-brainer. My stomach grumbled with hunger, but I'd rather die before losing this ego game with Dad. When everyone went to bed, I tiptoed my way down to the kitchen and ate three plates of leftovers. Then I went upstairs to the roof through the laundry-room window, and stargazed.

I spotted Mercury, Saturn, Venus, Mars, and Jupiter. If I squinted real hard, I could even pretend to see the rings on Saturn. Stars calmed me down. Their existence. The knowledge there were universes out there that were so much bigger than my shitty existence.

Proportions. Yeah, that's the reason I liked astronomy so much. It put everything in proportion.

The next morning, I was a no-show at breakfast. Conversation was tense as it drifted up to my room. Doug was cracking, knowing his sole heir would rather drink his own piss than share a dining table with him.

By noon, Dad and Miranda sent Gracelynn to knock on my door.

"Come in," I said, after letting her wait outside my room for nine full minutes, and even gritted out in frustration, "Come on now, I know you're there."

She pushed the door open. She'd gotten taller. There were pimples on her chin, and she had colorful braces. She didn't look good, and that made me happy.

I'd filled out during our time apart. I knew I looked handsome because I got hit on all the time. And I knew Gracelynn figured as much, because she couldn't stop staring at me.

She gnawed on her inner cheek, clenching the doorknob tightly. "We're going to the movies. Mom and Dad asked if you wanna tag along."

"She's not my mom, and he's not your dad," I said matter-of-factly, bouncing a tennis ball onto the ceiling and back to me repeatedly. "And pass."

"You don't even know what we're watching." She sounded whiny and a little stressed. She didn't want to disappoint Doug and Miranda. After all, being the favorite child was her full-time job.

"Unless it's a live show of you getting wedgied by every single person we went to school with, I remain uninterested."

"I see you haven't changed at all." Her pimply chin quivered.

"Of course I did." I smirked, my gaze still hard on the bouncing ball. "I no longer care for you. Not in the slightest."

"I'm your stepsister!"

"You're a liar."

She turned away and slammed the door behind her.

◆ ◆ ◆

The days passed slowly, but as they did, the determination inside me grew.

Doug broke first. He knocked on my door five days into our cold war, inviting me to go golfing with his friends. Saying no was no hardship—I hated golf and pretty much despised him.

The nights were much more pleasant. Quieter and less hot. I got on the roof with a flashlight and an astronomy book and a telescope I'd bought after working odd jobs between classes over the year. Doug had given me a credit card to use, but I never touched it, out of principle.

I read about dwarf galaxies and black holes and Higgs boson. I ate a whole day's worth of food on the roof, not bothering to clean the leftovers, knowing I'd attract all kinds of animals. I lay flat on my back, hands tucked under my head, and wondered. Wondered about what the girl I'd end up marrying would look like. I liked dark-haired women, so I guessed she'd be a brunette. I thought she'd be serious and smart. A scientist, maybe. And she'd have great tits. And she'd let me touch them all the time.

She'd be nothing like Miranda, like Gracelynn, or even like Patrice.

We'd get married, me and this hypothetical girl. And my "family" would attend the ceremony; I'd be cold and distant with them. And they'd know I didn't need them anymore. That I had my own family now.

This girl, my dream girl, she was going to come from a big, happy family. We'd spend all our holidays with them. We'd have traditions and matching ugly Christmas sweaters and holidays.

It was the dreams that kept me going. Because where there were dreams—there was hope.

After three weeks of solitude, Doug managed to drag me to the tennis court. He knew I liked to play and bribed me with a promise of Korean barbecue and beer afterward.

Dad tried in his own backward way. In the upcoming days, he let me drink beer with his hotshot friends at the country club after my tennis matches (I won them all). And he didn't force me to spend time with Miranda and Gracelynn.

In fact, I managed to avoid the duo for six whole weeks. Almost the entire duration of my summer vacation. Until one night, when I was on the roof, reading about quantum mechanics, I heard a noise coming from the opposite side of the chimney. I sat up, glancing behind my shoulder. I found Gracelynn standing on the ridge in her pale-yellow pajamas, fists on her hips.

She was just a foot from me, staring at me from above.

"In case you're wondering, things are perfect without you." She tried to force a smug grin, but I could tell she was nervous. Her eyes were wide and desperate.

"I wasn't, but thanks for the update," I said indifferently. "You can have both of them and this ugly-ass mansion. Life here is boring. I'm having fun at school."

Lies, lies, and more lies. Andrew Dexter Academy was strict and full of bullies and abusive staff, but I wasn't going to give her the pleasure of telling her that.

"You know." She tapped her chin thoughtfully. "I think about that night every day. How come you didn't try to tell your dad the truth? You just . . . dropped it."

I did try. He didn't listen.

I dog-eared a page in my book and put it aside. "Whatever for? I got what I wanted. Not seeing your ugly face every day."

"Did you really mean what you said? About not caring for me anymore?" Her facade dropped, and with it, her taunting smile.

"With every fiber of my body."

"Well, for your information, I hate you too!"

"Is this the useless-fun-fact awards?" I looked around us in wonder before reaching for my book with a yawn. "Why the hell do you think I care?"

The next part happened very fast. Gracelynn let out a growl and crouched down, trying to push me down the shingles. I stumbled, still a step away, before managing to grab the vent pipe. I was still a few feet away from the edge. Gracelynn groaned in frustration, using her legs to kick me down. She wanted to kill me. Straight-up break my neck. The girl was a psycho.

"Fall! Oh, die already!" She kicked her legs desperately, trying to reach my body. I curled one hand around the vent pipe and grabbed one of her feet with the other, then tugged her down to me. She gasped, turning flat on her stomach, trying to claw her way back up like a wet cat in a tub.

I didn't let go of her ankle, but I did climb up the ledge with her. When we got to the ridge, I flipped her flat on her back and straddled her waist. I couldn't take any chances that she'd try to kill me again.

She raised her fists in the air, attempting to catch my nose, my cheek, my neck. I grabbed both her wrists and slammed them down on either side of her head. She moaned in pain. It took everything in me not to hit her.

"What's your problem? Huh?" I screamed.

She panted underneath me. Her chest rising and falling. She wasn't wearing a bra. I swallowed, feeling weird and tingly and not half as furious as I should be. And it sucked, because even though I hated her, I didn't hate her body.

"Kiss me." She licked her lips, her dark gaze dropping to my mouth.

"*What?*" I asked, confused.

She tried to wiggle free, laughing. "Kiss me, you dumbass. I want you to be my first."

She hadn't been kissed before? She was almost my age. I was still a virgin, but I'd kissed plenty, made out, and even finger-banged two girls at a ski tournament last winter.

Plus, and more importantly—why me?

"You hate me," I spit out.

"'Hate and love are the same mistresses under a different mask.' I once heard this phrase somewhere, and it made me think of you." She smiled up at me, batting her lashes. And that's when I realized what was happening. She liked the struggle. The fight. The games. She saw Doug and Miranda's relationship and wanted to reenact it. What I saw as abuse, she viewed as passion.

My hand slid from her wrist to her neck. I put a little pressure on it. Not so much as to hurt her but enough to tell her I wasn't messing around. I lowered my face to hers. Her eyelids fluttered; her breath hitched. Her stupid body caved in, muscles going slack, as she readied herself for a kiss. I leaned forward. My lips were a hair away from hers when I stopped moving, letting that last inch between us feel like an entire mile.

"You foolish, foolish girl. If you ever try to kill me again . . ." My grip on her neck tightened. "I'm going to break your pretty little neck, even if I'll get locked up for it. Next time, you won't be crying wolf—you'll be eaten by it. Bones and all."

Before I could straighten my spine and get the fuck out of there, she leaped forward, and her lips touched mine. She stole a kiss. It was sloppy and full of tongue and metal. It tasted like venom. Like alcoholic mouthwash and a girl I had no business wanting, but I wanted all the same.

"You taste like poison," I whispered into her mouth.

She grinned, biting my lower lip real hard, until the metallic taste of blood exploded in both our mouths. "Maybe that's how I'll end up killing you." She licked the blood off my mouth. "With kindness."

CHAPTER SIX

ARSÈNE

"This might not mean jack shit." Christian inches in front of the billiard table, holding his cue like a rifle. He shoots a perfect cannon. "You're reading too much into this."

I'm perched on the recliner behind him at the New Amsterdam. A private gentlemen's club on the corner of Sixty-Ninth Street. It is the most exclusive club in New York, and therefore relatively empty.

Christian, Riggs, and I have been hitting the place ever since Riggs informed us we could no longer go to the Brewtherhood, our favorite pub, because he'd banged his way through the patrons, the pub goers, and some of the supply providers.

"Hardly." I flip a page in the astronomy book I'm reading, a pipe tucked in the side of my mouth. "I went to see his estate lawyer today. He couldn't give me details but said that Grace inherited something of value."

"That could mean anything. It could mean the good fucking china. When can you see the will?" Christian puts his cue aside to grab his beer and take a swig.

"A physical copy should be sent to me any day now."

"But why would your dad leave Grace anything?" Riggs frowns, moving around the billiard table to examine where he wants to take his best shot. "Wasn't she his former best friend's spunk stain?"

I put the pipe down. "Being a polarizing piece of work runs in the Corbin family. Giving her something he thought I'd want would be the ultimate fuck-you. I don't think he ever forgave me."

"For what?" Christian frowns.

"Being born." I smirk.

"You weren't the one who shoved his cock into your mom, excuse my French." Riggs takes a pull of his drink.

"Grudges, like crotchless underwear, make very little sense." Christian claps my shoulder. "What do you think he left for her?"

The hotel on Fifth Avenue? The yacht? The time-share private jet? The options are limitless. The Corbins are old money. So old you can trace it back to eighteenth-century France. My ancestors ate cake with Marie Antoinette.

"Hard to say." I toss my book onto a table. "Douglas had a lot of assets and zero scruples. The only thing I know for sure is that he couldn't have given her too much. We're not known for our generosity."

"There's a silver lining to all of this, though." Riggs leans against his cue like it's a cane, ankles crossed, a winning game show–host smile on his face.

I arch an eyebrow in question. "Enlighten me."

"He's dead now, and you get to make the final move. To leverage whatever's in the will to your advantage."

"Meaning?"

"Whatever she *doesn't* get, you'll dangle in front of her face like a carrot." Riggs uses his cue to scratch his back, his eyebrows arched. "You wanted to conquer her, didn't you? This is how you deliver the final blow. How you win."

I narrow my eyes. "I didn't peg you for the cunning type."

"Oh, I can be ruthless." Riggs waves me off with a chuckle. "I just never give enough damn to show that side of me."

Huh.

I'm going to make the most out of the situation.

Even if it means putting flames to Douglas Corbin's legacy.

Three days later it arrives. A signature-required manila envelope. Alfred from reception calls to let me know it is here. I charge out of my apartment barefoot.

"Who delivered it? UPS?" I pluck the folder out of the old man's fingers.

He shakes his head. "Hand delivered by some important-lookin' fella in a suit. I hope it works out well for you, son."

In the elevator, I muster every ounce of my self-control not to rip the brown envelope to shreds. That would be exactly what my father would have wanted. I can't risk the infinitesimal chance an afterlife does exist, and his spirit is watching me from above.

I flip the bird upward instead, then downward, toward the floor. "My inkling is you ended up in hell, but there's just enough chance you bribed an angel for a place in heaven."

When I return to my apartment, I frisbee the envelope atop my office desk, go to the kitchen, make myself a cup of coffee, and then return. I slit the envelope with my letter opener, then neatly pull out the stack of papers, reminding myself internally for the millionth time that I don't care either way.

But I do. I care, and it's fucking killing me.

I know my shine would dim in Grace's eyes if Doug made her as rich as I am. I dangle my pedigree, my prestige, my family's billions in front of her to keep her. If that goes away, she might leave for good.

And if she leaves for good, I lose. Truly and finally lose our three-decade war.

Here goes nothing.

I skim over the boring parts and dive straight to business. I begin reading through the items.

The majority of the estates, save for the office building in Scarsdale that went to Dad's business partner, now belongs to me.

The liquid money, bonds, and bank accounts go to me, in their entirety. His investment portfolio is mine now. His time-share private plane too. I even get the cars, antique furniture, and ugly heirlooms.

I get everything he's ever possessed.

Miranda Langston gets nothing. Not even the canned goods in the pantry. Not even his best fucking regards. Grace doesn't seem to be getting anything either. What the hell was the estate lawyer talking about? That he left her something of value?

I stare at the file in confusion. What am I missing?

And then I see it. At the very end of the will. Gracelynn Langston has received Calypso Hall. The small theater, a stone's throw from Times Square, is neglected and in desperate need of refurbishing. If it is functioning at all, it must be a money pit. I suspect the only reason it hasn't closed thus far is because too many tourists can't get their hands on Broadway tickets in time and end up catching a show there.

The place isn't worth the real estate it is occupying. And the best part is it's a historical building, so whoever is gonna buy it would have to keep it a theater. It is therefore unsellable. Not for a good price, anyway.

Grace isn't a penny richer than she was before this will.

Great news for me.

A bombshell for her.

I sit back, mulling this over—what was Douglas's angle? What was he planning to achieve by depriving me of this glorified shithole?

Then it hits me.

Calypso Hall was originally purchased when my mother first moved to the US. I'd overheard the servants say that she was lonely and bored out of her mind during her pregnancy with me. To pacify her, my father decided to gift her something to keep her busy and out of his hair. Since Patrice was an aspiring actress, he bought her this failing theater. He appointed her as the managing director and, in true Corbin fashion, told her to spare no dime in making it a success.

She'd spent days and nights there, fussing over every detail, each stage prop, each show. Some said she actually turned it around and made it profitable for a few months. My father didn't tell me a lot about her, but he did say that as soon as I was born, she tossed me into the arms of a wet nurse and continued working at the theater, and forgot all about my existence.

I was the only one who'd have you, Ars. It's you and me, boy. Forever.

One of Douglas's only saving graces was the fact that he took me on when my mother moved to Manhattan and lived a life without me.

I'm not sure why Dad thought giving Grace something my late, dysfunctional mother once loved would spite me, but he missed the mark by a thousand miles or so.

If anything, giving Grace something sentimental and of no fiscal value just shows how little he knew his stepdaughter.

Smirking, I spin my office chair to face the floor-to-ceiling window. If I got a copy, that means Grace got one too.

She is about to find out that I just became one of the richest men in the country. Minted beyond her wildest dreams. It is going to kill her—but it is going to lure her in too.

And thus begins another game between us. A game of chicken.

Who will cave in first, pick up the phone, and call? Admit defeat? Accept their destiny and finally bow to this sordid arrangement and all that it entails?

It is a good time to remind Grace of something she might've forgotten.

I always win.

64

CHAPTER SEVEN

ARSÈNE

Two weeks later

"Thanks for letting me crash with you." Riggs wobbles out of the taxi behind me, hammered as a thousand goddamn nails.

I glance at my watch. "*Letting* is a big word. You followed me home, asshole. I had little choice in the matter."

"C'mon, Ars. Everyone wants a stalker. Means you made it in life." He slaps my back good-naturedly, his golden curls tumbling down his wide brow as he shakes his head.

"You're an odd creature," I grumble.

"Said the pot to the kettle."

We make our way down the street to my apartment. I'd asked the taxi driver to drop us off before we reached our destination, worried my childhood friend would vomit all over his leather seats.

Riggs pushes his fists into his front pockets, whistling tunelessly.

"What's your next destination?" I ask, trying to quiet my mind. Grace hasn't contacted me these last couple of weeks. I know she's still digesting the loss of her edge on me. She and I both know that through this will, I became too important for her to continue playing games with.

She knows I will ask for concessions—heavy ones. And she's biding her time.

"North Jakarta," Riggs replies.

I *hmm*.

"That's in Indonesia, you uncultured swine." He chuckles.

"When are you leaving?"

"Next week." He kicks an empty soda can on the sidewalk straight into a trash can, in a curled free kick that would put Beckham to shame. "For three weeks. It's kind of a perk, since I won Photo of the Year last year."

The photo was of a lightning strike touching a sandhill crane's wing. He caught the entire flock lifting off at the same time, flying in the same direction. The background was all purple and blue.

I have no doubt Riggs is full of all the dark matter artists are born with. But whatever darkness resides in him, he makes sure not to let anyone see it. The happy-go-lucky, handsome man chasing skirt and adventure is the version everyone gets, his best friends included. In a way, I suspect that he's fucked up more than both Christian and me combined.

I shove the glass door to my building with my shoulder. We make our way to the elevator.

"Alfred, my good man." Riggs bumps fists with my seventy-year-old doorman while I drag him inside. "How's Suzanne doing? Hip surgery went well?"

"Beyond well, Mr. Riggs. Thank you for sending flowers—it was most kind of you. She's already up and about. Glad to have you back. Mr. Corbin, I—"

"Not now, Alfred," I bark, advancing toward the elevator. Riggs may be a nice guy to service providers, but he's also a goddamn 180 pounds of muscles to carry right now, and drunk as hell.

"But sir—"

"I said I'm busy."

Riggs knows Alfred's wife's name. Unbelievable. That asshole better rent an apartment in the city next year. My place is not a hostel, and he is starting to become too comfortable here.

We take the elevator up. Riggs squints at me. "Where are your manners, ass-face? Alfred is an elderly gentleman."

"I don't care if he is the pope himself." I push the door to my apartment open.

"Now make yourself useful and order us a bite. *Your* treat." I make it halfway across the living room before realizing Riggs has frozen over. He is standing in front of my couch, mouth open, eyes wide.

I stop.

Stare at my sofa.

Grace is sprawled on it, completely naked, save for a pair of red-soled high heels. She is sound asleep. Her pink nipples are erect, and there are goose bumps all over her skin.

What. The. F—

"Holy ravioli." Riggs whistles. "I'm starting to get the whole screwing-your-sister kink. Still not my jam, but I'm broadening my horizons."

"I'll be broadening your ass if you don't get out of here right this moment." I turn to him, trembling with anger and elation.

Finally. Fucking finally. What took her so long?

"But I need a place to stay." He grins provocatively, enjoying seeing me squirm.

"New York is the home of six hundred and seventy hotels. Go stay in one of them."

"Bros before hos." Riggs makes a show of yanking his bag from the floor and swinging it over his shoulder. He snaps his fingers, hanging his head down. "Oh, that's right. She *is* your sister."

He makes his way out the door, slamming it, but not before he salutes me. "Enjoy!"

I perch on the edge of the coffee table and stare at Grace for a few seconds. Her expression is peaceful. That's how I know it's all an act. Grace usually has a puckered frown on her face when she's asleep. Like she uses this downtime to contemplate world domination.

"I know you're awake," I say.

I figure she realized I wasn't alone when we got in and wasn't in the mood to explain her state of nakedness.

Her face doesn't flinch.

I sigh. "Riggs is gone, we have an important conversation that's overdue, and I may not be in a charitable mood tomorrow morning, once the alcohol wears off."

Her eyes flutter open. She sits upright, pouting like the spoiled princess she is. "Ugh, I hate most of your friends, but that one takes the cake, Ars. He acts like an actual frat boy."

I say nothing. It's been two weeks. She should be on her knees servicing me right now.

"I made you mashed potatoes with extra butter and onion bits, just like you like." She stretches like a lazy cat, shooting me a grin. "And there's a seasoned steak waiting to be thrown in the pan."

She examines me, waiting for my words.

I tilt my head in the kitchen's direction. "Well? Steak's not gonna make itself."

She stands up. I smack her ass lightly on her way to my kitchen, admiring her long legs in those heels. She rolls her shoulders as she takes the raw steak out of the fridge, probably to relieve the tension building in her body.

"Grace." My voice is cold as a sharp blade, traveling down her neck.

"Hmm?"

"Come here when you're done."

While I wait for my steak to fry, I enjoy a glass of Moet & Chandon and a hearty blow job. She is on her knees, bobbing her head enthusiastically back and forth, taking more of me in than she normally does.

I stand casually by the window, watching the darkness engulfing the tree-filled park while Grace fists my cock, sucking my balls into her mouth, her tongue massaging them.

I won. I know it. She knows it. Still, the satisfaction of having her in the palm of my hand is not as tangible, as glorious as I imagined it'd be. The fun part about Grace was always—*always*—the chase.

Dinner is pleasant. She smiles at me frequently, stroking my hand and asking if everything is to my taste. It is.

"Congrats on the will, by the way." She finally gets to the point forty-five minutes after I woke her up.

"Strange choice of words, but thanks. Congrats on the theater." I cut a juicy piece of steak and pop it into my mouth. "What're you going to do with it?"

"Oh, I don't know." She twirls her champagne glass by the stem, lost in thought. "I have a call with my financial adviser next week. I'll know more then. You don't think there's a way to turn this into a profitable venture, do you, Ars?"

I think it's an endless money pit designed to appease the females the Corbin men are enamored with and is a waste of brick and mortar.

"No."

"Maybe I'll sell it, then."

"Don't expect a substantial revenue. It'll take a lot of money and a few miracles to turn that place around and make it appealing."

"You're so smart." Grace sighs, beaming at me. "We'll revisit this subject after I take a good look at it. I'm sure you can help me out with that big brain of yours."

I put my fork down, tired of this tedious charade. "What took you so long?"

She knots her arms over her chest defensively. "What do you mean?"

"I mean coming here. Don't play dumb."

"Nothing. I . . . I don't know." She throws her hands in the air. "Can you blame me? I guess it's hard, coming to terms with the fact that you're in love with your stepbrother. A stepbrother you haven't always been kind to. It's been a pretty difficult month."

"In *love* with me?" I splutter.

The timing, the convenience of it, makes it all transparent. She isn't in love with me. With my money, maybe. And as much as I want to marry her, her lies are transparent at best and offensive at worst.

"Of course I'm in love with you, Arsène. Why else would I be with you for so many years?"

Because you're an attention-seeking Erinyes, and you simply can't let a good marriage prospect go to waste.

Grace is thirty-three. Still young, but not so young not to think about who she'd want to procreate with one day. She is a calculating creature, always five steps ahead in the game. When it comes to profitable ventures—I am one.

"You love me?" I ask again, sitting back.

"Yes." She narrows her eyes, shifting uncomfortably in her seat. "Why is this so weird to you? Don't you love *me*?"

"I'm not sure."

But I am. I'm sure and a half. I'm sure and fucked as a daytime hooker, because loving her brings me no joy. No fulfillment. I've come to think of love as a prison guard. Something you resent, not cherish.

"Your sudden declaration is awfully convenient. I'm going to need to ask for some receipts for this so-called love," I drawl out.

"You literally had your cock in my mouth not even twenty minutes ago. While you were texting on your phone!" she thunders, her cheeks hot with fury.

I offer her a cold smile. "You like to feel a little manhandled. Helps you loosen up after being a ballbuster all day at work."

She rolls her eyes. "You want proof, fine. What'd you have in mind?"

We are having this conversation like we are conducting business. I like it. How like minded we are.

"I want you to move in with me," I say dryly.

She nods. "Okay. I can do that. What else?"

"You will also marry me," I continue matter-of-factly. "Although I understand this can be delicate news to break, considering the timing and circumstances. I'll allow you a few months to smooth out the rough edges. Prepare the soil, so to speak."

"Marry?" Her eyebrows lift, her eyes widening with open, unabashed pleasure. She is keeping her excitement out of it, not wanting to acknowledge her own disadvantage in our negotiations. "I didn't peg you as the marrying type."

"Marriage is a perfectly pragmatic endeavor." I pick up my fork and take a bite of the rare steak, its bloodied juice running down my tongue. "I'm a fan of institutions. They stand the test of time because they're functional. Marriage is a good, low-risk investment. I need heirs, stability, and a house outside this goddamn city. The tax relief isn't lost on me either."

While this little speech is not going to win any romance awards, it hits the mark. Now that Grace knows Douglas didn't make her a multimillionaire, I have my foot on her throat.

"Is this a marriage proposal?" Her dark eyes nearly bulge out of their sockets.

"It's a declaration of intention."

"All right." She gives her shiny hair a pat. "Provided I get a ring big enough to be spotted from Mars. I want something gross and distasteful. Something that'll make every woman I know despise me."

I don't have the heart to tell her most women she knows already hate her.

Either Grace is shit at negotiations and I gave her far too much credit, or she is desperate for this bargain. At any rate, she's given up the fight too willingly, and I wonder why. She's spent the last decade dumping me every few months and dragging me through all her drama . . . only to say yes to a proposal? What's her angle?

"You'll sign a prenup," I announce.

Her face falls. "Why? It's not like we're ever going to—"

I lift a hand up. "I enjoy you, Grace. More than I should. But make no mistake. I trust you no more than tomorrow's *National Enquirer* headline."

She lets out a laugh. "You're terrible."

"That can't be news to you."

"Fine. But I reserve the right to have three lawyers go over this prenup."

"Have a hundred, sweetheart." It doesn't matter. I'm going to get my way and ensure my wealth is safe from her, just like my father had with her mother.

"Now, go wait for me in the bedroom while I wash the dishes." I stand up.

She hesitates at first, loitering, as if she has something more to say, then gets up on her feet.

My back is to her when she starts walking. I watch her from the kitchen window's reflection. "Did I say go? I meant *crawl*."

Turning my head, I watch her spine stiffen as she gives it a brief thought.

"You like to humiliate me, don't you?"

Not particularly. But I know she likes it, and I play our game very well.

"That's fine, Ars. The trouble is, I like to be humiliated by you too. I know you don't love me . . ." She draws in a breath. "No, don't even try to deny it. What you have for me is not love. It's obsession. It's always been obsession. I'll still take it."

Slowly, she lowers herself on all fours and crawls toward my bedroom, her magnificent ass in the air. I *do* love her. Of course I love her. Why else would I put up with everything she's put me through?

I want to tell her to get up. But something stops me. A searing pain that slashes through my chest every time I remember how she deprived me of the only family I knew. How cruelly she screwed me over.

I wash the plates and the pan, then rinse the champagne glasses. Drying my hands on my way to the bedroom, I hear the water running in the en suite.

Grace appears in the doorway a minute later, in a sexy black lace baby doll.

Baby doll. The nickname makes me shudder. Why am I thinking of that country bumpkin all of a sudden? Never mind. Her simpleton face has already disappeared from my mind.

Grace approaches me and drags her fingernail over my throat.

"I was thinking . . ." The tip of her tongue travels along her top lip. "How about I give you VIP access to my back end?"

I stare at her. Did she just offer me anal sex? Like we're teens? We've never discussed it before. I wasn't under the impression this was something she'd be interested in.

"Why?" I question.

"What do you mean?" Her smile crumbles. This wasn't the reaction she was shooting for. "I want to make things special for you. We're moving in together. We just discussed *marriage*." She swallows hard, taking a step back. "Plus, you've always liked unorthodox things. I thought maybe you wanted to get a little kinky."

I don't want her to give up things she doesn't want to give because the cards have shuffled and changed in my favor.

"Oh, come on!" She rolls her eyes. "Don't pretend like you don't like it when I squeeze my tits together and you fuck the gap between them until you come into my mouth."

We definitely have some room for growth on the sweet talk side.

I give her a leveled look. "That idea was born of you being bored and horny while you were on your period, remember?"

"Well, now my idea is to have anal sex!" She is shouting at me, never a good look when trying to seduce someone. "What's so hard to understand?"

"Let's pin this generous offer for when you're feeling less grateful and I'm not as power drunk." I fist the back of her hair, extending her neck. "Now be a good girl and get on all fours for me on the bed. It's your best angle, anyway."

She does, dragging her knees over the satin linen.

"Stare at the headboard. Don't take your eyes off of it." I circle her like a predator, knowing it's making her hot for me.

When I put on a condom and finally enter her from behind, I find her as dry as a bone. Confused, I pull out slowly, not wanting to necessarily hurt her.

"Would you like more time?" I clear my throat, feeling surprisingly out of depth.

She reaches over and grabs the hem of my shirt. "No. Continue. It's just . . . stress makes me that way sometimes. I'm having fun."

"No offense, but you feel like sandpaper," I say flatly. "Having sex is not mandatory." I pull away from her, about to rip the condom off my cock.

She turns around and tugs at my shirt desperately. "No, no. Please. You have to fuck me."

"Why?" I ask, flabbergasted. We've never had an issue like this before, but I don't see the necessity in fucking tonight if she is not up for it.

"Because!" She is on the verge of crying. "I've missed you and I want you inside me, all right? Stop asking so many questions."

I have an odd feeling that there is more to tonight than her not being wet. She usually bounces on my cock like it's Sky Zone. Something's up with her, but she'll never confide in me.

"Please." She pushes her ass toward me, her voice urgent. "Do it. Please. For me."

Begrudgingly, I fuck her, slow and careful, holding her by the waist, watching her silken, raven hair spilling over her smooth back. She is still mostly dry, but every time I see her wince, I push my fingers into her mouth and use her saliva as lubricant, massaging her clit in the process in the vain hope she'll get a little wetter.

"Are you sure this is okay?" I ask gruffly, feeling like a goddamn high schooler and hating every moment of it.

"It's amazing. Ohhh, just like that. Please."

"You don't feel like you're enjoying yourself."

"Men know very little about the female body," she barks out. "Don't tell me what I'm feeling. I have my own agency."

Closing my eyes, I try to finish as fast as I can. The sex is about as good as a week-old coffee. I'm half-mast, put out, and unsettled. So for the first time in my life I grunt a little, pretending to finish, then pull out as fast as I can.

When she rolls over underneath me, she grins up, cupping my cheeks. "That was so much fun, wasn't it?"

Like grinding my dick over a nail file.

"Epic," I mutter.

She leans forward to kiss the side of my mouth.

Subdued, I slide the condom off as I amble to the bathroom. I throw the condom into the trash and turn to the toilet to take a piss. Frowning, I crouch down to examine the pink residue around the rubber. Another unwelcome first.

"Grace?"

"Hmm?" she purrs from the room, grabbing the remote and flipping through channels.

"I think you bled."

Her metallic laugh is bone rattling as it echoes around my room. "Did I? Oh, it used to happen to me all the time in college."

"What does it mean?" I ask.

"No idea. I should really get it checked. I've been really stressed since the will. Didn't even use my vibrator once."

"Call your doctor tomorrow."

"Yessir."

I return to the bedroom and watch her, trying to strip down all the lies she is coated with to find out the truth. But she is so good at this. At the charade. She's always been a beautiful liar.

"All right, future hubby. Come here now." She reaches for me and drags me down onto the bed with her. "Let's cuddle a little."

Who. The. Fuck. Is. This. Woman?

"Since when do we *cuddle*?"

"Now we're going to have to start!" she exclaims, back to being fake cheerful. "We're about to get married, right?"

We try watching something together, but Grace is allergic to documentaries, and I don't give two damns about stupid reality TV shows where people drink, gossip, and sell houses.

In the end, I let her watch something on Bravo and fall asleep.

CHAPTER EIGHT

ARSÈNE

Three months later, I whisk Grace off to Martha's Vineyard. A quainter, less glamorous version of Cape Cod. The Hamptons without the shine.

I don't enjoy Martha's Vineyard any more than I do the nearest public restroom, but I know that renting a house there makes Grace feel like Michelle Obama.

"My goodness, Arsène, I feel like *royalty*. What did I ever do to deserve this?" Grace gushes expectedly, cupping her cheeks in faux amazement, twirling in the vast foyer of a dazzling Oak Bluffs mansion.

Managed to become unavailable to me even while living under my roof.

Foolishly, I thought moving Grace in would make us grow closer.

Almost the opposite has been true. Grace works insane hours and doesn't return home until nine or ten o'clock most days. These past two months alone, she spent half of her weekends in Zurich, working on a complicated merger between two small private banks.

She makes an effort—I'll give her that. We fuck like rabbits. She makes me breakfast, purchases my favorite ties and cologne, and is diligent about hanging on my arm during formal events.

The dry spell episode in which she bled was a one-off. We've been having noteworthy sex since. She has not brought up the anal suggestion again, and I am grateful for it.

She stopped introducing me as her stepbrother and began referring to me as her *partner in crime*. An unhappy medium between calling me her brother and flat out admitting my dick lives rent-free between her legs.

Manhattan's financial circles are abuzz with the news that, while waiting for my ban to expire, I've decided to move my stepsister in for my own pleasures, and she knows it. What's more, after years of Grace hammering it into their heads, many people simply think of us as siblings. After all, we do look alike. With our dark hair and eyes.

It is all incredibly messy and, therefore, for me, also exceedingly amusing.

"You deserve this getaway." I curl my fists inside my front pockets, watching her admiring the imposing columns and wall-to-wall bookshelves. "We barely get to see each other anymore."

"But when we do, it's so great. Don't you think?" She flings her arms around my neck, kissing me.

She rips her mouth from mine before I can kiss her back. "Have I told you how good you look today?" She beams. "Like a brusque king. God, Ars, I don't think I'll ever have enough of you."

She yanks me down the hallway, climbing me like a tree, peeling her clothes off in the process, ready for her first holiday treat. "I'm so glad we're doing this. I miss you so much whenever we're not together. I can't wait to quit this awful job when we get married." Her mouth is hot and eager on my jaw, making its way down my body. "You'll buy me a little business to keep me busy, right? A winery or something."

I snag the back of her neck and slam her against the wall, devouring her mouth in a punishing kiss as our bodies melt together. Heat swirls between us like fire.

"You're about to get everything your heart desires," I mumble into her hot skin.

Everything she doesn't deserve. For the Corbin men have one thing in common—they always know how to choose the wrong woman.

◆ ◆ ◆

The proposal is a quiet, dignified ordeal. I find it tacky when people ask others to marry them in public settings, where it's impossible for their significant other to decline.

I take Grace to a nice dinner, buy a fine bottle of wine, and, when we return to the rental house, present her with a mammoth diamond ring.

"My goodness. How unexpected! Is that the Catherine?" she coos, accepts, and gives me a twenty-minute blow job that results in two Tylenols for her jaw afterward.

She is happy. Happy enough to hum, and laugh, and even have a piece of cake for dessert. So happy she kisses me when we take walks on the beach and clings to me, nuzzling my neck, and can't stop talking about how she wants to start a charity when she quits work.

We are getting married. Mission accomplished. And yet. *And yet.* I can't say I'm truly satisfied. I've reached the top of Everest, only to find out I can barely breathe up there.

The evening before we go back to New York, I take Grace to a yacht club. She munches on her green salad and wiggles her delicate fingers, letting the engagement ring catch the last sunrays pouring through the glass windows.

Looking at it, I decide that Christian was right about what he said when I took him ring shopping earlier this month. Someone is going to cut off this woman's finger to get their hands on this piece of jewelry. I make a mental note to buy her a toned-down ring for everyday functions. I would strongly prefer it if all my future wife's extremities remain intact.

Grace is talking animatedly now. Something about our parents. My eyes keep darting to the ring. It is impossible to look away. It looks uncomfortable to wear. It takes so much space on her bony hand.

This is a statement. One old-moneyed people do not like to make.

I'm so rich I gross myself out. Bow down, you peasant.

This is the kind of piece I'd expect Cardi B to wear. Not a gently bred, private school–educated woman from Scarsdale. But Grace always felt less than. Maybe because her father moved to Australia before she was even born. Maybe because she was made in sin, in secret, in shame, for the sole purpose of hurting my father.

"Arsène, have you been listening to *anything* I just said?" Grace frowns, snapping me out of my reverie.

I blink, taking a sip of my sparkling water. "Sorry, I lost my train of thought. Please repeat that."

She flushes, looking a little embarrassed.

"I was talking about the will." She licks her lips, her eyes skittishly moving around the crowded room.

"What about it?"

"Well, now that we're engaged, maybe it's best if we write each other into our individual wills. You know, just in case."

"In case what?" My jaw hardens.

"Anything happens."

"Define *anything*."

Grace tried to kill me at least once in our lifetime (intentionally, unlike what I did to her). Which—call me a hopeless fucking romantic—was once more than your significant other should. It was a long time ago, but I wouldn't put it past my beautiful, cunning fiancée to try it again.

She is a highly resourceful woman, and I am a very rich man.

She flicks her wrist, chuckling pensively. "I know you're thinking about that time. That was just a stupid teenage retaliation. I was a *kid*. Hormonal as hell. Underdeveloped frontal lobe, et cetera."

"Your underdeveloped frontal lobe is not my concern. Your underdeveloped conscience is."

She pouts. "That's not a very nice way to talk to your fiancée."

I smirk, the back of my fingers brushing her cheek. "Niceness is not a trait we look for in one another."

"Won't you even think about that? For me?" Her eyes are two onyx diamonds. "Knowing how much that means to me. The trust, obviously. Not the money. Just the trust."

It's not like I have any living family to give my possessions to. If I were to die tomorrow, it *is* likely Grace will get at least a good portion of everything I own. Along with Miranda, someone I want nowhere near my shit.

Still, it doesn't take a genius to see Grace's intentions are anything but pure. We're both in our thirties, healthy, and in no immediate danger of cashing in our chips.

"No," I say flatly.

"No?" She blinks, looking genuinely surprised. She is not accustomed to that word, especially from me.

"No," I repeat. "I don't intend to think about it."

"Oh . . . well, I understand." But she doesn't. Which is why she deflates like a balloon.

"I plan on leaving everything I own to the Planetary Society," I continue.

She reaches for the pearls on her neck, playing with them. "That's fine. I . . . I shouldn't have asked."

Someone give the woman a Razzie Award. She is terrible at playing the innocent part.

"So you can call off the engagement right now," I urge her, almost tauntingly. "If this is a deal breaker for you."

She shakes her head, a shriek of laughter bubbling from her throat. "That won't be necessary. Really, it was only a suggestion. I'm okay with whatever you choose. I'm not marrying you for your money."

Of course she is. And the worst part is, I know I'm not going to deny her. Test her—sure. But I'll never follow through. She will get what she wants. I will write her into my will, and vice versa.

"Grace."

"Yes, my love?" She attempts a weak smile. Fails.

"We'll visit my lawyer this week and make the necessary changes."

Her shoulders sag in relief. She smiles—*really* smiles now—her entire features brightening up, like a flower angled up toward the sun on the first day of spring. I've never made her smile like this before.

A rush of possessiveness and desire courses through me.

She is mine. Her bony fingers. Her shrewd eyes. Her black heart. All mine.

"Thank you for trusting me." She reaches across the table, grabs my hand, squeezes. Her hand is cold and dry. "I love you."

I promise myself not to drink or eat anything she makes in the future unless she takes a first sip or bite.

"Love you too."

And I do. I love her. I'm sure of it.

But I also know one thing for sure—a leopard never changes its spots.

CHAPTER NINE

ARSÈNE, SEVENTEEN

I was home for Christmas. Or at least, at the place technically referred to as my home. If it were up to me, I'd have stayed at Andrew Dexter. With that moron Riggs, who was probably looking for creative ways to set himself on fire or jump from roof to roof to pass the time. Or Nicky. Quiet and reserved and sad as he might have been, he didn't make a bad companion. He wasn't a complete idiot either. Always a plus in my book.

The truth of the matter was, these two orphans felt more like my family than the heartless creatures occupying this mansion.

Said creatures were now bursting into the dining room, completely ignoring the fact that I was sitting there eating my breakfast while enjoying an astronomy book.

"You're a selfish bastard, Doug! That's what you are." Miranda sank her claws into the back of an upholstered dining chair, spitting fumes and fire at my dad, who—of course—had chased her here.

"Takes one to know one, honey. What'd you think, that I'd just let you hand over that estate to your mother?"

Uh-huh. Miranda crossed a line here. Never mess with a Corbin's property without permission. We were a stingy bunch. I flipped a page in my book.

"She had nowhere to live!" Miranda shrieked.

"We could've rented her a place. I have people leasing the property! Paying customers. What were you thinking?"

In other news, they were still completely oblivious to my presence. Not that I was surprised. I wondered where Gracelynn was. She'd been uncharacteristically quiet since I got there, no doubt thinking of ways to kill me without leaving traces.

"I was thinking I'd have my husband's support! Sue me for making the assumption." Miranda grabbed a vase from the center of the table and hurled it at him. He dodged artfully—expertly—reminding me that throwing objects at one another was a daily occurrence in this house, akin to passing the jam across the table at breakfast.

"Well, you now stand corrected. I *used* to care. I no longer do. You're not even half as beautiful as you were when we met, and twice as temperamental and problematic. I'm done."

I suspected Miranda and my father were on the brink of divorce. Not because she was terrible to him. She'd always been that. But because he was starting to notice, for a change, and it didn't look like he was as agreeable to her mood swings and demands.

Miranda stared at him with a combination of panic and disbelief. I sat back. I was enjoying this. Why shouldn't I? This woman had been nothing but horrible to me, and it looked like she was finally getting hers. As for my father, he was no angel, either, and watching him grow old alone was a sight I'd relish.

"What are you saying, Doug?" Miranda inhaled.

"I think you should spend Christmas away." He pushed off the wall, heading toward the door.

"Are you serious?" She rushed after him now.

"Yes. The kids can stay with me. The cook's making a big enough meal, and I don't want the food wasted."

Ho, ho, ho. Merry fucking Christmas. From my dysfunctional family to yours.

"One of them is sitting right here," I said blandly, highlighting a passage in my book. No one acknowledged me. "Speaking of food, you're ruining my appetite."

"I'll ask Gracelynn what she wants to do. I bet she wouldn't want to spend the holiday with you!" Miranda said spitefully.

"Don't be so sure," Doug replied, already halfway through the door. "She's fond of me, and I know for a fact she hates your guts."

Oh, lookee here. Trouble in paradise?

It was comforting to know that Gracelynn's childhood had ended up being just as fucked up as mine. Miranda lingered in the dining room, panting, when I took a bite of my oatmeal and flipped another page.

"I'm sure you're just delighted with this whole scene." Miranda pivoted my way with snark, trying to pick a fight.

I swung my gaze from my book to her, smiling. "I'm amused more than delighted. Glee is such an acute feeling—I doubt you could do or say anything that'd prompt me to such emotional heights."

"Ah, you and your stupid riddles. I never understand what you mean." She bared her teeth. "You've always been odd and awkward, just like your mother."

To this jab, I gave a full-blown laugh. "She was weird, awkward, and the first lawful wife of Douglas Corbin. The mother of his firstborn. His sole heir. And she might be dead, but these facts? They fucking *kill* you, Miranda."

"Tell me." She leaned forward, toward me, her eyes dancing in their sockets. "Why are you happy about all of this? It's not like you're having a bad time at Andrew Dexter."

Sitting back, I drummed my fingers on the back of my hardcover, giving it some thought. "Guess I enjoy seeing karma in action. You convinced this man to throw his son—his own flesh and blood—to the curb. And you expected him to stick around for you? Loyalty is not a tree. It doesn't grow with time. Either you're a loyal person or you're not. Douglas isn't loyal. What's more, I bet he isn't faithful either."

She still stared at me as I picked up my empty oatmeal bowl and my book and left the room, knowing that she wanted to hurt me but that she no longer had the power to do so.

◆ ◆ ◆

Dad turned out to be right. Gracelynn decided to stick around at the mansion for Christmas while her mother ran away to our Hamptons house, surrounding herself with her New York divorcée friends.

The benefit of this whole thing was that over the years, I'd relocated my residence whenever I was here for vacations, and I now lived in a separate wing of the house, far away from her. It was entirely possible for me not to see her at all if I wished to.

And I did wish to, because she was a pain in the ass.

I managed to avoid her the entire duration of the holiday, save for Christmas Day itself, on which the three of us exchanged gifts.

Dad got me a 1966 Shelby 427 Cobra and my stepsister a vintage tiara—the real deal, full of diamonds. Gracelynn got me funny socks and a sweater. I gifted Dad an engraved cigar box and for Gracelynn, arctic mice—snake food from PetSmart. The gift drew an awkward giggle from her and an annoyed hum from him, but he was too preoccupied with the collapse of his marriage to chide me for it.

I endured the day, hour by hour, minute by minute, until it evaporated into the night and I was able to breathe again.

Another day passed, and then another. It was a beautiful thing to look at the calendar and see that tomorrow I was going back to Andrew

Dexter, and Miranda was still not here, and Gracelynn, who *was* here somewhere, was as miserable and lost as I'd felt my first two years at Andrew Dexter.

The occasion called for a celebration, and I decided to go downstairs to the kitchen in the middle of the night to raid the wine fridge. I hadn't planned on drinking tonight, but I'd bring some bottles with me to the dorms. Riggs and Nicky would appreciate it, and we'd have enough alcohol to hold us over until Easter.

I made my way downstairs barefoot, opened a garbage bag, and started filling it with expensive bottles. Then I walked into the darkened pantry and began shoving junk food into a separate bag. That's when I heard a soft huff behind my back. More of a hiccup, actually. I turned around, thinking it was one of the staff, to find my stepsister standing right in front of me, looking like a ghost of her former self.

We stood in the pantry, staring at each other, the faint light from the range hood outside the room the only thing illuminating our faces.

"Are you crying?" I sneered. Her eyes were shining; her face was wet.

She wiped at her cheeks hurriedly, letting out a laugh. "Don't be ridiculous. Why would I cry?"

"Because your family life is nonexistent, you have no real friends, no particular talents, and once your average beauty fades, you're pretty much toast?" I offered chivalrously.

She let out a cackle that sounded like a nail scratching a blackboard, before breaking down in a feral wail. I didn't understand it. Any of it. She'd won. She was here, and I was gone. I hadn't forgiven her, no. In a sense that I'd still deliver vengeance, if and when the opportunity called for it. But I had accepted the situation for what it was over the years. And I never let her see how upset I was by it. Letting someone know you have an emotional reaction to them was the worst thing you could do for yourself. Especially if you didn't trust them with said feelings.

"You're such an asshole, Arsène, no wonder your dad likes me better than you!" She pushed at my chest, but she was still crying, almost hysterically, and we both knew this was just a weak attempt from her to save face.

I flung the bags of junk food and alcoholic beverages over one shoulder, shrugging. "Well, enjoy your meltdown, sis. See you next year. Unless Doug decides he's finally had enough of you Langstons."

I tried to sidestep her, but she shoved herself between the door and me. "No! Don't go."

This goddamn menace . . . I glanced at my watch. It was late, but even if it weren't, no time was a good time to listen to Grace bitch and moan.

"Do you want to talk about it?" I grunted.

"Actually." A slow smile spread over her face. It was a pleasant face, I had to admit. She had grown out of her awkward phase. And not only was she hot, but she was also completely off limits. Which, of course, spoke to my adolescent cock. "I could think of better uses for our mouths, seeing as you're about to leave here in a few hours."

I swallowed, watching her under half-lidded eyes. The self-respecting man in me wanted to tell her to go ride her own fingers in the shower. The hormonal teenager in me couldn't wait to know if she'd put that virginal tongue of hers to good use since we'd last kissed.

I arched an eyebrow, downplaying my interest. "I'm gonna need you to be more specific than that."

She grinned, masking her pain. "Like, tell you what I wanna do to you?"

"A demonstration would be best."

"All right, cowboy."

She closed the door behind her. I flicked the light on. I wanted to see everything when it happened. A part of me didn't believe this was happening (hormonal teenager). Another thought I was insane for letting her teeth anywhere near my cock (self-respecting man).

But as I was pushed back by my stepsister, my spine colliding with tall glass bottles of imported sparkling water, I decided to take the chance. Gracelynn dropped to her knees and worked quickly at tugging my pants down my legs. She didn't even want to kiss. My cock sprang free from my sweatpants. It was long and hard and engorged, having listened to the conversation between us and knowing the score.

She grabbed it by the base, looking a little hesitant. I was pretty sure this was the first time she'd come face to face with a cock. She looked up at me, under thick lashes.

"Do you sometimes think about me? When you're there, at boarding school?"

All the time. And not good things.

"If you're asking if I wanna fuck you, the answer is this." I thrust my hips her way, my cock poking her cheek.

"No, not fuck. Do you want more? Do you . . . do you like me?" Her eyes were pleading, but I knew better than to think she was genuine. She was just hurt. Messed up about our parents. If I showed her compassion, she would use it as a weapon against me.

I ran my fingers through her hair, moving it behind her ear with a smirk. "Gracelynn, I'm not here to tell you you're pretty. If you want to suck my cock, be my guest. If not, move along and let me get out of here. This is too little, too late."

This, ironically, made her spring into action. She became hot and needy for me. Turned on by the idea of trying to win me over. Her lips covered my crown, and she went to town on it. I tipped my head back, a grunt escaping my mouth. I'd enjoyed a few blowies in the past, but never with anyone I'd known. This felt different. Like submission. I decided seeing Grace submit to me was even better than making her cry into her pillow by being mean to her. Because when I hurt her—she only hated me. When I used her—she'd hate herself afterward too.

Somewhere in the back of my mind, I knew what we were doing was extremely fucked up. Wanting her to hurt. Putting myself in harm's way. All of it.

"Is this good?" she asked around my penis.

"Deeper." I grabbed her hair and tilted her back a little, shoving more of myself inside her. She gagged. I chuckled.

She gave it her all, and when I felt like I was about to blow my load, I said, "If you don't want my cum down your throat, now's a good time to pull away."

But she shook her head, giving me one thumbs-up and the green light to go to town. I did. It was a beautiful thing, watching Gracelynn on her knees for me, and I decided I liked it so much more than watching her cry.

I didn't know why she was doing what she was doing. All I knew was that when I came in her mouth, when her lips were wrapped around me, wet and inviting, I stopped thinking, I stopped hurting, and I stopped being mad.

The best antidote to love must be pleasure.

She pulled away, then clawed her way up to me, her fingers all over my chest, leaving marks. My cock was still half-mast, damp from her mouth and my cum. She kissed me hard, and I let her.

"Your turn, bro." She grinned into our kiss.

"Fair." I pushed her against the marble counter. The back of her head knocked over a few cereal boxes, and they rained down on us. I was between her legs in no time. I'd watched enough porn to know what I was doing, and by the quivering thighs wrapped around my ears, I knew I'd made her come.

"Just remember I don't do feelings." She squeezed my head between her legs.

"Way ahead of you in the sociopathic department." I bit her inner thigh. "Mark my words, Grace. No matter what happens, a part of me will always, always want to ruin you."

CHAPTER TEN

ARSÈNE

Four months later

"Darling, don't forget to email Makayla back about the guest list." Grace is standing at our apartment door, checking her pocket mirror for invisible lipstick smudges.

I never thought I'd find myself discussing the merits of beige and gray as a color scheme for a three-hour event, but life's good at throwing curveballs at you, I suppose.

"Forget? This will be the highlight of my day." I emerge from our bedroom, buttoning my dress shirt.

Grace is going to Zurich for another weekend of nonstop work. She rarely turns on her phone when she is there. I loathe it when I can't reach her. Which is why I'm heading out to meet Christian and Riggs at the New Amsterdam tonight. Time passes quicker when you drown in enough alcohol to fill an Olympic pool. "I'll email her tonight."

"Tell her I don't want to work with the flower shop she recommended. The one she claims Catherine and Michael used?" She is referring to Catherine Zeta-Jones and Michael Douglas like they live downstairs. "I read on Yelp that one delivery arrived at the venue with the flowers completely frozen. Oh, and she was supposed to send me the candle options. I hate to think she dropped the ball. Really, is it too much to ask for professionalism in this city?" She scrunches her nose.

"I won't forget." I lean down and kiss her long and hard, my mouth moving over hers as I add, "And if she drags her feet again, I'll show her the wrath of a thousand Corbin men."

She flings her arms over my shoulders, returning the sloppy kiss.

My hands slide down her back and cup her ass. "How about another quickie for the road?"

"Ugh. I wish I had time." She disconnects from me, flipping her phone in my direction so I can look at the screen. There is a notification letting her know her Uber driver is waiting downstairs.

"Rain check?" She grins.

"I'll hold you to it." I kiss her again. "Have a safe flight."

She lingers, smiling at me with something that almost looks like wistfulness.

"You know . . ." She trails off, her shoulders slumping. It's a rare sight. Grace is usually a stickler for good posture. "I really do love you, Arsène. I know you don't believe it. Not all the time, anyway. But it's true. I'm glad we chose each other. I'm glad you *won*."

My whole body beams. It is pathetic, how much I crave her approval. This must be the most pitiful form of mommy issues I've yet to witness.

"Hey, Grace?" I tug at her dark ponytail, winking. "I believe you."

"You do?" She brightens.

I nod.

"Forever yours." She kisses the side of my mouth.

"Forever yours." I kiss the tip of her nose. "What would you like for your welcome-home meal? Thai or Burmese?"

Grace likes to return home to find the dining table set and a warm bath drawn for her.

She turns around, wheeling her suitcase out to the foyer, then stops, flashing me a glorious smile full of white straight teeth. "Surprise me."

◆ ◆ ◆

The knocks on my door are persistent, yet oddly apologetic.

Like the person behind it doesn't want me to open. And for good reason. Not many people live to tell the tale of how they woke me up at ass-crack o'clock without notice.

What time is it, anyway?

Patting for my nightstand clock in the darkness, I bang on its head. The time says 3:18 a.m. *Christ.* Who the fuck decides three in the morning is a legitimate time for a social call?

Wait a minute. I actually *do* know someone as careless and reckless. And I'm happy to punch his face all the way to Antarctica for this disturbance.

Another bout of knocks sounds from the door.

Who let him in? This is why I pay an offensive amount of money every month for around-the-clock security. So people *don't* knock on my door in the middle of the night. Whoever is in charge of reception tonight is going to get the boot.

The doorbell chimes. Once. Twice. Three times.

"I'm coming." Never have I said these words with so little enthusiasm.

"Someone better be dead . . . ," I mutter as I shove my feet into my slippers, dragging myself to the door, wearing nothing but gray sweatpants and a scornful scowl.

Flinging my door open, I start with, "Listen here, you waste of worldly resources. I don't care if you're leaving for Africa on Monday and Christian doesn't want you to bring your hookup to his house like it's a low-budget Airbnb . . ."

The rest of the words die in my throat. It isn't Riggs. In fact, it isn't anyone I know.

On my threshold are two people—a man and a woman—in dark-blue NYPD uniforms and grave frowns. They both look like they've just swallowed a full-size hedgehog.

I've had my brush with law enforcement in the past, but it is usually the IRS and SEC who rain trouble on my ass, not the honest-to-God police officers. I'm a white-collar man, with white-collar problems. Perhaps someone decided to off themselves next door and they want to know if I heard anything. Damn socialites and their chaotic lifestyles.

Narrowing my eyes, I ask, "Who died?"

"I'm so sorry, Mr. Corbin." The woman bows her head.

Well, then. Someone *did* die, and it's someone I know.

I'm fresh out of parents, and my social circle is limited to those I absolutely must tolerate. I'm guessing . . . Riggs? He seems dumb enough to find his immature death. Maybe a Tinder date gone wrong.

Can't be Christian. He is too responsible to get himself into trouble.

The man says, "I'm Officer Damien Lopez, and this is my colleague, Officer Hannah Del Gallo."

"Thanks for the niceties. Now move on to the punch line," I bite out, not in the mood for chitchat.

"Are you Gracelynn Langston's fiancé?" he asks.

My heart, untouchable merely seconds before, now feels like it's being clenched in their fists. *Not her.*

"Yeah. Why?"

"We're very sorry." The woman bites on her lips. Her chin trembles. "But your fiancée was involved in a plane crash. She died on impact."

It's not true.

I can't really explain why it isn't true; I just know that it's not.

Which is why I don't call anyone.

It seems hysterical, idiotic, and unnecessary. I'm not going to believe it until they show me proof.

I make my way to the hospital's morgue in my own car to identify the body. The officers will meet me there.

One of the officers—Hannah—told me she called Miranda Langston, Grace's official next-of-kin. She said Miranda is coming down from Connecticut to the morgue, but that understandably, it might take her till morning. I haven't spoken to Miranda in over a decade, save for the taciturn exchange of condolences during Douglas's funeral. But it occurs to me that she might not even know her daughter and I are engaged. In the spirit of having a fucked-up relationship to the highest degree, Grace and I never really discuss her mother in any form or capacity.

Which clearly doesn't matter, since Grace is alive, and this is all a terrible misunderstanding that will end in someone being sued.

Grace can't be gone. We've only just begun our lives together. We have plans. A wedding to organize. A honeymoon booked. She still hasn't quit, birthed our babies, had her dream nuptials. Her bucket list is still full, sloshing about with plans and ideas.

Every time I stop at a traffic light, I scroll through the local news on my phone, trying to find reports about a United Airlines plane crashing. There are none. With each passing second, my suspicion this is a simple human error intensifies.

This is purely a case of identity mix-up. I'm sure of it. Grace flies United Airlines twice a month. The flight she is on is currently above the Atlantic, making its way to Zurich.

To think she is asleep, her cheek squished against a freezing window in first class, unaware of this entire mess floods me with warm satisfaction. I try to call her again, but her phone goes to voice mail.

This is not weird, I remind myself. *Her phone is always turned off when she travels to Zurich.*

Maybe it's all a big fat prank.

I arrive at the hospital in a daze. Park. Stumble out of the car.

Relax, idiot, she is fine. It's not her.

Even if it isn't, I'm not particularly hot on seeing anyone's corpse tonight, or any other night.

I head to the basement floor, where the morgue is, passing the loading dock area. The stench of hospital cleaning products assaults my nostrils. It deepens with each step I take, until my lungs burn. I need to get out of here.

The officers wait for me in the reception area. It's a small blue-green room, with a row of simple benches. The air-con is on blast. The walls are littered with plastic holders offering brochures about group therapy and funeral homes and casket makers. Zero points for subtlety.

"Was the drive here okay?" Officer Hannah asks sympathetically.

"A fucking delight." I pocket my car keys. "Let's get it over with. You have the wrong person, and I've no time for this bull crap."

Her concerned, poor-you frown doesn't waver. "So here's what we know so far. Miss Langston's private plane left Teterboro Airport at quarter past midnight this Friday—"

"See?" I sneer. "You've got your facts wrong. Grace boarded a United Airlines flight to Zurich. UA2988. She flew out of Newark. Jesus Christ, I can't believe my hard-earned tax money is wasted on you and your likes."

Officer Hannah's face twists, like I'm beating each word into her skin. Officer Damien remains calm, his expression unreadable, but he does write things down in a stupid little notebook.

Nice journal you have there, Gossip Girl.

"I understand this may be the information you have—" she starts.

"This is not a matter of *opinion*," I say sharply, losing all traces of decorum. "It's the truth. There was a computer mix-up or something. Grace flew commercial out of Newark. Check again."

"We were able to recover her passport." Officer Hannah clears her throat, her eyes meeting mine for the first time.

I'm rendered speechless. It can't be. Why would Grace lie about flying private?

Is it possible they got a perk this time around and she forgot to tell me? Unlikely, but not completely impossible.

I shake my head. "What about Chip Breslin? Paul Ashcroft? Pablo Villegas? Were they on the plane too?"

The two officers exchange glances. I want to grab them by the collar and shake the information out of them.

Suddenly, I'm on the brink of laughter. This is ridiculous. It is the kind of thing that happens to other people. People you read about in the newspapers. People who go on talk shows. Write heart-wrenching autobiographies. Not me. *Not. Me.*

"Look, Mr. Corbin, I understand you're upset. However, we—" Officer Damien starts.

The automatic doors behind us slide open. A small woman blazes inside. She's wearing a brown wig, a puffy yellow dress with a hoop, elbow-high satin gloves, and heavy makeup.

Because my life is not bizarre enough as it is tonight.

"Lord! Tell me it ain't true!" the strange woman wails in a southern accent.

Winnifred.

She either came straight from the theater or developed an extremely questionable fashion sense between Italy and now.

Her trim waistline doesn't scream pregnancy. I'd forgotten to ask Grace if she was knocked up. It seemed of no importance at the time, when we were neck deep in wedding preparations.

Now I'd never get the chance to ask Grace about the unlikely Ashcroft couple.

Never get the chance to do a lot of things with her.

"Where is he?" Winnifred demands, looking left and right frantically. "I need to see him!"

Two officers rush toward her, trying to calm her down.

Grace went to Zurich with Paul. Well, that makes sense. He was her boss.

"I'm going to see if they can accept you now." Officer Hannah rests her hand on my arm. "I can't find the receptionist, but someone should be here to help us. Officer Damien went to see if we could get the dental records of those who were on the flight. We'll be right back, Mr. Corbin. Please wait here."

The words brush past me. I'm more focused on Winnifred, who looks like the human answer to a dumpster fire, tears running down her face, leaving pale streaks of makeup. She is speaking to two officers. Maybe they have more information than the two clowns who knocked on my door. I strain my ears, piecing together parts of the conversation.

". . . private plane . . . certified pilot . . . a seasoned professional . . ."

". . . preflight inspection . . . poor tire condition . . . bear no legal responsibility, but a lawyer will be able to tell you more . . ."

". . . no one is certain . . . these things unfortunately happen . . . anyone you'd like to call?"

Sharp, intense agony slices through me for the first time since this shit show unfolded. The prospect is becoming real, and with it, the consequences of losing the only person in this world I truly care about.

Everything I didn't feel when Douglas died—the sorrow, the pain, the helplessness—is now cutting my inner organs into thin ribbons. I want to get closer, to hear everything. At the same time, I want everyone to shut the hell up. For this nightmare to go away.

Grace, enchanting as she is, isn't the most trustworthy person on planet Earth.

She lied to our parents about me.

Lied to the world about our relationship for years.

Nothing stopped her from lying to me about her flight details.

At some point, the two officers who speak to Winnifred step outside, and we are left alone. Her red, bloodshot gaze lifts from the floor. Once she registers me, recognition kicks in. She looks like she'd love nothing more than to club me with one of the empty benches in the waiting room.

"Stop looking at me like a fawn. It's not them," I bite out, baring my teeth like a ghastly beast. "They've got the wrong people. We'll be out of here before dawn."

"You can't be serious." She lets out a pained moan. "Do you actually believe it's an identity mix-up?"

"Yes," I say tersely. "And I'm not willing to be persuaded otherwise by a fully grown woman wearing a Disney princess dress."

She turns her head in the opposite direction and closes her eyes, pressing her lips together. Let her hate me. I care only about Grace.

I start pacing. What's taking them so long? You can't call people to recognize a body in the middle of the night and then keep them waiting for hours. After fishing my cell phone out, I google *private plane crash Teterboro Airport* and click on the news tab. There is one lone article about it, vaguely explaining there was a crash during takeoff and that the details are currently being investigated.

The officers return with a sleepy-looking receptionist and the two officers who came with Winnifred.

The four officers ask both of us to step aside with them to try to piece the timeline together.

"Do you know what the plane's destination was?" asks Officer Damien.

"Zurich," I say, at the same time Winnifred answers, "Paris."

I give her a pitiful look. "Not all European capitals are the same, Country Bumpkin."

It gives me sick pleasure to be cruel to her. I need to let my steam off somewhere, and she is the perfect victim.

"I can confirm the plane was headed to Paris." Officer Hannah is jotting something on a notepad she is holding, not lifting her gaze from it.

My jaw slackens. Paris? Grace went to Paris? Why?

"How many people were on the plane, as far as you're aware?" Officer Damien continues, turning his attention to Winnifred, who obviously has more information than I do.

"Three, minimum." She rubs at her chin, looking wide eyed and lost, like a stunned teenager. "Paul, Gracelynn, and the pilot. Although I suppose there might've been a flight attendant or two. And a copilot? Gosh, I know nothing about those things."

Fuck me. My source of information is currently wearing yellow plastic earrings.

"Is there any more information you can share with us?" Officer Hannah asks.

I stay silent. Whatever is happening, I'm not in the goddamn loop. Now, I'm just waiting for the officers to go away so I can interrogate Dolly Parton Jr. here.

She hesitates before shaking her head. "No. This is all he told me, sorry."

Officer Hannah looks pained when she asks, "Do you happen to know, Mrs. Ashcroft . . . did they travel for business or . . . um, *leisure?*"

Closing my eyes, I feel everything inside me collapsing, brick by brick. Everything I built over the years is gone, buried in ashes. The memories. The stolen kisses. The games. The stakes. The winning. All gone.

Winnifred's voice sounds far away. "I—I don't know."

"You don't know if they were traveling for business or pleasure?" Officer Damien repeats crassly.

"No."

"I suppose this means you didn't know that they were traveling together at all, then?"

"Stop that," Officer Hannah chides under her breath.

"No," Winnifred says, jutting her chin up, proud despite the ridiculousness of her outfit and this situation and this *question*. "He didn't tell me he was traveling with Miss Langston."

"All right." Officer Damien bites his inner cheek, frustrated. "Thank you, Mrs. Ashcroft. The good news—if you could call it that—is that the pilot had attempted to land safely in the Hudson, so the bodies are in, er, presentable condition."

"Fantastic news," I drawl, unable to stop myself. "So they drowned, didn't burn up in flames. Makes a world of difference. Country Bumpkin, aren't you proud your husband's funeral will be an open-casket event?" I throw her a deplorable smirk.

Winnifred gasps as if I just slapped her.

Officer Hannah puts a hand on Winnifred's shoulder. "People say terrible things when they're hurting," she says to comfort her.

"Oh, saying terrible things is his party trick. It's got nothing to do with what's happening here." Bumpkin side-eyes me.

Finally, Officer Damien gets a phone call, and the officers nod between them. "We'll be right back."

They all stride outside, mumbling between themselves, leaving Paul Ashcroft's wife and me alone.

I turn to her. "You need to tell me everything."

"Why! Are you talking to little ol' me?" She stubs her index finger in her chest, putting on her thickest Tennessee accent. "'Cause I don't know Rome from Reykjavík. So why don't you take your big, smart brain and giant, intolerable attitude and shove them up your bu—"

"Truce." I hold my palms up. "I know you know more than I do. That's clear to everyone within a hundred-mile radius. And though we didn't start on the right foot, it's also clear that we're both in the middle of a shit storm, so now would be a good time to excuse my manners and piece together what happened here."

"No," she says decisively.

I stare at her, transfixed. "Excuse me?"

"I won't do it." She folds her arms over her chest. "You can't go around treatin' people like they're dirt, Mr. Corbin. No matter how much money you've got in your bank account. Apologize first."

You little sh . . .

"My sincerest regrets." I bow with deliberate exaggeration. "I'm a thorny man used to getting away with deplorable behavior. I'll think twice before opening my big mouth and taking out my wrath on people from now on. Can we move on?"

She sucks in a breath, nodding.

"Good. Now tell me everything."

"Paul bought two tickets to Paris at the beginning of the month. It was supposed to be a romantic getaway. A reset button . . ." She hesitates, not wanting to unravel too much. "A chance for some one-on-one quality time."

At the word *Paris*, the full weight of the betrayal crashes into me. Grace went with Paul to the most romantic city in the world. *Alone.* It doesn't take a genius to know they intended on enjoying more than the local pastries and champagne.

I nod encouragingly. "And?"

"I told him I couldn't come. I'd just landed my first theater gig. It was a big deal for me. Tonight was my first show. I'm Belle from *Beauty and the Beast*." She smooths a hand over her stupid dress, like it's her most beloved possession. A tear slides down from her cheek, to her neck, and onto the dress.

This dress will forever be sullied with her tears. The role tarnished with this moment, this place, this scene. Just like I'll never be able to drive by this hospital again without thinking of Grace. Our lives are about to change forever.

I say nothing, letting her continue.

"Paul couldn't cancel the hotel reservations, so he asked if I'd mind if he took one of his college friends, Phil. I know Phil. He was his best man and always comes over to watch baseball games. I told him to go for it . . ." She trails off.

She doesn't have to say it out loud. The rest is abundantly clear. Paul didn't take Phil. He took Grace. And they were caught red handed. Only now they aren't here to face the consequences of their actions. My feelings veer dangerously from the *Good, fuck them* lane, to *Why did you have to get on that plane, Grace? Wasn't I enough?*

"Why didn't you tell them that?" I demand, looking to channel my anger at someone who is here, who is present, who is *alive.* "The officers."

Fresh tears fill Winnifred's eyes, and her nostrils flare. "I'm not jumping to conclusions. I trusted Paul."

"Clearly he misused this trust to spend the weekend screwing my fiancée."

"Maybe she caught a ride with him and had other business in Paris. We don't know what happened there, and I'm not going to have his name tainted like that." She tips her chin up.

She is still loyal to him, and that drives me nuts because the asshole not only cheated on her, but he did it with my goddamn future wife.

I want to shake the naivete out of her like she's a piggy bank.

Then it dawns on me. She has a role to play. The devoted, loving wife. The one who will later get the fat insurance check and the sympathy. It's not that Winnifred doesn't believe Paul and Grace had an affair—it's that she doesn't give a damn.

She probably didn't care who this white bread of a man screwed as long as she had access to his credit cards when he was alive.

"Believe what you wanna believe." I screw the soles of my palms to my eye sockets. "It's not my job to drag you kicking and screaming into the realms of reality, *Belle.*"

"Your version of reality is askew, anyway, *Beast.*" She huddles on the other side of the room and plasters her forehead against the wall.

I let out a bark of laughter. "Did you just call me a beast?"

"Yes, but I take it back," she bites out. "The Beast redeems himself. You would never!"

"How was Paul not arrested for marrying you?" I wonder aloud. "You're mentally twelve."

"Well, no one forced you to talk to me!" she hits back. Her accent is thicker than ever when she's angry. "Stay on your side of the room, and leave me the heck alone."

We are both shells of our former selves. I know exactly why I'm broken—I just lost the love of my life, or the closest thing to one I'd ever have. But what's her excuse?

Instead of processing the possible death of my fiancée, my mind begins swerving out of control, spinning wildly down an endless rabbit hole.

Did Grace love Paul?

Did she want to leave me for him?

What was the exercise of this pointless affair with him if she were to marry me? If she wanted to quit her job? Paul wasn't particularly handsome, nor did he enjoy a wealth of gray matter.

How long had it been going on? Were they already at it, harboring this secret, while all of us were in Italy?

Was Grace really at work in Zurich all those days, those weeks, those months? Or was she with him?

And where did they meet when they were alone? A hotel? An Airbnb? The apartment Grace had refused to stop renting, "just in case"?

I want to know each and every sordid detail. To gorge on my own sorrow until I choke on it.

"Mrs. Ashcroft?" A woman in a white robe walks out of a silver door. She takes off her thick glasses and cleans the lenses with the hem of her sleeve.

Bumpkin flattens her ridiculous dress, squaring her shoulders. The woman steps sideways, motioning for her to come with. Winnifred throws me one last die-in-hell glance. I want to tell her she can drop the whole wounded-widow charade. She got her wishes. She is a young, beautiful widow with millions in the bank, and no one can accuse her of foul play. Every gold digger's dream.

We hold each other's gaze for a moment. I hope my eyes convey what every bone in my body is screaming.

It should've been you on the plane.

You were supposed to die. You.

Unremarkable. Insignificant. Forgettable. Country Bumpkin.

Not my beautiful, sophisticated, math-wiz fiancée.

Not the cunning, alluring Gracelynn Langston. The spectacular woman only I understood.

"Please follow me." The woman in the white robe ushers her. Winnifred complies swiftly and comes back ten minutes later, looking ashen and pale. Her shoulder bumps into my arm as she leaves the room, but she doesn't even notice. I swivel my head to follow her movements. In the hallway, Winnifred collapses midstep, on the floor, back hunched, sobbing and sobbing and sobbing.

I don't need to ask. I know. It was Paul she saw in there.

The woman in the robe saunters out the door again. "Mr. Corbin?"

I close my eyes and press the back of my head against the wall.

Grace has somehow managed to slip through my fingers. Again.

I didn't hold her tight enough, close enough, good enough.

And this time? The water didn't save her.

PART TWO

CHAPTER ELEVEN

WINNIE

Eight months later

Momma always tells me that the cutest thing I ever did as a child was bawl my eyes out every time "Space Oddity," by David Bowie, came on the radio.

I'm talkin' full-blown meltdown, peppered with hiccups and uncontrollable emotions.

"You were so moved by it, no matter how many times you listened to it. It touched your soul. This was how I knew you were an artist. You let art touch you. So it was obvious to me, one day you'd be able to touch others with it."

These days, I can't shed a tear to save my life. Super Bowl commercials. Cheesy Hallmark movies. Women pushing strollers on the street. People without housing. Wars, famines, humanitarian crises. Expired yogurts that belong to Paul in the fridge. "Mad World," by Michael Andrews. The list of things that usually make me weep is long and tedious, but my body is all dried up. In an emotional coma, refusing to produce tears.

Cry. Feel something, darn you! Just one thing, I inwardly chide myself as I burst out of the theater, a blast of humid heat slapping my face.

New York wears her weather like a weapon. Summers are long and sticky, and winters are white and ruthless. These days, it seems like the entire city is melting into the ground like an ice cream. But for the first time in years, the heat doesn't get to me. All I feel is a mild chill, thanks to the fifteen pounds I've lost since Paul.

My eyes are still dry.

"No, you shouldn't cry. You're happy," I mumble to myself aloud. "Fine. Maybe *happy*'s not the right word . . . *satisfied*. Yes. You're satisfied with your little accomplishment, Winnie Ashcroft."

One good thing about New York is no one ever looks at you twice when you talk to yourself.

I stride along Times Square, oblivious to the sights, the scents, the festivity in the air. Putting one leg in front of the other requires enough effort these days.

My phone dances in my pocket. I withdraw it, swiping to answer my agent, Chrissy.

"Don't worry." I roll my eyes. "I didn't forget to attend the audition this time."

I've been very forgetful these past few months. Understandable, everyone keeps reassuring me, but I can tell some people are at the end of their rope. I rarely show up to auditions, meetings, and social functions these days. Forget to eat, to exercise, to call relatives and friends back. My niece's birthday came and went, and for the first time since she was born, there were no lavish gifts, no balloons, no surprise visit from Auntie Winnie. Most days I'm slumped on my couch, staring at the door, waiting for Paul to return.

Ma and Dad say I should cut my losses. Pack up and move back to Mulberry Creek.

There is a job with my name on it back home. Drama teacher for my former high school.

Ma says my childhood sweetheart, Rhys Hartnett, works there now as a football coach and can pull all kinds of strings. She claims it's a done deal. A great, comfy position to fall into while I figure things out. But the idea of leaving the apartment Paul and I shared makes my skin crawl.

Plus, taking favors from Rhys Hartnett after our messy goodbye just seems . . . wrong.

"Yes, I know you decided to grace them with your presence—very charitable of you, by the way." Chrissy chuckles on the other end of the line.

I shoulder past a flock of tourists taking selfies in front of billboards, giggling and squeaking, without a care in the world.

"How'd you know I showed up?" I toss my last few dollars into the open jaw of a violin case of a street performer without breaking stride. "You spying on me now, ma'am?"

"No, though sometimes I'm tempted, just to check that you're okay. You know I'm a fierce worrier."

Darn Chrissy and her heart of gold. I *do* know that. And, truth be told, she is one of the only people in New York who cares about me. She and Arya, the woman who runs the charity I volunteer for. Most of my social network is back in Mulberry Creek. Chrissy took me under her wing when I first signed up with her. I think she saw in me someone she once was. Young and impressionable, fresh off the bus. Easy prey to New York's bloodthirsty sharks. She came from Oklahoma. I, from Tennessee. But it's the same story all over again. Small-town girl trying to conquer the Big Apple.

"Well, missy, for your information, I'm fine and a half," I announce. "Been eatin' all my veggies and practicing self-care."

"If you think I'm buying what you're selling, you're in for some disappointment. But we'll revisit the subject later. Back to your audition," Chrissy says decisively.

It was the first audition I attended since the plane crash and the only role I cared about since Paul passed away.

I want this role. I need this role.

"What about my audition?" I ask.

"I have some news."

Oh, no. That was fast. Was I really that bad they couldn't wait to pounce on their phone and call my agent? *The woman doesn't belong onstage.*

"Listen, Chris. I tried. Sure did. I went in there and gave it my all. Maybe I—"

"You got the role, baby!" Chrissy announces.

I freeze midwalk. A couple of people crash into me from behind, muttering profanity. Making an unannounced stop on a sidewalk in Manhattan is a serious traffic offense.

Wait . . . I got the role?

I try to muster pleasure from the news. Some kind of contentment or something that imitates it. But my body is numb from the outside, empty from the inside. I feel paper thin. So light, so weightless, I could be carried with the next gust of wind.

Shed a tear, Winnie.

I'd always been such a good crier. Any occasion, good or bad, prompted the waterworks to start.

I'm going to work! Leave the house! Attend rehearsal! Memorize lines!

I'm going to have to be a fully functioning human being. But somehow, the only emotion I can muster is fear.

"You're going to be Nina," Chrissy wails, undeterred by my silence. "Can you believe it? Every actress's wet dream."

She isn't wrong. Since my Juilliard days as an aspiring actress, playing the role of Nina has been a fantasy for most of my fellow students. The beautiful, tragic, fame-hungry girl from Chekhov's play *The Seagull*.

The woman who represents the loss of innocence, emotional damage, whose dreams were crushed into fairy dust.

So fitting. Of course I got the role. I am the role.

"Nina," I breathe out, closing my eyes as herds of office folk rush past me, by me, *through* me. I'm caught in a wave of bodies. "I'm going to be Nina."

To feel the stage under my feet, the bright lights pounding on my eyes, and their warmth. To smell the sweat of other people again. Steal bites of energy bars between rehearsals. All that I dreamed about when I packed a small suitcase and left Mulberry Creek.

"I know things have been difficult, honey." Chrissy drops her voice. "But I think this is the beginning of the end. The caterpillar will soon become a butterfly. You earned it, baby girl. Spread those wings. Fly high."

I nod as if she can see me. I need a hug. I wish someone were here to wrap their arms around me. I also need buttermilk biscuits. Lots and lots of Ma's buttermilk biscuits.

"Tell me you're at least a little bit happy." The plea in Chrissy's voice is unmistakable. "You sound like you're attending your own funeral."

"Are you kiddin' me? I'm happy as a clam!" I swivel artfully to avoid stepping over a tiny Chihuahua rushing alongside its owner, lying through my teeth.

"Lucas, the director, was so impressed with your performance. He called it *electric*. They should get back to me with the schedule and contract in the next few days." There is a pause. "I'm sorry, honey. I'm all about business today. Would you like me to come over tonight? We can Hallmark and chill."

Chrissy and I both like our movies the same way we like our pizza—with extra cheese and cheap red wine on the side. Normally, I'd be all over the offer. But today, I'd like to be alone. This new job symbolizes my return to the outside world. I need to digest it all.

"I think I'll have a quiet one in tonight, if you don't mind." I smile, out of habit, to people on the street as I make my journey to my apartment block. They never smile back, not in this zip code, but it's a force of habit I find hard to break.

"You got it, Win. Just wanted to put the offer out there. Enjoy your night."

I kill the call and scroll through my phone to keep my mind busy. I have one unread message from Pablo.

Hey, sorry I missed your call again. I'm available if you want to talk.

It was sent at four thirty in the morning.

Pablo has been avoiding mc for the past eight months. So does the rest of the staff of Silver Arrow Capital. Chip, Dahlia from HR, and Phil, Paul's best friend. They've all been cagey about what they know—or don't know—regarding Paul and Grace's relationship. I still have no clue what my husband and that woman were doing together that day when their lives ended.

It's easy to speculate Paul and Grace had an affair, but something in me refuses to believe he'd so callously betray me.

Paul wasn't an angel, but he wasn't a villain either. Besides, he loved me—I know he did. And he'd never indicated Grace was someone he even liked. On the contrary. Many times I found myself chiding him when he accused her of being self-centered and high maintenance when he returned home from work.

Never met a bigger headache in my life. That Corbin guy must be a glutton for punishment. All she does is whine and make demands.

Over the last few months, I've been trying to piece together the reason why Paul got on that flight with Grace. Did he truly give her a ride? Or was this salacious? I think back to our conversations, go through his things in our apartment trying to spot clues.

I haven't found any evidence of an affair so far. Nothing to raise my suspicion. Everything he owned and kept close was so innocent. Photo albums, knickknacks, his stamp collection, signed baseball tees.

Sometimes I toy with the idea of calling that pompous creature Arsène Corbin. I bet he holds all the answers to my questions. For all his many glaring faults, he seems like a resourceful man. The kind who is quick to play catch-up.

I have no doubt he found out everything there is to know about the circumstances that led Grace and Paul to be on the same plane that claimed their lives.

But I can't bring myself to ask him for a favor. Now, if he were the one to approach me, that'd be a whole different ballgame. Wouldn't that be somethin'?

A dull pain thuds behind my forehead. I stop scrolling and call Ma. Rita Towles always manages to lift my spirits, even when they're in the dumpster.

"Sugar plum!" she yelps in delight. "Your daddy and I were just talking about you. He's right here beside me. Were your ears burnin'? He asked if I remembered the time you tried to walk in my heels when you were a kid and broke your ankle. 'Course I remember. I was the one to drive you all the way to the hospital while you were screamin' to the high heavens."

I still have a little scar on my ankle to show for that.

"It was a lesson well learned. Never wore heels again," I say with a wistful smile.

"Other than on your wedding day," she reminds me. My mood wilts again. All roads always lead to Paul.

"They were platforms, not heels, Ma. And I only wore them for the membership."

Paul and I had married in my local church in Mulberry Creek. We buried a bottle of bourbon upside down at the wedding venue and danced into the night, barefoot. When he whisked me off to my dream honeymoon in Thailand, I got on the plane in pj's he'd packed and bought for me ahead of time, my feet still muddy from the wedding. He rubbed them in his lap until I fell asleep on the long flight. It was just another way Paul was amazing. Considerate and always thoughtful.

Other than the times he wasn't.

"Lizzy's coming over for dinner tonight. And you know Georgie's always here. So I'm making peach cobbler," she says about my sisters.

"Darn. I wish I could be there."

"Oh, but you can! Just hop on a plane and come see us."

"About that . . ." I trail off. "I've news of my own."

"What is it, sugar plum?"

I gather oxygen in the pit of my lungs, preparing for my announcement. "I got a job! A new role. I'm going to be Nina from *The Seagull*."

The line goes quiet. For a second, I think maybe I lost reception.

Dad is the first to recover. "That so? Broadway and all?"

I wince. "Not exactly Broadway. But it's an established theater in Manhattan."

"How long's this gig gonna run for?" he continues.

"One year."

"How nice." Ma clears her throat, disappointment coating her voice. "This is . . . I mean, it's what you wanted. I'm happy for you."

I can see my Hell's Kitchen brownstone from the corner of my eye. My feet feel like lead. I know I saddened my parents, who thought I was warming up to the idea of going back home. There's still a part of me that wants to go home too. It's not small either. But this role is important for so many reasons. One of them I can't even utter aloud.

"Please, now. You're making me blush with all your excitement," I murmur, but there is no real bite in my voice. As much as it pains me to admit, I understand them. They want to nurture me, help get me back on my feet. Keep an eye on me while I'm close by.

"I just don't think it's a good idea that you're all alone out there," Ma says with a heavy sigh. "Maybe I should come? Just for a couple weeks? Make you that peach cobbler? I won't stand in your way at all. Don't worry. This old lady can find entertainment all on her own."

"Don't, Ma," I beg, panic taking over me. "I'm okay. I promise."

Our apartment—I guess it is *my* apartment now—is a modern two bedroom. With an open kitchen, eastern view of the Manhattan skyline, and what Realtors like to call character. I love everything about it. The quilted leather stools by the black granite island in the kitchen, the art pieces Paul and I collected from small flea markets on our honeymoon, and most of all, the way the place is still soaked with his presence. Swollen with the promise and expectation he will be back any moment now.

That he'd push the door open with his daytime-show-host smile and announce, *Honey, I'm hooooome!*

Sweep me off my feet, kiss me hard, and ask me how his favorite girl is doing.

His running shoes are still by the door. His toothbrush is tucked in a cup by our Jack-and-Jill sink, the bristles bent out of shape like a ripe dandelion. Paul scrubbed his teeth to the point of bleeding.

It gives me strange comfort that his yogurts are still in the fridge, arranged by now-expired dates, though I know they shouldn't be. That his spare contact lenses are still perched by the faucet of his sink, waiting expectantly to be put on.

It's why I don't want my parents to pay me a visit. I'm not supposed to keep these things. The everyday oddments he won't be using anymore. His orange-bottled prescription pills, the reading glasses on his nightstand, complete with the open newspaper he'd been reading, the article he never finished glaring back at me. "Mining the Bottom of the Sea."

The New Yorker is to blame for the ugly way we parted.

The last time I saw him, we'd had an argument.

I'd been pestering him about canceling our newspaper subscription. He never touched it, and I'm allergic to world news and the anxiety it induces. I grew up frugal, and didn't like how Paul threw money away for no reason other than he possessed it. He made a show of opening the paper that night, read half an article, put it aside, and promised he would read the rest when he returned from his Paris trip.

Don't close the newspaper. I'll get back to it, he'd warned. *By God I will. The only reason I'm not taking it with me is because Phil always wants to talk baseball when we take flights together.*

I never did. It stayed put. Each new paper I receive every day is rolled up and waiting in a pile in the pantry for Paul to arrive and read it. Like he might materialize one day, stride in here, and ask me what he missed these past eight months.

Pacing across the apartment, I run my fingers over the books on the shelves—a mixture of my favorite classics and his Jack Reacher—and the stainless steel appliances we chose together.

Reality nibbles its way into my gut. I can't afford to keep this place. Even though Paul had paid off the mortgage before we got married ("Bad investment," he argued, but I wanted to live in a place that was completely my own), and I inherited the property as his wife, there are too many bills piling up each month.

The property tax, parking, food, health care, and transportation make me dip into the insurance money I received every month since he passed.

Paul and I had signed an iron-clad prenup upon his parents' request, which means I'm not as well off as people might suspect. At the time, I didn't think much of it, because the idea of ever parting ways with Paul was crazy to me.

It's going to suck to sell and move away and leave all his memories behind.

Maybe this new role as Nina in *The Seagull* will help keep me afloat, but I doubt it. It's just a one-year contract, and not a Broadway gig. No big money to be made.

The doorbell chimes. I jump back, taken by surprise, before remembering I ordered Paul's favorite. Banh xeo and cha ca. I hurry to the door, tip the DoorDasher, and crack open a cheap bottle of red wine. I set two plates in front of the TV on the coffee table. I pour Paul a glass, too, and mound food on his plate, taking all the baby corn out manually because he hated it. Even though I'm starving, I wait until Netflix loads before taking the first bite. It was a pet peeve of his.

At least have the manners to skip the intro, baby doll. The food's not going to run away.

Am I being unhinged right now, serving a full plate to the ghost of my dead husband? Absolutely. Do I care very much? Nope. It's one of the rare perks of living completely alone. I don't have to tuck my crazy in.

"Tonight, my dear, we're going to watch *The Witcher*. I know it's not your cuppa, but Henry Cavill is mine, and there is nothing you can do about it," I joke, starting up the first episode as I take a bite of the fluffy stuffed rice pancake. "Executive decision. Should've been more careful. That way you'd have a say in the matter."

Wednesdays were our Vietnamese takeout and TV nights. Paul would pick up the food on his way back from work while I cleaned the apartment, got the groceries, and ironed his clothes. I keep the tradition alive, even though he isn't here anymore. Well, minus ironing his clothes. That part, I don't even pretend to miss.

I make idle conversation with Paul's side of the sofa while I eat.

How was your day?

Mine was pretty good, actually. I went to an audition and got it! Thank you for always believing in me. For telling me I was going to make it.

My role as Belle died a swift death the night Paul passed away. The next morning, Chrissy called the theater and told them about my situation, and I dropped out of the show. The loss felt miniscule in the grand scheme of things, but months after, I sometimes wondered if it would have been possible to push through. Maybe if I'd had something to keep me going, I wouldn't be so numb.

When the episode ends, I clear the coffee table and wash the plates. Double-lock and bolt the door.

In the kitchen, I fill myself three tall glasses of water and drink all of them. I like to wake up at least a couple of times each night. I do a little inspection around the apartment, making sure I'm really alone. I've always been scared of sleeping by myself. At Julliard, I had a bucketload of roommates, and before that, I shared a room with both my sisters. There's no doubt I'm not good at being alone.

I turn the lights off on my way to the bedroom but stop in front of a door when I reach the hallway.

Paul's office. The door is locked. I know where the key is, but I haven't used it since he's been gone.

Back when he was alive, Paul spent countless hours in his home office. I've seen it hundreds of times from the inside, when I came in to fetch him coffee, or water, or just to remind him it was time to take a break. It's just another office, with piles of documents, an Apple screen, and an unholy amount of filing cabinets.

He had asked me not to open it whenever he locked it.

Trade secrets, baby doll. Plus, I kind of like the idea of having an island of my own. A private place that only belongs to me.

And me, blindly loyal, unreservedly faithful, decided to never break this rule. Even now, after all these months, the office is still closed.

Waiting for me to betray him, just like he allegedly betrayed me.

CHAPTER TWELVE

"It's Elsa! Elsa's here!" Little Sienna, only six years old and a resident in the pediatric rehabilitation unit at Saint John's, calls out to me from her place in her bed. She reaches her arms, wriggling her fingers as I enter her room. I lean down to hug her, my fake, synthetic white-blonde wig tickling her face, making her giggle.

"You smell like plastic," she says.

No matter how down I feel, there is one thing I never miss—my volunteer work at Saint John's Children's Hospital.

More than it helps the little warriors to pull through, it soothes me. There is nothing like watching an innocent child fighting a grown-up battle to put your own troubles in perspective. I thank the Lord every day I found Arya Roth-Miller and was able to jump on board with her charity. That we got talking at this random party three years ago, and when she said she'd call and give me the details of her charity—she truly did. I not only gained perspective and something to nourish the soul—I also gained a friend.

"Why, if it isn't my favorite trooper." I plop next to Sienna in a visitor's chair, placing my makeup kit on her nightstand. A clear plastic box sits on it, consisting of dozens of small squares, pills inside them, along with half-finished bottles of water and some candy. "Where's your momma and daddy?"

"It's my little brother Cade's birthday. So they took him to Chuck E. Cheese to celebrate with his class. But don't worry! They said they'll get me something yummy." She flashes me a half-toothless smile. My heart melts in my chest.

Oh, Sienna.

"Good. I'll have you all for myself. So who do you want to be today?" I wiggle my brows. "Minnie Mouse? A butterfly? A dragon? I know! Maybe a rainbow?"

Sienna licks her lips, fixing the glasses atop her nose. She shuffles in her bed, reaching to scratch beneath the blanket covering her legs. Or, rather, her *leg*. Her left one was severed in a car accident three weeks ago. She has a case of phantom limb, and she keeps feeling the leg that isn't there.

"I want to be Mirabel from *Encanto*!" she announces. "Because you don't have to have a superpower to be a hero."

"That's the spirit, Si!" I'm already on my phone, looking for tutorials of how to draw Mirabel. "Superpowers are boring. They have no merit. It's the power we find in ourselves that matters."

Now if only I can listen to my own advice.

Sienna is a delight to put makeup on. Usually, I chat up the kids as I work on their faces. Sienna tells me she might get discharged at the end of the month and will return back to her class.

"And at first, they'll give me a wheelchair, but after, they said they'll fix me a supercool bionic leg and it'll be just like before the accident!" she says excitedly. "I'll just have to put it on every morning when I wake up."

I pull away when I'm done, grinning back at her. "That sounds like the coolest thing *ever*!"

"Right?" Her eyes light up.

"For real. You could walk, dance, swim, do anything!"

After Sienna, it is Tom's turn (spine surgery), and after Tom comes Mallory (cystic fibrosis). I make the round, and time passes by without the usual pain that accompanies breathing and operating in the world without Paul.

When I'm done, I call the elevator. It slides open, and out pops Arya Roth-Miller, the director of the foundation I'm working with on this project and the only other friend, other than Chrissy, who bothers to visit me once a month.

"Winnie." She smiles, stepping back into the elevator. "Just who I was waiting to bump into. Let me see you out of here."

I follow her into the elevator and hit the ground floor button, smiling at Arya. I love that she has her own PR business, a family—a *baby!*—but still finds time to do this work.

"Am I in trouble?" I laugh. "Why'd you want to speak to me?"

"Trouble?" she asks, frowning. "Do I already have a crabby-mom expression? Why would you think that?"

I shrug. "You normally like to catch up over coffee, not in the elevator."

"Well, first, I wanted to congratulate you on getting the Nina part. Chrissy told me. I'm so proud of you!"

Blushing deeply, I nod.

"Second, I'm throwing a charity ball in a few weeks, and I would love for you to come. It's a three-K-a-plate thing."

Bless her heart. What'll they be serving at this event, a steak made out of pure gold?

"Thank you so much for offerin'. I'm not . . . I mean, you know how I like to keep to myself . . ."

Translation: I'm so poor I might as well have a tumbleweed as a pet.

"Jesus, you won't have to pay!" Arya waves her hand. I feel my ears pinking in shame. "But I do want you to be there. You're one of our most dedicated volunteers. No one cares about those kids like you do,

Winnie. And they always ask for you, specifically. Some of the parents are going to be there, and, well, I can't afford not to have you there."

"Then I'll be there."

It'll be the first public event I attend since Paul passed away, but at least I have a good excuse. Charity. Plus . . . I kind of miss seeing people. Dancing. Puttin' on a nice dress.

"Brilliant!" Arya claps just as the doors to the elevator slide open and I stumble outside. "I'll tell Christian. He's going to love seeing you again!"

I bet he would. Christian, her husband, approves of everything his wife loves, including her friends. I turn around, smiling weakly at her. "Well . . . see you later."

"No way!" She shakes her head as the doors close. "Not later. *Sooner.* We'll hang out soon. I'll call you tonight. Hey, and Winnie?"

I turn to look at her.

"You're loved. Remember that."

◆　◆　◆

Four weeks later

"Think of me sometimes?" I rest a hand over Rahim's face, staring into his dark eyes.

He strokes my hand. I let out a soft gasp at his touch. A smile curls at his lips. "Of course I will. I'll think of how you looked in sunlight—remember? In that wonderful dress . . ."

His lips draw closer. I feel their heat. The cinnamon gum on his breath. The afternoon whiskers adorning his cheeks. Can I do this? Can I really kiss another man? So soon?

With every inch he eats between us, my heart sinks lower. I feel it sliding down my body. Seeping to the floor, bleeding into the cracks of the worn-out wood. I can't breathe. I can't do this. His lips get closer, hotter.

Get me out of here.

I want to run. I *can't* run. I'm paralyzed. Rahim's lips nearly brush mine . . .

"Aaaaand, cut!" Lucas pops his gum, falling onto a burgundy seat in the first row of the theater.

"Saved by the bell," Rahim whispers into my mouth, leaning down to kiss my cheek softly.

I jerk back like he just slapped me. He clasps my shoulders, righting me up.

Blush creeps over his tan cheeks. "Sorry, Winnie. I didn't mean to make light of it. I mean . . . I'm not gonna kiss you during rehearsals if I can help it. I'm sure Lucas will understand."

"Gosh, no! I was just . . . I blanked out." Embarrassed I've been caught losing it over an onstage peck on the lips, I duck my head and pretend the last few minutes hadn't happened.

"Okay, let's run this scene one more time, this time with a smooch." Lucas flips through the play's pages, leaning sideways and saying something in his assistant's ear.

"Hey, Winnie, remember the cookies you brought over on day one of the rehearsal?" Rahim asks.

"Memaw's kitchen-sink cookies, yes." I smile. Whenever I go anywhere new, I always bring a fresh batch of cookies. A Towles woman tradition to sweeten every relationship.

"There was a secret ingredient there, I'm sure of it." Rahim snaps his fingers. "What was it? The texture was amazing."

"Add another yolk and extra brown sugar for moisture." I wink. "I'll send you the recipe if you promise not to show anyone."

"The women at my felting club are going to be disappointed, but I'm sure they'll understand," he jokes.

Calypso Hall is otherwise empty. There are more people backstage, but here it's just Rahim, who plays Trigorin; Lucas; his assistant; and me. And—of course—the golden-arched stage, sea of claret seats, mezzanines, and box balconies as our audience. It's an old theater. Small and cozy and in need of repair. But it still feels like home.

"Same scene. From the top." Lucas taps his beret. "Actually, no. Give me the resolution scene again. We need to nail it down, and right now you're not sparkling for me. Sparkle, unicorns! Sparkle."

I've memorized *The Seagull* by heart. Each word is carved into my brain. I daydream Nina's aspirations every day. Feel her desperation at night, when I toss and turn in bed. It's liberating, slipping into a fictional character's mind. Experiencing the world through the eyes of a nineteenth-century troubled Russian girl.

We do as we're told, diving right into the resolution scene. Rahim fires his lines at rapid speed, flourishing under the harsh lights. His charisma is addictive. I follow his lead, coming alive on this square, magic stage that offers me complete freedom to be someone else. Even though we're at the changes, score, and blocking part of the rehearsals, I already feel like her. Like this naive, superficial girl who thinks she is in love with a novelist. I push at Rahim's chest, fling my hands in the air, laugh like a maniac, and whirl around like a storm.

Nina. The hopeless, risk-taking, dream-chasing provincial girl.

The door to the theater flings open. From the corner of my eye, I can see a demon-like creature. Tall and dark, filling the frame like a black gaping hole.

The energy in the room shifts. The little hairs on my arm stand on end.

I force my attention back to Rahim.

Focus. Focus. Focus.

Trigorin and Nina are fighting. I spew out my lines. But I no longer shine under the theater lights. Cold sweat gathers at the back of my neck. Who is this person who just came inside? This is a dry rehearsal, closed to the public.

Lucas and his assistant still haven't spotted the intruder. But I seem to be attuned to him as he descends the stairway toward the stage. He's not alone. There's someone trailing behind him. His movements are sleek and smooth, tigerlike.

Trigorin is on the verge of a breakdown. Nina soldiers ahead.

I tell Rahim that I loved him. That I gave him a child. My eyes scald with unshed tears. This part feels like digging into my own gut with a rusty spoon. It's the part where Nina comes to terms with her shallow, artificial existence.

I'm in the middle of my monologue—*that* monologue—the one every aspiring actress finds herself reciting in front of her dorm mirror, using her hairbrush as a mic—when I see Lucas jumping to his feet from the corner of my eye. He rips his beret off his head and squeezes it like a beggar, waiting for the tall figure to approach.

"Cut . . . *cut!*" he coughs out manically. "Take ten, guys."

Rahim and I stop. My gaze trails to the two men who entered the theater.

When I see his face, the sharp planes of his jaw, the black irises, no part of me is surprised.

He is the only person who has ever managed to make my skin crawl and my mouth dry with a simple stare. His mere existence turns me inside out.

Arsène Corbin.

He stands out like a coyote in a henhouse, wearing a pair of black slim-cut slacks, leather strap shoes, and a cashmere sweater. Maybe it's too far away to tell, but he doesn't look too heartbroken from where I'm standing. No obvious telltale signs of bloodshot eyes, unkempt hair, or a five-o'clock shadow.

This man is dressed to the nines, has seen his barber recently, is closely shaven, and would fit right into a fancy gala.

I want to lash out at him. To scream in his face. To tell him that he's a horrible human being for his behavior during the night we found out our loved ones were gone.

"Winnie?" Lucas curves an eyebrow impatiently. "Did you hear what I said?"

He wants me gone. Whatever's happening here is private. But I can't move. My feet are frozen on the worn-out stage.

"She heard. Her legs must be cramping from all the standing." I hear Rahim chuckle good-naturedly. He laces his arm in mine and drags me backstage. My feet slog across the hardwood.

Through a toothy smile, Rahim hisses, "Please tell me you're okay. I skipped the first aid tutorial they made us take when I temped as a lifeguard in the Hamptons. Not my proudest confession, but I haven't the greenest clue what to do if you're having a stroke."

"I—I'm not having a stroke," I manage to stutter.

"Thank God. We could all use more of your memaw's cookies."

Backstage, Renee, who plays Irina, hands me a plastic cup with water. Sloan, who plays Konstantin, ushers me to sit down in a folding chair by a rack full of costumes.

Sloan puts his hands on my shoulders. "Deep breaths now. Is she asthmatic? Allergic? Do we need an Epipen?" He turns to Rahim.

Rahim shrugs helplessly.

"I'm neither," I answer, still shaky, even though I don't think Arsène has even noticed me. "Just a little shell shocked. Sorry."

"What was that all about?" Renee lifts an eyebrow.

"I just had this awful cramp in my foot. I couldn't even move," I lie brazenly, raising the plastic cup in thanks, taking a sip of water. "I feel better now."

"I get that in the middle of the night sometimes." Sloan nods sympathetically. "You should supplement with magnesium. Life changing, girl."

"Who was that guy?" Rahim—young, striking, with one failed Broadway show under his belt—points at the stage. "He just walked right in there like he owns the place."

"That's because he does," Sloan, who looks like every blond heart-throb you've seen in movies, deadpans. "Arsène Corbin. Wall Street hotshot by day, owner of half this city by night. Not sure what brought him here, though. He doesn't give much damn about this little theater. He's not the artsy type. Probably just came here to flex and remind Lucas who's pulling the purse strings."

"What purse strings?" Renee bites out bitterly. "The place is a dump, and he's not spending a penny on it."

"How do you know all this?" I ask Sloan.

Sloan shrugs. "People talk."

"Well, do they say that he is an absolute, horrible prick?" I grind out, unable to stop myself.

"They do, actually, but now that you've mentioned it, I'd *love* some tea." Sloan's eyes brighten. "I've yet to hear you use foul language, little Winnie. He must be awful. What's he done? More importantly—*who's* he done? The man is delish."

My colleagues know I'm a young widow, but they don't know much about Paul. They don't know about his maybe-affair with Grace. They don't know Arsène and I are bound together by an awful tragedy.

My heart is still out of whack when Renee, Rahim, and Sloan all lift their eyes to glare at something behind me. Their mouths slacken collectively.

"What?" I sigh, turning around. And there he is again. Arsène Corbin, this time up close. Beautiful, yes. In the same way an active volcano is. Fascinating from a safe distance, but not anything I'd like to touch. And now I see it. The one and only sign of heartbreak. The same thing I see every day in the mirror. His eyes, once sharp, sultry, and full of sardonic laughter, are now dull and dim. He looks like the angel of death.

"Hi!" Sloan greets him brightly, as if he hadn't just asked me to spill the goods on him. "Mr. Corbin, it's lovely to finally mee—"

"Mrs. Ashcroft." Arsène's voice is velvety. "Follow me."

I have no intention of giving him the drama he craves. I've seen this man's smug smirk when he grilled me in Italy. I stand up and trail behind him, giving a little beats-me shrug on my way out. No need to raise the other actors' suspicions.

"Where to?" I ask as we cross the stage and proceed toward the dressing rooms. "Hell?"

His back is muscular and lean. It is obvious he's still active, athletic, working out. Heartbroken my foot. I bet he's having the time of his life.

"Absolutely not. That's my natural habitat, and you aren't invited in my home."

"In that case, leave me alone," I bite out.

"Afraid I can't do that either."

He stops by one of the dressing rooms and pushes the door open. He motions for me to get inside first. I hesitate. Arsène doesn't seem the type to physically assault a woman—doesn't seem the kind to sully his precious zillionaire hands by touching a simpleton like me—but I know his words might be more lethal than fists.

He watches me with a mixture of impatience and curiosity. Now that we're up close and alone, his indifferent mask falls a few inches. His jaw is clenched; his mouth is turned downward. The last months haven't been easy for him, I realize. He keeps his emotions exceptionally close. It is the first time I consider us to be in the same crappy boat. What if we're both miserable, and he is just better at hiding it?

"Would you like a special invitation?" Arsène inquires dryly when I don't make a move to enter the room.

"Would you issue one?" I ask cheerfully, knowing just how much my accent grates on his nerves.

He sneers. "I suggest we get it over with as quickly as possible. Neither of us wants to prolong this, and at least one of us has better places to be in right now."

I step into the dressing room. He closes the door. The place is tiny and jam packed. My back is pressed against a vanity table littered with makeup. Open tubs of setting powder, eye shadow, and brushes. Broken lipsticks are thrown about like crayons. Buried underneath them are batches of fan mail and greeting cards.

Arsène crowds me. I don't know if he does that intentionally or if he is simply too physically imposing for this shoebox of a place. Nonetheless, he is standing close enough for me to smell his aftershave, the mint on his breath, the hair product that makes him look as sleek and shiny as a titan.

"You need to leave," he says decisively.

"You asked me to come here." I fold my arms, intentionally playing dumb.

"Nice try, Bumpkin." He flicks invisible dirt from his cashmere sweater, as if his presence here is dirty. "You're fired, effective immediately. You'll be compensated for your ti—"

"You're not the director, or the producer." I let out a shriek, anger rising up through my chest. "You can't do that."

"I can and am."

I thrust my palms forward, pushing him. He doesn't budge. Simply stares at me, bored pity in his expression.

Gosh. I physically *touched* him. This is not assault, is it? I come from a place where a slap in the face, in the right context, is understandable, even warranted. New Yorkers, however, abide by different rules.

But Arsène doesn't look like he is in danger of swooning or calling the police. He wipes down the lint where my hands have just been. "May I remind you, Mrs. Ashcroft, I own Calypso Hall. I get to say who stays and who goes."

"May I remind you, Mr. Corbin, that your director, Lucas Morton, hired me. We signed a contract. I've done nothing wrong. The play premieres in two weeks. The backup actress hasn't even learned the entire play yet. You won't be able to find a sufficient replacement in time."

"Everyone is replaceable."

"Is that so?" I arch an eyebrow, knowing we're both thinking about the same people. The people who left glaring holes in our hearts.

"Yes." His nostrils flare. *"Everyone."*

I can't lose this job. For too many reasons to count.

"Not Nina, though." My voice drops as I meet his gaze head-on. "Nina is a once-in-a-lifetime creature. I know you probably haven't read *The Seagull—*"

"A lovestruck, ignorant country girl desperate to become a part of a world she doesn't belong in?" he asks smoothly, his voice as dry as the Sahara Desert.

Well, then, I suppose he did *read it.*

He reaches to clasp my chin and closes my mouth with a movement so soft I can't fully trust that he actually touched me. "Don't look so surprised, Bumpkin. My former boarding school is the unofficial feeder of Harvard and Yale. I'd learned them all. The English, the Russians, the Greeks. Even the few Americans who managed to weasel their way into the world's famous literature."

I almost forgot how awful he is. Condescending, patronizing, and worst of all—gleeful about it. Then I remember the last thing he told me when we were at the morgue. How I was a gold digger who was probably happy to be rid of her rich husband.

I decided to use his jadedness against him.

"Fine." I swat his hand away. "Fire me. See how that works out for you."

He gives me a once-over, trying to read between the lines.

"Right, let me spell it out for you, in case your big ol' brain can't figure it out." I put on my thickest accent, stubbing my chest with my finger. "This country bumpkin is gonna run to the nearest tabloid and sell her story. Don't you know actresses? We're a fame-seeking breed, Mr. Corbin. And what'd Andy Warhol once say? Ain't no such thing as bad publicity." I wink at him. "Plus, my story fits into the current cultural narrative like a glove to a hand. A rich, white, billionaire male going after a helpless widow just tryin' to make it in the cruel Big Apple." I press my palms together, looking heavenward. "Think about it. Our story is so juicy. Tongues would waggle for months! My loving husband caught with your fiancée, red handed, heading toward a romantic vacation in Paris. Why, I bet neither of us will be able to leave our apartment without getting caught by the paps!"

There is absolutely no way I could ever bring myself to do such a thing, but he doesn't know that. He thinks the worst of me.

He believes me. He is also a highly private person. I know, because when news broke about Paul and Grace, someone—from Arsène's camp, I always assumed—sold the newspapers the same story. About a work trip gone wrong. A terrible accident that claimed two coworkers, endlessly devoted to their significant others, out to get an urgent merger deal signed. There was one article on TMI, an online gossip site, speculating Paul and Grace were more than colleagues, but it was taken down within minutes.

Corbin's arm is long, powerful, and within reach of most things in this town. But he can't be in charge of every tabloid, every newspaper, every TV channel. Someone would want to buy what I am willing to sell, and we both know that.

He inches forward. The scowl on his face makes him look like a pagan god. This man is used to scaring people. Well, he ain't going to scare me.

"Your presumption, that anything—least of all you—can touch me, not to mention humiliate me, is endearing." His gaze moves down my features like a blade, a sardonic smirk tugging at the side of his lips. "You're lucky I'm a big fan of opportunists. They're my favorite breed of people. Now, any other backup plan to stop me from giving you the boot? And drop the exaggerated accent. You're fooling no one, Bumpkin."

My stomach is full of venomous snakes. I hate Arsène for making me fight for my hard-earned job. I passed the audition on merit. He has no right to do this.

Suddenly, I remember this man's love language—money.

"Sure. Other than the gossip part, there's also the legal matter. I can blow up whatever's left of this place and make it an even more expensive venture for you. Imagine the headline, Mr. Corbin." I frame my fingers in the air. *"Actress Winnifred Ashcroft Sues for Wrongful Termination."*

"It's not wrong to want the woman whose husband *fucked* my dead fiancée far away from me."

"New York is mighty big, and as far as I'm aware, you haven't set foot in Calypso Hall for decades before today." I loop a curl that escaped through my ponytail along my finger. "Y'all never paid any attention to this place in the decades your family owned it. Didn't spend a dime on restoring it either. It was only when I saw you here that I remembered what Grace had said in Italy—"

"Don't speak her name!" he lashes out, baring his teeth like a monster.

Arsène's neck flushes. It surprises me, and I realize I never considered him to be fully human. He is so formidable that the only thing that seems remotely mortal about him is that he apparently cared for his fiancée.

Bringing this man down a notch or two is soothing. I'd been at a point of disadvantage both times we'd met. While he's still technically my employer, at least this time around I don't have to deal with an immediate calamity like I had in Italy and at the morgue.

"Tell me, Arsène." My voice softens. "Are you still on your trading ban?"

"No," he says flatly.

"I see." I pout, tapping my lips. "Wouldn't want to rock the legal boat again, would you?"

"There's absolutely no connection between Calypso Hall and my SEC ban."

"No," I agree. "But you know how slow and grinding the wheels of the law turn. Not to mention all those legal fees you'll have to shell out on this failure of a theater." I look around, fanning myself. "You're going to be deep in the red if I sue. And I will. Because we both know you have no good reason to fire me."

"If you stay . . ." He chooses his words carefully. My corroded heart beats wildly in my chest, reminding me for a change that it is here, that it's still working. "I'm going to make your life so miserable you're going to regret the day you were born."

Leaning forward, I get so close to him our noses almost touch. He smells of sandalwood, moss, and spice. Like dark woods. Nothing like Rahim. Nothing like Paul. Nothing like anyone I've ever known.

"I understand, Mr. Corbin, that you're used to getting your way since people either fear you, loathe you, or are indebted to you. Well, we have a saying in the South. *You look rode hard and put up wet.*"

He frowns. "Sounds like a dirty pickup line."

"Horses break a serious sweat when they run fast. Especially under the saddle. A good rider always takes care to walk their horse and let it cool down before they bring it back to the stable. Then brush it dry. You . . ." Now it is *my* turn to give him a cool once-over. I don't know what comes over me. I'm usually the nice one, the dependable one, voted Most Likely to Run a Charity in high school. But Arsène forces me out of my restraints. He is wild and barely civilized. And so I decide to leave my God-fearing-gal persona at the door. "You look haggard. Sure, you still dress the part, and your haircut probably costs more than my entire outfit, but there's no light behind those eyes. No one's home. I can take you down, Mr. Corbin. And you can bet your last dollar that I can hold my own."

Since I know darn well this is the best monologue I've ever delivered that wasn't written by a playwright, I decide to retire while I have the upper hand. I shoulder past him, knocking over a stack of sheet music on my way out, along with a vase of flowers. My hands are shaking. My knees bump together.

Pushing the door open, I tell myself it's almost over. I'm almost out of harm's way.

But then he opens his mouth, each of his words like a bullet through my back.

"It should've been you."

I stop. My feet turn to marble.

Move, my brain instructs them desperately. *Don't listen to this awful man.*

"I think about it every day." His voice drifts along the room, like smoke, engulfing me. "If only you hadn't been given that stupid role, she'd still be here. Everything would have been fine."

Would it?

Would Grace still be his, even though she went to Paris with another man?

Would Paul still be mine? Even if I didn't turn out to be the woman he'd wanted for himself when he married me? Did we really know the people we loved?

"Oh, Mr. Corbin." I let loose a bitter smile, glancing behind my shoulder. "Maybe you'd have been happy, but you can't say the same for your fiancée. That's why she was on that plane to Paris." I deliver the final blow. "To be loved by someone who knows how to love."

Finally, I manage to move my legs. I stalk off before the first tear falls.

But then I remember: I don't have the simple pleasure of crying anymore.

CHAPTER THIRTEEN

I don't know what surprises me more. Seeing Winnifred Ashcroft in my domain, or all the fresh anger that ignited in me when her blue eyes met mine from across the theater.

The pain, anger, carnal agony slammed back into me in full force. Like the last nine months never happened.

She seems to be a decent actress. This, of course, has nothing to do with why I've decided to keep her. Neither did her little stunts about suing me or leaking it to the press. All of them were puppy bites— meant to hurt but nothing but amusing.

"Let's head back to my office." Ralph, my estate lawyer who came with me to Calypso Hall to give me a ballpark estimate of what this shithole might be worth, gestures to the street.

We're standing on the pavement outside the place I've inherited from Grace. I've been ignoring this financial pit for the better part of the year, while I worked extra hours to reinflate my client list and deploy different mathematical models to make investment decisions with mouthwatering returns. Business is booming, which helps me forget that Grace is no longer here, at least until the night crawls in, and with it, the memories.

"Give me a second to think." I raise my palm to Ralph, massaging my temple with my free hand.

I don't particularly enjoy plays, or any form of nonprofitable art, and I'm no sentimentalist. There's no reason for me to keep this theater. The only person who liked it was my late mother, and as far as humans go, she had a reputation for being a terrible one.

This is why I came here today. To get a number I could later give to potential buyers and get rid of it. Sticking it to my dead mother is just a bonus.

"Sure thing. Coffee while you put your gray matter to work?" Ralph throws a thumb behind his shoulder, pointing at a Krispy Kreme.

"Black, no sugar."

Like your heart, Winnie's annoying voice points out in my head. She's there now?

"Gotcha." He salutes and disappears inside.

Ralph pops back out of the Krispy Kreme to hand me a white cup. "Ready to talk some hard numbers?" He flashes me a jovial smile. "Let's walk. My office is down the block, and Becky always nags me about my ten thousand steps a day."

"Actually, I decided to think it over."

Choking on his coffee, he coughs out midsip. "Think what over?"

"Selling."

"What? Why?"

"Didn't realize I needed to rationalize my decisions with you, Ralphy."

"No!" He waves a hand, pinking. "You just seemed so sure—"

"The only thing I'm sure about right now is that I don't care for your opinion."

"All right, all right. Just keep me in the loop, will you?"

I pivot on my heel and stride toward my apartment.

The reason why I decided to spare Winnifred's job is simple. I still have questions about the night that changed my life.

And Winnie? She might have the answers.

CHAPTER FOURTEEN

WINNIE

Chrissy slides a piece of her rosemary focaccia onto my plate. I finish slurping my pasta napolitana. "Thanks. Want some of my pasta?"

"Want? Always. Should? Not in this lifetime." Chrissy moans, taking a sip of her fat-burning tea. "You need to eat, and well. Otherwise, your family will hold me accountable."

"Ma's all bark and no bite. Don't pay any heed to her." I know my shameless family emails Chrissy about me, asking for weekly updates about my life. I also know that Chrissy basks in it. She loves being my designated BFF/savior.

"She's not wrong, though. You're all skin and bones." My agent throws me a worried look. "Didn't you hear heroin chic is out? This is our era, girl. Curves for miles and appetite are *in*."

"Like I'm going to let the people at *Vogue* tell me how much I should weigh," I huff.

We decided to have a quick brunch before my rehearsal. We invited Arya, but she was too busy with work to come. It's been a week since Arsène strode into the theater and left me reeling. He hasn't visited the place since, but hasn't fired me either. When Rahim, Sloan, and Renee asked me why he took me aside, I lied and said he wanted to ensure I was okay after my cramping leg.

You know, health and safety liability. The last thing he needs is for us to get injured and complain about the sagging wood on the stage.

I hate lying. Not just because of the moral implications. I'm a *terrible* liar. Comes with the territory of having a really bad memory. But no one can find out what binds Arsène and me together. I don't want to be pitied, whispered at, judged; most of all—I don't want them to think the worst about Paul. Not when even I still can't digest the idea that he was unfaithful.

Chrissy puts her fork down and gives me the Stare. The one Ma perfected when I was in high school and snuck out to make out with Rhys right after Sunday church.

"Winnie, we need to talk."

"Oh, I know that line." I break another piece of bread, dip it into the olive oil and vinegar, and pop it into my mouth. "You can't break up with me, Chris. You're the only friend I have in this godforsaken city."

"You have to move on." She remains serious.

"Move on?" I choke out, genuinely appalled by the idea. "It's been less than a year!"

She cannot seriously mean I should date again. Maybe she is thinking I should adopt a pet or get out more. Not that these ideas seem more appealing than dating—*nothing* has sounded appealing since Paul's been gone—but at least they're not outrageous.

"Don't give me that." Chrissy takes a sip of her smelly fat-burning tea. "Paul wasn't some tortured saint. He was a cheating scumbag."

"That's pure speculation. We don't know that," I grind out.

"*We* do." Chrissy slams her tumbler back on the table. "*You* don't. Everyone around you knows. They just don't say anything because you've been through enough."

Do my parents and sisters think the same thing? That Paul had an affair?

"You have no reason to sit and pine for him. Ordering him food, doing the whole preaccident ritual," she says with conviction, spinning in her chair to signal our waitress to bring the check. Her eyes remain on me.

Yeah. Chrissy may or may not have caught me keeping up with my takeout tradition with Paul.

"Look." I groan. "Even if he did cheat on me—which I'm not saying that he did—we'd shared an entire history together. We'd been through a lot. I can't just forget about him. It's not that simple."

"My point exactly! Another reason why you should move on. If he did this to you *after* everything you'd gone through, then I'm sorry, but he shouldn't be forgiven, nor mourned. No one's gonna judge you if you move on."

The delicious food tastes like mud in my mouth. The waitress slides the check between us. I attempt to grab it, but Chrissy is faster. She grins, wiggling her eyebrows as she drops her credit card into the black leather bill holder and hands it back to the waitress.

"Point is, it's time for you to move on, before the world moves on without you. Tough times never last, honey. Tough people, however . . ." Chrissy reaches to pat my hand as the waitress hurries along with her credit card. "Life is beautiful and wild, and it doesn't wait for you to decide to participate in it. You need to jump into the water headfirst. And when you do? Make sure to make a splash."

◆ ◆ ◆

An hour later, I walk into Calypso Hall for rehearsal. Since the place is closed until the matinee shows start, Jeremy, the daytime security guard, unlocks the door for me.

"Miz Ashcroft. Lovely day out, isn't it?" he greets me.

I smile back in response, handing him a biscotti and coffee I purchased from the Italian place before coming here. "The loveliest, Jeremy. Here. I hope this sweetens up your day."

"You're too kind for this city, Winnifred." He sighs.

I make my way backstage. Jeremy waves a frantic hand to stop me.

"Hey, wait, Miz Ashcroft! Have you seen this? Impressive, don't you think?"

I turn around, coming face to face with something I have no idea how I missed when I walked in. It's a floor-to-ceiling poster of *The Seagull*. Rather than displaying all the actors, it's a close-up of Rahim and me.

Anton Chekhov's The Seagull.

Starring: Rahim Fallaha, Winnifred Ashcroft, Renee Hinds, and Sloan Baranski

The shot is of me staring at the camera, Rahim standing behind me, whispering in my ear. It is beautiful, tender, and erotic. But I can't muster any excitement and pleasure from it. My heart doesn't skip a beat, nor does it beat faster. This is the height of my career—something that would have made the old me leap in excitement, gather Jeremy into a hug, kiss the poster, take pictures, and send them to everyone on my contact list.

I feel so empty I want to scream just to fill my body with something.

Shed a tear. Just the one. To show yourself that you can. You're an actress, for crying out loud!

"Good for you, Miz Ashcroft." Jeremy tilts his hat in my direction. "Well deserved."

Somehow I get through the entire rehearsal without having a meltdown over *not* having a meltdown about the poster. Am I ever going to feel anything again? Joy? Pleasure? Jealousy? *Hate?* I'll take anything at this point.

Rahim is in high spirits. He rushes to admire our poster when it's time for our break.

"How sad is it that this place sucks so bad we get excited over a *poster?*" Rahim clucks his tongue, examining himself on the floor-to-ceiling thing once again. "Do you know how much money they poured into *Hamilton's* marketing?"

Lucas walks around like a peacock between rehearsals. Apparently, for the first time in twenty years, actual critics are going to attend a premiere at Calypso Hall. He smiles and laughs with the technical crew, doesn't complain when two of the sound guys go home early, and *hugs* the set designer when she accidentally breaks a prop.

When rehearsal is over, Renee and Sloan dash to an amateur production by a mutual friend that's premiering tonight.

"See you tomorrow, Win. Oh, and my girlfriend says thanks for the cookie tip." Rahim kisses my cheek, also on his way out. "The yolk and brown sugar? Godsend!"

"Tell her to call me whenever. This thing is full of recipe hacks." I knock on my temple. "But remember, no sharing trade secrets with your felting club!"

He laughs, turning around and heading out the door. I amble into my dressing room.

It's a tiny space backstage, but it's all mine. I close the door behind me, plaster my forehead to the cool wood of the door, and suck in a cleansing breath.

"You're fine. Everything's fine," I tell myself out loud.

"I beg to differ," someone drawls behind me, making me jump out of my skin. "Not many people who talk to themselves are considered fine."

The voice, wry and amused, belongs to the only man I *do* have some feelings toward these days. Pure loathing, to be specific. I find Arsène sitting on a tattered yellow couch, one leg crossed over the other, the forbidding emperor that he is.

"Mr. Corbin, what a surprise." My heart ripples in my chest. It's the first time I feel the organ in months, and I don't like that this Byronic, tortured man is the reason. "What brings you to my little den?"

"I'm currently between meetings. I'm thinking of acquiring an escape room on Bryant Park. Medieval-dungeon themed. They seem to be all the rage."

"Thanks for sharing. It means a lot. Now, let me be specific. What are you doing in *my* room?" I gather my hair into a ponytail.

"*Your* room?" He arches a skeptical brow. "I hadn't realized you're so fiercely possessive of it. Grew up with siblings, huh?"

Yes, but I'm not going to give him the satisfaction by sharing this piece of information with him. Also, I hate how his tone is always friendly and mocking, like he can stand me more than I can stand him.

"You grew up with a sister too. Though I can't say you felt very brotherly toward her at all." I cross my arms over my chest, leaning against the door. "Cut to the chase. I have things to do today."

"I didn't know they taught you sarcasm in God's Country, Bumpkin." He runs a hand over his athletic thigh, and I resist the urge to follow the movement with my eyes. "I think it's time we exchange notes about what happened that night." He drapes his arm along the back of the couch. "Everything we found out in the aftermath. I'll show you mine, and you'll show me yours, so to speak."

"I don't like to be shown anything by you." I wrinkle my nose.

Truthfully, I want to do this. Badly. The amount of times I've considered reaching out to this man to ask him what he knows is countless. But I also don't trust his intentions, considering our brief history.

His lips twist in a grin. "How many Hail Marys do you need to say for lying, Winnifred?"

"I'm not lying."

"Yes, you are." His smirk widens. "I know because your lips are moving."

"Even if I do want to exchange notes"—I roll my eyes—"how do I know you'll tell the truth? You could lie just to spite me. What if I fulfill my part of the bargain and you bullshit your way out of it?"

"I've no particular interest in hurting you," he assures me calmly. "Nor sparing you any pain. I simply want to put together the most accurate picture of what happened."

"And you want to get this information from a—quote—*gold-digging bitch* like me?" I fail to keep the hurt out of my words.

"Winnifred, darling!" He tips his head, roaring with laughter. I really want to stab him. Right in the throat. "Don't tell me you got offended? Sweetheart, you being a gold digger earns you nothing but brownie points from me. Don't forget I work on Wall Street, where greed is welcome—even celebrated."

"You're a horrid person." I shake my head.

"Why, thank you. At any rate, as I said, I have a few spare minutes and some information I'm sure you'd be interested in. I gathered that Lucas's rehearsal is over, so if you feel like exchanging notes, there's no time like the present."

I finger my chin, my curiosity piqued. The need to know what happened is greater than the desire to stick it to him. Plus, I have nowhere else to be right now. My schedule's wide open and consists mainly of staring at the walls in my apartment.

"All right." I cross the tiny space between the door and my vanity, plopping onto a chair opposite him. "But be quick about it."

He shakes his head. "Not here."

"Why?"

"We could be seen."

"And?" I narrow my eyes at him.

"And I don't want to be affiliated with you for numerous reasons, all of them highly logical." He spells it out for me. "The main one being that, technically speaking, I'm your employer. We shouldn't be in a closed room together."

"Gosh, *employer*. That's a big word for someone who barely pays us minimum wage around here."

He grins again, satisfied with the trouble I'm giving him. "It's a free country. If you wish to be employed somewhere else, I'd be the last person to stop you."

"I'm not going to your apartment." I bring the conversation back to its original topic.

"You wound me, Bumpkin." He stands up, buttoning his blazer. "I'd never make a pass at an employee. That's bad taste and dubious ethics."

"Aren't those your defining traits?" I arch an eyebrow.

To this, he full-blown laughs. "I'll call us two separate taxis. What's your pants size?"

"Hmm, let me see." I twist in my seat, tugging at the size tag of my jeans. "Says here none of your business."

Another sincere laugh escapes him. "My apologies for upsetting your southern notions. See, here in New York, women don't let their dress size define them."

"My size doesn't define me. My right not to answer your personal questions does."

"Humor me anyway, just for funsies." His smile—when done right—can make a woman weak in the knees. Dimpled and boyish, with just the right amount of snark. Poor Grace stood no chance. I wonder if they got it on while they were under the same roof. *Of course* they did. Well, that's kind of hot.

Since when do I think about things that are hot?

"Small or medium." I purse my lips. "Now my turn to ask a question—how old are you, exactly?"

"Exactly? Thirty-five, seven months, three days, and . . ." He glances down at his watch. "Eleven hours, give or take."

He feels much older to me, and I'm twenty-eight. Maybe because he has that larger-than-life aura.

"A taxi will arrive for you in eight minutes. But first, go change into men's clothes," Arsène instructs, standing up.

"What's wrong with my current clothes?" I look down. I'm wearing a pink tank top and a pair of casual jeans from the GAP. My sandals are a hand-me-down pair from Lizzy.

"Nothing at all," he assures me smoothly. "All the same, I do need you to look a little more masculine."

"Masculine?"

"Yes. You need to dress as a man."

"Where the hell are you taking me?"

He is already out the door, his back to me. "You'll see."

The taxi pulls out in front of a white beaux arts building. It is vast and stunning and looks ancient. What is it? A hotel? An office building? My senses kick into overdrive. I haven't had this much adrenaline coursing through my veins since . . . since . . .

Never. No one ever pushed you that far out of your comfort zone.

"That's you, sir," the taxi driver announces.

Sir. After my bizarre exchange with Arsène, I went and grabbed some clothes from a pile of extras for a Victorian-era musical. I'm wearing an ivory cotton shirt, a double-breasted vest, a dinner jacket, and some slacks. My hair is stuffed inside a brown newsboy's hat, concealed from view. I'm pretty sure I look like Oliver Twist.

I push the taxi door open and take the steps to the building two at a time. I don't have Arsène's number, so I have no idea if he is already inside or not. When I reach the large black door, I see a golden label on it.

THE NEW AMSTERDAM.

A GENTLEMEN'S CLUB.

MEMBERS ONLY.

I had no idea gentlemen's clubs still existed. I raise my fist, about to knock on the door, when a voice behind me booms.

"Wouldn't do that if I were you."

I turn around, and of course, it is Arsène, who is in the habit of materializing out of thin air like a demon, narrating my every move. Out here, in the concrete jungle of Manhattan, in broad, natural daylight, I am forced to see that he is not only a man, but a striking one at that. His thick, jet-black hair; square jaw; prominent chin; and high cheekbones give him the appeal of an old-era gentleman.

"That's a peculiar look, Bumpkin." His pleased voice is oddly addictive. I wonder if he's moved on from Grace yet. If he is seeing someone else. Somehow, I think not. Arsène is the kind of man to have a very particular taste.

"You said to dress like a man." I scowl.

"One born in this century."

"Sorry, we ran out of hipster Brooklyn men with plaid shirts, waxed beards, and Warby Parker glasses," I bite out.

He shoulders past me to punch in a secret code into the electric lock of the door. "You do amuse me, Winnifred. You haven't surrendered your odd individuality in order to fit in just yet. This uninhibited, innocent vibe? It's growing on me."

"I'm sure there was a compliment under all that patronizing mumbo jumbo, but if it's okay, I'd like to keep things between us professional." I step away from him, just to prove to myself that I'm not flattered. And really, I'm not.

"Well, it's time to put your acting skills to good use, because if they find out you're a woman, there's a teeny, tiny chance you'll get arrested for trespassing."

"Excuse me?" I thunder, finding myself yet again riled up by this impossible man. "What on earth were you—"

He nudges the door open with his shoulder and gives me a light shove inside. I'm thrust into the situation. It's a vast hallway, all limestone pillars and columns and rich beige carpets. Men in suits and expensive golf wear pass us by. Some of them nod in acknowledgment to Arsène. Everyone looks like variations of Paul's Wall Street friends.

I follow Arsène's brisk steps, trying to rein in my panic.

Sweat gathers under my armpits and on the back of my neck.

"What if I get caught?" I whisper-shout to him.

"Just say you're Jupiter."

"Jupiter?" I ask, confused.

"That you're the cleaner. You know that Jupiter vacuums and absorbs comets and meteors? One estimate I read suggests if Jupiter didn't suck objects into its sphere, the number of massive projectiles hitting the Earth would be ten thousand times greater."

"That is . . . good to know."

Arsène approaches a vast reception area.

"Cory, I need a private space for my nephew and me. What's available?" He snaps his fingers to the man behind the reception desk.

"Mr. Corbin." Cory smiles, typing on his keyboard. "I didn't know you had any nephews. Is he from around here?"

"The sticks." Arsène waves a hand. "It's his first time in New York. He's a little starstruck."

He's about to strike you in the back if you're not careful.

"We have billiard room number two, or the tennis court."

Arsène aims his hawkish gaze at me.

"Billiard room." I drop my voice low. I'm great at pool. Rhys taught me when we were dating. We even went and won a few amateur tournaments together.

Cory, who hears me, gestures to the right side of the foyer. "Gentlemen, I hope you enjoy this establishment, and Manhattan."

Five minutes later, we're in an empty billiard room full of shelves laden with antique books and a fully stocked liquor bar. Leather upholstered chairs are scattered around us.

Arsène steps behind the bar, clearly in his natural habitat. "What can I get you for your troubles, my dear nephew?"

I look around me, still mesmerized. I hadn't stepped into the world of the rich and corrupt since Paul passed away. I haven't missed it, but I forgot how it made me feel. Like I'm wearing someone else's skin.

"Anything I can't usually afford." I shrug.

"They don't keep the exclusive stuff in the open bar. Let's see." He runs a finger over a row of bottles. "Will Bowmore do?"

I pin him with a what-is-that? stare.

Another devastating smirk. "Scottish. Single malt. More or less your age."

"And how old do you think I am?"

"Twenty."

"Eight," I correct. Twenty-eight.

"You're *eight*? Well, may I suggest a visit to the dermatologist? You certainly look past puberty, and now I feel all kinds of guilty for entertaining improper thoughts about you in Italy."

He did, now? I push this little nugget of information to the back of my mind—there's no trusting that it is true—and give myself a tour across the grand room.

Arsène pours a glass for each of us, ambles over, and hands me mine. I take a slow sip. The amber liquid is warm at first, scorching a path down my throat. Then a calm feeling washes over my limbs, like I just entered a relaxing bath.

He motions with the hand that holds the whiskey to the chairs. "Sit."

"I want to play."

I haven't done anything fun since Paul passed. Now that I'm here, I'm thinking . . . why not? Everything else about this situation is strange. Surely, getting a game of billiards out of this won't be such an awful betrayal against my late husband.

"I don't."

"Why?" I ask, gulping more of the liquid.

"I never play to lose."

I find it refreshing that he doesn't assume I'm a bad player, like many men did before him.

"You might not lose." I lick the whiskey residue from my bottom lip.

"I will." He seems completely at ease about his weaknesses, which is also interesting.

"How do you know?"

"You haven't talked yourself into any corners so far." He strides across the room, his back to me, and examines the bookshelves. "If you want to play, that means you're good at it."

Maybe it's the whiskey, or maybe it's just the fact I haven't really interacted with anyone other than Chrissy, Arya, and my colleagues in a while, but instead of letting it go, I pick up a cue stick. After moving over to the fuzzy green table, I arrange the triangle rack on top of it.

"You little rebel," Arsène says, picking up his own cue. "Fine, I'll play."

"It's been a while since I did something fun." I readjust my hat, tucking a ribbon of strawberry blonde hair back inside.

"What are we playing for?" he asks.

I think about it. "If I win, I want you to pay for a huge billboard sign and advertise *The Seagull*. You know, one of the fancy Times Square placements. Three days minimum."

"I'll do you one better. An entire week, best block available. And if I win, you quit," he fires back, standing on the opposite side of the pool table from me.

Sourness explodes in my mouth. He still wants me gone.

"And here I thought you were mildly human," I huff. "I should've—"

"Winnifred." He smirks, delighted.

"What?"

"I won't win."

"But you—"

"And just for the record, I love that out of all the things I could've done for Calypso Hall—repair the floors, the seats, put a fresh coat of paint on the walls—you chose something for yourself. Very telling. I find altruism such a boring trait."

I blush furiously because he is right. I could've asked for him to fix the theater. I never considered myself to be selfish, but something about this man inspires me to want to get things for myself. Maybe because he is so unapologetically self-serving.

He takes my limp hand in his, shakes it, and starts playing.

Arsène is, in fact, exceptionally bad at this. He doesn't give excuses or get frustrated like Paul did whenever he proved himself to be less than adequate in axe throwing or basketball. On the contrary. Each time I slide another ball into a pocket, he lets out a delighted laugh. I'm never sure if he is laughing with me, because of me, or at me. But for the first time in months, I'm actually having fun, so I choose not to ask.

The first few minutes, we play silently. So I'm nearly caught off guard when he starts speaking.

"I suppose our starting point is that we both agree they were having an affair."

My cue stumbles on the surface, creating a train of bald patch as I lose my grip on it. I straighten up. "No. We don't."

"They did." Arsène stands back, his voice steady and low.

"Why? Because you always choose to believe the worst about people?" I lean against my cue.

"For at least nine months." He ignores my question.

"*Nine* months?" Something inside me goes slack. That can't possibly be right.

"Yes." Arsène takes his turn, striking the stripy red ball straight into a pocket.

"How do you know?" I try to angle my stick on the table and, again, it slips.

If this is right . . . if Arsène is telling the truth . . . then that means . . .

For the first time in months, I *feel*. Oh, do I feel. Anger. Wrath. Pain. I want Paul's blood. I want to resurrect him and kill him all over again. How could he do this to me? How could he?

It's not that I haven't suspected it. It's that up until now, I told myself there could be other explanations. And I kept thinking that even if they did have an affair, it was recent. Not an ongoing thing. A month-old thing, maybe.

"I hired a private investigator." He crosses his ankles. "Grace and Paul had been frequenting a hotel not very far from their office. All the receipts are from the nine months prior to the plane crash. All paid in cash."

I drop the cue noisily. I stagger to the bar to fill my empty whiskey glass to the brim with more liquor, as if it's sweet tea. I take a swig. "When's the earliest receipt from?"

Arsène's face is unreadable, a blank mask. "September thirteenth."

"The thirteenth, you say?"

He nods. I close my eyes, bile coating my throat.

"I'm missing context here." Arsène's voice seeps into my body. "What's significant about the date?"

I shake my head. It's too personal. Besides, it has nothing to do with why we're here.

"I need a minute." I put my glass down, my drink sloshing every-where. "Where's the restroom?"

Silently, he points me in the direction. I make my way there in a daze. I lock myself in one of the cubicles, rip my vest off my chest, stuff it into my mouth, and scream into it until my vocal cords are raw. I bite down on the fabric until my gums are bleeding.

I want to torch the entire city of New York to the ground. To go back in time. To stay in Tennessee, in the comfort of my family. I could've had a good life. Yes, I wouldn't be an actress on Broadway—but I'm not one now. At least I'd have Rhys—sweet, dependable, chivalrous Rhys—and a secure job at a high school, and people to lean on when things got tough.

Even through all this pain, all this heartache, I can't find my tears. I blink fast, trying to produce moisture in my eyes, but to no avail.

"Oh, Paul!" I howl in the cubicle, punching the wall. "You asshole!"

Allowing myself a few minutes to recompose, I make my way back to the billiard room. Arsène waits where I left him, by the pool table, his posture imperial.

When I walk in, he frowns at me.

"What're you looking at?" I lash out. "Never seen anyone have a nervous breakdown before?"

"I've seen plenty. And believe it or not, yours doesn't even give me particular joy," he says dryly. "But your hat's off, and so is the vest. I take it you want to spend the night at the police station."

I look down and realize that he is right. I stuffed the vest into a trash can after bleeding on it in the restroom, and now it is visible that under my cotton dress shirt, I have breasts. My blonde hair is spilling over my shoulders.

Still, I can't muster enough energy to care.

I return to my whiskey glass, take another sip, and fall down into a leather recliner. "Tell me something nice about space."

"What?" He lifts an eyebrow. I caught him off guard.

"Distract me!" I roar.

"All right. Close your eyes."

Unbelievably, I do. I need a second to breathe, even if my designated therapist right now is Satan himself.

"About three billion years ago, Mars probably looked like a tranquil resort by the ocean. There's some interesting fossils and craters on Mars that suggest a river ran through it. This means that, possibly, there *was* life on Mars. Maybe not as we know it, but life nonetheless."

"Do you believe in aliens?" I murmur, eyes still closed.

"*Believe* in them?" he asks, surprised. "I don't know any, so it's hard to say I put my faith in them. Do I believe in their existence? Certainly. The question is, Are they close enough to be discovered, and more importantly—do we *want* to discover them?"

"Yeah," I sigh. "Maybe not. Humans have let us down. Why try our luck with other species?"

He laughs, and I realize that he is oddly entertained by my humor.

"I do think it's only a matter of time before we find biology somewhere that's not on planet Earth. It's extremely vain to think we're alone in a billion-galaxy space, consisting of more stars than there are grains of sand, and billions of planets."

"I don't want to meet them," I say.

"I don't think you will. Not in our lifetime, anyway."

"Thank you," I say.

"For what?" he asks.

"For putting my mind off that thing I thought about when you said September thirteenth."

There's a brief silence between us. I'm the first to speak again.

"Paul had an apartment in Paris."

"Come again?" Arsène takes a seat opposite to me, attentive and alive all of a sudden.

"After he died, I started taking care of the bills. He was good with numbers, so this was normally his jurisdiction. One of the outstanding bills was an overdue rent payment on an apartment on the eighth arrondissement." I stare into the bottom of the glass.

"The Champs-Élysées area," he supplies.

I nod. "Nice geography. I Google Mapped it."

Arsène considers my words. I can tell he's already digesting this information, fitting it into a puzzle in his head.

"Don't look at me like that," I hiss out defensively. "His parents are building a house in Provence. I thought he helped them with accommodations, what with all of the back-and-forth."

Now that I say it out loud, it does sound like a weak excuse. Why would Paul hide such a thing from me? Not to mention, Provence isn't even close to Paris.

"Hadn't he told you he made reservations for a hotel in Paris?" he asks. "That time you were supposed to go with him on a romantic trip?"

"Well, yeah." I munch on my bottom lip.

"Have you ever seen those hotel reservations?"

"Now that I think about it . . ." I take another sip. I haven't. I'd taken Paul's word for it.

Arsène stares at me, but doesn't say anything. He doesn't need to. I feel stupid enough already.

"He never intended to take me with him." I let my head slump between my shoulders.

"It's possible he knew you'd get the job. It was a small production, wasn't it? He could've even pulled a few strings to make it happen. Silver Arrow Capital has a wide range of clients. Some of them are on off-Broadway boards."

Leaning forward, I bury my face in my hands. My hair spills out on either side of me. Arsène doesn't say anything. I don't expect him to. In a way, I even prefer it. I'm tired of empty words. The amount of clichés that are hurled at me is exhausting.

It gets better, kiddo.

This too shall pass.

Have you tried therapy? It did wonders for my niece . . .

"Mr. Corbin?" I hear Cory's voice. "I just wanted to make sure everything is to your satisfa—"

The words die in his mouth. My head snaps up. I know I've been caught. He can see, by my hair and slight frame, that I'm a woman. I stare Cory in the eye. Arsène stands up. He is about to say something. I don't want to stay to find out how much trouble I'm in. And I'm *definitely* not spending a night in jail. I grab my messenger bag and bolt out the door, pushing Cory on my way out. His back slams against the wall.

"Sorry, sorry," I mutter. "I'm so sorry."

I don't look back.

Don't falter when I hear Arsène calling my name.

I continue running, blasting through doors, through corridors, through air, pushing guests and waiters and employees. I spill onto the street and rest my hands over my knees, the sun beating down on my back.

Paul cheated on me.

Chrissy was right. He never did love me.

When I get home, my answering machine is flashing red. Even though I'm a wreck, I decide to listen to the messages. I can always give Ma a call back tomorrow, and hearing a friendly voice might do me good.

I hit the button as I make my way to the dishwasher, then fish out a clean glass and fill it with tap water.

The voice that fills my room doesn't belong to any of my family members, but it is one I can recognize in my sleep.

"Winnie? Um, yeah. Hey. It's Rhys." Pause. Uncomfortable laugh. Something twists in my heart, cracking it open, letting nostalgia trickle in. "We haven't spoken since I came to Paul's funeral. I don't know why I'm calling." Another pause. "Actually, I do. I do know. I wanted to ask how you're doing. I know you just landed a huge gig—congratulations, by the way. Didn't I say you were too big for this town?" His soft laugh rings through my apartment like church bells, bringing me back to the comfortable, to the familiar. "Anyway . . . just checking in. Your momma gave me this number. No rush in gettin' back, I imagine you're mighty busy over there. Things at home are fine. Normal. Boring." Another snicker. "Guess I've always been kind of boring. That was my problem, huh? So, yeah. Call me. Miss you. Bye."

The message ends. The glass slips from between my fingers and shatters on the floor noisily.

Rhys Hartnett is wrong. He was never boring. He was always perfect in my eyes. But perfection is something that's easy to walk away from when you are eighteen, just got an acceptance letter from Juilliard, and the dreams in your head grow wild and long and free like weeds.

Another message rolls through. This time from Lizzy, my sister.

"Hey, Win! It's been a hot minute, so I thought I'd see what's going on with you. We love you. We miss you. Kenny wants to say hi to her favorite auntie. Right, Kenny?" A child's laughter fills my apartment, making my empty stomach clench.

"Hi, Auntie Winnie! Love you! But I love Auntie Georgie too," Kenny coos.

"Anyway," Lizzy butts in. "Call us back. Bye!"

There is one last message. This time from Chrissy.

"Oh, and another thing." She starts straight from the middle of our conversation earlier today. "Not only was Paul an obnoxious human being—not to your face, but behind your back—but he was also terrible in bed, remember?"

I choke out a chuckle. He wasn't *terrible*. I'd had better. That's all I ever told her, one drunken night when Paul was in Europe, ironically probably screwing Grace.

"You told me the best part of your sex life was your foreplay. That's like enjoying the complimentary bread more than the entrée! I rest my case. Now go open a Tinder account and live your best life. Doctor's order."

I pull myself up, deciding the crushed glass could wait until tomorrow to be cleaned. I walk into the hallway. Stop in front of Paul's office.

Betraying him and opening the door doesn't seem like such a sinful act anymore, knowing what I know after my conversation with Arsène.

Paul never loved me.

This much I now know to be true. But because a part of me still loves him, I pass by the door and not through it.

One day, I promise myself. *But not today.*

CHAPTER FIFTEEN

ARSÈNE

Tonight I'm expected to be the last thing I want to be—a respected, civilized part of polite society.

Arya Roth-Miller is throwing her annual charity ball. It's for a good cause—Saint John's Children's Hospital—something that, in itself, would not make me leave the house in a million years.

No. I'm here because the pain in the neck she refers to as her husband used every tool in his arsenal to ensure my presence.

The general idea is to make a fat donation, take a few photos with people whose names I will forget before they even utter them to me, and go back to my apartment to read an astronomy book and eat leftover takeout.

I spent the afternoon hitting the bottle, pregaming before the ball. There's nothing I like less than having to tolerate people I don't know for long stretches of time sober.

"Arsène, you look amazing in that tux!" Arya pounces on me as soon as I walk through the door of the Pierre hotel's grand ballroom. It's an exquisite space, with dripping chandeliers and enough curtains to conceal New Zealand in its entirety. Grace would've loved it.

"I know." I kiss both her cheeks.

Christian appears beside her, snaking an arm around his wife's waist. "Return the compliment, you swine."

"Arya." I take my best friend's wife's hand, bringing her knuckles to my lips. "You'll look amazing in my tux too."

Arya, who is wearing a pastel dress, laughs, swatting my chest. "I don't even know why I like you."

"You like me because I'm direct, and fun, and I keep your husband on his toes," I supply.

"Don't forget humble. One of my favorite things about you. Well, enjoy."

"He'd never enjoy something as wholesome and uplifting as a charity ball." Christian shakes his head, but his wife is already swaggering away, approaching the guests trickling into the room.

He hands me a glass of champagne. "I know humans aren't your thing. You surviving?"

I down the entire thing like it is water, then toss the glass onto a tray held by a waiter who's passing by. "Just barely. But I'll do better after five more of these."

"Drinking away your problems is such a fucking cliché."

"Away?" There's already another glass in my hand. I smile wryly. "I can assure you, Christian, my problems can outrun Usain Bolt. No part of me is dumb enough to think I can escape them."

"Then why the shit are you drinking?" A hand claps my back. It's Riggs. I turn around to look at him. I find him in a tux that doesn't suggest it's been stolen from Salvation Army—a welcome improvement from his usual attire—and a tan he must've gotten in Antarctica. There's a pretty redhead on his arm.

"Gentlemen, it is my pleasure to introduce you to—" Riggs is about to tell us the name of his date—if he even remembers it. I wave him off.

"Spare me. If I allowed room in my mind for all the women you introduced to us, I'd need more cloud storage."

Christian half winces, half chuckles. "My apologies." He turns to the scarlet-haired beauty. "Our friend Arsène is frequently blunt, but rarely wrong."

Riggs punches my arm. "What crawled up your ass, Corbin?"

"Grace," Christian answers on my behalf. "Who else would be foul enough to get anywhere near his private parts?"

Ah, Grace. Even in death, she is their public enemy number one. And that's without them even knowing anything about the Paul bull-shit. I haven't said a word about my late fiancée's affair. I didn't need to look pathetic on top of being an unlucky, grieving bastard.

"Just to keep you informed." Riggs turns to her. "Christian just threw a dig at this asshole's dead fiancée. We don't do boundaries here."

She sucks in a breath, looking at Christian with abhorrence.

"Don't pretend like you'd fare better if something happened to Arya," I murmur into my drink.

Christian gives me a pitiful look. "No, I'd die right along with her. With one distinction—Arya never tried to kill her stepbro—"

"I really do insist you meet my enchanting date." Riggs pivots the conversation before a fistfight ensues.

Christian introduces himself to Riggs's date. The two are locked in polite conversation after he explains to her that no one liked my fiancée very much. My gaze drifts unenthusiastically to the other people in the room. I finish the second glass of champagne and reach for a third. Galas and balls were Grace's favorite thing. This is the first time I've attended an official function as a single man.

The newness of crawling back into the world without her on my arm feels like carrying a three-ton phantom limb. More specifically, the idea that Grace is no longer the endgame. The trophy. The ultimate prize.

In the sea of blow-dried dos and painted faces, I find one that I recognize.

A mass of strawberry blonde hair arranged in a high, unfashionable ponytail. I can tell it's her even when her back is to me. She is wearing a spaghetti-strapped flowery dress to a goddamn *gala* and still manages to steal the entire show. Her neck is long and elegant, swanlike even, and seems just as fragile.

As if sensing my gaze on her, she turns around. Her face is wide, open, smiling. She is radiant, and I remember the last time we met, when she almost gave Cory a heart attack and nearly annihilated me in billiards. She also drank like an Irish sailor, defended that idiotic late husband of hers, and exhibited general adorableness I couldn't decide whether revolted or amused me.

She also took interest in my astronomy obsession. Nobody else ever did. Which is the *only* reason why I'm not completely disgusted by seeing her here.

I lean back against the wall, watching her laughing and talking animatedly with a crowd of eager-looking men. She is significantly underdressed, but a genuine smile is a jewel more priceless than any diamond necklace one could purchase.

Riggs, naturally attuned to anything with a pair of tits, follows my gaze and *hmm*s in agreement. "Our boy is showing signs of life. Can't blame him, though." Riggs grins into his drink. "Those legs would look great wrapped around my neck."

"Winnifred Ashcroft," Riggs's date provides readily, glad to be of use. "She's an actress. Came here with her agent. Well, *our* agent," she amends, a brittle bite in her voice. "Chrissy has her favorites, obviously."

I'm not particularly unhappy to see Winnifred here. I am, however, considerably drunk, which means now's not the time to talk to her. She is not as easily maneuvered as she seems, and I still haven't squeezed all the information I need from her.

Turning back into my group of friends, I say, "I'm heading back home."

"Not before Arya makes a speech." Christian moves in front of me to block my way. "She worked really hard putting together this event."

"I don't think you understand." I smooth my tux. "This wasn't a request, but a stated fact."

"Why, if it isn't my favorite boss," a sweet southern drawl greets me from behind.

"Boss?" Christian asks in surprise, peering behind my shoulder. "Arya's not gonna love *that.*"

"You must have the wrong person, sweetheart." Riggs flashes Winnifred a smile, clapping my shoulder. "This man right here can't be anyone's favorite anything. He's about as lovable as a juicy, pus-filled zit."

"Thanks for the image." I shake his touch off, turning around to face her.

"Hey, Winnie." The redhead air-kisses Winnifred.

"Hey, Tiff! Heard you killed it in that romcom pilot." My employee gives her a warm hug. Her need to be cute and selfless grates on my nerves. She turns her attention back to me. "Didn't know you were the philanthropic kind."

"He isn't." Christian tucks a hand into his front pocket. "I dragged him here kicking and screaming."

"Don't forget the wailing," I deadpan. "I was inconsolable."

Despite being an annoying Goody Two-shoes, she doesn't look horrid in her simple dress and ponytail. The realization is unwelcome and alarming. I don't even like blondes. This must be Mother Nature's way of telling me it is time to stick my dick somewhere wet and warm. It's been almost a year, after all.

"Arsène?" Winnifred frowns. "Everything okay?"

I haven't acknowledged her existence in the two minutes she's been standing here. *Oops.*

I clasp the small of her back, brushing my lips against her cheek noncommittally. "Winnifred, would it be improper to tell you that you look beautiful?"

"No, which is why you wouldn't do it."

I laugh. The most surprising thing about this boring, one-dimensional, cookie-making blonde is that she possesses wit. Or something that resembles it, anyway.

She studies me intently, like a concerned parent. "Are you . . . okay?"

"Never better."

I'm waiting for her to leave. I'm drunk, tired, and not in the mood to milk information out of her.

"You sure you don't want me to call you a taxi?" She frowns.

And she would. Little Miss Sunshine.

"Positive, but thank you."

"Well . . ." She lingers. "Enjoy your night."

"I intend to."

When she leaves, both Christian and Riggs look at me, openly aghast.

"I've never seen you like this." Riggs's smile is slow and taunting.

"Like what?"

"A teenager ushered into the ER with his ball sack stuck between his girlfriend's metal braces," Christian articulates poetically. "You looked flushed. Uncomfortable. Dare I say it? *Embarrassed.*"

"Mortified." Riggs knocks back a drink. "He blushed. I saw him. Did you see him blush, Tiff?"

"Yes!" Tiff, grateful to be more than a decorative ornament at this point, joins my two friends eagerly. "His face is all red. That's so sweet. Winnie's a great gal."

I've managed to get through an entire week without cornering Winnifred at Calypso Hall for more information. The rented Paris apartment was a big revelation. What else does she know? What else did she *miss*?

Bringing her back to New Amsterdam is a big no. She assaulted Cory. The man had to get two stitches, which I generously paid for to keep his mouth shut. I bet it was her first brush with doing something less than perfect, and I take pleasure in knowing I corrupted her, even if just a bit.

"I didn't blush," I say shortly.

"Yes, you did. You're going to have to explain the last five minutes to us," Christian announces.

"Nothing to explain. She works at Calypso Hall," I say.

From the corner of my eye, I catch Arya moving in our direction at rapid speed. Time to wrap up this little girl talk.

"And, for your information, even if I wasn't still mourning the untimely death of my fiancée, pursuing an employee is tacky and frowned upon."

"I'm getting weird vibes." Riggs licks the ball of his index finger and raises it in the air, closing his eyes. "Yup, there it is. There are horny winds coming from the east."

I stand to the moron's east.

"Even if there are *hurricanes* of horniness, I demand you don't act on them." The voice belongs to Arya.

I turn around, studying her. "I don't like to be ordered around. What's your angle?"

"That girl is an angel on earth. She visits the children at Saint John's hospital once a week. Dresses up as a fairy and paints their faces. They love it. They love *her*," she says desperately. "And I love her! She's a widow, you know. She knows what pain is. I don't want her to get hurt again."

So she heard, but she doesn't know how it happened. Good job, Winnifred, on keeping our shit private and not letting people put two and two together.

Christian watches Winnifred as she makes her way back to who I assume is her agent. "Met the girl before. She seems kind, talented, and attractive. Don't worry, my love. Arsène doesn't stand a chance even if he tried."

"Money talks," Riggs points out. "And our boy has plenty of it."

"She doesn't care about money." Tiff, his date, reminds us of her underwhelming existence. "She was married to someone super rich and signed a *really* shitty prenup or whatever. Then when he died, he left her with pretty much nothing. She's been doing odd jobs to make ends meet."

Collective murmurs fill the air. My eyes follow Winnifred. Is this true? Was she really left with nothing? Knowing what I know about her late husband, I wouldn't put it past him. And she's naive enough not to protect herself.

"Anyway, she's off limits." Arya snaps her fingers in front of my eyes, trying to catch my attention. "Got it?"

"My apologies, Arya. I must've given you the false impression I give two craps about what people think." I flash her a sincere smile. "Once I make up my mind about a woman, no one can save her. Not even God."

I walk off, leaving my cluster of friends behind. I drift toward the outdoor balcony. This room is too crowded, too hot, too pretentious. The night breeze hits my face. I splay my fingers over the wide, blond-bricked banister. When I look down to Fifth Avenue, the people below appear as ant-like dots. Tightroping the banister is the last thing my drunk self should be doing.

Then again . . . what's to lose here?

I've no mother, no father, no fiancée. As Riggs pointed out charitably, I'm not exactly the most lovable person in this zip code. There is nothing to tie me down to this universe, and I'm starting to suspect this is precisely the reason why people take mortgages, pop out kids, make commitments—so that suicide wouldn't be a valid option when things are in the shitters.

Not that I'm contemplating suicide. This banister is wide and not very long. I can do it.

Just one time, for old times' sake. Grace's voice is throaty and tempting in my head. Even beyond the grave, she entices me to do the wrong thing.

Glancing behind my shoulder, I make sure the coast is clear. It's just me outside. I hop on the banister, righting myself until I stand up straight across the surface. I don't look down.

The first step is solid. The second makes me feel alive. I spread my arms in the air, like Grace and I used to do when we were kids. I close my eyes.

"Time me," I mouth.

And I can hear her in my mind answering. *Three. Two. One. Go!*

I take another step, and then another. I'm almost at the end. One more step . . . and my foot doesn't land the hard surface this time. It's all air beneath it. I sway. Lose my balance. Tip to the left. It all happens fast. The memory of Grace falling slams into me again.

The tears. The pleas. The silence.

I'm going to be pancaked to the street in a few seconds.

You shouldn't have done that, idiot.

I'm falling.

Out of nowhere, sharp, desperate claws sink into my right arm. They rip at my suit, pulling me back into safety.

My body slams against a hard surface. The balcony's floor. I'm a jumbled mess of limbs. Not all of them mine. Some of them small and lean and hot and all foreign flesh.

Count your blessings, asshole. You aren't dead.

I open my eyes, rolling onto my back. I prop myself on my elbows, looking to see who my savior is.

A cherubic face shoves itself into my line of sight. Familiar and angelic and absolutely, beyond any doubt, pissed.

"Now you've really done it, you conceited fool!" Winnifred growls, balling my bow tie in her hand, shaking a fist to my face. "What the heck were you thinkin'? What'd have happened if I weren't here? I've no words to describe you!"

She is standing above me, her face as red as a ripe tomato, her eyes so big I can see my reflection in them.

"You don't?" I ask casually, lounging on the ground as if it's the most comfortable spot in the building. "Well, here are some useful suggestions: idiot, moron, drunkard, imbecile, reckless asshole—technically, that's two words, but—"

She tries to slap me. I catch her wrist effortlessly, stopping her from doing so. Drunk or not, my instincts rarely fail. I stand up, her delicate wrist still captured between my fingers. She stares at me with undiluted hatred. It shines from her sapphire eyes. I find it disturbing that I can't hate her as properly and thoroughly as I should. She is a simpleton. An anecdote in my life. Nothing more.

"I'm sure you'll find a good reason to slap me in due time, but that time hasn't arrived just yet. You were saying?" I smile cordially when we are both standing in front of one another.

She shakes out of my touch, jerking her hand back.

"You're a bastard!" she spits out in my face. "Tell me what you were thinking. Have you had these thoughts long? No one just gets up on a banister like that. In the dark too! When I saw you through the window, I thought . . ."

She fires venom and wrath at me with her words, her voice drifting into one ear, exiting the other. I'm not suicidal. Tanked up? Sure, but nowhere near the realms of self-harm. Nonetheless, Winnifred succeeded in saving me, whereas I failed in saving Grace. *Twice.*

My eyes are still focused on her lips. Pink, narrow, and luscious. She is impossibly sweet. That combination between virtue and rage is downright sinful. They don't make 'em like this anymore. Especially in

Manhattan. My mind may be slow, but my senses are sharp, and I know an opportunity when I see one.

My lips crash against hers clumsily. I cup the back of her head and draw her to myself. Arya's warning is a distant memory. So is Calypso Hall, and the fact that we are both in love with other people, and that those people are dead. Reality ceases to exist, and the only thing I'm focused on is the person in front of me.

She is soft and sugary and different. So different I cannot close my eyes and imagine she is Grace, like I want to. There's not a hint of alcohol on her breath. No bitter bite of an overpowering perfume. She is all toffee apples and lazy Tennessee summer nights. She is church bells and sweet tea and Moon Pies.

The very thing I frown upon.

Our tongues dance together. She fists the lapels of my tuxedo like I might run away. I'm not going anywhere. I want to pick her up and take her to my apartment and fuck her senseless. I want that girl who ate a peach like she was a forbidden Lolita under the Italian Riviera's sun, oozing reckless sexuality.

Reckless sexuality. Jesus. Who am I? I need to screw this woman out of my system, ASAP.

My thumbs are on her cheeks, under her lashes, as I deepen the kiss, crowd her until her back is flat against the wall . . .

Winnifred rips her mouth from mine the minute her exposed back touches the concrete. Breathless, she raises her hand and slaps me. This time, my right cheek flies sideways. It stings like a motherfucker. I rub my palm along my cheek, smiling.

"You darn well earned this one," she hisses.

I bow my head. "When you're right, you're right, Bumpkin. Back to your words from a few minutes ago—I'm not suicidal. I am, however, shitfaced, which could explain why I overstepped the line."

"Overstepped?" she chokes out in anger. "You pissed all over the thing!"

I laugh but take a step back regardless. Sexual predator is not a look I'd like to try. "You kissed me back."

"I did no such thing!" She blushes guiltily. *Oops.* This is the second time I drag Winnifred out of her perfect Stepford Wife comfort zone.

"What annoyed you about my existence this time?" I inquire pleasantly. "And please spare me any claims you didn't enjoy it. Your toes curled in your sandals, and I felt the goose bumps all over your skin."

Her eyes narrow as she tries to figure out where and how to aim her next verbal blow. We're playing a game here. But unlike my games with Grace, this one is competitive without being hostile. We both want to win, but no part of me is worried she is capable of poisoning or killing me in the process. Most important of all, we share the same endgame— we both want to know more about the lovers who left us behind.

"You know." She smiles sweetly, reaching to dust off my blazer. "I forgot to mention at the New Amsterdam that I have a room full of Paul's belongings that I haven't opened yet. He asked me to never set foot in it, before he passed away. Wonder how many Grace-related things we could find there?" She looks up at me with her bluebonnet eyes. "The options are limitless."

My grip on her waist tightens. I don't stop to think why the fuck I'm holding this annoying woman in the first place. "And you're just telling me this now?"

"My bad, was I supposed to be on your timeline, Mr. Big Brain?" She catches my hands, rips them from her waist, turns around, and walks away midconversation. I follow her. She opens the door to stroll back into the buzzing room. I'm on her heel, transfixed. She slides gracefully between dancers. I shove and elbow my way to keep up with her. We're a hungry cat and a very smart mouse.

Fifteen seconds later, we're out of the ballroom. Winnifred calls the elevator and pivots in my direction.

"Why astronomy?" she demands.

"Why ast . . . ?" I stand between her and the closed doors of the elevator, confused. "Do *not* change the subject. Tell me more about the room."

She shrugs. "I'll do whatever I want. You're the one at a point of disadvantage here."

"How'd you figure that?"

"Because you want to know more about what happened with Grace and Paul, whereas I'm terrified of the truth."

I don't really believe her. I think she is just as fascinated with what happened between our lovers. But calling her out won't change her stance.

"How'd you figure I'm into astronomy in the first place?" I turn the conversation back to her. I forgot to ask back at the New Amsterdam.

"There's always an astronomy book tucked under your arm. There was one in Italy, when you were on the balcony, and one the first time you came to Calypso Hall. It's almost like your anchor. It grounds you, doesn't it?"

"It's not a security blanket." I scoff.

"I think it is." She arches an eyebrow.

"Luckily you're not paid to think, but to recite lines better thinkers have written."

"Spare me." She raises a hand. "If you thought I was this stupid, you wouldn't giggle like a schoolgirl every time I made a joke. Now tell me about your fascination with astronomy."

She is not going to let it go. I might as well throw her a bone.

"Astronomy is physics, and physics is absolute. It is factual, and therefore real. Some people turn to God for answers. I turn to science. I like the mystery of the cosmos. And I like to unravel it. Think about it this way—the Earth will explode in about seven billion years. By this time, most life on it will probably be extinct. Whoever is unfortunate enough to survive will have to watch their own demise as the sun absorbs the Earth, after we enter the red giant phase and expand beyond our current orbit. At this stage, it would be nice to have a plan B in place. No doubt neither of us will be here to execute it, but to think you and I could be a part of the solution—that excites me."

And that's when I realize no one's ever asked me about my love for astronomy before. Grace treated my books, my degree, my passion, as if they were no more than a plastic houseplant. Riggs and Christian largely ignore it. Dad never understood the fascination—he never understood anything that couldn't make him more money.

Winnifred actually cares.

The elevator slides open. We both walk inside. I have no idea where we're going. Actually, I have no idea where *she* is going. This woman is not going to let me tag along, wherever she's headed.

"So why did you opt for hedge funds? Why not NASA?" She studies me.

"I knew from a very small age that I'd inherit the Corbin fortune and portfolio. In order not to shit all over the family legacy, I needed to work in finance."

"Do you care about your family legacy?"

"Not particularly," I admit. "See, we Corbins have a curse. Two curses, to be exact. One of them is we always try to outperform the last person we inherited the empire from."

"So you want to be better than your dad, even though he's not here to witness it. Gotcha. Makes a lot of sense. And what's the other one?" She tilts her head sideways.

Smirking, I lean back against the mirror. "We always fall for the wrong girl. In fact, all of the last seven generations of men in my family ended up divorcing their wives."

"That's really sad."

"I could think of sadder things to torture your mind with."

"I'm sure you can." She smiles wanly. "You like torturing people, don't you?"

"I actually don't care enough," I say casually. "Unlike you, who cares too much. The charities, volunteer work, the cookies, the smiles. You need to live a little more for yourself and a little less for everyone else."

She stares at me, but doesn't say anything. I hit a nerve, and I know she'll think about it when we say our goodbyes. Nonetheless, we still have a few minutes to burn together.

"So tell me—what are you passionate about, Winnifred?"

She rubs at her chin, a tic she cannot conceal. "Mostly theater. Since I was a little girl, the stage has been my escape."

"What did you escape?"

"The same thing we all escape." She runs a finger over the rim of the elevator's mirror, just to do something with her hands. "Reality, mostly."

The elevator slides open. She is quick to get out.

"What was so wrong with Winnifred's reality, growing up?" I'm a dog with a bone. I'm chasing her across the lobby, making a spectacle of both of us, and I don't care. I won't care tomorrow either. I never cared what people thought of me. It was always Grace who gave a shit.

"Well, if you really must know, I hated to be the small-town gal, with the big aspirations, who knew full well people like you would always stand in my way, ridicule and belittle me whenever possible. I wanted to believe I could be something amazing, and the world didn't always let me."

I stop on the pavement, just as a black Toyota Camry Uber stops in front of us. I get it now. This is why Winnie resents me with so much passion. I represent everything she fears and feels insecure about. And I've been taunting her with it from the moment we met.

Maybe because I, too, resent what she represents. An easy, laid-back life. Where running after money and prestige breathlessly is tacky, not honorable.

She pops the back door of the Camry open.

I want to chase her. To steal another kiss, while the getting's good. Perhaps even tell her my sole reason for taunting her in Italy was because she was alluring, too damn fuckable, and I hated her for it.

But what's the point? Winnifred is too engrossed in her love for her dead husband. Even if she wasn't, I've only ever wanted one woman. Wanting another one seems foreign; unlike riding a bike, it is not a skill you can neglect and pick right back up.

"Oh, and by the way." She throws one last look at me, clutching the door. "That kiss? Four out of ten. Maybe that's why Grace cheated on you. You're a bad kisser."

She dips her head and disappears inside the vehicle before closing the door. The car slides back into traffic, leaving me in a cloud of exhaust smoke.

I laugh to myself, shaking my head.

Bumpkin is ten out of ten entertainment.

CHAPTER SIXTEEN

WINNIE

Then

It was my first time in Italy—anywhere outside of America, actually—so even the old seemed new. The ancient pastel buildings stacked together like colorful ice cream flavors. The yellow August sun that painted the landscape in an antique brush.

Everything in Italy was smaller—rooms, roads, cars, stores. The food tasted different too. The cheese and herbs and cold meats were more pronounced, sharper in flavor.

Paul, red nosed and extra freckly in the heat, plastered me against the banister of our hotel balcony. His hands wrapped around my waist, his erection digging into my stomach. I took a juicy bite of the peach I was holding as he nibbled his way up my throat, sucking on the nectar residue.

"So tasty . . . so addictive . . . ," he murmured, dropping his head farther down, between my breasts. I wore the same burgundy dress I'd attended senior prom in. While I was no longer that girl who had to count her pennies, using Paul's money to pay for expensive dresses didn't feel right either. Even if he begged me to do so, and often.

"It *is* a very good peach." I kissed his ear, playing innocent.

Paul pulled away, the heart-stopping smile that I loved so much—fresh faced and shy and good—on full display. "I'm talking about the woman I married. I still pinch myself every morning seeing you next to me. How'd I ever get so lucky?"

Somewhere not so far away, music blasted from one of the houses kissing the promenade. A classical piano piece. I wrapped my arms around my husband. The peach dropped from my hand. I kissed him deeply, and it was perfect. Sweet and needy, with a promise for what's to come. In a minute, we'd go upstairs to the restaurant, and Paul would throw himself into his role. A member of the boys' club. Indifferent to sexist jokes, conceited, and aloof.

Paul was the first to pull away. His blue eyes searched mine. "Let's take it to the bedroom. We still have a few minutes before dinner."

My stomach dropped.

Just spit it out, Winnie. There's nothing to be ashamed of.

I kissed the tip of his nose. "No can do, cowboy. Aunt Flow's in town, and she brought her distant cousins, Sore Boobs and Pimply Chin."

"You got your period?" His smile vanished. His hands turned stiff and cold around me. I told myself I shouldn't be offended or even mad. He was just as disappointed as I was. That was a good thing. How would I like it if Paul was like Lizzy's husband, Brian? Before they had Kennedy, my niece, they'd tried for three years. Brian had always been so apathetic whenever Lizzy got her period. He'd just pat her head and tell her it'd be okay.

"Yes." I scraped the pimple on my chin. "On the flight here. I didn't want to—"

Tell you.

Disappoint you.

Have you look at me the way you are right now, like I failed some kind of test.

The frustration was unspoken. Paul was too dignified to say something insensitive. Still, I could feel it in the way he touched me on the days and weeks after I told him I got my period. The miles he put between us. Between our hearts.

"You know." He walked over to a small table on the balcony, unscrewing a bottle of sparkling water. "If you really can't get pregnant naturally, you should bring your doctor up to speed. I don't mind jerking off into a cup. You know I'm a modern kind of guy." He shot me a charming smile from over his shoulder. "But we need to get things moving, baby doll. Mom's not subtle about wanting to become a grandma, and God knows Robert is not gonna make her one."

Robert was his brother, and he was a self-proclaimed eternal bachelor. There was a lump in my throat the size of Mississippi. I tried to swallow it down, to blink away the sting in my eyes.

"My doctor says I'm still young, that I should try naturally for at least four more months before we discuss the next steps."

"Well, then, maybe it's time to change doctors?" Paul smiled encouragingly, taking a sip of his drink. It wasn't what he said, and not even the way he said it. But something was off whenever we broached the subject of reproducing. After all, I was the one who had told Paul on our third date that I didn't want to waste any time. That I wanted a big family and would like to start working on one right away. He seemed enthralled by the idea. Our courting period was quick and intense. He asked me to marry him before we'd even officially moved in together and seemed delighted when I'd asked if the wedding could be in Mulberry Creek.

He was perfect. The opposite of the relationship-phobes I'd found myself dating since first landing in New York. Paul wasn't a boy—he was a man. He knew exactly what he wanted: Four, maybe five kids. White picket fence. A house in Westchester. A big one, with white columns and black shutters and a rose garden. He wanted boys. Hopefully athletic ones. I still remembered how he fell all over himself the first time he heard Da got a full ride in college for baseball and Lizzy was a nationally acclaimed gymnast.

"Gotta love your genes, Winnie. We're gonna make gifted children together."

Paul and I had started working on having children the first night of our honeymoon. And every single week thereafter. It'd been months, but still, no luck.

"I'll think about it." I turned my back to him, staring at the Mediterranean Sea. Truth be told, I wasn't going to think about it. I liked Dr. Nam. I trusted him too. I didn't want to take medicine and start going through IVF before I absolutely had to. And I hated the suffocating pressure of falling into bed with my husband, knowing what he had in mind was impregnating me alone.

Then again, I'd always had irregular periods. Heavy, sometimes painful ordeals. I always chalked it up to the stress of school, work, and auditions. Maybe Paul was right. Maybe there *was* something more to it.

"You do that." Paul's voice was decisive behind my back. "Oh, and remember what my friend Chuck said."

His friend Chuck, whom he played golf with, and was an MFM doctor. Apparently, over lunch at our local country club, Paul saw fit to tell him about our issues conceiving.

After all, I hadn't delivered the goods. We had an unspoken deal. Marriage. Babies. I hadn't fulfilled my side of the bargain thus far.

"He said"—I heard Paul speaking over the piano tune from one of the balconies—"and I quote, you 'should stay away from alcohol, energy drinks, smoking, and caffeine.' Now that I think about it, you do drink a lot of coffee, don't you think?"

I swallowed hard. "Two cups a day are fine. You drink four Ventis. On a mild day."

"Winnie, please. You know I can't stand it when you're mad at me." Paul dropped a kiss on the back of my shoulder. "I'm just worried for us. For the future of our family." He clasped his arms around me from behind, his fingers splayed over my flat stomach. I wanted to throw up.

"I love you, okay?" His lips brushed against my ear.

"Love you too. I just need a minute."

"All right. I'll wait inside and jerk off. Seeing you in this dress was too much."

The minute I heard the glass door close behind me, I let my head drop and started crying. My tears were hot and furious. Unstoppable. It felt like the weight of the entire world rested on my shoulders. I wanted to stop struggling to carry it. I wanted to sink, let it bury me underground. Suddenly, I was tired. Too tired for this dinner, for the mingling, for everything else that I signed up for by marrying him.

Angling my face up to the sun, for it to dry my tears, I looked upward. A few floors up, I noticed another person sitting at his hotel balcony. A man. Tall and tan and maybe older.

My hands twitched. I was tempted to wipe my face clean so he wouldn't see me cry.

But then I realized he was staring at me so openly, with such intense interest, there was no point. I was busted.

I met his gaze head-on, daring him to say something, to do something.

He looked like the angel of death. Not beautiful. Not homely. Just . . . different from everyone else. In an impressive, frightening way. He was holding a hardback with a photo of outer space on the cover.

Why are you here, in the most important moment of my life? Why do you care?

He stood up, turned around, and walked away.

CHAPTER SEVENTEEN

WINNIE

The wine-red curtain falls over the stage. Rahim, Sloan, Renee, and I clutch each other's sweaty hands in death grips. We're all shaking. I can hear my own heartbeat through the sound of cheers and claps.

You survived a human experience. Congratulations.

"Hey, Nina." Rahim bends down, whispering in my ear. "You killed it out there. Proud of you."

Letting out a nervous laugh, I rise on my toes to hug him, then the others. We just delivered the first, full-audience show of *The Seagull.*

Not only did everything go smoothly—the acting, the lighting, the design, the music—but there were actually four important critics in the audience.

"Who did you spot out there?" Sloan elbows Renee as we rush backstage, cheeks flushed and exhilarated.

"The *New York Times, The New Yorker, Vulture.*" Renee rips the wig off her head, wiping the sweat from her brow. "The big dogs, Sloan. I can't remember the last time there was a full house in Calypso Hall, let alone one where critics attended!"

"And did you see the Times Square billboard?" Sloan slaps his own cheeks, squealing. "My boyfriend sent me a picture between acts. I almost *died* on impact. I can't believe Corbin shelled out the dough for marketing. He doesn't give a rat's ass about this place."

"Times Square billboard?" I whip my head in his direction. "He did that?"

"Yes, girl." Sloan gathers me into a hug, spinning me in place. "And it's big and glorious. It's only got your face on it, but all of our names. You should take a picture of it on your way to the bar."

Arsène humored my one, sole selfish desire. Allowed me the indulgence of a billboard with my face on it. Even though we left off at the New Amsterdam without finishing our game. But why?

Because he wants you to give him all the information that you have about Paul and Grace. He doesn't care one iota about you.

But there was something else too. I have an inkling Arsène really wants to bring out the self-interested side of me. To show me that I, like him, care about myself. It makes me feel uneasy. Mostly because I think he's right. I think deep down, there is a part of me that's selfish. I've just never let it loose.

Was he here tonight? Will he attend the after-party down the street? There's no telling with this man. He comes and goes as he pleases. A renegade in a suit.

I can't stop thinking about our kiss. I'm not sure if it made me exhilarated, offended, delighted, or all three. It was so urgent, so dark, so desperate that it felt like sipping a magic potion. I haven't heard from him since the night at the gala, which, I remind myself, is a good thing. We'll have enough time to find out what happened between our loved ones. There's no need to form a relationship with the awful man.

The cast changes into their party clothes. I slip into a pair of jeans and a strapless black top and put on some lip gloss. The entire time, I remind myself that I hate Arsène Corbin. And even if I want to see him tonight, it is only because he is the main source of entertainment in my life these days. Nothing more.

Renee and Sloan cab it together to the venue. Rahim and I do the same, making a stop in front of the neon Times Square sign so I can pose in front of the billboard.

We arrive at the Brewtherhood to find it brimming with the entire cast and crew, their friends and family, and some industry people. We advance toward the bar. Rahim spots his girlfriend ordering a drink. He gives my arm a squeeze. "I'll go get Bree and get you a drink. What's your poison?"

My Tennessee heart wants whiskey, but after the New Amsterdam incident, I suspect spirits may not be my friends. "White wine. Make sure it's not too tasty. I really can't afford to get drunk."

"One gross-ass chardonnay coming right up."

I scan the room, knowing exactly who I'm looking for. I give myself a mental slap on the wrist.

What's wrong with you? You're exactly like Nina. Drawn to an impossibly tragic hero. A Trigorin. A misunderstood rebel with a cause. A fallen foe.

A magnetic force pushes me to look to my right. There, I find him. Leaning against the wall, a beer bottle in his hand, an unfathomable expression on his face. He wears elegance so well. He wears *everything* well. Even . . . depression? I cannot help but wonder whether he intended to fall that night at the Pierre, or if it was just a drunken, foolish mistake as he said.

Maybe he is regretting the kiss that came after it too.

Maybe he doesn't even *remember* kissing me. Why do I care? I'm a widow still very much in pain from losing her husband. I shouldn't give a darn what he is thinking.

That's when I notice he isn't alone.

He brought a date?

Yes, he brought a date. So what? Again, you don't care, remember?

She is standing right next to him, and they share a pleasant conversation. She is beautiful. Tall, razor thin, with long black hair and midnight eyes. Unlike me, she is dressed to impress, in a white gown, with fitted bodice and exposed back.

My stomach rolls. It can't be jealousy. Me? Jealous? Ha. I wasn't even jealous when Paul invited all my good friends to slow dance at our wedding, including Georgie, my sister. *Twice.* Even when it stopped being appropriate and started looking a little weird (*Big city people!* Ma laughed it off).

But this girl . . . she is so lovely, and so much to Arsène's taste. Dark haired and mysterious, like Grace.

"Surprise!" A pair of hands grabs me by the shoulders from behind. I gasp, swiveling around. Ma—yes, *Ma!*—is standing in front of me, arms stretched wide.

My momma, in the flesh! With her big grin and wide eyes and short, no-nonsense hairstyle and gemstone-beaded necklace that makes her fancy herself a real first lady.

"Sugar plum! You bright shining star of mine!"

I fling myself into her arms, clinging to her for dear life. "Ma! What're you doing here?"

She wraps herself around me. "What do you mean? I wouldn't have missed your premiere for the world. Oh, Winnie, look at you. You're all skin and bones! Your daddy was right. I needed to buy a ticket six months ago and drag you back home with me."

I unglue myself from her, peering into her face. She looks the same as always. Same clothes, same hair, same smile. It brings me a lot of comfort knowing my parents are exactly the way I left them.

"You're staying?" I ask, realizing she is going to get into my apartment and see Paul's shoes and yogurt and newspapers are still very much there, eagerly awaiting his return.

"Oh, sugar plum, I wish I could. But Kenny has a recital tomorrow, and Lizzy's going to kill me if I miss it. Not to mention Georgie is down with her allergies again, and Daddy . . . oh, you know Daddy! He can't do anything without me. I just wanted to be here for you today."

"When did you land?" I hold her hands as if she is a hallucination, about to disappear from my view any minute now.

"This morning," Chrissy answers, inserting herself between us, a ceramic travel mug with her fat-burning tea in hand. "I spent the day showing her around. We didn't want you to know before the show. Figured you were already a nervous wreck."

I don't need to ask Chrissy to know she bought Ma the tickets. My parents aren't poor, but they'd never splurge on a few-hours trip. I'm so grateful I could cry.

"Oh, Chrissy." I make a face, hugging her. "Thank you," I whisper in her ear. "Thank you, thank you, thank you."

"I'm heading back to the airport in a couple hours," Ma announces, taking the scene in with haunted eyes. She's never been a fan of the Manhattan scene. "All I really wanted was to make sure you're okay."

"I'm okay. Better than okay!" I smile brightly, hoping she buys it. If I can convince her of that, I am ready for my Oscar performance.

Ma's eyes are misty and skeptical as her gaze swipes over me. Her hand is still on my arm, like she, too, cannot bear the idea of my evaporating into thin air.

"I don't think New York's good for you," she says, finally, through pursed lips. "It's cruel and hectic. It doesn't understand your soul, sugar plum."

"I couldn't agree more, Mrs. Towles." Chrissy jumps into the conversation artfully. "In fact, I was going to broach this subject with your daughter tonight."

"You were?" I frown. This is news to me. Chrissy always tells me I have nothing to look for in Mulberry Creek. That my future awaits somewhere big and polluted and full of opportunities.

"Yes." Chrissy takes a sip of her tea. "You should be heading to Hollywood as soon as *The Seagull* ends. If you make it there by June next year, we can book you a ton of auditions for pilot season."

"Hollywood?" Ma rears her head back like Chrissy slapped her with the word. "Why, that's even worse than New York!"

"How come?" Chrissy asks, blinking innocently. "It's nice out there. Sunny. Open spaced. Everyone's a health fanatic. And I'll tag along for a few months, Mrs. Towles. Make sure our girl is all settled."

"Sounds like you got it all figured out." I eye my superagent. I wish I had made a pit stop at the bar. I could have used a glass of something strong and preferably poisonous for this conversation. "But I'm not sure about it at all. What about the apartment—"

"You can lease it," Chrissy butts into my words, and by the glimmer in her eyes, I gather pulling me out of the space I shared with Paul is a part of her elaborate master plan. She wants me to get rid of his things. To move on.

To make it on my own and stop apologizing for who I am.

"I'll think about it," I lie.

"Think about what?" Lucas strides to our corner of the room and hands me a glass of wine. "A knight in shining armor thought you needed one and sent me over to save the day."

"A knight, you say?" My heart leaps in my chest, and I feel my neck flush. "Who would that be?"

"Rahim, of course. Who else?" Lucas laughs, giving me an are-you-okay? look. "He didn't want to interrupt this little reunion. Isn't he darling?"

Disappointment slams into me. I'm so stupid. Did I actually expect Arsène to notice? To send me wine? The man brought a *date* here after kissing me silly, minutes after I saved him from *death*. He is a train wreck and the last person I should be warming up to.

"Rahim's great," I mutter, taking a generous sip. Gosh, it *is* a bad wine.

"Mrs. Towles, your daughter is an absolute gem!" Lucas explodes. "The best Nina I've seen with my own eyes, and that includes Saoirse Ronan and—God help me—the love of my life excluding my dear husband, Carey Mulligan. I cannot wait for the reviews to pour in. She was stunning, *stunning*. Even if she didn't cry."

Because she can't, I want to scream. *Tears are beyond me.*

"She was always like this," Ma boasts. "Did I ever tell you how she cried her eyes out the first time she listened to 'Space Oddity'?"

A happy, loud conversation ensues among Lucas, Chrissy, and Ma. At some point, Rahim, Renee, and Sloan join us, along with their partners. The jolly, victorious mood is addictive, and I forget myself for the next hour, until everyone fades to their own corner in the bar, and Ma and I are alone again. She tilts her head, the dreamy smile wiped clean from her face.

"Now that everyone's gone, tell me—how've you really been?"

"Honest to God, Ma, better than you think. Working hard on the play, of course, but it's been a welcome distraction. And the paycheck!" I rave. "I might be able to keep the apartment now. Things are looking up, Ma. I swear."

"What about going to the doctor?" she persists, her eyebrows puckered. "Please tell me you have an appointment. You've been neglecting it for months."

The words hit me like a bucket of ice-cold water. I've done my best to ignore this subject—this *problem*—since Paul passed away. Everything took a back seat after the funeral, my health included.

"I haven't forgotten," I mutter.

"What're you waiting for?" She tries to catch my gaze, to no avail. My eyes are firmly stuck on an invisible spot behind her.

"I'll do it next week."

"No, you won't. You haven't done it so far!"

"It doesn't even matter right now." I roll my eyes, feeling like a teenager again. "I feel fine. Healthy. Good."

"Says *who*?" The plea in her voice undoes me. "My lord, sugar plum—"

"Ma, not here." I stomp, desperate. "Please let it go!"

My last words come out more harshly and loudly than intended, drawing a few curious looks from people around us. Ma looks around helplessly, like she is waiting for someone to step in, to talk some sense into me. Usually, that person would be Georgie. She always likes to club me with the truth stick. But Georgie is not here to tag team me.

"This conversation ain't over." She wiggles her finger in my face. "Not if I have to drag you to the doctor myself. Now, let's talk about something else before you tell your momma goodbye. Something pleasant. Oh, did you know Jackie O'Neill had a baby? A good-lookin' one too. I have a picture on my phone somewhere . . ."

We talk about other things, but the damage is done.

I can't unthink about what she said. Because she is right.

I'm not well.

I do need to go to the doctor.

Sooner rather than later.

◆ ◆ ◆

Ma leaves in a flurry of kisses, tears, and hugs. We stand on the curb outside the pub. I insist on coming with her to the airport, but she refuses. This goes on and on until the cab driver interferes and says, "Ladies! Please just say your goodbyes so I can carry on with my shift!"

"You can't come, sugar plum. It's your big night. Stay with your friends. I'll call you tomorrow. Love you."

With that, she kisses my cheek, enters the taxi, and drives off. I'm left on the curb, watching as the taillights of the cab disappear. The thought that something could happen to her on the plane occurs to me, but I squash it as soon as it floats into my head. *Nope. Not going there.* I have more issues than *Harper's*, and there is absolutely no reason to develop a crippling fear of flying on top of everything else.

I don't want to go back to the party. Now that the adrenaline of the show has worn off, I'm not in the mood to pretend to be jolly. Usually,

Paul was the one to pull me through moments like this. He was my crutch.

But bailing without saying goodbye is rude. Reluctantly, I drag myself back inside. I see Lucas's trilby hat in the distance. He's bobbing his head, talking animatedly to a few Broadway-type people. Moving toward him, I feel fingers wrap around my wrist. I stop, looking up to find Arsène's dark, hooded eyes on mine. His lips are drawn in a shrewd smile.

"Bumpkin. Was that your mother?"

Remembering he brought a date, I shake out of his touch with a scowl. "What's it to you?"

"She's an impressive woman." He ignores my attitude, his charm jacked up to the max. "Which is very good news to future sixtysomething you."

"Why, twentysomething me wants you to take a hike. How about you try being a gentleman and cater to me once?"

The cad *kissed* me and didn't even address the subject.

"Now, Winnifred, don't be a sourpuss. It's your big night."

"It's diminishing, now that we're talking," I murmur.

He tips his head back and laughs.

"Here. Have you met Gwendolyn?" He motions to his date with his beer bottle. She steps forward and smiles at me, offering her hand for a shake. "Gwen, this is Winnifred. She plays Nina, as you've gathered from the play."

So he *did* come to see it.

With a date, Winnie.

I shake Gwen's hand. "Nice to meet you. I hope you enjoyed the show?"

"It was fantastic. You and Trigorin knocked it out of the park." Gwen looks delighted and genuinely impressed. "And I've seen a lot of versions of *The Seagull*, if I may add."

She is striking, intelligent, and eloquent. There is nothing I can dislike about her, other than her existence. For some reason, it suited me better to think Arsène would never move on from Grace, just like I'm stuck on Paul.

"That's kind of you." I dip my head down, blushing. "Well, I don't want to keep you two. I should go and say my goodbyes—"

"Leaving so soon?" Arsène gives me a faux-wounded look. "The evening's just begun."

"For you, maybe. I'm calling it a night."

"Before the cake's been cut and speeches are made. My, my, you're not even trying, are you?" Arsène steps between me and the door's direction, an easy, albeit intentional, buffer. "Especially when the future of Calypso Hall is hanging by a thread. You do know, Winnifred, I'm not a big fan of theaters, and even less of slacker employees."

"Yes, I'm aware." I cross my arms over my chest. Gwen grins privately, amused by our exchange. "I'll take my chances. Any parting words?"

"You seem preoccupied. What's on that simple mind of yours?" He tilts his head sideways, entertained more than worried.

"None of your business." I bypass him and head straight to the door, goodbyes be damned. I can barely handle him on a good day, much less on one when I'm reminded of my health issues.

I'm almost at the wooden door when something occurs to me. I stop, softly curse myself, then turn around sharply and head straight back to where he's standing. Which is exactly where I left him. There's a cocky smirk on his face. He leans against the wooden bar nonchalantly. The jerk *knew* I'd make a U-turn. It's written all over his face.

"One more thing." I raise a finger between us.

"Hit me with it."

"The billboard."

His eyes turn from mocking to alert, but he says nothing.

"Why did you do it?" I ask. "You didn't have to. We never finished that billiard game."

"Chivalry, of course." He opens up his hands theatrically. "You told me to start somewhere, didn't you?"

Yeah, but that was a second ago.

"I doubt you can spell the word, let alone practice it."

He laughs, pleased. "You're right. I did it for purely selfish reasons. I wanted to ensure a good return on my investment, and *The Seagull* looked like it might actually make a few bucks."

"That can't be it either." My fists ball beside my body. I'm losing my patience. I'm tired of being mocked by him. Of being pushed out of my comfort zone. "There are many ways to advertise a play that don't include stroking my ego."

"Ah, so you admit that you have an ego."

"A small one." I pinch two fingers together.

"Yes, yes, I know. I'm trying to change that. No one likes altruism, Winnifred. It's such a boring trait."

"Is that why you gave me a billboard? To prove to me that I'm vain?" I press.

He steps forward, his mouth a breath away from my ear. The back of my neck blossoms in goose bumps, and my breathing becomes labored.

"Maybe I simply needed a bait to lure you into the conversation you walked away from that night at the Pierre. Have I succeeded?"

Of course he has. I am here, after all. Drawn to him like a moth to a flame. Praying like a desperate schoolgirl for his lips to graze the shell of my ear.

I jerk back from him, realizing that he has me exactly where he wanted me. "What do you wanna talk about?"

"We only have one mutual interest, and it keeps both of us awake at night."

Grace and Paul.

"Actually, judging by tonight, what keeps you awake at night has nothing to do with your late fiancée." I glance coolly behind him, looking for Gwen.

"Jealous?" He lifts an inquisitive eyebrow.

"Don't flatter yourself," I splutter.

"I should be so lucky. A young, beautiful admirer. Fresh out of the Bible Belt too."

I laugh incredulously, pushing him away. "I'm not the dumb farm girl you think I am."

"Oh, yes. You're very observant. I'm in awe of your watchful skills." He casually glances around him, which makes me do the same. And that's when I realize . . .

"Wait, where's Gwen?"

His white teeth gleam. He is enjoying this exchange too much. "Who, now?"

"Your date!" I'm about to kill him. I'm sure of it.

He looks around, as if just realizing she is gone. "She must've left. Beats me as to why."

"You gave me more attention than you did her," I say hotly, knowing I'm falling right into his trap. "Which is incredibly rude."

"Rude?" He looks genuinely surprised. "Grace used to love it when I brought dates over and neglected them in favor of her halfway through the night. Dare I say, it was her favorite pastime."

Grace sounds like a real piece of work. "I take it this was a reoccurrence?"

He shrugs, tucking his hands into his front pockets. "She liked to be reminded of her loveliness often, and preferably by disparaging others."

"Well, some girls are confident enough in their skin not to bring down others. Your relationship was seriously messed up."

"While I second your statement, I think we can both agree Paul wasn't the stuff dreamboats are made of either."

I open my mouth to argue with him, to defend Paul, but the right words escape me. He is right. Paul cheated on me with Grace. He has the receipts to prove it. It is foolish to pretend our relationship was bulletproof.

To the expression on my face, he grins. "What, no comeback? Very good, Winnifred. I'm seeing progress, and I like it."

"So?" I ask dispassionately. "Where are you going with this conversation?"

"Since you're obviously as uninterested in this place as I am, I thought we could head over to Grace's apartment and go through her things. See if you recognize anything of Paul's."

A smart woman would say no to this offer. We've already established Paul and Grace bumped uglies behind our backs, and often. What's the point in poking this open, raw wound?

My suspicion is that Arsène and I keep doing it because it makes us feel something; otherwise we're completely numb. Pain is a great substitute for pleasure. Both are radical feelings, even if one is positive and the other negative. And maybe, just maybe, Arsène is as lonely as I am, and this project reminds him that once upon a time, he belonged to someone.

Isn't that what we crave, at the end of the day? To belong. To a family, to parents, to partners, to communities?

"Well?" he asks. "What do you say?"

No.

I have an early morning tomorrow.

All we're doing is hurting ourselves.

This is going to bite us in the ass.

In the end, though, I'm just like Arsène. Addicted to the feeling that comes with the pain.

"Call a taxi."

CHAPTER EIGHTEEN

WINNIE

Grace's apartment is luxurious and chic. Everything is in either black or white. There are expensive throws everywhere and vases that were once stuffed with fresh flowers, I'm sure. I give myself a tour of the place while Arsène turns on the lights.

"And you keep paying rent on this place?" I glance around at the glass fireplace and custom-made curtains. Surely, it's $15K a month minimum, before utility bills.

"Yeah," he answers shortly, ambling to the kitchen and getting both of us bottles of water. It soothes me to see her apartment is still equipped with refreshments. It makes my Paul mania seem almost normal. Arsène is keeping this place livable too.

"Why?" I turn around to face him. "You always lecture everyone about smart investments. How's paying rent for your dead fiancée's old apartment a logical decision?"

"It's not." He leans a hip against a kitchen island, taking a sip of his water. "I don't usually do irrational splurges. This is a rare indulgence, and I'm hoping after we're done with each other, I'll find it easier to terminate the lease."

His words hit me somewhere deep, because a lot of the time, I wish I could hate Paul too. It'd be the easiest way to get over him.

Approaching Arsène, I grab the small water bottle he handed me and unscrew it. "And when do you expect us to be done with each other?"

"That depends on your cooperation, Bumpkin."

"Stop calling me Bumpkin."

"Stop being offended by it," he fires back. "You shouldn't care what anyone thinks of you. It never does a person any good. And, at any rate, people's opinion of you is a reflection of themselves. Not you."

"I always feel like you're expecting me to be embarrassed about where I come from."

"And what if I do?" He lingers on this point. "Why should you succumb to other people's wants and expectations? You have free agency and an admirable mind. Keep shutting me down. Fight back. Never be ashamed of where you come from. A person has no future without first owning up to their past."

"And you?" I tilt my head sideways. "Have you owned up to your past yet?"

His eyes meet mine. He looks pensive. "Next question."

I grin. I got him there. It's a small win, but a win, nonetheless. "You're hiding something."

"We're all hiding something." He rolls his eyes. "Some of us are just better at keeping secrets."

He has a point.

"So . . . where should we start?" I look around us.

"Her bedroom." Arsène pushes himself off the island and advances toward the hallway. "Where they probably spent most of their time together. The bastards."

Not that it should surprise me, but I do find things that place Paul and Grace at the scene of the crime together.

There's a stainless steel watch with a mother-of-pearl pink dial, identical to the one he gifted me for Christmas, in Grace's jewelry box. Both watches are engraved, and with the same font. There is also a hoodie Paul used to wear that mysteriously disappeared on one of his business trips neatly tucked inside her closet, and a jar of a very particular type of moon cakes in her kitchen, which Paul was obsessed with, and I'd had to find for him even when it wasn't Lunar New Year.

His DNA is all over this place. And they hadn't even been here often. Arsène had keys to this apartment, which means Grace could only host Paul here when he was out of town.

"You know what? I actually expected to find more," I murmur when Arsène and I both collapse on Grace's couch. "Seeing as they'd had an affair for at least nine months."

"But consider this," he counters. "She knew I let myself in here whenever I pleased. The cookies are telling, Bumpkin. They show a level of intimacy. If this was a passing fling, they wouldn't know each other's culinary preferences."

I fling my head against the couch, closing my eyes.

"Why didn't they leave us?" I croak, opening my eyes. I find Arsène looking at me in a funny way. Something between annoyance and surprise.

"Well." He smiles wryly. "Because I was too rich, and you were too good a catch to give up. I don't think Paul and Grace planned to leave us for one another. They simply wanted to stick it to us. For Grace, it was about not belonging to me. This was her way of assuring herself she hadn't given in to me completely. With Paul . . ." He trails off, giving me a sidelong glance. "Hmm, now I wonder. What did you do to piss him off? Burned your famous apple pie?"

If only . . .

I know exactly where I fell short for Paul.

Of course, I'd rather die than share this with Arsène.

"You don't have to say." He pats my knee. "The answer's plain on your face. Poor Winnifred."

I feel myself turning crimson, and I'm about to lash out at him, give him a piece of my mind. Then something occurs to me.

"You know, I think Paul was mad about who I was. I mean, I think he liked me as an idea, not a person. The wholesome little blonde wife with the cute accent who made cookies and volunteered in hospitals and knew how to throw an axe. But then he saw how his colleagues looked at me—Chip and Pablo and even Grace—and he was . . . I don't know, *disappointed*."

"Disappointed how?"

"They didn't really see me as their equal. A worthy opponent. Oh." I wave my hand, laughing through the pain. "It's not that they didn't like me. They did. But kind of how you like your pet dog. They saw me as adorable and disposable. And then after the plane crashed, when I called Chip and Pablo over and over again, asking, *begging* for answers, for them to shed some light on why Paul and Grace were together, neither of them took my calls. At first they were apologetic about it, but then soon I stopped even getting their awkward text messages and started getting their PAs'."

"They treated you like you were garbage," he says plainly.

I shake my head. "They treated me like I was powerless, because I was."

"To *them*," he highlights. "Never put yourself in a position where you let people think you're powerless again, Winnifred. They'll always take advantage of it. I know I did."

I know he is talking about our exchange in Italy, and my stomach turns.

He stands up and saunters toward the door. "Let's grab something to eat. All this talk about infidelity and betrayal's making me hungry."

I glance down at my phone. "It's one in the morning."

"Yes, it is, and neither of us had dinner. I know because I've had my eyes on you for the last six hours."

This foreign feeling of flourishing under unexpected sunlight crashes into me. He did? He looked? He noticed? It is tempting to pretend he likes me, even if I know it can't be true.

"I don't think we have the same culinary preferences." I try to dodge the offer.

"You'd be surprised."

"Where do you want to go?" I'm on my feet before I know it, following him.

He waves me off. "You'll see."

◆ ◆ ◆

Ten minutes later, we're in a hole-in-the-wall type of restaurant, tucked in the back of a Cuban deli that's open throughout the night. We pass through the actual bodega before descending the few steps into its basement, where there are a handful of round tables, loud Cuban music, and waiters and diners laughing and talking joyously. A thick cloud of cigar smoke hangs over the room. I'm surprised that Arsène frequents this place. It's not gold plated and doesn't have any Michelin stars.

We're seen to a small table. I order the calamari in garlic sauce, and he orders the lechón asado. The food arrives in record time, served on plates you'd find in your auntie's kitchen. They don't even match, which I love. For the first time in months—maybe years—I feel at ease in Manhattan. This place feels like somebody's home. It lacks the glamour and pretense that's usually stapled to anything in this zip code.

"I like this place," I admit.

"Figured." He is concentrating deeply on his food.

I should be tired, but I'm not. Maybe it's the adrenaline from the show, or seeing Ma, or maybe it's going to Grace's apartment and coming face to face with Paul's wrongdoings. No matter what it is, I'm actually wide awake as we tuck into our food.

"So have you been going out with people regularly since Grace . . . ?" I broach the subject while munching on a gummy piece of calamari.

"I haven't dated since Grace passed. Nor do I wish to. I've never been a relationship kind of guy."

"You've been *engaged*." I spear another calamari with my fork, pointing it at him.

"Grace was a once-in-a-lifetime woman." He takes a generous bite of his asado. "I only have one lifetime; therefore, I don't expect to find someone like her."

"So you never plan on moving on?" I ask, oddly sad, even though I shouldn't care for him.

"Do you?" He looks up from his plate.

Biting down on my lip, I think about it. "I hope so. Logic dictates that I will, at some point. And to be honest, ever since I found out he really *did* cheat on me . . ."

"It should make things easier," Arsène completes. "Emphasis on the *should* part."

He gets it. Just because they didn't deserve our love doesn't mean that we can stop loving them.

"So what was Gwen all about?" I persist.

He waves a dismissive hand. "Gwen's an old friend. We sometimes do each other solids. I didn't want to be bothered by the Calypso Hall crew tonight, and she was a buffer between the little people and me."

The way he says it, *little people*, like he is no mortal, reminds me that despite his surprising tenderness toward me, he is still a dangerous creature.

I lean back in my seat. "And look at you now. Sitting here with a southern bumpkin, no less. Oh, how the mighty have fallen."

"We both know why we're here. No pretense. No illusions about who we are and what we want." He finishes his last bite, and before he even swallows, a waiter jumps between us, handing him a hand-rolled cigar and lighting it for him.

"Want one?" Arsène points the lit cigar in my direction.

I shake my head. As if reading my mind, Arsène makes a face.

"C'mon, Bumpkin. Give it a try. Breaking the mold should be at the top of our priorities right now."

The waiter lingers, staring down at me with open curiosity. I decide to comply, mainly because I've never smoked a cigar, and because Arsène, for all his many, glaring faults, is shaping up to be an enjoyable foe.

I take one, allowing the waiter to light it up for me.

"Don't inhale," Arsène instructs, his eyes studying me attentively. "You absorb the nicotine through the mucus membrane in your mouth."

I do as I'm told, coughing a little anyway. "My gosh, it smells like socks on fire."

"Oil and tar." He laughs. "Neither is supposed to be consumed by the human body."

"You're a bad influence." I side-eye him, holding the cigar away from my face. I'm done. I came, I saw, I coughed out a lung. No more.

Arsène leans forward, catching my gaze. "I wish someone had corrupted you long ago, and thoroughly enough for you to sniff out a weasel like Paul Ashcroft and never give him a chance. I could've spared you a lot of heartache, you know. If I'd met you first."

"You were with Grace."

"On and off." He hitches a shoulder up. I'm confused as to why we're talking about a hypothetical scenario where we could've dated. "Warning you off Wall Street wolves would've saved you from that asshole."

"No one could've known." I put the cigar out in an ashtray.

"Oh, I could." He sits back. "Back in Italy, when I roasted you publicly and he turned a blind eye."

"Well, what does that make you?" I flash my teeth angrily. "If not an even bigger asshole than Paul."

He nods, unperturbed. "True, but my fiancée had known that about me all along. She never needed a prince. Only an interesting enemy to pass the time with."

Whenever I think about these two's relationship, I want to cry. There seemed to be so much hostility and sadness between them. Then I remind myself I shouldn't pass judgment. At least Arsène and Grace knew one another for what they truly were. I never got to know the man who shared an apartment, a life, a *bed* with me.

After we're done, we pour ourselves out into the night. I start walking in my apartment's direction, and he follows. Our time is coming to an end, and I'm both relieved and disappointed. I'm not sure how I feel about this man. One moment, I find his presence comforting and uplifting. The other, I want to stab him in the neck.

"Are you really going to sell your family's theater?" I ask as we make our way down the street.

"Yes."

I wrap my arms around myself, feeling the night chill. "Good. Maybe the next owner will actually put some effort into it. Fix all the things that need to be fixed."

"Don't count on it." He tsks. "No offense, but the place is a real money pit. Now, how about we get back to the matter at hand. Our transaction. More specifically—Paul's office." He stops abruptly in the middle of the sidewalk, making me come to a halt too. We stand in front of one another. His face is grave, for the first time in a long time. I find myself wanting to smooth the creases between his eyebrows.

"I want you to let me inside it."

"Is that why you let me into Grace's apartment?"

Even though we're not friends, I find it disappointing that everything he does to me, for me, *with* me, is always as a result of his obsession with Grace.

"Yes," he says honestly. "And I've no issue with you coming to my apartment and going through it. Although, I should warn you, there are cameras everywhere in my building, and the chances Paul had ever been there are akin to my spontaneously giving birth to an eel."

"I can't let you into his office. That would be a breach of Paul's trust in me," I say slowly. "Even though he was a certified dirtbag, I hold myself to a higher standard."

"But don't you want to know?" His eyes twinkle mischievously.

"Know what?"

"What other cards I hold up my sleeve. I still have more info about him," he coaxes. "So much more for you to explore, to learn, to hate."

"I want to see the file first," I say. "From the private investigator."

"Knock yourself out." He chuckles.

"And there's a ground rule I wanna lay out right here and now, before we continue this journey toward detonating our loved ones' privacy and our loyalties to them."

"Lay it on me, Bumpkin."

I bite down on my lower lip. "Never, *ever* kiss me again."

There's a beat of silence before he throws his head back and laughs blithely.

"I give you my word. I'll keep my lips—and other organs—to myself."

"It wasn't so easy for you to do that at the gala." I resume my walk, trying to keep the insulted bite out of my voice. He falls into my step, letting out a sexy, throaty laugh.

"Yes, well, as established, I was very drunk and very lonely. Not a good combination, I'm sure you'll agree."

"Spare me your excuses. Just never touch me again."

"Why?" he asks, genuinely interested. "Forgive my honesty—not many people use it these days—but it's not like you betrayed Paul. He is currently six feet under, in an advanced stage of decomposition—"

"Arsène!" I roar, stopping in place again.

"—after cheating on you, for the vast majority of your short marriage." He ignores my outrage, soldiering through. "While I'm right here, very much alive, and dare I say—more attractive than that oatmeal with legs and a crew cut. And you can't tell me you don't find me attractive, either, because I might've been drunk during that kiss, but my ears were working fine. And I remember, Winnifred, your heartbeat slamming against my chest. How you moaned and trembled—"

"Stop!" I push at him desperately, jerking him away, my face hot with shame and something else. Something dark and depraved. Need? "Just stop! I don't care that he cheated. I don't care that he was a scumbag. He was still my husband."

Arsène stares at me nonchalantly, waiting for the storm to be over.

"Now please leave me alone. I can walk home by myself."

"No," he says flatly. "I'll see that you get there safely."

I start moving in my apartment's direction again. "Aww. You sound like a good southern boy."

"No need to hurl insults my way." He resumes his walk. "Going back to our original conversation—you're welcome to see the private investigator's file whenever you please, provided you'll give me access to Paul's office afterward. Furthermore, whenever we see each other, I promise not to kiss you."

"Thank you," I say primly.

He grins. "You'll be the one to kiss *me* all on your own."

"Dream on!" I cry out childishly.

We're almost at my apartment, and the sun is beginning to peek from the rooftops. Where'd the night go? I've spent ten hours with this man without even realizing it.

I stop next to my front door and lift my chin up. "I'll reach out when I'm ready to see the file."

"One last question." Arsène leans an arm close to my ear against my building. He is so nonchalant, so beautiful, it is maddening to think he is—was—one woman's man.

"What's that?"

"I overheard your mother saying you should go to the doctor. Are you okay?"

Yes. No. I don't know. I'm too scared to check.

Laughing carelessly, I say, "Goodbye, Arsène."

I fling the entrance door open and slam it in his face.

After all, for him, this would be another exotic tidbit to laugh about on his way home.

For me, it is my life. My destiny. My heartbreak.

I wake up to the sound of my phone, alarm clock, and doorbell all chiming simultaneously. Groaning into Paul's pillow—I still like to sniff it at night, pretending his scent lingers on—I unplaster myself from the warm sheets.

I bang the alarm clock on its head. By the time I reach for my phone, the call dies. I squint at it, the screen too bright for my sleepy eyes. A chain of text messages rolls in quick succession.

Lucas: TELL ME YOU READ THE TIMES. TELL ME YOU DID. OH MY GOD. OH MY GOD. YOU ARE FAMOUS, BABY.

Rahim: We need to ask for a $$$ raise after this, LOL.

Rahim: BTW, did u get home OK?

Ma: Hey, Sugar Plum. Made it back home safe. Flight was blissfully uneventful. Everyone says hi. We love you and are so proud of you!

Chrissy: Sure you don't want to think about Hollywood? This is shaping up to be Winnie Ashcroft's year. You're hot right now, boo.

The doorbell chimes again, and I jump out of bed, bumping my toe against the bed frame on my way to get it. "Mothertrucker . . . ," I mutter as I fling the door open. I expect to see Chrissy on the other end, but instead, it's a delivery guy in a purple-and-yellow uniform. He thrusts an iPad with a touch screen pen into my hands. "Winnifred Ashcroft? Sign here, please."

I do. After I'm done, he passes me a thick stack of newspapers and magazines.

"Wait, who sent me this?"

The guy shrugs. "I'm just here to deliver stuff, ma'am."

He turns around and walks away.

I splay all the magazines on my dining table and open the theater section in each of them. There are four new reviews for *The Seagull*.

"In an ensemble full of relatively seasoned actors, Ashcroft shines as the tragic heroine of the play, with her silken, dreamy look and coquettish fragility."

"Broadway has a lot to answer for. It is unheard of, almost criminal, that Winnifred Ashcroft has yet to grace any of its stages."

Even the less eager reviews are still somewhat favorable.

"While Calypso Hall cannot be accused of producing high-quality, thought-provoking work in recent years (or at all), Lucas Morton's take on one of Chekhov's more famous plays may not be a reinvention of the wheel, but provides a solid, riveting escape from reality."

I put the newspapers down and dig my palms into my eye sockets. Of course I looked tragic up there onstage. That's because I *am* tragic.

The first sprouts of true resentment spring inside me whenever I see the last name Ashcroft next to my name. It seems all wrong. I'm not an Ashcroft. Paul's parents barely take my calls anymore, whenever I try to reach out and check on them. I'm a Towles. Always have been.

And it's not just that. The true meaning of what Paul has done is finally beginning to sink in. He burdened me with his last name when I should've always been *Winnifred Towles*. The starry-eyed girl from Mulberry Creek who dreamed big, and finally—accomplished it.

Arsène is right. Paul and Grace don't deserve our sympathy, our loyalty, our devotion. He's right about a lot of things. I should never feel powerless. And it *is* okay to have a bit of an ego. It's better than cancelling yourself just to be "the Wife of."

And there's one more thing he is right about . . .

Call your doctor.

I pick up my phone and make the call.

"Sullivan OB-GYN Medical Group, how can I help?" a chirpy voice answers. I open my mouth to make an appointment, but no words come out.

I need to see my doctor.

There are tests I need to have run.

I'm not okay, I may never be okay, and I'm scared of what it might mean.

"Hello? Hello?" the receptionist asks on the other line.

I hang up, shoot up to my feet, and storm into the bathroom. I grip the edges of the sink and stare at myself in the mirror. "You're such a coward, Winnie Ashcroft. Such a darn coward. I want Winnie Towles back."

For the first time in a long time, I recognize the face staring back at me. I see the girl from Mulberry Creek. Her freckles. Defiance. Hopes. Dreams. The laughter in her eyes.

"Winnie!" I bracket the mirror with my hands. Wonder and relief swirling inside me. I see the girl who visits kids at the hospital to make them happy. The girl who snuck around with Rhys Hartnett, captain of the football team, during prom night and lost her virginity in the boys' locker room while he apologetically muffled her moans with his kisses. The very same girl who showed up at the Nashville airport with half the town behind her when she bid Tennessee farewell and moved to New York.

The girl who taught the neighbors' kids to do cartwheels on her dewy front lawn. Who secretly enjoyed going to church every Sunday, because it gave her a sense of community, of grounding. Who read the classics and dreamed big, imagining herself in the shoes of Jane Eyre and Elizabeth Bennet.

I love this girl. She is still here, and she was the one who saved me on that stage last night.

"It's good to have you back." I finger the mirror, smiling. "Now, can you please tell your new self you need to get checked?"

I blink, and in a heartbeat, it's all gone. It's me again. Winnie Ashcroft. Sunken cheeked and beaten up by life. Betrayed and unsure.

Only this time, I know exactly who I need to be to get my life in order.

Winnie Towles.

CHAPTER NINETEEN

ARSÈNE

Two weeks later, I sit in front of Archie Caldwell at a restaurant. Archie is an old acquaintance from Andrew Dexter Academy. He lives in London, and whenever he's in New York, he drags me to the most awful establishments. Michelin starred, with extra-white tablecloths, minimal designs, and food that looks like Costco samples served on oversize china.

"How are you handling the whole . . . you know." Archie makes a face.

"Death of my fiancée?" I supply blandly, taking a spoonful of caviar nestled in a bowl of ice. "Life moves on," I drawl.

"Now, that's the spirit, mate." He reaches across the table to pat my arm awkwardly. "It's not the end of the world. Oh, I suppose for her, it is. Anyway, shall I order us another grapefruit rosé and some dessert?"

"You can, if you wish to seduce me, but I'll be honest, Archie. You're too married and I'm too straight. Your chances aren't looking good."

Archie and I, although friendly, haven't been close in years. Which means he called me here for a reason. I can sniff people's intentions from miles away. Archie's here to present a business offer. I'd like to hear it more than his mindless chatter about I bonds and stock dividends.

Archie chuckles and scratches the back of his neck, not used to being called out. "Fair enough. If nothing else, I can appreciate your bloody honesty. The truth is . . . well, let's start from the beginning." He clears his throat, signaling a waiter for the check. "Sadie and I are moving to New York this January."

"You are?" I ask dispassionately. Sadie is his wife. Third wife, to be exact. He goes through them like socks.

"Yes. See . . . we've had our own little tragedy happen in our family." Archie's face is crestfallen.

"Oh." I sit back.

"We lost our dear, dear Daisy prematurely."

"I'm sorry," I say. "I hadn't realized you and Sadie were expecting."

"Expec . . . ?" Archie's face twists in confusion before he waves his palms around. "No, no, you misunderstood. Daisy was Sadie's King Charles spaniel. Such a darling dog. I gifted her Daisy for Christmas, but the poor pup died of canine distemper shortly after. Sadie took it hard. She was an absolute wreck for the longest time."

A dog.

He is comparing Grace's death to a *dog's*.

My face is expressionless, I know—I've practiced the art of not giving a fuck for many years—but inside, I'm burning with rage.

"Please." I raise a palm. "The story cuts too deep. Say no more. So you're moving to New York?"

Archie, picking up on the sarcasm, looks flustered. "Well, yes, and see, Sadie is going to be so very bored here while I help Papa with that god-awful building he is trying to buy—"

"Bottom line, Archie." I glance down at my watch.

". . . and I heard through the grapevine—mates from Andrew Dexter who frequent New Amsterdam—that you're in the market to sell that quaint little theater of yours. Calypso Hall, was it? Sadie always had a passion for theater—she loves the West End—and with *The Seagull* already a smashing success, I think it'll give her something to do while she's here. A sense of purpose, if you would."

I stare at him, wondering idly what makes him the way he is—an abundance of stupidity, or privilege? Perhaps a combination of both. I've no doubt his family's name is on Cambridge's library, where he went for higher education. There's no way this dimwit got in on merit.

I open my mouth to answer him, but he beats me to it.

"Before you say anything, I have an offer you cannot possibly refuse."

"Sounds like a challenge." I smirk.

"They say Calypso Hall is worth six point two."

"They say a lot of things." I play with the napkin on the table. Said rumor was started by me. In practice, Ralph told me, it is worth a lot less.

"I'm offering you eight million dollars if you sign this week."

There's a beat of silence while I digest his offer. It is unorthodox, maybe even a bit extreme, to bid so high on such a pitiful business venture. There's no logic behind it, just the need to pacify his high-maintenance wife.

Every pragmatic bone in my body tells me to take it. A better offer won't come, with or without *The Seagull*'s success.

Maybe it's because Archie compared Grace's death to that of an inbred dog, or perhaps it is because he didn't even bother to make it to my fiancée's funeral. Hell, it might even be the sudden, unexpected success of Calypso Hall these past couple of weeks, but I find myself in no particular hurry to sell it, whatever the sum.

"It's an obscene number, indeed." I look up to find his eager gaze clinging to my face.

"Told you." Archie clucks his tongue, satisfied. "Shall I talk to my solicitor, then?"

"If you wish, and enjoy a pricey conversation." I stand up, smoothing my cashmere sweater. "Unfortunately, Calypso Hall is not currently for sale. No deal."

I dig through my wallet for a few bills and throw them in Archie's general vicinity before making my way out of the restaurant. The air is no longer acidly hot, marking the first signs of fall. I let my legs carry me aimlessly around the streets. I've nowhere to go and no one to see.

There is something about my showdown with Archie that troubles me. I don't normally let my feelings dictate my actions. I'm a pragmatist. Ordinarily, Archie comparing Grace to his dog would not be a reason for me to reject a perfectly good offer. I've always been able to successfully separate my feelings from my business decisions.

Until now.

Why?

It's not like my love for Grace has grown in the past few weeks.

I come to a stop in front of Calypso Hall, surprised to find myself here. It's not even on the way to my apartment.

It has been two weeks since Winnifred told me she'll be in touch about our information exchange, and so far I haven't heard from her. Seeing as she doesn't know my number or my address, I'm not exactly shocked. Making myself available to her constantly is bad form, but a little nudge in the right direction wouldn't hurt.

As long as you remember it is not infatuation—it is business. The woman is a bore. Naive, sweet, and beneath you. Remember that.

I step into the theater, strolling by the ticket booth and concessions. On a bad day—which is most days in Calypso Hall—the place is empty, save for a few art students and unenthusiastic tourists. Now, it is buzzing with families, couples, out-of-towners.

After pushing the door with my shoulder, I saunter into the theater midplay, leaning against the wall. I expect to see Winnifred, but instead, it is her replacement, who works twice a week when it's Winnifred's days off. A girl named Penny.

Fuck you, Penny.

She rushes across the stage, cries, wails, throws herself onto Trigorin. But she lacks that special Winnifred thing that turns Nina from a tragic heroine to a perilous creature. Penny's Nina is simply tragic. Nothing more. Nothing less.

But Winnifred's? She's a force gaining power and speed.

Nice one, idiot. Not infatuated at all.

I leave with a huff, knowing deep down that I should sell this damn theater, and yesterday.

Another week passes.

Riggs is in town—back from Finland. Arya took Louie to visit a friend in Omaha, which means Christian is not out of commission for a change. We meet at the Brewtherhood. Riggs is wearing a baseball cap and keeps his head down, trying to go incognito. I never understood his fascination with women. I find tolerating one person to be too much, let alone multiple every week.

I knock down one Japanese beer after the other and flip through my astronomy book every time the conversation takes a boring turn, which is often.

At some point, the discussion spills into the territory of parents. All three of us are orphaned. In fact, I'm the only one who had a father not so long ago. Christian and Riggs have been like this since early adolescence. Not that Doug could be considered anyone's parent.

"We know your father was a poor excuse for a dad, but what about your mom?" Riggs elbows me to catch my attention.

I dog-ear a page and send him a disgruntled stare. "What about her?"

"You never told us about her."

"She passed when I was six. I hardly remember what she looks like, not to mention any personality traits."

And what I do remember, I don't trust. I grew up with the notion Patrice Corbin was a real monster, an agenda promoted by Douglas. The gist of it was that she cared more about Calypso Hall than about me and spent her days as far as humanly possible from the Corbin clan.

I knew she had an apartment in Manhattan, and that she stayed there regularly when I was a child. She also had a lover, Douglas made a point of lamenting to me, probably in order to erase his own wrong-doings. From my few recollections of her, Patrice was mild and pretty. But again, what did I know? I was just a stupid kid.

"Did you have a good relationship?" Christian asks.

"I was *six*," I reiterate. "Back then, I had a pleasant relationship with everything other than broccoli."

"We're just trying to figure out what made you the way you are," Riggs explains, grinning from ear to ear. He flings an arm around my shoulder. "You know, a total nut job who thought Gracelynn Langston was a good idea."

"Ah, yes. Because I'm the only one here who has a messed-up relationship with the fairer sex." I return my attention to my book.

"It's not just that," Christian explains. "That you don't remember your mother very much is not out of the ordinary. The fact that you haven't put any effort or resources into learning anything about her . . . now, that smells fishy to me."

I down my beer, pick up my book, and bow them farewell. "Thanks for the psychological assessment, gentlemen. Keep your day jobs."

With that, I leave.

At home, I take out an old photo album—the only one I have— and flick through pictures of my mother and me before her boating accident. Christian and Riggs aren't completely wrong—I haven't spared a minute of thought about my mother in decades.

There was little point. She was a terrible human, possibly worse than my father.

The first picture is of her holding me when I was a newborn, staring at me with pride. She looks exhausted, so I'm guessing I was as difficult a baby as I am an adult. The second is of her standing above me, holding my hands, as I wobble in what must've been my first steps, wearing only a diaper. In the third one, we're both throwing yellow-orange leaves in the air, dressed for autumn. The fourth is of Patrice and me making a cake together, looking messy and happy.

She doesn't look like the devil my father made her out to be. In fact, she very well could have been a saint. I will never know since both of them are completely and thoroughly dead.

The truth, unfortunately, was laid to rest right along with them.

CHAPTER TWENTY

WINNIE

"What do you mean, gone?" I ask Jeremy four weeks after *The Seagull* premieres.

"Disappeared. Not here anymore. Missing. *Poof!*" Jeremy snaps his fingers in a magic gesture.

"How can the poster just . . . vanish?" I look around us in the lobby, still hoping to find it rolled and tucked in a corner. "It took over the entire hall."

Jeremy flings his arms helplessly. "Sorry, Miz Ashcroft. When I got here this morning, it wasn't there anymore."

The big poster, starring Rahim and me, is no longer here. My guess is some punks took it. Stealing Broadway memorabilia was big when I attended Julliard. But people usually stole small stuff. Keychains and tiny props left onstage. Not an entire poster.

"We'll get to the bottom of this." Lucas wiggles his finger in the air, already on his phone. He is so distraught his hat fell off, and he hasn't bothered to pick it up. "I'll go up to management and ask to see the tapes from last night. Could be the cleaning people, trying to make a fast buck on eBay."

"Come on now." Rahim puts a hand on my shoulder. "We have a show to do. Don't worry about the poster. We'll get it back."

"But what if we don't?" I ask. "It's an expensive poster. And it was good for business. People could see it from the outside. We had walk-ins because of it."

We're already at a point of disadvantage, with virtually no budget, without losing the poster.

"Don't think about it now," Rahim says. "There's nothing we can do but kill it onstage."

And so we do. The show is explosive. I feel like a different person onstage. Maybe because I *am* a different person once the bright lights hit my face. I'm the old Winnie. The one I left behind in Mulberry Creek. She takes over every night and saves the day.

As soon as I step down from the stage, reality catches up with me, and I feel worn out. The last couple of weeks have been rough. I'm still adjusting to the knowledge that Paul had a secret life, and not one he'd have been proud of. Four days ago, I finally washed his pillowcases. Shoved his running shoes in the shoe rack. Being reminded every second of the day of the man who romanced his colleague doesn't comfort me as it used to, knowing what I know now.

I step out through the back door of the theater. There are still a few theatergoers lingering, hoping to get an autograph. I smile, take pictures, and sign tickets and postcards.

After the crowd disperses, I make my way to the end of the alley to catch a taxi. I'm almost at the curb when a hand grabs my arm and tugs me up a small flight of stairs leading to the back of a restaurant.

Gasping, I yank myself away and start for the street. Firm hands wrap around my waist before I'm able to take off. They jerk me backward, and my back slams into a firm, muscular torso.

"*Bumpkin*," Arsène taunts into my ear. The small hairs on the back of my neck stand to attention, but it's not just fear I'm feeling. It is a *thrill*.

I recognize him like an old lullaby. His smell. His height. The firmness of his body. Gosh, I'm beyond screwed. "You're a hard woman to pin down."

"Pinning me down shouldn't be on your to-do list," I grind out. "This is sexual harassment."

"My apologies." He takes a generous step back, allowing me the space to turn around and give him the stink eye. "Been waiting to hear from you about our little information exchange."

Right. Why else would he seek me out? To ask how I've been? Pay attention to Calypso Hall, heaven forbid?

"Actually, it's good that you're here." I straighten my spine. "I have a bone to pick with you."

He cocks his head. I have his full attention now.

"Someone stole *The Seagull*'s poster from the lobby." I park my hands on my waist. "It's gone."

"That's what security's for. Did management pull out the surveillance videos?"

"Lucas is working on it right now. In the meantime, I know you're not a fan of spending any money on the theater, but we need a new one."

"Talk to accounting." He leans against a metal banister, looking bored and put off. "I've no direct involvement with the theater, and now that I'm hell bent on selling it, you're lucky I still pay the electricity bill."

"They're gonna jerk us around." I shake my head. "No poster, no deal."

His mocking chuckle reverberates inside me, dark and demeaning. "Why, Winnifred, this sounds a lot like extortion. Have you sprouted another inch of that spine I've been recommending you grow?"

How is this man still alive? How did no one kill him?

"Spare me the third-grade taunts." I lift a hand. "We both know you want in Paul's office more than I want my hands on that file."

His dusky eyes glitter in the dark. "This is very decadent and improper. Did you ever do this to Paul?"

No. I've never done this to anyone. He is the only person who makes me feel emboldened.

"How dare you?" I bark out. "Don't even compare yourself to him. He was—"

"The patron saint of fidelity and refinement. I know, I know." He pushes off, striding down the stairs with a provocative yawn. "If you ask me, every self-respecting millionaire should be blackmailed by the woman he loves, at least once. It's very thrilling for a powerful man of his position. The idea of handing over control."

I've no idea what he's talking about. Paul would have been horrified if I ever pulled this kind of thing on him.

"Are you getting us another poster or not?" I bite out impatiently, following him.

He glances behind his shoulder, throwing me a grin. "Yes. But this time, with the entire cast on it. You haven't proved yourself to be a resourceful ally. You don't deserve the perks."

"I already told you." I throw my hands in the air. "We'll do it."

"When? There's no time like the present. Come to my apartment now and look at the file, and we can set up a date for me to come to your place to look in Paul's office."

"I can't do it tonight," I say hurriedly, catching up with him as he walks toward the main street. Since when am *I* chasing *him*?

"Why, pray tell?"

Because then you'll be gone from my life and I'll stop feeling those butterflies that I get in the pit of my stomach every time you're around. I don't want to stop feeling. I haven't felt in so long, and I think I'll go mad if I go back to being numb.

It's pathetic, but as long as Arsène keeps seeking me out, I don't feel so alone in this place.

"I have plans tonight." This, surprisingly, is not a lie.

"Great. I'll join you."

"What? No!" I stop at the curb, craning my neck to try to flag a yellow taxi down. "You're not invited."

"Why not?" he inquires casually, not one bit offended.

I look around myself, wondering if he is for real. "Has it ever occurred to you I might have plans with people?"

"What people?"

"Friends."

"You don't have any friends." He chuckles easily. "You're an outcast, like me. Well, not like me," he amends, waving down a taxi. He is much taller than me and is probably visible to drivers all the way from Long Island. "I do have some friends, though I try my best to avoid them. But you, all your real friends are miles away. You miss company, and you don't have it. Really, I'm doing you a favor."

A taxi signals in our direction. The familiar pitter-patter of my heart beating out of whack makes my chest cave. This is exactly why I haven't reached out to Arsène these past few weeks. Even though I've been dying to know more about Paul, I couldn't risk it. This feeling. Of falling again. And with yet another rich New York jerk. No doubt, this is another Winnie Ashcroft error. Winnie Towles would've found herself another nice, dignified Rhys Hartnett.

"I don't want you to tag along." I spit out the words.

The taxi pulls over and stops in front of us, and Arsène casually places a hand on its roof to stop it from driving while we finish this conversation.

"You'll just be talking about Paul and Grace nonstop, and I'm tired of the heartache," I add.

"Cross my heart and hope to die, you will not be hearing their names from my lips tonight." He raises his fingers in a Boy Scout motion. "Now, where're we headed? Do they serve alcohol there?" He opens the door for me, and I slide into the back seat, with him following behind.

◆ ◆ ◆

Twenty-five minutes later, we're sitting on a redbrick wall, our feet dangling in the air. In front of us, there is a sea of parked cars. And in front of *them* is *Breakfast at Tiffany's*, playing on the back of a stark-white building in Brooklyn.

"Let me get this straight." Arsène rips open a bag of Skittles. "You were going to go to a drive-in without a car?"

"Yes."

"Alone?"

"Also yes." I bury my hand inside a bag of popcorn. The salt and butter cling to my fingers. "I like sitting outdoors while the weather's still warm. Reminds me of home."

Only it's not warm at all tonight. Autumn is bleeding into the remainder of summer, and the air is cold and biting. I have a cardigan, but it barely helps keeping the shivers at bay.

"It's not safe," he points out.

"I've survived thus far. Have a little confidence in people."

"Never." He peers around us, then scowls at me. "You're freezing. Wait here."

He hops off the wall, disposing of the opened Skittles bag into my hands. I try to turn my attention to the movie, but it's no use. My eyes follow Arsène religiously. I'm curious as to what he'll do next. He saunters nonchalantly across a row of cars, passing pickup trucks and Teslas. He stops in front of a BMW, leans forward, and knocks on the driver's window. What the heck is he doing? I prop myself closer to the edge, desperate to hear the words he exchanges with the person behind the wheel.

"How much to rent your car for the rest of the night?"

"Fuck you, man." The guy inside laughs incredulously.

"Sex is not a currency I trade in, but I appreciate the offer. You bought this car for . . . what? thirty-five K? After adding all the perks?

It's five years old. I know the model. A car loses seventy percent of its value within the first four years. I'll give you ten grand if you lend it to me for the night. You can pick it up from here tomorrow morning."

"Yeah, buddy. Right." The guy scoffs. "And you expect me to believe it?"

"I expect you to use your brain cells, take the once-in-a-lifetime offer, and call yourself a cab, sooner rather than later."

I can't decide if what he's doing is romantic, crazy, stupid, or all three. I wonder if Arsène used grand gestures on Grace. I decide that, yes, he did. He's a nonconforming, eclectic person. Then I wonder what kind of fiancé he'd been to her. Somehow, I don't see him stressing out about babies in the same way Paul had. He seems eerily self-assured and calm. He'd be in no hurry to reproduce just to prove something.

"How're you gonna pay me?" the guy asks.

"Apple Pay. Right now." Arsène raises his phone between them, arching one thick eyebrow.

"Fine." The guy turns his attention from Arsène to his girlfriend in the passenger seat. "Sorry, babe. I'll make it up to you." Then he turns back to Arsène. "Why're you doing this, anyway?"

"My date is cold." Arsène gestures toward me. I duck my head and pray no one can see my face.

"That's one expensive date if you ask me. She better put out." The guy gives Arsène his phone number and steps out of the car. "C'mon, babe. I'm taking you to Peter Luger. We'll order all the starters too."

Arsène signals for me with his hand to join him, and we both slide into the BMW. It's weird to be in someone else's car. With the scent of their deodorant, the half-finished gum pack in the cup holder, the unfamiliar tree-shaped air freshener dangling from the rearview mirror.

"You're so embarrassing," is my thank-you to Arsène as we resume watching the movie.

"You're so welcome," he replies generously, making me pink again.

"Please, I wanted to die."

"Yes. Of hypothermia. And I was going to be an accessory, the last person to see you alive."

"I can't figure you out." I squint at him. "You do nice things for me, but you are an asshole about it all the way through."

He returns his attention to the screen. "Sounds like the antithesis of your late husband, who said all the right things but acted like an asshat."

We're more than halfway through the movie, though I cannot for the life of me concentrate, when Arsène speaks again.

"I don't get it." He tosses a handful of Skittles into his mouth. "The heroine is essentially a criminal and call girl, and her love interest, Paul, gets paid for sex. What's so romantic about this film?"

"It's about a girl in her prime!" I cry out. "She's trying to survive and support herself and her brother who's at war."

". . . by sleeping with strange men," he finishes. "Didn't women spend the last few decades burning bras to defy these kind of stereotypes?"

"Hold on." I frown, tossing my gaze to him. "Aren't I supposed to be the prude here?"

"If it helps, I think Paul's a piece of work too. They deserve each other."

"*Which* Paul?" I fire out. "This one or mine?"

"Ah!" He grins at me, and I feel beautiful and alive under his gaze. Like he is the Italian sun, nourishing me in ways I can't explain. "Not so dull, are you, Bumpkin? The answer is both of them."

"Well." I tuck a lock of hair behind my ear. "Women love this film."

"I bet." He looks around us, surveying the drive-in. Sure enough, it's mostly couples, with some mother/daughter and girlfriends combos in the cars. "I don't know why, but I've a feeling my mother loved this film. It reminds me of her."

"Loved?"

"She died when I was six."

I feel like I unlocked an impossible level in a video game, and now I need to really concentrate to pass it. This man has never opened up to me like this before.

"How'd it happen?" I shift my full attention to him.

"The usual rich-person way. A boating accident." His jaw tics.

"You don't like talking about it."

"It's not that." He rolls his index finger over his five-o'clock shadow. "I'm just not used to it."

He looks at me with a mixture of gratitude and relief. Really, no one spoke to him about this before? "Not that it matters. Apparently she hated my guts. Well, my father claimed she spent four weeks in total with me the entire time we were both alive."

"What do *you* think?" I ask.

It's wild that he was expected to believe the worst about his mother. Even if she wasn't the best mom, why would you let your child know this about his late parent?

"I don't know," he admits. "She doesn't seem like a villain from pictures and my very vague recollections of her, but as we know, Satan tends to arrive in a pretty package and a satin bow. Ask Gra—" he starts, then stops, remembering we're not supposed to talk about them tonight. His expression turns flat. "Ask anyone who's ever played with the devil."

"And this is why you decided to play with it?" I press. "The devil, I mean? Because you thought you'd find your mother in her?" I'm talking about Grace now. Paul had told me, in passing, about the turbulent relationship the stepsiblings had back when he spoke about her.

"I never thought about it that way." He leans backward, smirking, the cynicism returning to his features. "I suppose I do have mommy issues. I had poor views about my mother, so I chose a woman who was just as lacking in the maternal department. What made you choose *your* devil?"

Leaning back against the headrest, I frown. "No daddy issues here, sorry to report. I grew up hearing from people that I couldn't make it. That I'd never get out of the small town I grew up in. Pau—*my devil*"—I correct myself, smiling now—"was a worldly man. Rich, up and coming, innovative, all the things I thought would get me out of my small-town-girl rubric. His very existence in my sphere held a promise I'd lead a big, shiny life. It worked, for the most part. Because during the good times . . . he was great. The best."

He tsks. "Too bad we're not measured based on our good times. It's how we perform in the bad times that makes us who we are."

I stare at him in wonder. He is right. Paul was brilliant when things were good. But when we ran into an obstacle, I couldn't count on him. Not in the places that mattered.

Our eyes are locked in this strange stare, and I don't know why, but something about this moment feels monumental and raw. Suddenly, and for the first time in maybe years, I feel my womanhood acutely. Not just as a fact—but as a being.

"Stop looking at me like that," I say, finally, though I can't seem to look away either. It's like we're in a trance.

"Like what?" He arches an eyebrow.

"Like I'm raw meat."

"You are chewable to a fault," he teases, a ghost of a smile passing over his face. "All right. You go first."

We're still staring. Lord, if my sisters were here, they'd burst into a fit of laughter. I've never been good at hiding my feelings.

It takes everything in me to tear my gaze back to the movie. A few moments pass, and my stare drifts back to him, only to find he never stopped looking at me.

"We should leave." He straightens suddenly, his voice gruff.

"Why?"

"Because I'm about to do something we'll both regret."

I swallow hard, licking my lips. The dare is on the tip of my tongue. His eyes are hard on mine, waiting, assessing, pleading. I feel naked suddenly. The way I did when he looked at me in Italy. Like there are no barriers between us.

"I'm not going to regret it," I whisper, finally.

"Fuck." He closes his eyes, tipping his head back. Two things are obvious to me—he is attracted to me, but he doesn't want to be. "Yes, you are."

"No, I won't," I say, louder now. "Trust me."

"Good." He erases the space between us within seconds, next to me all of a sudden. "Because I never regretted that first kiss. Not for a nanosecond, Winnifred."

He grabs the back of my head and jerks me closer, and his lips crash against mine. The kiss is tender at first, like he is checking the temperature. When I open my mouth, signaling my final surrender, he groans. His tongue wraps around mine, deepening the kiss into something entirely different. Hungry and desperate. The world spins around us. I can feel my grip on gravity loosening, but still, I kiss him even harder, draping my arms around his neck. And when it's still not enough, when the center console insists on keeping us apart, I do the unbelievable and spring up, hoisting myself on top of him, straddling his lean waist.

He tastes of Skittles and Coke and someone new and exciting. He buries his fingers in my hair, which is gathered in a ponytail, before using it to pull my face up and extend my neck. His tongue rolls around my neck, tasting the sweat that still lingers on me from the show tonight. He makes happy noises I've never heard a man make. A mixture between a murmur and a moan. His face disappears between the valley of my breasts through my top.

"I've wanted to do that since Italy. Since I saw you on that balcony and you looked like a present." His voice is barely a whisper. So much so, I don't even know if he really said it or it's all in my head. But the thought that he's wanted me for so long makes me feel drunk on power.

Vengeful against Paul and Grace, and so incredibly hot for him. I push my hand into his slacks and cup him. He's blazing hot and hard as a rock. I watch the top of his head as it bobs. He is licking a trail, the outline of my breasts through my shirt.

I squeeze his cock. "More."

He looks up at me, dazed and a little flushed. "You sure?"

I nod.

I pepper encouraging kisses all over his face, lips, neck. His movements are quick and desperate, and it brings me pleasure to see him urgent for once, and especially because he is urgent for *me*.

His cock springs up between us, long and hard, and I slide my bottom off the seat, toward the floor, before catching the tip of it in my mouth, still in a daze that I'm doing this. With someone else. Someone new. Someone frightening.

"Oh, shit." He fumbles with the side of his seat, trying to find a way to pull back the darn thing, to allow me more space to take more of him. "Stupid BMW. Give me a minute, Winnie."

Winnie. He never calls me that. It amuses and surprises me that I'm Winnie in his head, even when he insists on calling me Winnifred. I don't comply. I wrap my fist around his cock and lower my head, swirling my tongue against his tip. He hisses with pleasure so intense I swear it is dipped in pain. "Fuck. Please."

"Please what?" I tease.

"Just wait a second. If I don't find the right button, I'll just rip the damn seat from its base. It'd still be worth it, but I won't be able to look at myself in the mirror quite the same again."

I laugh, my mouth still around him. A salty pearl of precum hits the tip of my tongue. And then—lo and behold—he finds the button and pushes the seat as far from the steering wheel as possible. He reclines the back of it until he is almost lying flat. I take all of him into my mouth, dropping to my knees on the sticky floor, gum wrappers and crumbs of food digging into my knees. The windows aren't even tinted. Just what am I doing?

He pushes one hand into my hair and watches me through hooded, drunk eyes. He looks so into it I think I might come just from watching his expression. Our eyes meet across his lean torso. I'd love to see him without a shirt. But, I remind myself, I'd never let myself go this far. Already I've crossed too many lines with this man. Next time I'll see him, it's going to be to exchange information, and then we'll be done. We have to be done. His heart still belongs to a dead woman, even if mine is beginning to slowly come alive from the hibernation Paul has put it in.

"Stop." He groans, stroking my hair. Not like a quick date you meet on an app, but like a lover. "I'm about to come, and I don't want it to be all over this poor asshole's car."

The permission to let him finish inside my mouth is on the tip of my tongue. By a miracle, I manage not to utter it. We're not together, and I know that come tomorrow morning, I'll regret it. He tugs me up before I find my footing, somehow maneuvering me so that I'm flat on my back on the seat he was just occupying. He's on top of me now, hovering like a dark shadow. He grins down at me. My heart jackrabbits in my chest. Uncontained. This is the word I'd use to describe myself right now.

"Regretting me yet?" He dives down to kiss me hard. I shake my head, not wanting to break the kiss.

"Good," he murmurs into my mouth.

His hand snakes between us, fumbling with my jeans. The top button loosens free, and Arsène drags the zipper down. Rather than pushing his hand into my underwear, he slides the fabric to one side, stroking my center, finding me wet and warm.

Another grunt slips between his lips.

He doesn't ask me what I like, the way Paul did when we first fell into bed. I'd told him, of course. Gave him a full, detailed list of dos and don'ts. Paul did everything right, patiently bringing me to my climax, the gentleman that he was. But he never did anything unexpected either.

Arsène isn't patient or unsure. He strokes and dips his fingers in, exploring with barely controlled eagerness, rolling his thumb over my clit, until he tentatively finds a spot that makes me squirm with desire and writhe beneath him. He stays on that spot, his mouth moving from my lips to my right breast. His teeth peel down my top and bra, and his tongue swirls around my tight nipple.

He is turning me inside out, making me feel sixteen again, like it's the very first time my underwear got all sticky and wet in the back of Rhys's truck. I feel cherished and beautiful and sensual. His fingers inside me alone push me close to the edge. My whole body is trembling with need. I'm about to fall apart in his arms, and I don't even care. I'll have a lifetime to give myself excuses for what's happening right now. For once outside of the stage, I'm fully immersed in a moment.

"I'm close . . ."

To my words, he strokes me quicker, deeper. The pleasure is so intense I squirm and hiss, unraveling at his fingertips, all loose threads.

A knock on the driver's door brings the moment to a halt.

Oh gosh.

Swiftly, Arsène reaches with his free hand to cover my modesty, draping it across my chest, while he turns his head toward the window. He makes sure to cover most of me, so I can't see the knocker, and they can't see me.

"Yes?" he asks, composed and detached. "How can I help you?"

"You can stop knocking boots with your wife in your front seat while there are children watching the movie," a woman, by the sound of it, huffs in annoyance.

Wait till you hear I'm not his wife, but his dead fiancée's lover's widow . . .

"Can I try to bribe you to take your precious children and whatever's left of their innocence and get the hell out of here?" Arsène asks pleasantly.

"Not on your life!" She raises her voice.

"How about ten K? Number negotiable, of course."

"I'll call the police!" I can see from the corner of my eye that she is shaking her fist at him, and a snicker escapes me. Arsène is quick to move his hand, plastering his palm over my mouth to muffle my giggles. The space between my thighs is still throbbing, hot and needy. I can feel my pulse there.

"I'll take that as a no," he drawls.

"Get outa here!" she shrieks. "And don't think I didn't take your license plate."

"Oh, I hope you did." He laughs, rolling the window back up.

When the coast is clear, his gaze drops down to me. We share a quiet moment before bursting into laughter together. I don't think I've ever laughed this hard in my entire life.

"I'm afraid you're going to have to do the walk of shame with me, seeing as I told the dudebro I got this car from that I'd leave it here."

"I'm oddly okay with it." I grin up at him. "And I'm not even sure why."

"Because then we'll get the chance to exchange numbers, so I don't have to chase you again for our business transaction."

All the air rushes out of my lungs, like he poked a needle in a balloon.

Even when he doesn't say their names, they hover over us. Drenched in the air. Soaked into our skin.

Grace and Paul. Paul and Grace.

We just shared an intimate moment—our very first sexual encounter since losing our loved ones—and this is what he has in mind.

Not wanting to show him just how hurt I am, I let out a throaty laugh. "Well, then. First things first, do unplaster yourself from me, *boss*."

He complies quickly, rolling onto the passenger seat. "Anything for you, employee of the month."

CHAPTER
TWENTY-ONE

W I N N I E

Two days later, I give Arsène a call. We arrange to meet in the evening at his place. We're professional and curt, almost clinical, and I wonder how a person can kiss you one way and treat you another in the same exact week.

Since I have the entire day off, it leaves me an abundance of time to overthink. I stay in my jammies, make myself a cup of coffee (three shots. Take that, Paul!), power up my laptop, and Google my condition. It's stupid, I know. The first thing doctors tell you *not* to do is go on the internet and self-diagnose. "Every ingrown toenail becomes the c-word," Ma used to tell us when Georgie, Lizzy, and I crumbled in fits of hysterics whenever we woke up with a blue mark on our skin.

I type in all the symptoms I've experienced throughout the last few years. Awful menstrual cramps, paralyzing pains, infertility, random cramps . . .

The same word keeps popping up on the screen over and over again. *Endometriosis.* I click on the definition, suck in a breath, and brace myself for the worst.

Women who suffer from endometriosis have trouble conceiving and, in fact, may not conceive at all.

It says the condition is incurable. Can be medicated—but never healed. In other words, I may never, ever have biological children of my own.

And just like that, the heartache of Paul's death and betrayal shrinks into a Post-it Note–size issue, making room for something bigger in my chest. It swells, and rises, suffocating me.

Permanently infertile.

I'm in full-blown meltdown mode, pacing back and forth. And still. *And still.* I can't bring myself to cry about it. About the terrible prospect of never birthing children. What's wrong with me?

I charge toward my bedroom. Pick up Paul's stupid alarm clock and hurl it across the room. It breaks in two.

Time. You were never on my side.

I grab his newspaper next, rip it, and toss it on the floor. Trudge into the en suite, open a cabinet, and take out all the half-empty pregnancy tests and ovulation kits. I toss them into the trash. They aren't needed anymore.

Finally, I fall into my bed and scream into my pillow.

That's not the end of the world, now, is it? a reasonable voice inside me soothes. There are still ways. Adoption. Surrogacy. But they're all expensive and drawn out and demand bureaucracy. Moreover, pregnancy is not only about the end goal. My sense of failure as a woman is so immense that I loathe myself in this moment.

A knock on the door makes my head snap up from my pillow. I'm not expecting anyone. Which means it could be Arsène. Couldn't he wait until tonight?

Maybe he misses me.

I roll over to my back, about to shove my feet into my slippers and head for the door, before I hear a voice.

"Winnie? It's me, Chris. Open up! I know you're there. It's your day off and you have no life." She lets out an awkward laugh.

My heart sinks. It's all the evidence I need of the fact that I'm royally and seriously messed up. Why did I think it'd be Arsène? Why did I *want* it to be him? He belongs to someone else. His heart, dusty and crooked as it may be, will always beat to the rhythm of Grace's drum. I bury my face back in the pillow, ignoring the persistent knocks and the doorbell, not feeling even half-guilty for it.

Endometriosis.

Oh, Paul, aren't you glad you aren't here? You'd have had to pretend not to be disappointed. You'd have had to do your part, say all the right things, be a gentleman about it, but it wouldn't have changed how you felt. Played—by the sweet, naive woman you thought you could tuck away in the suburbs and make babies with. If Paul were here, if he knew, he would stick around for a year, maybe two. Before his affair—or several of them—would intentionally come to light. Before he'd start to manufacture fights.

He'd make me leave him. Tweak the narrative to fit his good-guy universe.

It just didn't work out. We tried. Sometimes people just grow apart.

It reminds me of the whole Brangelina debacle back in the day. People lashed out at Jennifer Aniston—why hadn't she given him babies? Was she too obsessed with her figure? Was she too selfish? Too self-centered? Too infertile? Either way, inexcusable! And then, of course, came Angelina. Who made him a father. Suddenly, they were a *brood*. We all know how that turned out. Children are not glue. They cannot fix a marriage. Just like infertility isn't a hammer. It cannot—*shouldn't*—break one.

The doorbell continues to chime, but I ignore it.

Chrissy can wait. For now, it's just my new best friend and me.

Agony.

◆ ◆ ◆

I arrive at Arsène's fifteen minutes late. I don't want him to know I've waited for our meeting all day. How I was ready three hours in advance, tucked inside my most flattering pair of jeans, cute black sweater, and the only pair of nice shoes I own.

Not wanting to look eager, or worse—interested—I kept my makeup to a minimum. A little bit of foundation, mascara, and a pink lip gloss, which I also tapped lightly on my cheekbones to create a shiny blush.

He opens the door in his work clothes, the top of his dress shirt unbuttoned to reveal a mat of dark hair. He is barefoot and talking on his phone, motioning with his hand for me to come inside.

This throws me off. After all, at the drive-in, he was acutely attuned to me. Generous, playful, almost romantic; now he is the same cold statue I met in Italy.

Arsène turns his back on me and advances toward his kitchen. I follow, straightening my spine and ignoring the obvious signs of obnoxious wealth dripping from every stainless steel appliance and piece of furniture in his domain. If Grace's apartment hints at wealth, his downright screams it. His view alone is mouthwatering.

"Right out the gate, I'd move away from crypto. Too vulnerable to government crackdowns. If there's one thing we can always count on, it's the government's ability to fuck up a perfectly good investment channel," he says to the person on the other line.

I glance around myself uncertainly. I was not expecting this kind of welcome.

"Hmm," Arsène answers to his client. "Not sure about this one. Let me run the numbers and double-check." He points at a seat at his dining table, and I assume position, taking it. "Hold on a sec, Ken. What can I get you, Winnifred? Coffee? Water? Tea?"

I was hoping we were going to have something stronger. Clearly, he and I aren't on the same page tonight. Anger begins simmering in my veins, diluted by humiliation. *You stupid, stupid woman.*

"Water's fine, thank you," I say formally.

He gets me a bottle of FIJI Water and disappears into his hallway, then returns with a thick manila envelope, which he dumps in front of me on the table.

"No surprises there." He laughs, deep in conversation with *Ken.* "Stock-oriented hedge funds have low net exposure. I hardly ever deal with those time wasters."

It's all gibberish to me, so I open the manila folder without waiting and pull out the heavy stack of papers. It's mostly pictures, which I wasn't expecting. Largely printed and in good quality. I'm not even sure what I'm looking at. How could the private investigator capture pictures of Paul and Grace *after* they've passed away?

And yet that's exactly what I'm holding in my hands.

The first picture is of Grace perched in Paul's lap, grinning at the camera. The picture is taken by someone else, and the backdrop seems to be a party. A company party, to be exact. Why would they be so openly intimate in public?

Maybe their affair was Silver Arrow Capital's worst-kept secret.

This explains why none of Paul's colleagues wanted to answer my questions about him. Chose to send me flowers rather than pick up the phone.

The second picture is of both of them in Paris. *Paris.* Where they shared an apartment. A second, domestic life full of bliss. The window behind them is open, overlooking the Eiffel Tower. They're not touching each other, which is somehow almost worse. Grace seems to be serving food to a small group of people while Paul cracks open a bottle of wine. This goes beyond betrayal. This wasn't an affair, I realize—it was a love story.

The third picture is peculiar. I'm not sure what to make of it. It's of Grace only. Puffy eyed and tired. She is slung over a bed, her mouth in a surly pout. There's an Instagram caption under her face that reads, *miss my baby <sad face emoji>*

Said baby, I'm going to take a wild guess, is my late husband.

The final picture is the one that breaks me. It's a picture of Paul and Grace kissing—full-blown kissing—in *Italy*. I recognize the background like I do the palm of my hand. The yachts. The bay. The pastel-colored buildings. I can almost smell the brine and the olive oil and the blossom of the nearby trees. They were at it when their partners were nearby.

With a soft gasp, I grab a pile of documents and throw them on top of the pictures so I don't have to look at them. They'd met privately in Italy. Before that awful dinner, seeing as Arsène and Grace left hastily in the middle of it.

Paul kissed her before he kissed me on that balcony.

Been inside her before his mouth roamed the most sensitive parts of my body.

Then he shared a peach with me. Told me he wanted to have a child with me. Gave me hell for my *coffee* intake.

"My apologies." Arsène slides into the seat next to me, tossing his smart phone to the other side of the table. "New client. I had to pretend to care."

I'm already full to the brim with rage. Lashing out at him, the man who not only showed me more evidence of Paul's indiscretions but treated me like I was an unwelcome cold caller since I walked into this apartment, is a no-brainer.

"Where'd the private investigator get all these pictures?"

"Grace had a secret Instagram account," he supplies. "Finstagram, I think the clued-in youngsters call it."

"Why would she be so mindless?" I roar.

Arsène shrugs. "I don't have any social media, so the prospect of being caught by me was slim. Plus, it was set on private. It allowed Paul to leave her flirty comments without you seeing them."

"From his real profile?" I splutter. He nods. I want to throw up.

"They really loved each other, didn't they?" I worry my lip. How else can I explain the frequency, the intensity, with which they carried out their affair? It was almost like they were begging to be caught.

Arsène's eyes hunt my face for something, for a reaction I don't deliver. After a moment, his attention returns to the thick file. "Yes. I suppose they did love each other. We were their safe bets. But they were each other's safe haven."

◆ ◆ ◆

I go through the rest of the file. It's comprehensive. Not that I would expect less from a man like Arsène. Though it must be said, he doesn't look half as heartbroken as I thought he'd be when we go through the material.

Paul and Grace shared an apartment in Paris and biweekly trips to their favorite Manhattan hotel. They also went to Saint Moritz together for a skiing trip, were treated as a couple by their colleagues, and were planning to *buy* an apartment together in SoHo, not too far from my place. They'd already put in an offer at the time of their deaths. The contingency fell through when they passed.

There were presents, and holidays, and plans for the future. Romantic dinners, shopping sprees, and even nicknames. He called her Gigi.

Gigi is so much better than baby doll.

I don't lift my head from the papers for hours. Maybe more than hours. Maybe days. Who knows? I'm so engrossed in all this new information . . . the details . . . the messages . . . the *emails*. There are so many work emails. How did the private investigator get his hands on those?

"I think it's time we crack open the brandy." Arsène swoops up everything in front of me in one go, arranges the pages and pictures neatly, and tucks them back into the manila folder. He stands up and returns with two snifters and a decanter. He pours both of us a generous amount, shoving mine across the table until it hits my elbow.

"You need a distraction," he muses.

"I need a bullet to the head," I murmur.

He studies me for a long moment. "You know, Mars is red because it's covered in iron oxide, which is essentially rust. It is also the prime candidate to be the next place humans would live on."

"What's your point?" I look up at him with a sigh.

"My point"—he takes a sip of his drink—"is that just because something doesn't work properly, or is rusty—like your heart—doesn't mean it can't survive."

"Still not following," I lie.

"Come, Bumpkin. You dodged a bullet. Can you imagine finding out all of this when you're forty-five, after you've given Paul all of your best years, plus two unplanned C-sections, saggy breasts, and a shattered Broadway dream to show for it?"

To this improper joke, I answer with a snarl.

I cover my face in my hands. My snifter knocks over, spilling all over the floor. The glass breaks. I don't even have it in me to mumble an apology. At least up until now, I could tell myself that Paul had been letting off some steam with Grace, after all the tension that had been building up in our marriage. Now, even that weak excuse is gone. What he had with her wasn't dirty and salacious. They were in love. All in. Just merely tolerating Arsène's and my existence.

"Winnifred." Arsène's voice is harsh now. He stands up. I don't lift my head to look at him. "Stop this right now. You must've had an inkling. People don't carry on months-long affairs if they don't care for each other."

"That's not why I'm broken." I use the sleeve of my black sweater to clean my nose. I don't even care that I'm a snotty, ugly mess. A wad of clean tissues materializes in my periphery, and I snatch it, dabbing my nose with it without so much as a thank-you. And still, no tears. No tears. No tears.

"Why're you like this, then?" His voice is patient but not at all emotional.

"Because I can't blame him." I look up at Arsène, with his tar-black eyes, hard jawline, imperturbable expression. "I hadn't delivered on all the things he thought he'd get when he married me. I'm not the woman you saw in Italy. I'm not all sweetness and warmth and peach cobblers. I don't . . . I don't even know how to make a peach cobbler!"

I throw my hands in the air, then bury my face in them.

"I wasn't ready for this kind of confession," he drawls sarcastically. "Should I loop in the feds? Maybe Interpol? This is too big a secret to stay within these walls."

"Be serious for a second. I'm telling you I'm a huge disappointment."

"I *am* serious," Arsène says tonelessly. "You're a complex human being, not a stock he gambled on. If he thought he had a sure bet, he's the idiot. Not you."

"Just stop!" I dart up from my seat. Glass crunches beneath my shoe. "Don't defend me. I'm not that little southern girl Paul had fallen in love with. I'm the bitch who tried to get a job at Calypso Hall—and succeeded—so she can get closer to *you*!" Now that the confession is ripped out of my mouth, I can't stop. "I wanted to meet you, Arsène, because I knew you were a man of resources who could shed some light on what happened between Grace and Paul. I wanted your knowledge, your information, your means. Wanted to use you to get closer to the truth. I knew you owned the place. It was all premeditated. I wanted you to think it was *your* idea to exchange notes. But I only took the job because I needed my hands on this file." I point to the manila folder.

"I'm a manipulative, weak, gross excuse for a woman, and I wanted to use you. I'm selfish, just like you said!"

Rather than look stunned, hurt, annoyed, surprised—any of those things—he smiles that lopsided, worldly smirk of his that makes me crazier than a sprayed roach.

"Why, this is wonderful news, Bumpkin! Drink." He thrusts his brandy glass in my direction. I gulp half of it in one go.

"The only reason I let you keep your job is because I wanted us to exchange notes," he continues. "And I always knew you were selfish. You're human. It's in the DNA. I just wanted you to own up to it so you can start asking things for yourself."

"That's what I mean." Miserably, I shove the snifter back into his hand. "We're both deplorable creatures."

"I prefer resourceful. And I'm sorry to be the one breaking this to you, but you're not half as cunning and corrupted as you think you are. You taking a job at Calypso Hall hurt absolutely no one. Grace was a million times more shrewd and heartless, and as you can tell, Paul didn't care one iota. At any rate, in case you need to hear this—you're still the most wholesome person I've ever met in my entire life. Please don't thank me—I don't consider it a compliment." He raises his hand and shakes his head, like I'm a lost cause. "And I *still* think you're too good for Paul."

I can't believe this is almost over. That soon, he'll come to my place, get into Paul's office, and find what he's been looking for (or not), and we'll never see each other again.

"Paul liked that I was good." I cross my arms over my chest.

"Paul never understood you," Arsène says bluntly, completely unfazed by the idea of upsetting me further. "He thought of you as a stereotypical southern belle. You were a status symbol, akin to an Italian car, a nice suit. The minute you fell short of his *Little House on the Prairie* idea, he lost interest and moved on. By then, though, you had a ring on your finger, so he figured why not make you the baby maker and go find his true love? I doubt he thought you'd ever catch him."

This hits too close to home and explains too many things I couldn't understand about my relationship when Paul was alive.

Taking a deep breath, I collect myself. "Thanks for sharing your unsolicited opinion with me. I think I'll head back home now. We can arrange for you to come over at—"

"Stay." It's an order, not a request, and before I know it, he pulls me to his living room and places me on his couch. I comply, stunned. He tucks his snifter between my fingers and says he'll be right back. In the sideline of my vision, I see him cleaning the mess I left behind. All the broken glass. I sip the brandy. It rolls down my throat smoothly. After a few moments, Arsène joins me with a snifter of his own.

"Do you think we'll ever do it?" I ask him but stare down at the bottom of my drink.

"Do what?" he asks.

"Occupy Mars."

He smirks, recognizing I don't want to know about the planet—I want to know about my heart.

"I think maybe there *was* some type of life on Mars at some point. At any rate, right now it's too cold, too dusty, and too dry to be hospitable. But this could change. I can see us investing in making artificial habitats and becoming Martians if we really put our minds to it, if we *really* try." His eyes bore into mine, intense and urgent. When I don't say anything, he shrugs. "I mean . . . not us. Humanity in general. It'll take some time."

I nod, nestling inside the silence for a few minutes.

"Tell me what's in that little head of yours," he says.

I swallow before I speak.

"I just think it is so symbolic that what brought us together, you and me, was a play that's all about unrequited love. Because that's what we're both experiencing. Think of how it all starts. Nina is courted by

Konstantin, who is in love with Masha, who, in turn, is also the object of Medvedenko. No one gets what they want. Everyone's love life is unfulfilled. Everyone's unhappy."

"That's right, life is a messy business. Living is a lesson in endurance." Arsène nods. "And endurance is a lesson in humility. The problem with humankind is that everyone wants a simple, comfortable life. But that's such a terrible existence. How could you ever appreciate the good moments if you haven't braved the bad ones?

"And," Arsène continues, watching me as I sip the rest of my drink. "You keep forgetting one thing—Nina survived. She found her way. She *endured*."

"Do you think you'll ever move on from Grace?" I place my empty snifter on the coffee table. I'm fairly intoxicated by now, having drunk on an empty stomach.

"No." Arsène is quick in refilling my drink with more brandy. My heart drops, and I realize this confession really and truly hurts my feelings. "I haven't made any celibacy declarations. And no part of me *wants* to keep pining for her. But I'm a practical man, and, practically speaking, I don't think any woman could ever compare."

I drink some more to shake off the uneasy feeling that accompanies the realization that Arsène is never going to be in the market for love. "Maybe I should go back to Mulberry Creek."

"And do what?" He eyes me mockingly, that taunting smile ready on his face. "Milk cows?"

"First of all, we don't even have cows." I pin him with a look. "I'll have my family, my friends, my circle. I'll have . . . Rhys."

"Who's Rhys?"

"My ex-boyfriend. We broke up when I moved to New York. We were really good together. He's a nice guy."

Arsène rolls his eyes. "Please kill me if the first adjective that springs to mind to describe me by my ex-girlfriend is *nice*."

I laugh. "Being nice is a great trait."

"That will not get you in the history books." He salutes me with his drink.

"Not everyone wants to get into those books," I point out.

He makes a disgusted face. "Oxygen wasters."

This makes me laugh. "I don't hate you quite as much as I did weeks ago," I admit.

"Well, then here's some food for thought." He pivots toward me. "You broke up with Rhys for a reason. Never forget that."

The brandy decanter gets emptier as the night progresses. Arsène brings over the file, and we go through the pictures together again, but this time, it's not as gut-crushingly terrible to watch as the first time around. At some point, the doorbell chimes. He ordered food. *Soul food.* My favorite. Fried pork chops, collard greens, cornbread, mac 'n' cheese, and apricot jam tart. No sign of a peach cobbler. He really does think of everything.

We tuck in, washing it down with lots of water, and then we drink again.

I get brazen. Maybe even a little reckless. After all, this is Arsène. He will never love me. Not that I want him to. But he'll never betray me either.

Because he'll never be mine.

"I have a confession to make." I tuck my hands between my thighs.

"Is it as big a bombshell as the peach-cobbler one? My heart can only take so much." He places his hand over his sculpted chest.

"You have to promise not to tell anyone." I ignore his jest. I think I'm slurring, which is an excellent reason *not* to tell him what's on my mind. But I'm heavy with food and easy with alcohol, and the mood between us is so different than it was at the drive-in. Tonight, he put on a different air. The best friend one. The guy who can be trusted. And it's not like I have anyone else to talk to.

"You have my word. Unless it's really juicy—then out I go with it to *The Enquirer*."

Groaning, I shove at his shoulder, hoping it'll stir something inside him to prompt him to kiss me. No dice. He is different tonight. Cocksure, as always, but also reserved.

"I'm probably infertile."

The words explode between us. Taking a breath, I continue.

"Well, not probably. More like certainly. Remember when you saw me in Italy? I was a whole blubbering mess in the bathroom."

My ears get hot when I think about that moment. He nods slowly, staring at me.

"That was because I had a bad argument with Paul about it."

"I see." He strokes his chin. "That first time we talked about them—in the New Amsterdam, remember?—you seemed to have had a drop-of-a-penny moment when I told you when they started having an affair. Why was that?"

Swallowing, I look down at my feet. "Because it was around the time Paul and I had spoken about my possibly having fertility issues. It felt like he gave up on me and moved on with her."

Arsène doesn't say anything for a while, almost like he hasn't heard me. This was clearly a mistake. I get embarrassed waiting around for him to reply, so I stand up.

"Where's the bathroom?"

"Second door to your left in the hallway."

After emptying my bladder, I return to the living room to find him sitting in the same position on the couch. I regret telling him about my infertility. I don't know what I expected—but it wasn't complete apathy.

"I'm happy for you," he says from his spot on the couch.

I blink, thinking maybe I misheard him. "*Happy* for me?"

He nods.

"Why?"

"Because you're not really heartbroken about Paul. You're heart-broken over the way you two ended your relationship, and that he didn't love you enough to accept you despite what you view as your imperfection. That's an excellent starting point. You'll move on, find someone else. Someone who realizes the value of a person is measured not by their reproductive system and have a good life. Probably with Nice Rhys or a guy of his brand. Paul will become a distant memory, an anecdote."

Narrowing my eyes at him, I shake my head. "You're such an asshole."

"Why?" He watches me grabbing my little clutch bag and my phone.

"You're so callous about everything."

"You wanted me to be devastated for you?" He stands up to follow me across his apartment.

Yes, yes I did.

I stop at the door, turn around, and fling out my arms. "I wanted you to comfort me!"

He stares at me, a little confused.

"Why're you looking at me like that? What's so bad about wanting to be comforted? Have you never consoled anyone in your life?"

We're still for a moment before he speaks. "No."

His voice is quiet, forlorn. "Never," he admits. "I'm not sure where to start."

Vacillating between scolding him and teaching him, I decide to go for the latter. After all, I know what his childhood was like. Distant father, no mother, and a stepmother who banished him from his home.

"There are a few ways." I munch on my lower lip. "My favorite is just to cuddle and sleep in each other's arms. My momma always used to hug me to sleep when I had a bad day. Even when I was a teenager. Cuddling is a great destresser."

He squares his shoulders. "Cuddle. Right. I can do that."

"Why, though?" I stare at him with a mixture of disbelief and suspicion. "Why humor me?"

He throws me a sarcastic smirk. "Because you haven't fulfilled your part of the bargain yet, why else?"

I'm not sure I believe him—I don't *want* to believe him—but I still trudge my way to his open arms like a moth to a flame. I plaster my cheek over his chest, hoping to feel his heart racing the way mine does.

"If we cuddle in your bed, I want no funny business." I speak into the rich fabric of his shirt.

"I . . . no, you can't go into my bedroom." He places his hand on the small of my back, ushering me to a small guest room down the hallway with a queen-size bed.

"Why?"

He looks around himself, as if looking for an excuse. "I don't let people in my bed."

"You've never mentioned it before." I frown.

"I've never discussed my bedroom antics with you either," he says easily, but something's off. This man doesn't seem sentimental enough to vow not to bring a woman into his bed because Grace once slept there. Luckily for him, I'm too drunk and exhausted to grill him about it.

Minutes later, I'm in a strange bed, his arms are wrapped around me, and his lips are in my hair, and my breathing is all calm.

"There, there," he says. "Everything'll be all right. Am I doing this okay?"

"You're doing just fine."

CHAPTER TWENTY-TWO

ARSÈNE

"I'm not in love."

"I know this one. Who is *10cc*?" Riggs presses on an imaginary buzzer à la *Jeopardy!*, then knocks back his drink.

My lips thin in annoyance. Christian slaps my shoulder, his shit-eating grin on full display. "Sorry, pal, but it kinda sounds like you are."

"Because I let a random woman whom I'm conducting business with sleep in my *guest room*?" I sneer, abhorred.

Not that I made Winnifred's stay at my place public knowledge. No, that was Riggs's fault. True to his nomad ways, he showed himself into my apartment the morning after Bumpkin stayed over, bearing gifts in the form of coffee and bagels. Alfred let him in. I was up by then, showered, shaven, and after my tennis practice. Winnifred, however, wasn't. And when she gingerly tiptoed out of the room, a shy smile on her face, Riggs jumped to conclusions like an Olympic athlete.

"No. Because you never let anyone into your apartment, ever, and she looked at *home*," Riggs counters.

Christian waltzes over to the bar at the billiard room in the New Amsterdam. After lying low for a few weeks and letting Cory recover from his little meetup with Bumpkin, I'm finally able to be seen here again. Or at least, I was, until these two morons started ripping me a new one.

"She looked like a woman who'd just woken up and felt awkward being around two strange men," I correct him. "There's nothing going on between us. As I said before, her husband worked with Grace."

Over my dead body am I going to admit to Riggs and Christian that they were right about my late fiancée all along. That she two-timed me. Which, unfortunately, makes Winnifred an unlikely, albeit important, ally. Even my sour ass needs someone to speak to.

"This is all very convincing, not to mention fascinating." Riggs stands up, tucking his phone into his front pocket. "But I gotta run. *Discover* magazine is doing a big editorial about historical shipwrecks, and I want to be commissioned. It's a five-destination assignment. I have a meeting with their editor in chief."

"Are these magazines even making money anymore?" I cross one leg over the other. Print is such an outdated industry.

He rolls his blue eyes at me. "Not everything's about money."

"All the important things are," I counter.

Riggs smiles at me with pity. "This is why you've never been truly happy. You're still trying to find the price tag on joy."

"Okay, Dr. Phil."

"Actually, I got that one from a fortune cookie at Panda Express."

With that, he swaggers out of the room. Christian hands me a fresh drink before sitting down.

"Back to the conversation at hand." He smooths his tie. "I believe Arya already mentioned she doesn't want you anywhere near the Ashcroft girl."

"And I believe I aptly mentioned to *her* that I don't take orders from people who don't pay me a hefty percentage for my services."

"Look." He cuts to the chase. "Arya is not prone to dramatics. If she cares about someone, I'm inclined to believe they're somewhat special. There are plenty of fish in the sea. If sex is what you're after—"

"Sex is never about sex." I stand up, buttoning my blazer. "It's about power, pleasure, gratification, but never about just sex. Which means that no matter what I want from her—sex is not it."

Not that it didn't cross my mind to have Winnifred the night she stayed over. It did. A million times. But what would be the point? We're going our separate ways in a few days, and there is no need to make things unnecessarily harder for her.

She is a good kid, even if a little too innocent and doe eyed for my taste.

She's been through enough without throwing a salacious affair with another grade A bastard into the mix. "And I don't owe you an explanation. What I do with Winnifred, to Winnifred, and *for* Winnifred is our business only. Not sure what authority you have to be the knight in shining armor. You almost ruined your wife's life back when you two were 'just having sex.' Stay out of my lane, and I'll stay out of yours."

I make my way to the door, stopping only for a moment. "Oh, and send my regards to little Louie."

CHAPTER TWENTY-THREE

WINNIE

Two days after my self-diagnosis, Chrissy shows up at my door. She is armed with an unholy number of brochures and articles. She flings them onto my coffee table in triumph, her version of hello.

"What's all that?" I crane my neck from the kitchen.

"All kinds of useful information." Chrissy perks up, throwing me her sunniest smile while sucking on her electronic cigarette. "Mainly about how people *do* get pregnant with endometriosis. I mean, it's not impossible. There are ways, treatments, cures. A whole lotta options, actually."

She arranges all the brochures in a line on my table. I'm starting to regret telling her about my suspicion. I know she means well, but I don't like to poke at the subject. I put an old-school cube of sugar into each of our coffees and take the hot drinks to her. She takes a sip, closes her eyes, and moans.

"How do you make it taste so good?"

"Real sugar, chicory, and just a drop of sorghum. That's how Memaw used to make it."

I take a seat on the couch, and she is quick to follow and launches into talking shop.

"Spoke to Lucas yesterday. He said you guys are all sold out for the next three months. He thinks they might continue for a second year. How do you feel about that? I know we discussed Hollywood—"

"I'm not going to Hollywood." I place my cup on the table. I hate to disappoint her, but giving her false hope would be worse. Chris's mouth curls into a pout, but she doesn't say anything.

I place my hand on her knee. "Thank you for the suggestion. I really appreciate it. But I don't think I'm ready. In fact, I really wanna take it one day at a time after we finish *The Seagull*. I don't think I fully allowed myself to recover after what happened."

"You mean, you're not sure if you're going to sign for a second year with Calypso Hall either?" Chrissy frowns.

Nodding, I lick my lips. "I'm not saying yes or no right now. All I'm saying is that I'm done giving myself a deadline to 'get better.' I'll do whatever is right for me mentally. Right now, I don't know what that is. But I know going to Hollywood is not something I want to pursue. I don't care about fame and glamour. I care about art."

"Oh, Winnie." Chrissy sighs, puts her coffee on a coaster, and scoots toward me. She wraps an arm around my shoulder. "How on earth did I manage to find the one actress in New York City who doesn't care about all the gravy? You were always about the main dish, hon."

I chuckle. "Maybe you chose wrong."

"Oh, I chose the best." She stands up, wiping at her eyes. She looks around herself, as if suddenly realizing where she is. "The place looks better. I don't know how to explain it, but it does."

Other than stuffing Paul's running shoes in the shoe rack, I haven't made any changes. But I think I know what she means. Even the furniture doesn't look like it's holding its breath waiting for my husband to come back.

"Thank you," I say.

"Just promise me one thing," Chrissy says. "You'll take a look at the brochures I brought over. I'm not blowing smoke up your cute little butt, Win. I know you're in a state of despair, but there's so much more in life ahead of you. And some of it? It's really *darn* good, as you say."

◆ ◆ ◆

By the time Chrissy goes home, I feel a lot better. This, of course, doesn't last very long. Fresh dread floods me when I glance at the overhead clock in my kitchen while making a half-hearted attempt to tidy up the place. Arsène should be here any minute now. Together, we're going to raid Paul's office. Paul's *shrine*, which has been locked for almost a year, ever since he died.

Arsène is late. I use the time to go into my bedroom and change into a casual sage housedress. Nothing fancy, but it's one dress I know I look good in. The doorbell chimes. When I hurry to zip my garment, my skin catches in the zipper. "Ouch. Darn it."

I groan as I make my way to the door. When I fling it open, he is standing on the other side, and it's like we've never said goodbye. There is something so familiar about him. So dangerously comforting.

"You're late." I lean against the doorjamb. How else can I greet this man, who spent the entire night two days ago holding me, brushing my hair back, whispering in my ear that everything was going to be okay? Then, the day after, when I woke up and his friend was there, Arsène looked distracted and impatient, just barely holding himself back from kicking me out of his apartment.

"Time is a subjective experience, Bumpkin." He sails past me like he owns the place, walking into my apartment, giving himself a tour. He is taking it all in as I stand by the door.

"So this was Paul's domain."

I lean over the kitchen island, feigning disinterest. "*Our* domain. We designed the place together."

Tonight smells, and tastes, and feels like goodbye. The finality is thick in the air, suffocating me. After this, Arsène and I will go our separate ways. No more secrets to uncover, no more wounds to poke. He is going to walk out of my life, and probably sell Calypso Hall in quick succession.

"That's sweet," Arsène drawls, ripping his eyes from a painting on the living room wall to glance at me. "You said you have infertility issues. Did you ever freeze your eggs? Better yet, embryos? You could still have a nice little bundle of joy from him."

I blink, digesting the offhanded way in which he broached this personal subject. I don't know if I should be outraged or amused.

"How is that your business?" I ask.

"It's not." He approaches the credenza and sifts through items like it's a crime scene. "But I'm a problem solver, and when presented with one, I usually find a solution."

"And then what? Get a surrogate? They cost a fortune."

"In North America, yes. But there are agencies—"

"Well, we didn't freeze anything," I answer shortly.

And even if we had, I wouldn't want to use it, knowing everything I know.

"Too bad." Arsène puts a vase back in its place and pivots in my direction. "Now, where's the key?"

I withdraw the small thing from my dress's pocket and dangle it between us.

"Do you think we're going to hate whatever we find out?" I swallow hard.

"I hope so," he says. "Makes it easier to let go."

And then we're right there. In front of the door I've been staring at for months like it was the open mouth of a lion. Before I turn the key in its hole, I take a deep breath.

"God, you're still in love with him. That's pathetic." The words crawl over my back from behind, like claws.

"Pot, meet kettle," I murmur.

A chuckle escapes him. "Oh, Winnifred."

What? I want to lash out. *What am I missing? How are you and I different?* But it doesn't matter, and it wouldn't bring me closer to inner peace.

I turn the key and push the door open.

Paul's office is a vision of averageness. Files tidily stacked on his desk. A row of three screens adorned with Post-it Notes. There are filing cabinets, dusty pictures of us on his desk, and a stress ball. Nothing stands out. Nothing screams scandal. Adulterer. Cheater.

Arsène moves swiftly to one side of the room. "I'll take the filing cabinets, you check his desk drawers."

He pulls every single file out of them, then each filing cubby, turning them upside down and patting them from all angles to see nothing is hidden inside.

"Be careful. There's no need to destroy his things," I grind out.

"Bumpkin," he answers, already sitting on the floor, sleeves rolled up to his elbows. "You have to stop being loyal to people who haven't been loyal to you. It's not a gracious trait. In fact, it's a little off putting."

"This is not about Paul." I shove my hands into drawers, rummaging through notes, pens, a calculator, and some highlighters. "It's about your hunger for distraction."

"At least I'm hungry for something." His words cut straight into me. "When you're done with the drawers, power up that PC and let me know if it requires a login code, will you?"

For the next hour, we work silently. The PC doesn't require a code. At the same time, we don't find anything of interest on it. The filing cabinets turn out to be duds too. We go through letters, flip open the pictures, roll the carpets, seeking hideout spots where Paul could've kept something secretive, but it's one disappointment after the other. There's nothing in the office to suggest Paul had ever been anything more than a boring, married hedge fund manager.

At some point, I start feeling foolish and actually—*bizarrely*—become mad at Paul. I've built up this office to be the holy grail of all secrets, and nothing is coming out of it. I feel like I'm disappointing Arsène.

Why I care about disappointing this man is beyond me, but I do.

Another hour ticks by. We recheck everything we looked into before. Our nerves are shot, and the silence piles up on us, like deadweight. No stone is left unturned. But we're no longer friendly, or hot for each other, or even mildly civilized. The tension is everywhere, tangling around our limbs like ivy.

"Stop." Arsène's voice slices through the silence. It is sudden and makes me gasp as I browse through another one of Paul's clients' files. "You and I both know we're not going to find anything here. It's a waste of time."

"That can't be." I clutch the file closer to my chest. "Paul was so uptight about his office. So secretive—"

"That's because he has sensitive information here about companies worth billions of dollars. Not because he kept Grace's panties under the printer." He stands up from the floor. A thin film of sweat coats his forehead. "We gave it our best shot."

Is that all? He can't leave! Not like this. Not so soon.

I follow him out of the room, dejected. "Well, you know. It's late, and I haven't even offered you anything to eat, not to mention drink . . ."

He rolls his sleeves down his muscular forearms. "Don't worry about it. I have some leftovers in my fridge."

Still, I trail behind him. Out of the hallway, to the living room, and toward the door. Panic flares in my chest. Arsène may be callous, cold, and full to the brim with venom, but he's been a friend for the past few weeks. A brother-in-arms of sorts.

"Have a good life, Bumpkin." He swings the door open abruptly.

"*Stop!*"

This shrill, foreign voice, I realize, came out of me.

He does stop, his back still to me. He doesn't move, waiting for the other shoe to drop. I need to say something. *Anything, Winnie.* Finally, I find my voice.

"There are still some things I want you to see. Albums . . . stuff like that. Maybe I've missed something."

Arsène turns around to face me. His expression is utterly unreadable.

"I know it's hard. There's a level of acceptance attached to us saying goodbye. We found out everything there was to find, and none of it was good. After I leave here tonight, we probably won't see each other again. And your last connection to Paul will be gone. I get that." But he doesn't get it at all. My grief for Paul is independent from my relationship with him. To me, Arsène became his own entity. Not just means to an end. "But it's better to Band-Aid it."

"We can Band-Aid it tomorrow," I hear myself say, though nothing in my brain authorized these words to leave my mouth. "Tonight, we can avenge what they did to us. Come full circle."

"How?"

I lick my lips, staring down at my feet. "We can have sex."

His stare alone gives me whiplash. I can tell he thinks it's a terrible idea.

"Are you drunk?" He narrows his eyes.

I huff. "Don't tell me you haven't thought of it."

"*No,*" he drawls. Then, in case he wasn't clear: "I mean, yes, of course I've thought of it, but this is a terrible idea. Even for you, Bumpkin."

Though as he says this, he is also closing the door behind himself to allow us some degree of privacy.

"Why not? You were the one who couldn't stop kissing me—"

"The problem's not attraction." He steps forward and wipes a strand of hair from my face. "The problem is it's going to complicate things, resurface issues, and very possibly make your bleeding little heart confuse rebound sex with feelings. Plus, there is still the little issue of my technically being your boss."

"Not for long," I point out. "You want to sell Calypso Hall. And don't be so sure I will magically like you just because we sleep together." I lie brazenly. "Plus, think about the revenge—"

"Retaliation is a primitive, self-defeating notion. I won't do or not do things based on what Grace would have thought about them."

Darn him and logic. I can tell he's made up his mind. He pulls away.

I collect the shreds of my pride and take a step back. No need to beg.

"Well, then." I straighten my spine. "I won't keep you any longer. I hope you have a good life, Arsène."

"Chances aren't looking good, but thank you. Same goes to you."

He turns around, opens the door, steps away, and shuts it softly.

I stare at the door for a few moments. Then I sink to my knees and let out a self-pitying whimper. I wish I could cry about it, but, as usual, the tears don't come. The heartbreak, however, is real, and I don't know why. If it's because of the rejection, the disappointment, or the idea that another chapter regarding Paul is over in my book.

It takes me a few minutes to collect myself. When I finally do, I stand up and turn toward Paul's office. Intuition tells me I'm missing something. The doorbell chimes. I freeze. I'm not in the mood for company. I take another step toward Paul's room.

"Open up, Bumpkin."

After approaching the front door, I plaster my forehead against it, closing my eyes. "Why?" I sigh. "Give me one good reason."

"One?" His voice is so close I know he is leaning against the door too. "Because we fucking deserve this."

I swing the door open, and he is standing there, panting, like he ran up the flights of stairs. His hair is a mess. His cheeks are flushed. He looks alive. I don't remember the last time this man looked like more than a perfectly handsome preserved corpse.

"Let me make one thing clear." He raises a finger. "After tonight, we're not going to see each other again. You were born for greater things than being the arm candy to another man who could never love you."

"Yes," I answer, just as breathless. The only thing that stands between us is the narrow space of the threshold.

"After this, there will be no more dinners, no more movies, no more cuddles."

"No more schemes, no more information to share," I add, nodding.

"This." He points between us. "Is consensual, correct?"

"Yes." I angle my chin down, watching him. "I want to have sex with you."

"I want to have sex with you too," he admits on a choke, tipping his head back, closing his eyes. "*Fuck*, I'm hard pressed to think of anything I've ever wanted more."

Anything? Even Grace?

We collide and explode into one unit, his hands in my hair, my lips fused to his. He is stumbling into my apartment, one hand tight around my waist, kissing me frantically, desperately, while he struggles to peel my dress off. My arms snake around his shoulders. My back hits the wall, but his hand cups my head, protecting me.

"Where's the goddamn zipper?" He groans into our kiss, his tongue swirling around mine, dipping down to my neck.

"The side of my dress. But be careful, the zipper—"

Before I can complete the sentence, the zipper rolls down, catching the skin around my ribs. I let out a hiss. Arsène rears his head back, sobering up.

"Sorry. Fuck. Slower." He rubs his thumb over the flesh where my skin is reddening. "You good?"

I nod, unbuckling him while my dress drops to the floor. I kick it off. He unclasps my bra, his tongue and mouth already where I want them to be. His shirt is off. His pants too. In less than a minute, we are completely naked in front of each other. He rips himself away from me suddenly, taking a step back.

"Wait." He is heaving. "Let me look. I wanna have my fill. I've been fantasizing about this moment for far too long to devour you quickly." He shakes his head, laughing at himself a little.

I stand with my arms at my sides, my chin up, like the *Venus de Milo* sculpture, proud and tall and unbothered. I examine myself through his eyes. My modest height, my too-small breasts, my wobbly knees. My un-Grace-ness. But no matter how self-conscious I am, satisfaction is written plainly over his face. He is enjoying every inch of me.

"You know." He circles me lazily, completely naked, a predator on the prowl. "When I saw you in Italy, I had the acute sense that Paul chose you because he saw you as an investment. A piece of art bound to increase in value over the years. Something different, precious, one of a kind; he was right. You are not like the rest, Winnifred." He stops behind me. He buries his face in my shoulder, his hot lips skimming over my skin. He is bracketing me from behind, his entire body flush against mine. "You are nothing like other women. Nothing like other *people*. But, like all pieces of art, you are bound to break."

His lips trail my neck again, his hands cupping my breasts from behind. My head falls sideways, allowing him access to work his magic, while I arch my back, digging my behind against his erection.

"Break me, then."

"I can't." His lips touch the shell of my ear. "You're already broken."

I turn my head, catching his lips in mine, and we kiss again. I'm ready for him. The emptiness inside me intensifies. Somehow, we find ourselves on the floor, starving and half-civilized, kissing, dipping fingers, stroking and licking and demanding more of each other.

"Tell me you have a condom around here." His hands part my thighs, roughly pushing them apart. "Otherwise I just might die from blood loss on my journey to the nearest bodega."

"No, no condom. But I'm clean . . ." I hesitate. "And as established, can't really get pregnant."

He stops kissing me. His eyes meet mine. There's struggle behind them. "I'm clean too."

The rest is unspoken. He positions himself between my legs, and in one swift push, he is inside me, filling me completely. I've never felt so desired, so sexy, my entire life. He starts moving inside me.

"Ah, this is no good." He drops his head to my chest, kissing the valley between my breasts.

I run my fingers through his silken hair, dread filling me. "It's not? Do you want me to . . . ?"

"No, you're good. Shit, you're *perfect*." He is still inside me. "What I mean by this is no good, is that it's *too* good. Way too good. I'm about to come, and I'm two thrusts in. I've never . . ." He raises his head, and he is thoroughly blushing. What a wonder. "Never without a condom."

"Oh." Relief washes over me, and I hug him tighter, moving underneath him, rolling my hips, making him go crazy. "Come whenever you want. I'm close too."

"God, Winnifred. You're so sweet, even when you're killing me."

We find our rhythm. It's fast and intense. Urgent and needy. When he comes inside me, I stifle a cry it feels so good.

He stays over afterward. Sleeps in the bed Paul and I once shared. Or, rather, lies in Paul's spot. Taller and larger in frame. His dark eyes watching me, instead of those sunshine baby blues I've been used to seeing from across the pillow.

There is very little sleep involved on our last night together. We have sex, then we pull away, talk a little. His arm is draped over me in a possessive gesture I'll miss. And then he is inside me again, kissing, biting, moaning. Sometimes we fuse together before we even finish a conversation. We're a jumbled, delicious mess.

When the sun rises, I'm dead to the world. The good kind of exhaustion takes over me. My bones feel heavy, and I'm lulled into a deep sleep. When I wake up, the clock says 11:20 a.m., and Arsène is nowhere in sight. I peel myself off a bed that smells like a stranger and make my way to the kitchen. Half-exhilarated after the night I've had, half-devastated that this is the end.

There's a note waiting for me, stuck on the coffee machine, where he knows I will see it. It's his parting gift. His white flag.

> Call the doctor.
> —A.

◆ ◆ ◆

And so I do.

I call my OB-GYN. This time, I don't hang up. I don't let panic take over me. The receptionist announces cheerfully that they actually have an opening tomorrow, at around noon. I take it with both hands and thank her approximately five hundred times.

Before she ends the call, the receptionist reminds me to bring my insurance card, along with a photo ID. After I hang up, I rummage through my wallet. I can't find the darn insurance card. It's been a hot minute since I took care of myself, having spent the majority of this past year in deep hibernation.

Then I remember that Paul put our insurance cards, along with our passports, birth certificates, and social security cards, in the safe in his closet.

I walk over to our room, ignoring the mangled sheets, and open Paul's closet. The safe stares back at me. I don't have the combination for it. Paul didn't share it with me. I never thought much of it at the time. Trust hadn't been an issue in our marriage—or so I thought.

My extensive knowledge of movies reminds me I have only three tries before the safe self-locks. I rack my brain for what the code may be.

I try his birthdate first. Fail.

I try my birthday, letting out a wry chuckle when the light blinks red. No surprises there.

My Spidey senses tell me it has to be a birthday. It must. Paul lacked the creativity to come up with any other combination. He always used birthdates. I used to make fun of him about it. His Gmail, Facebook, Instagram passwords . . . all birthdates. Usually his own. He didn't remember his parents' birthdays. He was sure about the months but never about the days. His secretary had to remind him a week in advance to buy presents and schedule a call on his calendar.

Which leaves me with one other person.

After making my way to Paul's office, I power up his computer and log in to his company email, which is surprisingly still working. His name pops green on his company's internal software. My heart beats hard in my chest. *Oops.* He's online. Let's hope no one thinks he's back from the dead.

I scroll through his emails until I find what I need. A birthday sheet shared by a few of the PAs that includes all of Silver Arrow Capital employees and their birthdays.

I find Grace's. January ninth. I make my way back to the safe, crack my knuckles, and hit the numbers 010991.

The green light flashes, and the safe slides open effortlessly. Nausea rolls through my stomach, the bile tickling the back of my throat. What a darn cheater the man was. I grab a stack of plastic cards wrapped in a rubber band from the safe's jaws. Sort through them. Find the insurance card. I pocket it in my sweatpants with shaky hands, shoving the rest of the cards back. Something draws my attention just before I turn around to leave. A box, no bigger than a mug, in the corner of the safe.

It is brown and plain. Months ago—weeks ago, even—I would have left it alone.

Now? I want to know. I grab it and flick it open. There's a lot of scented black tissue covering whatever's underneath. I toss the wrappers away, my heart pounding so loud I can feel its thuds between my ears. The first thing I see is a USB stick. The second thing is a piece of paper rolled like a map. No, a few pieces of paper. Square. White. I unroll the batch, and what I see stuns me.

No. No. No.

I gallop toward the bathroom, kneel in front of the toilet, and throw up, retching uncontrollably. Tears run down my face. My whole body is trembling.

Standing up on wobbly legs, I stumble back to the box, which is flung over the bed, and pick up the pictures again. Yes. It is exactly what I think it is. Ultrasound pictures, indicating a small little bean of a baby swimming safely inside its sack. I turn the picture to the other side.

First scan. 6 weeks. G + P = PJ!

Paul and Grace were pregnant.

They were going to become parents together.

Arsène was wrong. They *were* going to leave us for one another. Paul never would have let another man raise his child. For all his faults, he'd always wanted children. *A herd of little stinkers to call my own.* He'd pat my ass after we'd have sex. His way of wishing I'd get pregnant.

Which begs the question—what happened? Where had their plan gone sideways?

I examine the ultrasound photos again, more carefully now, as adrenaline gives way to far deeper emotions. Rage. Pain. Shock. The name of the clinic, and the date of the scan indicates it was done some time ago. Mere weeks after Italy.

Suddenly, I remember the picture in Grace's Instagram account. The one that was in the private investigator's file.

Miss my baby 😞.

Innocently, I thought she was referring to Paul. But she wasn't.

She was referring to her miscarriage.

That's what went wrong for them. Grace had had a miscarriage. Bad omen? One of them had chickened out and decided to stay with their partner. Probably Grace, knowing what I now know about Paul.

Grace shone where I had failed. She almost gave him a baby.

My marriage was a sham.

The so-called love of my life was a joke.

I'm all fired up and shaking with anger as I make my way back to Paul's office. I've never been this affronted, this wounded in my entire life. I can't think clearly, and it scares me, because I'm not completely in control of my actions right now.

I shove the USB into Paul's computer and wait for a new folder to pop up on the screen, bracing myself for the worst. Once it does, it presents a few dozen videos. By the thumbnails alone I can tell these are old videos. It is apparent that they were transferred from a videotape. I click on one and don't recognize the people in the video. This is not Paul's family. Not his mom, not his dad, not his siblings. These are complete, beautiful strangers. I've never met them in my life.

Who are they? Why did Paul have this? Was he keeping it for a friend? A colleague?

Then I realize . . . these people in the videos are not strangers at all.

At least, I know one of them. Intimately.

Gosh, Paul, why did you take part in this awful woman's schemes?

The next half an hour passes in a daze. I shove the USB and ultrasound pictures into a FedEx envelope and call a courier to send it to Arsène's apartment. There is no reason to pick up the phone and call him. We decided not to see each other again. It's for the best, seeing as what I'm about to do will shock him and those around him to the core.

Next, I give Chrissy a call, informing her that I'm dropping out of *The Seagull.* She doesn't answer, and I go straight to voice mail, which is a huge relief.

Finally, I text Lucas, Rahim, Renee, and Sloan a heartfelt apology.

Dear Seagull Cast,

I know you're going to hate me, and to be honest, you have every reason to.

What I'm about to do is put myself first and disregard your best interests.

I'm going away for a while. As some of you know, I lost my husband almost a year ago.

Well, what you don't know is that in recent weeks, I've lost much more than that.

I lost my hope. I lost my faith in humanity. I lost the precious memories I have from my late spouse. I lost everything. But I think I'm beginning, for the first time in years, to gain something too. Perspective.

Even if I stayed, I'm not sure I would've made a valuable contribution to Calypso Hall. I know Penny will do an amazing job as Nina.

Though I do not expect you to forgive me now, I hope that one day, in the distant future, you will.

Love with all my heart,

Winnie.

I am being selfish. I am putting myself first. I am taking a leaf out of Arsène's book.

The last step is to do what I should've done the week after Paul had passed away.

I pack a small bag, buy a one-way ticket to Nashville, and turn my back on New York City for good.

CHAPTER TWENTY-FOUR

ARSÈNE

I avoid going back to my apartment after my rendezvous with Bumpkin. Staying in the city, in proximity to the scene of the crime, would be a mistake of epic proportions. Instead, I opt to stay at the Scarsdale mansion, working remotely, at a safe distance from her.

One of us needs to make logical decisions here, and that someone isn't the charming, strongheaded woman I left in a Hell's Kitchen apartment. Winnifred is lovely, in the same way a piece of art is—enticing beyond my comprehension. Better left for someone else to appreciate. I have nothing to offer a woman in the romance department. Even if I had, she'd be an unsuitable partner. And I am, after all, a man who prides himself with following reason.

I don't make my way back to my apartment until the end of the week, when I finally decide to drive back to the city. I saunter into my building, dipping my head in acknowledgment as I pass Alfred at the reception.

"Mr. Corbin, there's a parcel waiting for you." He raises a finger before I get into the elevator. He crouches down behind his desk and produces a small cardboard thing. I take it.

"Did I have any visitors while I was gone?"

"No, sir."

"Good." *Fantastic*, even. Bumpkin got the message. No calls. No unexpected drop-ins. Good girl.

I make my way up the elevator, enter my apartment, and fling the parcel onto the dining table. Probably work-related shit. It can wait.

I forget about it for the next few hours while I catch up on emails and get a phone call from Riggs, who is in Naples sampling more than the Italian food, and from Christian, who for some reason has appointed himself as the designated responsible adult and asks how I'm doing like he is my mother.

It is only shortly before I go to bed that I'm reminded of the parcel waiting in my dining room. I pick it up and rip it open carelessly. The first thing to drop out of it is a sequence of sheets . . . *ultrasound pictures?*

Confused, I turn over the package and glance at the sender's address for the first time. *Winnie Ashcroft.* I turn over one of the ultrasound pictures.

First scan. 6 weeks. G + P = PJ!

Well, then. Turns out, there *was* something interesting lurking in the Ashcroft household after all. Where did she find it? And why on earth am I so indifferent to the idea of Grace being pregnant with Paul's baby?

Paul's baby. The meaning of the words sinks into me now. Grace had always insisted we use condoms. I guess she didn't extend this rule to Paul. Otherwise, she wouldn't be so sure about the father's identity.

So Grace wasn't against forgoing contraception. She was against forgoing contraception with *me*. Perhaps the idea of a Corbin sperm swimming inside her repulsed her.

Wondering about the timeline of this entire shit cluster, I examine the pictures more carefully. I see the timestamp printed on the bottom of the ultrasound page. Three weeks after Italy. After Grace was emotional, distraught, not herself.

Three weeks after she'd asked the driver to pull over so she could throw up in the bushes and made me wonder if she genuinely did give a damn about Doug dying.

The pieces fall together. Including the period in which she must've lost her baby. First, she'd disappeared. I thought it was because of the will, but it was because she was going through loss and grieving. Then, she came back unexpectedly the night Riggs was supposed to crash at my house, waiting for me, eager to please, to entertain, to win me over. A decision had been made then. Paul wasn't a safe bet anymore. Maybe he decided to stick it out with Winnifred, after all.

After I'd kicked Riggs out, when we tried to have sex, Grace had been in pain. The sex was awkward at best, and I wanted to stop. There were blood traces on the condom. She claimed it was stress. It wasn't. The truth was, her body was healing from trauma.

I'm more disturbed by the fact I'd had sex with a woman shortly after her miscarriage than I am about how close Grace had been to leaving me.

So. Grace wanted to leave me *and* have another man's child.

This leaves me with the mysterious USB. The last piece of the puzzle. Bumpkin did well by sending these here. I'm surprised she didn't try to hand deliver them herself.

You told her not to. You specifically said you'll never see each other again.

Plus, my inner mentor is proud that she decided to ditch a deadbeat like me. This is exactly what I wanted her to do. Start putting herself first.

I shove the USB into my laptop. An array of videos appear in quick succession. I click on the first one. On the screen pops the face of a youthful-looking, tired-yet-happy Patrice Corbin.

What. The. Fuck.

It takes me a full minute to get over the initial shock and focus on what's happening in the video. By then, I have to replay it. Patrice gurgles and smiles at a surly-looking baby—supposedly me—before putting me to her breast. Baby-me sucks hungrily, one fist curled around a lock of her raven hair to ensure she is not going anywhere. She strokes my head—it is full of black straight hair—and laughs softly.

"*Oh, I know,*" she says in French. "*Your meal is not going anywhere, and neither am I.*"

Something weird happens inside my body. A rush of nostalgia, or maybe of déjà vu. An awakening. Clicking open another video, I see baby-me wobbling around in nothing but a diaper in an apartment I don't recognize. I'm guessing it is the apartment Patrice had rented in New York. The one she supposedly lived in by herself.

My mother runs after me, giggling. There's a conversation in French in the background, possibly between members of her family, who must be in town. When she finally catches me, she flings me in the air and blows raspberries over my belly, and I laugh, delighted, my chubby arms reaching to hug her.

Another video. This time at the Corbin mansion. I'm about three and helping Patrice wrap Christmas gifts. We talk in length about butterflies and boo-boos. Every so often she stops, puts a hand on my arm, and tells me, "You know what? You're so smart! I'm so glad I have you."

Another video. Mom and me on a ski trip. I try to eat the snow. She pours juice concentrate over it. I brighten up, and we eat it together.

Another video. We're making a cake. She lets me lick chocolate off the whisk.

At a swimming lesson, we wear matching swimsuits—me in trunks, she in a bikini—same lobster pattern.

Flying a kite. I bump into a bench, fall, and start crying. Patrice rushes to me, sweeps me up, and kisses my knee better. We choose a superhero Band-Aid together. It's the last Spider-Man one, so she suggests we go to the pharmacy together to get some more.

Who took these videos? Who was behind the camera?

I sit back, rubbing at my temple. Though I have no memory of any of those things happening, now that I've seen these videos, blurred pieces of my past click together into a bigger, more elaborate puzzle. I *do* remember the Manhattan apartment, cramped and out of style. I remember going to Calypso Hall with my mother when I was very little. Remember being carried in her arms often.

I remember her fights with my father, though unlike his relationship with Miranda, there wasn't a lot of screaming and no hurling objects at one another. Patrice was quiet and fierce and knew exactly what she wanted. And what she *didn't* want—my father.

I remember her to be good. Kindhearted. A free spirit. Not absent, uncaring, and disinterested. And I remember the day she gave up, packed us a bag, and moved us to Manhattan. How she apologized to me ten thousand times as she secured me in my car seat and said, "I know you deserve better. You *will* get better from me. I promise. I'm just figuring it out."

Tipping my head back, I close my eyes and grimace, the rush of memories moving through my body like an earthquake.

My mother wasn't a thoughtless monster. She was full of passion, fun, and compassion. And my father had resented her because all those positive traits were never directed at him. He chose Miranda, and Patrice chose to move on. The mere idea of her moving on without him, not fighting for him, made him deliver the ultimate punishment—he'd poisoned me against her. Tarnished the one thing she valued. My good memories of her.

It takes me a couple of hours to go over all the videos. I watch them on loop, in a trance, inking every single moment into memory. When I'm done, I save all of them to my Dropbox and remove the USB.

I wonder why, of all places, this thing has found its way to Paul's. I guess the content of the package I received today was Paul's little Grace shrine. Grace was in possession of this USB and decided to keep it somewhere I'd never find it. That couldn't have been her apartment. I had the keys.

Why hadn't she given it to me?

The answer is clear. She didn't want me to have it because a part of her loathed me enough to deny me this peace of mind. My thinking Patrice was an awful monster worked to her advantage. The more broken I was, the less I expected of her. My expectations from the fairer sex were so low that I'd readily accepted a woman who tried to kill me when we were teenagers.

Grace never loved me. I always knew that, deep down, but this USB is the final blow.

The surprising part is that I never loved her either. As I sit here, in front of a mountain of evidence of her affair, it is clear to me that this asshole Christian was right.

I was obsessed with her.

I mistook fixation for affection. But wanting my stepsister had very little to do with Grace as a human and a lot to do with proving something to myself. That I'd won, after all. The endgame—the biggest game of all—wasn't something I could afford to lose. Funny thing is, I lost it, anyway. And survived to tell the tale.

The only thing I ever wanted from Grace was her full and complete submission. Not her body. Not her love. Not her babies.

This explains everything. For instance, why I felt cheated and robbed more than heartbroken when Grace passed away. Like the universe had fucked me out of a perfectly good deal. My business sensibilities had been affronted. I'd invested time and resources in that woman, and it frustrated me when I didn't see a return.

The proximity to Bumpkin didn't make matters better. Seeing the woman turn inside out as she mourned her husband only highlighted the fact I really didn't care all that much for my fiancée.

Hold up. Rewind. Shit, shit, shit.

Winnifred.

She knows that Grace was pregnant. How must she feel, after struggling with her own infertility?

Glancing at my watch, I see it's already well past eleven. I call her anyway. She's up till late, what with her show schedule. Still, she doesn't pick up. I send a text message. **Answer me.**

Nada.

I call again. It occurs to me that something very bad could've happened between the last time we saw each other and now. Why did she send the package? Why not bring it over so we could both hate on Grace and Paul over a bottle of wine, like civilized people, before fucking each other's brains out?

Sure, I told her not to, but since when does this woman listen to anything *anyone* has to say? Least of all me.

What if Bumpkin is in trouble?

The thought unsettles me more than it should. I grab my keys and head to the parking lot, taking the stairs three at a time. The elevator may take several minutes, and time is of the essence.

I try to call her as I drive toward her apartment. The call goes straight to voice mail. It's like the time I went to identify Grace at the morgue all over again, but somehow, a thousand times worse. I'm appalled by my reaction to Winnifred not answering me, how out of proportion it is in comparison to the way I felt when I went to look at my fiancée's dead body in the middle of the night, all calm and collected.

I park in front of her building and run up the stairs, convincing myself the entire time my sense of responsibility stems from everything we've been through together, and not, Science forbid, because I've developed those pesky things called feelings. I just want to be on the safe side. The woman is obviously distraught after hearing about her dead husband's love child. I'm just being a Good Samaritan.

You? A Good Samaritan? Riggs's voice chuckles in my head as I fling myself over the banister to save time. *If the world depended on your good intentions, it'd have detonated a thousand times over.*

When I get to her door, I pound on it with both fists. Hysterical is not my most attractive look, but I'm not here to chase tail.

"Bumpkin!" I roar. "Open the goddamn door before I kick it down."

Tonight may or may not end in my arrest. I will never live it down if Christian releases me on bail.

"Winnifred!" I rap the door again. I can hear movements coming from behind nearby doors. People are probably peering out through their peepholes, trying to gauge how much danger I pose to their beloved neighbor.

"Answer!" I slam my shoulder against her door with a growl.

"The damn!" I thrash into it again.

"Door!"

Finally, I hear a door creaking open. Unfortunately, it's not the one I'm assaulting. A woman appears on the other end of the hallway. She is wearing a green face mask and has rollers in her hair.

"As much as I appreciate the romantic gesture—and don't get me wrong, I totally do, unless you're here to collect drug money—Winnie's not here."

"What do you mean, not here?" I spit out, panting. *The Seagull* should've ended two and a half hours ago.

She tightens her bathrobe over her waist. "I saw her leave maybe a couple days ago with a suitcase."

"A couple of . . . *what?*" I jeer. "She couldn't have. She's in a goddamn show. *My* show. I pay her a salary. We have a contract. She can't leave."

"Well, she did."

"That's impossible," I insist. "Where'd you get this dumb idea?"

"Don't shoot the messenger."

Then don't tempt me.

"I wonder why she left, though. You seem like such a great boss."

"The little, reckless, egotistical, sh—"

"Stop it right there." The woman lifts a hand, shaking her head. "Don't finish that sentence. That girl you're talking about is one of the kindest women I've ever met. You know, the other day I caught her asking our neighbor for a cup of sugar. The woman is a single mother and works two jobs to keep her kid in this school district."

Blinking slowly, I ask, "So fucking what? She asked a single mother for a cup of sugar, you wanna give her a Nobel Prize for it?"

The woman reddens under the neon-green mask slathered on her face. "So I asked Winnie why she did that. Winnie's a responsible human, and she bakes. There's no way she needed sugar. You know what she told me?" She licks her lips. "She told me that every now and then, she goes downstairs and asks her neighbor for something small and cheap so that the neighbor would always feel welcome to ask Winnie for things too. Food items, toothpaste, soap. This was her way of making sure our neighbor knows they're on equal footing. I don't know what your story is with this woman, but I can tell you she is not egotistic. She's an angel on Earth, and if you lost her, well, I'm inclined to believe you deserved it."

I never had her in the first place.

I make my way downstairs, head pounding, heart thrusting. The lady has some nerve to just up and leave the city as though she hasn't any responsibilities. How dare she? This is my theater. My show. *My* business.

And you care about this business since . . . ? Christian taunts in my head.

"Shut the fuck up, Christian," I murmur aloud, pouting myself out to the street like a goddamn teenybopper.

I scroll through my contacts until I find Lucas Morton's number. He is the director. He'll know where she is. Lucas answers on the third ring.

"Yes?"

"It's Arsène."

There's a pause before he answers, "Mr. Corbin . . . ? Is everything—"

"Where's Winnifred Ashcroft?"

"Oh, goodness." He sighs in a don't-get-me-started way. "Finally, someone to talk to! She bailed. Skipped town. Her agent just called me out of the blue two days ago. So unprofessional. Penny had to step in and work every night. We should sue her!"

"Where'd she go?"

"How would I know?" he cries out. "She just wrote us a text saying she was going away for a while. Where is 'away'? What is 'a while'? This is what I don't like about working with actors. They're prone to dramatics. What're you going to do about it? This is a real problem. You know how difficult it'll be for me to train someone else now? I don't have time to find and teach—"

I hang up the phone on him, and I'm back in my car, calling Christian now.

Because Christian has Arya.

And Arya knows Winnifred, and her agent.

CHAPTER TWENTY-FIVE

WINNIE

The first day coming back to Mulberry Creek was a hectic one for sure.

"Auntie Winnie!" Kenny throws her arms around my neck, peppering my face with sticky marshmallow kisses. "I missed you so!"

"I missed you, too, pumpkin!" I nuzzle her close, my nose inside her curly blonde hair. I pull away, grinning. "How's my favorite girl been?"

"No complaints. Well, actually, my back's a little sore, but what can you expect when you're thirty-five weeks pregnant." My sister, Lizzy, answers the question directed at Kenny. She wobbles into the room, her belly preceding her. I stand up and hug her. I'm not so pure hearted as to not be jealous of her, even though it's Lizzy, my big sister, who taught me how to braid my hair and cut my jeans into Daisy Dukes with surgical precision.

It is absolutely possible to be happy for someone and still be jealous of them to the point of tears.

"You look amazing," I whisper in her ear.

"You look *hungry*," she counters. "Have you been taking care of yourself at all?"

This is the part where I say *sure* and hope they buy it. But lying doesn't seem so appealing anymore. There's something liberating about breaking apart in my momma's old kitchen and having my loved ones help me pick up the pieces.

"I haven't been, but I'm about to change that."

"Well, then!" Ma claps in the background, sounding cheerful. "Speaking of food, how about some apple pie and sweet tea?"

We sit down at our small kitchen table, eat our weight in gooey pie with vanilla ice cream, and drink buckets of sweet tea. Kennedy shows me her new ballet moves, and I ooh and aah.

Dad comes home from work, hugs me, and tells me he loves me. I dissolve like butter in his arms.

Then Georgie, my baby sister, bursts into the kitchen, back from her job as a Pilates instructor. She jumps on me, trapping me in her limbs.

"My God, Georgie. You're like a Labrador!"

"Damn straight. I've always been your favorite bitch!"

Once Lizzy and Kenny say their goodbyes, friends from town stop over to hug me and catch up. I grab a quick shower and slide into my pajamas, then check my phone for the first time today. I have several missed calls from Chrissy, Arya, and Rahim. None from Arsène. Guess once he got over his initial ire over finding out about Grace's pregnancy, and how she kept his mother's videos for herself, he moved on.

A knock on the front door snaps me out of my reverie. Ma and Dad are in bed, and Georgie just stepped into the shower. I pad barefoot to the door and fling it open.

On the other side of the door stands a man I didn't think I'd see again.

My unfinished business. The love I left behind.

Rhys.

The man hasn't changed at all. He still has that same triangular baby face. With his toothy smile and half-lidded puppy eyes. He's wearing khaki Bermuda shorts and flip-flops and a burgundy Henley. He looks like the same old boy I left behind. Only I don't know if I'm the same gal I was.

"Winnie." His eyes light up.

"Rhys Hartnett, gosh!" I pull him into a hug. He laughs good-naturedly, hugging me back with one arm.

"Wait, hold on. There's a pie between us. Persimmon pie, to be exact. Your favorite. When Momma heard you were in town, she insisted on making you one."

I pull away and take the pie from his hands. "How's Mrs. Hartnett?"

"Fantastic!" He smiles. "My brother gave her a new grandchild last month, so obviously, they're keeping her busy."

Apparently, I cannot avoid the subject of children and babies.

I usher him to the rocking chairs on our front porch. I slide the pie onto the table between them and take a seat. "Sorry I didn't get back to you after you called me. Things have been really hectic."

"Figured." Rhys takes a seat next to me. "I can't even imagine what you've been through. Are you okay now?"

"I'm getting there." I smile. "How've you been?"

"Great," he says, and I believe him. Men like Rhys tend to do good, be good, and feel good. "Other than that small moment of relapse when I accidentally started dating a fugitive two years ago."

"A fugitive!" I choke on my saliva. "Spill it, Rhyssy! I want all the tea."

"All right." He runs his fingers over his perfect mane. "But promise not to laugh."

"I promise *to* laugh. You clearly dodged a bullet. A convict, wow!"

"A fugitive!" he corrects, making me laugh harder. "It makes a world of difference. About two years ago, a woman named Jessica moved to Mulberry Creek out of the blue. She rented out the house on the corner of Main and Washington. The Bradleys'. Started attending all the festivals and town meetings. Sent her first grader to the local elementary school. She was great. Both of them, really. The kid too. People said she divorced an oil tycoon and moved here to get away from the city. That's why she was so well off."

"Was she, though?" I examine him, knowing there's a twinkle in my eyes.

He shakes his head, slapping a hand over his forehead. "Elder fraud."

We talk into the night. About Paul's death and the months that came after it. We reminisce. About his football games and our make-out sessions and that time I lost a bet, and, after he scored a touchdown, I let him suck my toe publicly.

When the sun's just about to peek out, Rhys stands up and dusts off his khakis. "Well, looks like I've taken enough of your time. Sorry about that."

"Don't be." I stand up, too, reaching for a hug. "It was great to catch up. I needed that."

He hesitates, throwing an uncertain look behind his shoulder, at his truck.

"So, um, please feel free to say no. But, I was wondering, if maybe, since you're back, and I'm here, and this town hasn't got a lot to offer in the entertainment sector in comparison to Manhattan . . ." He sucks in a breath, laughing awkwardly. "Would you like to have a cup of coffee with me? Maybe? Sometime?"

I take his hand and squeeze it. "I would love that, Rhyssy."

CHAPTER TWENTY-SIX

A R S È N E

I arrive in Nashville, Tennessee, ready to commit capital murder. The only thing stopping me is the fact that the woman I'd like to strangle will be missed by many, including, to my great fucking shame, myself.

Nashville is busy and colorful and entirely too cheerful for a big city. The sun paints everything in a buttery-yellow filter.

I slip into a taxi and hand the driver the Mulberry Creek address I've been given. Arya made me promise not to give Winnifred shit, a vow I wholeheartedly intend to break. She was the one who gave me Chrissy's number. And Chrissy? She only asked me to keep her posted.

I haven't seen or heard from Winnie since she took a flight back home. Please, if you go there, tell me how she's doing.

It was her one and only request in return for her client's address. But now, as my phone flashes with her name, I can't help but send her straight to voice mail. In a way, I partly blame her for this blunder. She should've kept her client on a tighter leash. Should've stopped her, through blackmail or reason, from leaving New York.

What kind of woman ditches a leading role at a Manhattan theater without so much as a two-week notice? And what kind of person *lets* her?

It's a one-hour drive from Nashville to Mulberry Creek, and a whole lot of open fields and nothing between them. Wide-open spaces spark an uneasiness in me. Though I largely spent my youth in a boarding school in a mansion on the outskirts of New York, there is a certain state of mind, a quietness to the endlessly stretched fields, which I find disconcerting.

I arrive at Winnifred's childhood home when the sun dips behind ancient red oaks. It's a small white cottage with a sagging front porch, rocking chairs, a swing, and potted plans. There's a pink toddler bike tipped over on the front lawn.

"Wait here," I instruct the driver before getting out of the car. I've very little faith that I can change this stubborn woman's mind. Much less that I can appeal to her common sense. First, because I came here without a plan. Second, because Winnifred (since when do I call her Winnifred and not Bumpkin?) never valued common sense very much. This is what makes her unpredictable, different, and fresh. Her ability to easily and happily choose the road less taken.

I go up the steps to her house and knock on the door. The telltale noises of a family dinner in progress assault my ears.

"Georgie, aren't you going to eat any of the crawfish? For goodness' sake, you're not on one of your vegetarian spells, are you?" I hear Winnifred's mother.

"It's not a spell, I'm on Lent!"

"It's not even February."

"Winnie hasn't eaten any, and I don't see you complaining about her. And at least I'm being a good Christian."

"The bleachers of our local high school would beg to differ," Winnifred sasses back to her sister. I grin despite my best intentions.

Just fucking admit it, idiot. You don't hate this woman as much as you want to. Not even close. Not even close to close.

"Are you ratting me out?" Georgie gasps. "Because while we're on the subject, Ma and Dad may want to know about your little meet into the night with—"

"Are you ratting *me* out?" I hear my employee retort. "You haven't changed at all, Georgie!"

"Of course I have. I'm now skinnier than you are!"

I rap the door again three consecutive times and step away. It doesn't sound like Winnifred is having a terrible time. Her family seems to be nice. But she still owes me a show, and I do not like to be robbed of things.

The door flings open, and in front of me stands a woman who must be Georgie. She appears to be exactly Winnifred's age, only taller. Her hair more rusty red than Winnifred's vivid shade of orange blonde, her bone structure less refined and pleasing.

"Heya." There's a piece of string bean tucked into the corner of her mouth, like a cigarette. "How can I help you, you strange, good-looking city boy?"

So Winnifred got the personality and beauty. Poor Georgie.

"I'm here for Winnifred." The words, although true, surprise me. It occurs to me that I've never stood in front of a girl's door before, asking for her to come outside. I'd rarely dated before Grace, and when I did, I limited my communication with the said dates to sordid liaisons. Then Grace happened, and we either lived together or had our own apartments. There was no mystery, no added stress or value to pursuing her. Throughout my life, I had been spared the basic embarrassment of standing in front of a complete stranger, asking to see their beloved relative.

"Who's asking?" Georgie arches an eyebrow and grins.

"A strange, good-looking city boy," I say flatly.

She laughs. "Be specific."

"Her boss."

"Boss?" Georgie's grin melts into a frown. "You look like a big-shot businessman, and she works at the theater."

"Not for long, if she doesn't come here promptly and explain herself."

"Wait here." Georgie disappears into the house, half closing the door behind her. A minute later, Winnifred is outside, wrapping her cardigan against her shoulders. She tips her chin up to look at me, and all I see in her Nordic blues are dread and mild accusation. She wasn't expecting anyone to make the trip here and confront her. Her New York world and Mulberry Creek world have been separated thus far, and she thought she could keep it that way.

"Hello, Winnifred."

"Hi." She turns bright red the minute our eyes meet. "What are you . . . doing here?"

What a question, Bumpkin. If only *I* knew. Sure, you screwed Calypso Hall over, and I don't appreciate lazy employees, but I have people on my payroll with the capacity to do my dirty work and seek you out themselves.

The truth is, I haven't the greenest clue why I'm here.

"We need to talk somewhere private," I say.

"Are you going to yell at me?" She narrows her eyes, her defiance back in full force.

I give it a moment of consideration. "No. You'd just yell louder if I do."

She nods. "There's a river about a mile down from here. Let's walk."

"Shouldn't you tell your family where you are?" I ask.

She gives me a once-over, then smiles. "Nah. If someone's gonna drown someone, it's going to be me."

We both step off the porch and down the loosely paved road of her neighborhood. Each house is acres apart.

"How've you been?" she asks as we make our way on the shoulder of the road.

"Fine. Great. Why wouldn't I be?" I bark out.

She turns to me slowly, a funny look on her face. "No reason, I was just making polite conversation."

"We were never polite to each other—why break a perfect streak?"

She gives me another look. Why am I nervous? I'm a grown-ass man.

"How about we jump right to the important stuff." I clasp my hands behind my back. "You owe me a love interest."

"Excuse me?"

"A *Nina*," I specify. "You bailed on *The Seagull*. Your replacement is not well received."

Lucas has been calling me nonstop, begging for me to try to find the star of his show. Penny is not holding up very well. Perhaps *begging* is not the right word. But he did call once. It was by accident, but he did. And when I asked him how Penny was doing, he replied "Oh, well, a theater critic from *Vulture* described her the other day as 'possessing the charisma of an ingrown toenail.' So all in all, I'd say things could be better."

"Since when do you care about Calypso Hall?" Winnifred narrows her eyes.

"Of course I care about it. It's my family's business."

"You want to sell it."

"All the more reason for me to want it to function well and turn a profit."

"And yet, you wouldn't invest a cent in it, even though it's falling apart."

"The next owners will renovate it." What a maddening woman. What is she getting at?

"I'm sorry," she says, crossing her arms over her chest as she speeds up. "I realize my actions have consequences, grave ones, but I had no choice. I was in a really dark place. I couldn't stay in New York after what we found out."

"You did a lot of growing up in the last few months," I point out.

"I really did," she says. "So did you, though."

The elephants in the room—Paul and Grace—have been acknowledged, and now would be a good opportunity to broach the subject of the pregnancy, of my mother's videos, of the betrayal. But I don't. This will not serve my purpose. I'm here to bring her back to New York, not remind her why she ran away.

"Darkness is all I know," I reply tersely. "And yet you don't see me dropping commitments left and right just because I'm in a bad mood."

"It's not a bad mood." Her tone changes, the edge in her voice more prominent. "I couldn't stand the idea of staying in that apartment."

"Why didn't you say anything? We'd have found you appropriate accommodations in Manhattan." I kick a small rock on the side of the road.

"It's not just about the apartment." She shakes her head. "It's about my future."

"You'll have no future if you don't return to New York immediately!" I stop dead in my tracks, a few hundred feet from the river she was telling me about. I'm screaming. Why the *fuck* am I screaming? I don't think I've screamed my entire adult life. No. Scratch that. I never raised my voice when I was a child either. It is such a common thing to do.

I turn to her, and for the first time in months, no—years—I am thoroughly and royally pissed off. "I'm going on a flight back home in five hours, and I expect you to join me. You have an annual contract with Calypso Hall. I don't give a shit about your mental state, just like no one gives a shit about mine. Contracts are meant to be honored."

"Or what?" Her face hardens. Sweet Winnie Ashcroft is sweet no more. Maybe she was never that bundle of innocence and oatmeal cookies people pegged her to be. Or maybe she is simply growing up right in front of me, and she will no longer be pushed around by anyone. Paul. The world. Me.

"Or . . ." I lean forward, a mild smirk tugging on my lips. "I'll sue you, and you'll have to come back, anyway."

A second ago, I didn't think it was possible for me to hate myself more than I already do. But I was gravely mistaken. Because the look on Winnifred's face makes me want to vomit my inner organs and then feast on them. For the first time, disappointing someone means something to me.

She opens her mouth. Closes it. Then opens it again.

"You mean to tell me that after everything we've been through together, you're going to sue me because I skipped town and your theater has to make do with a temporary actress, for a role that had over *two thousand* women auditioning for it?"

"Yes."

"This is how little everything that's happened to me, to *you*, means to you?" She searches my eyes. She is not going to find anything there. I perfected the art of not showing any emotions decades ago.

"Oh, gosh." She steps back, shaking her head on a dark chuckle. "You really don't care, do you?"

I say nothing. How am *I* the bad guy here?

She is the one who left without even saying goodbye.

She is the one who quit on her role.

"You've given up," I reply mildly. "What was the point of this entire journey? Of us meeting? Finding out the truth? If you refuse to stay and fight for what you came to New York for? You just ran back to your mommy and daddy. To rainbows and pies. To the place you know damn well is too small for you, too uninspiring for you, too *wrong* for you."

"Our needs change as we get older." She throws her arms in the air. "It's okay to settle for comfort!"

"It is *terrible* to settle for anything," I grit out. "Comfort is the last thing an ambitious, talented twentysomething woman should be feeling. You shouldn't even be within a hundred-mile radius of comfort."

She stares at me with bone-deep frustration.

"I'm not coming back," she says, finally.

"Of course you are. You'll finish your post; then you'll leave. Don't worry, I'll be happy to pay for your ticket back to Shitsville." I glance around, scowling.

She presses her lips together, closing her eyes. "Maybe you'll never understand, and that's okay. Every person's journey is different. But I should've done this months ago. Come here, sort out my thoughts, make sense of everything that's happened to me. I'm sorry I ignored my responsibility. I know it isn't fair to Lucas, the cast, and you. I wish I could turn back time and not take the role."

I cannot believe I'm feeling disappointed. I never feel anything about other humans' actions. Putting your faith in someone else goes against everything I taught myself over the years. I want to scream in her face. To tell her it isn't fair.

She sighs, looking down at her slippers, which are now covered in dust. "A big part of why I took it was to get closer to you, anyway. But I can't go back. Not now. Maybe not ever. This is my time to put me first. No matter the price."

And so, on the side of the country road, and for the first time in my entire life, a girl ditches me.

She turns around and walks away, leaving me in a cloud of yellow dust.

CHAPTER
TWENTY-SEVEN

WINNIE

The next morning I go to the local OB-GYN and get lots of tests done. Ma and Georgie are there to hold my hand. They are also there afterward to drag me to Cottontown for brunch and some retail therapy to keep my mind off the results, which should arrive in the next four weeks.

It's when we browse through dresses that Georgie parts a rack full of garments between us like it's a confession-booth window, staring at me wide eyed. "I need to tell you something."

"I know you were the one who stole and destroyed my favorite dress Memaw made for me senior year," I say tonelessly, tugging on a price tag of a cute yellow sundress.

Georgie shakes her head. "Oh, Winnie, I'm denying destroying that dress until my last breath. It's not about that. I need to tell you something I never had the guts to. Ma knows. Lizzy does too."

"Okay . . ." I lift my gaze to watch her. "Go on."

Georgie's throat moves with a nervous swallow. "Paul." She licks her lips. "The night you got married . . . he was really drunk . . . he tried to kiss me. Right before the ceremony. Didn't force himself on me or anything like that, but tried. I pushed him away and gave him an earful—then I ran to Ma and told her all about it."

I continue staring at her but don't say a thing. What is there to say? I believe Georgie. Would have believed her if she'd told me back then too. Which is why, I'm guessing, Ma told her not to.

"What'd she say?" I ask. I care more about how my family reacted to this than about Paul. I already know he's a scumbag.

Ma is outside the shop, fetching us iced coffee with extra whipped cream.

"She said to let it slide. That it might be the nerves on his part. But that if it happens again, we should definitely tell you."

So this is why my family hasn't spoken about Paul since the funeral. They saw through the good guy charade. They didn't like him. Or at least, they had some serious reservations.

"You're not mad, are you?" Georgie asks, giving me her puppy face.

I smile. "No. But next time, always tell me. I'd want to know."

◆ ◆ ◆

The day after, Georgie drags me along for two classes of Pilates, and the day after that, Lizzy absolutely insists I help her put her new nursery together.

I slip into my pre-Paul existence like it's an old prom dress. Effortlessly, and yet it feels weird wearing my old life. My days are a whirl of social calls, cozy dinners, backyard parties, and leisurely walks by the river.

Three weeks after I get to Mulberry Creek, I decide I have too much free time on my hands. I take a volunteering post three towns north in

Red Springs, on the Kentucky border, as a theater director for a *Romeo and Juliet* production, set by a group of underprivileged youth.

I spend the car rides rolling down the windows and putting country music on blast. I make cookies without feeling like a dumb hillbilly about it—and give them away to complete strangers. I write to Arya and Chrissy and attend baby showers. I eat home-cooked meals and hug the people I love, and whenever Paul enters my mind, I don't push the thought away like it's a hot potato in my hand. I let myself feel the pain. And move on.

It's only when Arsène slips into my mind that I find myself doubting why I'm here. Which is silly. He told me time and time again we are nothing to each other. Proved as much, too, with his surprise visit where he berated me like he was a teacher. And yet, if he is planning to sue me, he is not being quick about it. I check my mailbox every day. Nothing but bills and paper-wasting ads is ever there.

I still don't cry, unable to produce tears, but I'm no longer anxious about it.

My friends and family are incredibly supportive. Rhys, especially, is an absolute star. We meet for billiards once a week and talk about our high school years, about all the things we used to talk about. Nothing about our hangout feels like dating. The first time we met up over a beer and a quick game, I told him plainly that I'm not ready to date.

"Honestly, I figured as much." He smiled and threw the cue-stick chalk across the table. "Can't blame you, after what you've been through. But I'm willing to wait."

Those words haunt me for two reasons. The first—because they contain a declaration of intention. He is willing to wait for me, which means he is waiting for *something*. He wants to pick up where we left off. I realize now that despite the last year, despite my idolizing what Rhys and I had after what I found out about Paul, I don't necessarily think it's a good idea to spark this old flame. "A wet match never reignites," Memaw used to say when she was alive.

The second, more pressing issue with what Rhys said is that my reason for not moving on has nothing to do with Paul.

It's been almost a year. A year to digest what happened, what he did, the things that can never be undone. I paid my widow dues. I grieved. I wept. I broke. Mended myself together, then broke all over again. Paul didn't deserve me: this much I can now tell. He saw me in the same light as all his friends did. Those gently bred, private-schooled, helicopter professionals he brushed shoulders with. I was a trophy. A status symbol. Nothing more.

No. The reason I cannot move on from Paul isn't Paul. It's someone else.

Rhys tells me there's a job waiting for me at the local high school, and now that I'm working with youth, I'm starting to seriously consider it.

Is that what I wanted to do with my life when I was a teenager? No. I wanted to act. To be onstage. But dreams change. People morph into different versions of themselves. And comfort is . . .

Terrible, Arsène's voice completes in my head.

When the call from the OB-GYN arrives, and they ask me to come back to the clinic, I don't fall apart like I imagined I would. I book a time, inform my mother and my sisters, put on a sunny dress, and grab my keys.

I have a love story to direct.

People need me.

Arsène was right. Commitment is bliss.

One month turns into three. Arya calls every week to ensure I'm okay and cement to me that she is not angry for bailing on her charity. Chrissy goes a step further and pays me a visit. It is a charged, albeit pleasant one. She is still unhappy about my decision to up and leave.

She was the one who stayed behind to clean up my mess. But I'm also encouraged by the fact she is truly more than just an agent. That she made the trip to Mulberry Creek to see me even though my future at her agency is hanging by a thread.

We go out for a girls' night in Nashville.

"Welcome to our Broadway." I stretch my arms as I take her through the neon-soaked streets of Nashville. The redbrick, low-built buildings are laden with signs of guitars and beer. It might not be as ritzy as New York, but it's entertaining. We enter a honky-tonk hole-in-the-wall where the floor is sticky and the playlist consists of Blake Shelton and Luke Bryan only.

We knock back shots, order a basket of beer-battered mushroom caps, and wash them all down with a local brew. While sucking on her electric cigarette, Chrissy tells me she is seeing someone. That he lives in Los Angeles and that she is considering moving there.

"It's been on your agenda for a while." I sip my ice-cold beer. "Moving west. Maybe it's the final sign you should take the leap."

"Maybe. We'll see." Chrissy frowns. "What about you? Please tell me you've been seeing someone and that you're no longer obsessing over him."

When she says *him*, I immediately think of Arsène, even though I know it is Paul she means.

"I'm not obsessing over him," I confirm, which is true. About Paul, anyway. "But I'm not seeing anyone either. Just figuring out fertility stuff. Life-plan things."

We talk some more. She doesn't ask about the tests, and I don't volunteer any information. I'm not embarrassed per se. Just a little more guarded than I was in New York, when I saw everything through the red-hot and frantic haze of the possibility I'd never be a biological mother.

I want to bring Arsène up in the conversation. To ask if she's spoken to him lately. I know he found out my address through her. I would love to have a crumb of information about him. Anything would do. Now that I haven't heard from him in months, I hate myself for every second I didn't appreciate when he was here in Tennessee. I should've prolonged it somehow. Invited him in for dinner. Asked about the videos. What he thought of them.

I was so busy being on the defense that I didn't have time to enjoy his proximity.

He came to drag you back to New York by the ear, I remind myself. *Hardly a grand romantic gesture.*

"Hello? Win? Are you there?" Chrissy snaps her fingers in front of my face.

I sit up straight. "Yeah. The shots got me, I think."

"Did you hear *anything* I said?" She knots her arms over her chest.

"Something about Jayden, right?" Jayden is her new boyfriend.

She rolls her eyes, sighing. "All right, spill. What is it?"

"What's what?" I blink, confused.

"What is it you've been wanting to say and/or ask since I got here? I know you're holding out on me."

I worry my lip. A telltale sign I am beyond nervous. But ultimately, I can't stop myself.

"Have you spoken to Arsène at all?" I blurt out.

She sits back, smiling like the cat who got the cream. "Ah, Arya owes me fifty bucks. My senses never fail me."

"Arya?" I blink, confused. "Why did you talk to Arya about this?"

"Well, initially, she didn't think it'd be a good idea to give Arsène your address. Said he was a grade A bully. But I thought there was more to it. A man doesn't up and leave to chase after an employee. It takes passion to arrive somewhere uninvited."

"And what did you tell her?" I demand.

"That as far as I know, you and Arsène had a cordial, professional relationship and shared some notes about your late loved ones, but that's the extent of it. She agreed with me."

I nod, relieved.

"But." Chrissy knocks down the rest of her beer and slams the mug against the sticky bar. "I also thought he likes you as more than just a friend, which, Arya said, was impossible, because he apparently doesn't do feelings. Well, I don't care what he *wants* to do, in practice, he caught a lot of feelings toward you, and there ain't no cure for that."

She pauses, tilting her head to examine the issue more carefully. "And I also thought it peculiar that you decided to ru—*move* after you managed to pull through Paul-less in New York. The timing was suspicious."

"I didn't run," I grit out, remembering Arsène's words.

"Sure, honey. Sure."

"You haven't answered my question." I pop the last of the mushrooms into my mouth and chew. "Have you spoken to him recently?"

She shakes her head. "Not recently, and not really at all. He hasn't been taking my calls. Apparently, he ripped your contract up for all to see the day he came back from Tennessee—made a whole big stink about it, Lucas said. That was the last anyone has heard or seen of him at Calypso Hall. He's a hard man to pin down. I could, obviously, work my contact with Arya, but what's the point? I wanted to talk to him about some of my up-and-coming actresses, and I'm pretty sure that bridge is burned."

I don't feel half as guilty as I should be about this piece of information. In fact, I'm more concerned with his public display of scorn for me. Ripping my contract in front of an audience? It is so different from the man I grew to know back in New York. The indifferent, aloof creature. He seemed like the kind of man who wouldn't take anything seriously. He must really hate me.

"Please don't make that face." Chrissy sighs. "I wish I hadn't told you. Who cares what he thinks, anyway? It's not like he owns Broadway. And he's a well-known asshole in town, anyway. No one's gonna judge you for bailing on him."

I let out a half-strangled laugh, just because I know she is expecting some type of reaction. But deep down, I want to weep.

CHAPTER
TWENTY-EIGHT

A R S È N E

"Maybe he's dead."

I hear Riggs's voice before I feel something—a stick?—poking the side of my neck. I'm tempted to grab the thing and snap it, but then think better of it. If I ignore them long enough, they might leave me alone.

"He's not dead," Christian says with conviction. "That'd be too convenient for us. No. He is going to drag out this existential crisis until my son is college bound and you run out of places to visit in the world."

The astronomy book I've been reading slips from my chest to the ground. I keep my eyes shut. It was Riggs's and Christian's idea to whisk me to an exclusive compound in Cabo like I'm a goddamn socialite they want to woo. No part of me understands the plan. First of all, I am perfectly okay. Second, even if I wasn't, a sunny villa is the last place you'd catch me in voluntarily. Third, and to top all that, I have work to tend to back home. This is a nuisance. Not a luxury vacation.

"How long has he been lying here like this?" Riggs asks.

"Two hours, maybe more?" Christian replies. "Oh, hell, maybe he *is* dead. Let's just leave him here and go back to the compound. If he's dead, we'll come back to find his body medium well."

I hear them gather their belongings, and after a few minutes of silence, when I conclude the coast is clear, I open my eyes.

I'm immediately met with two pairs of eyes staring back at me. I sit upright, letting out a roar. "What's the matter with you, idiots?"

"He's alive! *Alive!*" Riggs turns his palms heavenward, à la Frankenstein. "And can I just say—only slightly better looking than a reanimated corpse."

I pick up the book I dropped and shove it into my duffel. We're sitting by an edgeless pool that's built on a cliff, right above the Pacific Ocean. The rocky formations, including the famous arch of Los Cabos, are sprawled in front of us, basking in magnificent shades of pinks and yellows as the sun sets. This place is on the edge of perfection, and yet the world never looked as flawed as it has these days.

"We're leaving tomorrow night." Riggs falls on the edge of the lounge chair I'm occupying. "And you still haven't told us what makes you pout like a cakeless birthday girl."

"Actually, we know exactly why he's being a cakeless birthday girl." Christian takes the seat opposite to us, and this feels a lot like an intervention.

Passing my gaze between them, I shrug, refusing to budge.

"You're in love," Christian announces, point blank. "You haven't been able to think of anything else, to date anyone else, to do things worth doing. You need to tell her what you're feeling."

"Am I supposed to wait for her to answer? Because dead people aren't known for timely correspondence," I reply with utter indifference.

"I'm not talking about Grace," Christian says almost softly.

"Me either," I say easily, standing up and hoisting my duffel over my shoulder. "I'm talking about Winnifred Ashcroft, who is very much dead to me after what she did to Calypso Hall."

"You give zero shits about Calypso Hall." Christian is at my heel, refusing to pass on the opportunity for confrontation. Riggs is another story. He lingers behind, after his gaze landed on a pretty woman in a hot-pink bikini on the other side of the pool. "You choose to be mad at her because anger is a great distractor. So useful for masking love. It's the oldest trick in the book."

"I can't fall in love." My slides slap against the hot floor noisily as I take the stairs to our compound. "Always been incapable of it. The closest feeling I have to it is obsession, and the last time I was obsessed with a woman, it ended badly."

Understatement of the goddamn century.

I stop in front of our metal door, punch in the code to open it, and walk into the cool, monstrous complex.

Christian grabs my shoulder and turns me around violently. My duffel bag drops. I stare at him, unsure if I should punch him in the face or be glad someone actually gives a shit.

"Look, I've seen you these last few months. You're not you. You were more you when Grace *died*, for crying out loud. At least then, you made a conscious effort to be a part of the world. Or at least pretend you were. Winnie took away with her your entire lust for life. And there wasn't a lot of it to begin with. Cabo wasn't my idea for an elaborate bachelor's party. It was a last-ditch effort to get you to clear your mind and hopefully see that you might be missing out on something here—"

"On what?" I bark out, tired of this nonsense. "What, exactly, am I missing out on, O wise one?" I laugh in his face, pushing him away. "News flash: Grace cheated on me with Paul, Winnifred's husband. They had an affair. That was the thing that glued us together. Our mutual heartbreak and disappointment. I'm not one to kiss and tell, but I will in this instance, only because I know this'll never leave this room—Winnifred and I slept together. We connected. It felt good. It also felt like revenge. No part of her wants anything to do with me. And even if she did want me, as I said—I don't do love. Only obsession, and she, unfortunately, deserves more."

I turn around, making my way up the carved stairway.

"You fool!" Christian runs to the bottom stair and grips the banisters tightly. "You goddamn idiot! Do you know how to differentiate between love and obsession?"

I halt midstep, mildly curious. I've never paid attention to those pesky things before. *Feelings.*

"When you love someone, you generally do the right thing for them." I hear Christian's voice from the bottom of the stairs. "Even if it's not the right thing for *you*. You never left Grace alone, did you? Even though you knew you guys were toxic for each other. You played with her like a worm on a hook. But look at you now. You're a coward. You're so scared of fucking up this thing with Winnie you won't even start it. Instead, you'll sit and mope around and pretend everything is all right. Drown yourself in more work. More alcohol. More meaningless events. Buy more assets you don't need. More stock you'll never sell. Take more risks. Don't you get it? You'll never get that same high that comes with kissing the one you love. Only one thing will give you that high—stop being a coward."

◆ ◆ ◆

When I get home, the first thing I do is check the mail. It is futile. Winnifred has not contacted me for months, not since we left things off sourly in Mulberry Creek. There's nothing in the mail but invitations to events, charity balls, and conferences. I drop everything in a heap on the dining table and proceed into the shower.

My phone buzzes with an incoming call when I get out. With the towel still wrapped around my waist, I swipe the screen. *Arya.*

What could she possibly want? Normally, I wouldn't care enough to pick up. But now, seeing as there might be a chance she is still in touch with my disappointment of an employee, there's a reason for me to hear her out.

"I knew you'd answer." She sounds cocky.

Translation: I know you're hoping for crumbs of information on Winnifred.

"You're a genius, Arya. How can I help you?"

Making my way back to my bedroom, I choose a nice suit and a smart tie. No reason to sit around and sulk tonight. Christian is right. Life needs to move on, and I intend on taking up one of the many invitations sitting on my dining table.

"Oh, I don't know if you can help me, but I know I can sure help *you.*"

I put her on speaker and button my dress shirt.

"You sound like a salesperson who's about to screw me over. Just say what you want to say."

"I just got off the phone with Winnie. I called her to catch up, as I do every week."

"And?" I ask casually, my heart already beating faster.

"And she told me she took a job in Mulberry Creek. She's staying there, Arsène."

A rush of nausea takes over me. I ignore it. *It's fine. It was never meant to be.*

"Good for her," I say, my mouth sour with bile. "I hope she's happy in Mulberry Creek, because she has nothing to look forward to in New York when it comes to employment."

"Arsène," Arya reproaches. "Go talk to her. Seriously."

"I thought you told me to stay away from her."

"That was before!"

"Before you got a brain implant?"

"*I can hear you. You're on speaker,*" Christian bellows in the background.

"Before I realized that you *care*." Arya sniffs.

I press my lips together. I want to scream.

"I don't care any more about her than I do any other successful employee who helped me make money," I insist. "Now I ask that you and your nosy husband keep out of my business. Winnifred Ashcroft means nothing to me."

I hang up.

I go out. A dinner party two blocks down from my apartment. I mingle. I flirt. I discuss work. I even contemplate taking someone home. Riggs, Christian, and Arya are wrong. I *am* having fun. Even if I don't remember the name of the host or what the fuck we're celebrating here.

"Hey, Arsène." I turn around after dessert, in the drawing room, to find a man I faintly recognize as Chip, Grace's boss from Silver Arrow Capital. Draped on his arm is a woman who is not his wife, and he is not even a little embarrassed by this fact. I smile ruefully. Hedge fund management is great for your pockets and disastrous for your morals.

"I thought it might be you." He claps my shoulder.

Chip. Chip who kept Paul and Grace's secret. Chip who knew. Chip who ignored Winnifred for months when she begged for answers. Chip, Chip, Chip.

Turning around completely, I decide to play his game. "Chuck, right?"

"Chip."

"Right. I remember, from Italy." I snap my fingers, then turn to his companion. "Mrs. Chip, my sincerest apologies, I didn't catch your name in Italy. What was it again?"

The woman has the decency to look mortified. She untangles herself from the man and introduces herself as Piper. She is a good-looking thing. In an obvious, sorority-girl way. Tightly woven blonde curls, nice rack, and a smile I bet cost her parents a small fortune but got her through a few beauty pageants. Chip ignores the very deliberate blow on my part.

"Saw you on the *Post*'s fifteen top hedge fund managers list. Why are you not expanding your company? A lone wolf is weaker in front of a pack," he says.

"That's okay. I'm no wolf. I'm a motherfucking tiger."

"Still." He laughs, shifting uneasily.

"You just said you saw my name in the *Post*. I didn't see yours. Perhaps I should be the one handing out unsolicited advice."

Chip's face falls. "Am I missing something, Corbin? Have I done something to upset you?"

Other than keeping the affair between Paul and Grace a secret, nothing much. I'm not even upset about that part. But the way he and Pablo treated Winnifred after the fact still grinds my gears. She didn't deserve any of this.

"Nothing at all." I smile.

"Because . . ." He hesitates before glancing sideways and dropping his voice. "I always had an inkling, but never a concrete idea of what was happening. You must know, Corbin, we have a strict no-fraternization policy at Silver Arrow Capital. Sure, Paul and Grace seemed close, but never beyond what I considered normal."

Seeing as he is giving me this little speech with a woman who could pass for his daughter draped on his arm, I'm going to go ahead and file this in my big-pile-of-bullshit folder.

When I don't answer for a whole excruciating minute, letting him know I'm not buying what he is selling, Piper shifts and turns to me. "Would you mind giving me a ride home?"

"Not at all." I smile cordially at Chip before turning my back to him. "I'll wait for you at the door."

Ten minutes later, Piper and I are in my car. She gives me her address—she lives all the way over in Brooklyn—and apologizes for the long journey.

"You're fine," I say tersely. It's not like there's anything waiting for me at home. Every minute away is a minute I'm not tempted to call Winnifred.

"Or . . ." Piper bites down on her lower lip, glancing my way in the passenger seat. "We can just go over to yours, and I can catch the train in the morning? It'll save you the trouble."

I'm not sure if Piper knows who I am and what I'm worth, or if she is just looking for a good time, but I don't care either way. She'll be a delightful way to get my mind off Winnifred. I haven't been with a woman since Bumpkin, and this could be one of the reasons why I keep thinking about her so much.

Yes. That's just it. I'm so used to being consumed by the woman I sleep with, and Winnifred is nothing but an extension of my fascination with Grace. Piper is just what the doctor ordered. She'll be *manageable*, as my dad and Miranda liked to say.

"We could. Though I should be clear—I'm not looking for a serious relationship. My fiancée passed away a year ago, and I'm not ready to commit to anything beyond tonight."

I slow the car, giving her a chance to tell me she changed her mind and to take her home. I'm indifferent either way. But Piper squares her shoulders, nods, and says, "One night's fine by me. I'm on the rebound, anyway. This Chip guy . . . he didn't tell me he was married." She sighs and then adds, "Oh, and I'm really sorry about your loss."

We get to my apartment, and Piper, after gasping out loud at the sight of my living room, asks me where the bathroom is. I point her in the direction.

"Can I get you anything? Water? Coffee? Wine?" A taxi back home? *Wait, where did that come from?*

She shakes her head and smiles. "I'll be right back. Don't go anywhere."

Ah, yes. Because there's nothing I want more than to get out of here and leave a complete stranger in my apartment.

While I wait, I walk over to the dining table, where I disposed of all my mail earlier. The stack of ultrasound pictures and the USB Winnifred sent me all those months ago are still there. I plug the USB into my laptop and sit down. Double-click on one of the videos of my mother and me and rub my temples.

God dammit.

The loss that slams into me is a two-fold one.

First, I feel the pain of not knowing my mother. Not spending time with her. Of living the last three decades thinking she was nothing but a self-centered narcissist when, in fact, she adored and loved me more than Douglas ever did.

And then there is Winnifred. Who thought it was important for me to see these clips. Who made sure I'd have these memories.

I go through the videos, one after the other.

It is possible Christian is right. That I am, in fact, in love with Winnifred.

That what I have for her isn't obsession. Which is exactly why I keep my distance. I am poison, and she deserves better.

Shit. I'm in love, aren't I? How pitiful. And with Bumpkin, no less.

Piper comes out of the bathroom, yanking her minidress down her thighs with a giggle.

"Ready when you are," she announces.

I look up from my laptop, close the screen, and sigh. "Sorry, Piper, but I think I'll take you home. I can't give you what you're asking for tonight."

CHAPTER TWENTY-NINE

Winnie

Romeo and Juliet is a smashing success.

Ma, Dad, Lizzy, Georgie, Rhys, and my friends all arrive to show their support. My students *nail* it, every single part of the play, and hope gathers in the bottom of my belly.

Sure, it's not what I grew up dreaming I'd do. The scent of the worn stage floor, the bright lights in my eyes, the waiting glances—these are the things I live for, but directing is close enough to acting. And it's fun working with kids. I don't regret taking the job offer from my old high school to run the theater club.

Not when Whitney, who plays Juliet, gives her final monologue on stage, and I repeat the words, transfixed, my lips shaping out her words soundlessly.

Not when Jarrett, who plays Romeo, drinks the poison, and tears almost run down my cheeks.

Not when the audience gives the kids a standing ovation.

When the curtains fall.

When I think about a certain man who lives states away from here, and the fact that he is obsessed with Mars almost as much as I'm obsessed with Bowie's "Space Oddity," and isn't that a coincidence?

No. I don't regret taking the job at all. Because even if there is life on Mars . . . there's not one for me in New York.

◆　◆　◆

Two weeks after *Romeo and Juliet*, I cave in to Rhys's requests, and we go out. This time, it's a date-*date*. Rhys knocks on my door, a bouquet of flowers in his hand. I peek at him from my bedroom as Georgie leans one hip against the front door, slurping iced tea.

"My dad's out for today, so consider me the designated worried parent. What are your intentions with our Winnie, Rhys Hartnett?"

"Dine her, kiss her, and down the line wed her," he replies without missing a beat.

Georgie tips her head back and laughs. "My God, Rhys. Still cheesy as a chicken parmesan."

I emerge from the bedroom. Funny, I don't feel the usual butterflies that accompany a date. I chalk it up to Rhys being Rhys. *My* Rhys. My safety net. Not everything needs to be electric and exciting. A relationship can also be stable and comfort—. *Nope, not gonna say that word. Not even in my head.*

I gather the roses into my hands. "Thanks for these."

"Well, I got them for your momma, but since I see your parents aren't here . . ." He winks. "I'll just have to give them to the most beautiful woman in Tennessee."

We get into his car and drive south to Nashville. I don't ask where we're going. I'm guessing it's an Italian restaurant named Bella where we had our first date.

Turns out I'm not wrong. An hour later, we *are* in Bella, and we're even being seated at the same table.

When the waitress arrives to take our order, Rhys and I glance at each other from over the rim of our menus and share a conspiratorial grin.

"I'll have the meatballs," I say.

"Calzone for me, and the best wine on the menu." Rhys hands her our menus back. We both ordered exactly what we did the first time we were here, minus the wine. And the time after that.

"We used to come here every anniversary and order the same thing, remember?" Rhys turns his attention to me, taking a sip of his wine.

I nod. "It became such a thing for us I was almost superstitious about it. Even when I wanted to order other things on the menu, it seemed wrong. Because what we had worked so well."

I'm not just talking about Italian food right now.

Rhys reaches across the table and takes my palm into his over the red-and-white-checked tablecloth. "I like how this place works. I like that the menu, the tablecloth, the staff doesn't change, and neither do we."

I've changed, I think. *I've changed a lot. That's the problem.*

"And just think." Rhys looks around himself, at the brick walls, at the candlelit tables, at the giant pizza trays splayed on tables. "We can come here next anniversary, say, after we're engaged. And then again, when you are pregnant. Year after year. Baby after baby. We'll bring our kids here. Our . . . our grandkids!" His eyes light up animatedly. "This could be our thing. A tradition. That's why I brought you here." He stares at me with eyes so fierce, so hopeful, I want to cry. "To remind you what we had was good, and real, and worth it. We can still get it back, if you're willing to try."

Instead of feeling giddy, all I feel is dread. I've done this before. I've seen this movie. And I'm starting to suspect there was more to the breakup with Rhys than my Juilliard dream.

"I don't know," I admit quietly. My hand slips from under his, just as the waitress approaches to refill our wineglasses. I tuck my hands between my thighs, looking down. When she leaves, I continue. "There is a part of me that wanted to give us a second chance ever since Paul died. I think, in a way, you always symbolized to me the qualities a good man should have. I know you'd never cheat on me, never lie to me, never put yourself before anyone else. And those things are still true . . ." I suck in a deep breath. "But Rhys, you are wrong. We have changed. I got a taste of the big city, and now I'm addicted. I went after my dream . . . and you went after yours."

I look around myself, realizing that Rhys never wanted the life I wished for myself. He's always been happy here. And why shouldn't he be?

"And these lives of ours." I lift my eyes to look at him, and his expression makes my heart break. He knows what's coming, and he is bracing himself for it. Every muscle in his face taut. "They're not meant to be together. I realize that now, in this restaurant. I don't want to know where I'll be next year. Or in five years. Or in a decade. I want to go where my job takes me. I want life to surprise me. It might not be the most rational thing in the world . . . but it's what I want."

He swallows, about to say something, when the waitress interrupts us again, this time bringing our dishes. I look down at my meatballs, and all I can think is that I should've ordered pizza. And that says it all. Things don't feel right with Rhys. Maybe they hadn't for a while, even before I left Mulberry Creek.

Just because a man is perfect doesn't mean he is perfect for *you*.

Rhys turns his plate around a few different ways, rearranging it on the table as he clears his throat. "Can I be honest with you?"

"Always."

"I had a feeling." He breaks the edge of the calzone, where it's all crusty bread, and pops it into his mouth. I know this is not a you-can't-break-up-with-me-because-I'm-breaking-up-with-you scheme, because it's not Rhys's style. "At first, when you came back, I was excited. I used to think—or maybe hope?—that the acting bug was just a phase. That you would grow up and realize your place in the world is here. But even though you've done some pretty awesome healing here, I'm not gonna lie, you don't look happy. And I've seen you happy. Something is missing, and that something isn't Paul. I know, because I've seen videos of you on YouTube when you were performing in *The Seagull*. You looked alive on that stage. You look less alive now. And the truth is . . ." He smiles sadly. "I deserve more than an unhappy, unaccomplished girlfriend who'd always wonder what could have been. And you deserve more than settling for a job you didn't want in the first place."

Like magnets, we both stand up from our seats, fumbling away from the table, and crash into a hug. My face is buried in his shoulder. I whimper, and for the first time in over a year, I feel like I'm on the verge of crying. I don't know what devastates me more. The fact that Rhys is not my one, or the fact that I know who is.

A man who is never going to have me.

An enigma who has love only for his dead fiancée.

The day after my date with Rhys, I wake up to an empty house. With Georgie at work and my parents gone for the weekend for a wedding, I decide to tidy up the place. Afterward, I pay a visit to Mrs. E, an elderly neighbor. I promised I would drive her downtown for a book club meeting. We stop beforehand to enjoy a key lime pie and some tea and catch up.

When I pull my parents' car in front of my porch, an odd vision comes alive in front of me. Of a man standing in front of my door, his silhouette tall, imposing, and dark—so dark I can feel the temperature dropping around him—holding a bouquet of flowers. I kill the engine and sit back, glaring at the unbelievable sight in front of me.

I can't see his face, because he has his back to me, but I can see the flowers, and they're not the romantic red roses Rhys brought over yesterday. No. They're gorgeous and colorful and surprising. Red dahlias and purple orchids and pink tulips and yellow gazanias. Pale lilacs and orange marigolds and beautiful daisies. It is rich and dazzling and giant and *messy*. So messy. It takes my breath away, just like the man who is holding it.

My pulse quickens under my skin, and my stomach dips. I draw in a breath, the oxygen hitting the bottom of my lungs. I push the driver's door open and make my way toward him, up the stairway to the front porch. He turns around when he sees me through the reflection of the screen-and-glass door, his face betraying nothing.

I stop in front of him. I want to fling my arms around his neck and hug him, but I don't know what's appropriate and what's not. I don't know what we are to each other. He is the kind of man who never shows you where you stand with him.

"You're . . . here." I blink, still wondering if it's all a dream.

A dream or a nightmare? Can you put your heart on the line again?

He hands me the flowers, completely at ease, like the last time he was here didn't end up in a third world war.

"For you."

"That's . . . a lot of flowers," I observe.

"One for each facet of your personality," he remarks dryly. "I've yet to determine whether you're too sweet or too assertive."

"You didn't sue me." I narrow my eyes at him.

"Yeah, well, I thought it would be a terrible inconvenience if I ever decided to date you."

"If *you* decided to date *me*?" I arch an eyebrow, grinning. This is *not* how one asks a woman on a date. At the same time, every cell in my body blossoms. I'm so excited, there's a real possibility I am about to throw up on his shoes. Which I absolutely cannot afford to replace, seeing as I've yet to start my new job and am still paying the bills on a vacant apartment in Manhattan. "Last I heard, you shredded my contract in front of an audience at Calypso Hall. Not exactly the stuff love declarations are made of."

He strolls over to one of the rocking chairs on the porch and takes a seat, crossing his legs at the ankles on the table. "Come on, Winnifred, it's unlike you to hold a grudge."

"It's unlike you to care so much about an employee." I remain standing, folding my arms over my chest. "Why're you here?"

He looks up at me, and the mocking scorn is gone. I don't think I've ever seen his face so naked.

"You know why Mars was named after the god of war?" he muses, squinting up at the sky. "It's because it has two moons called Deimos and Phobos. The two horses that pull the god of war's chariot. For me, those horses are my friends, Riggs and Christian. They have an annoying habit of talking sense into me."

"Are you impaired?" I squint. "I just asked you why you're here."

"I'll tell you exactly why I'm here. But first, sit." He pats the chair beside himself. "And tell me all about your new life in Mulberry Creek. Spare no detail."

It is a bizarre situation, but then again, everything about my interactions with Arsène is usually on the weird side. I think that's what drew me to him in the first place. The delicious feeling of never knowing what I'm going to get from him next.

I sit beside him, worming my fingers together to keep myself from rubbing at my chin.

"Tell me." He leans forward, elbows on his knees. "What have you been up to?"

The words pour out of me without warning. Without heed. Like I've been saving them all for him. I tell him about my sisters, about Lizzy's new baby, about my volunteer work, and *Romeo and Juliet*, and my upcoming job. I try to sound upbeat, still unsure about his motives and not wanting to look desperate for him.

He said he *might* decide to date me, not that he has any intention of ever asking me out. And even if he does want to date me—should I want to date him? He is a million times more dangerous than Paul was. More sophisticated, quick tongued, and ruthless. If losing Paul broke me into pieces, losing Arsène would shatter me into dust.

Last but not least, Arsène lives in New York. As of now, I live in Tennessee and have made a commitment to a job that's due to start in three weeks. That's plenty of reason to keep my cards close to the chest.

"And Lizzy's baby, Arsène. Oh, she is a little doll. Too squishy for words!" I gasp.

"Speaking of Lizzy's baby." He sits back in his recliner. "Have you seen the doctor to discuss your future procreation options?"

"That's one of the first things I did when I got here," I confirm.

"And?"

"I was right," I say quietly, staring down at my hands in my lap. "It is endometriosis. An outgrowth of tissue around my uterus. Mine's at a moderate stage, also known as stage three out of four. It's not a complete disaster, but it's going to make my journey toward motherhood a lot more difficult." I haven't spoken about the diagnosis with anyone other than my doctor. It surprises me that I open up to Arsène so easily when I haven't had this conversation with Ma or my sisters yet.

"What's the next stage?" he asks.

"Well." I gnaw at my lower lip. "My doctor says I should freeze my eggs. Or, better yet, embryos. They last longer and have a better success rate."

"But . . . ?" He searches my face, leaning forward. He is doing that thing again where his body is in complete sync with mine. It reminds me that having sex with him is a euphoric experience. The back of my neck tingles, and my palms get sweaty.

I decide to go for broke and just tell him the God's-honest truth.

"I still need to think about it. It's very expensive, and I can't afford it. Not *all* of it, anyway. Especially now, when I don't have Paul's . . . er . . ."

"Sperm," Arsène finishes for me, standing up abruptly, businesslike. "Well, I'll give you both."

I peer at him through my lashes, confused. "What do you mean?"

"You need money and sperm. I'll give you both. I will do that for you," he says decisively.

"But . . . why?"

He opens his mouth to answer. I hear a car door slam in front of my porch, and the sound of it being locked automatically. Arsène's mouth shuts into a tight-lipped scowl. I stand up and peek at the person making their way up the stairs to the porch, and my heart sinks.

Talk about worst timing ever.

"Hi, Rhys." I hope I sound friendly and not murderous. It's not Rhys's fault I was in the middle of the most important conversation of my life. "What're you doing here?"

Rhys eyes Arsène with surprise and dissatisfaction, lifting my cardigan in the air between us. "You forgot this in my car yesterday. I'd have given it to you earlier, but practice ran late."

My eyes snap to Arsène. I can see he's done the math, that he gathers Rhys is my ex-boyfriend. The very one who got away. Arsène plasters a cocksure smirk on his face and sits back like a bored king, a sign his hackles are on the rise.

"Er, thank you. Rhys, this is Arsène. Arsène, this is Rhys."

They shake hands, with Arsène not even bothering to stand up.

"An old friend?" my ex asks politely.

"God, no. I can't befriend women I want to fuck." Arsène laughs, deliberately crass. "No, I'm here to make Winnifred an illicit proposition."

Rhys's face pales, and his eyes bulge out. *Christ.*

"Well, thank you so much for the cardigan! You know I run cold. Ha ha." I place a hand on his arm, ushering him back to his car. I am all but kicking him out, and I don't feel good about it. On the other hand, I think I might die if Arsène and I don't finish our conversation soon. My ex-boyfriend stumbles his way toward his car, glancing behind his shoulder.

"Who's this guy, Winnie? He sounds like Satan's big brother."

"Don't worry about him," I singsong. "He's surprisingly tolerable once you get to know him."

"I don't know." Rhys stops in front of his Jeep but doesn't make a move to enter. "I feel like I should stay here, make sure you're okay."

"I can handle this on my own." I smile tightly.

Please, please leave.

"But . . ."

"My goodness!" I throw my hands in the air, losing patience. "I know you mean well, but please, Rhys, just let me handle this. I'm a big girl, and I've been doing my thing for over a decade without your help."

I finally get it. It all comes rushing back to me now, at an incredible speed. The reason why I left here. Not all of it was Juilliard. Some of it was the suffocating feeling of being coddled by everyone, including—but not limited to—Rhys.

While it is true that he always meant well, he also frequently overstepped. He had defended me tooth and nail in front of Mrs. Piascki, our physics teacher, when I'd failed her class in tenth grade, which made her hate me for the rest of my high school years. When Georgie and I had gotten into arguments, he'd always plead my case and beg her to talk to me, when I simply wanted to be left alone. And whenever I'd gotten upset with him, which wasn't often, he'd chalk it up to me being bored or on my period.

I didn't like it then.

I don't like it now.

Rhys stares at me in horror. "No one said you can't handle yourself."

"No, you didn't say it, but you keep thinking it. Otherwise, you wouldn't be acting this way."

This makes him shut up. He presses his lips together, shooting his gaze to where Arsène is waiting on my porch.

"I guess you're right. I'm sorry, Winnie. Sometimes I just . . . I don't know. I get carried away when I care about people."

"I'm fine." I wrap my arms around him and squeeze, reassuring him that I'm not mad at him. "I'll call you tomorrow, okay?"

He slides into his car and—thank heavens—drives away. I return to Arsène, who is waiting for me on the porch with his usual amused smile, like this is all a big fat joke to him. Only now I'm onto him. He isn't amused. And he *does* care. This is just his defense mechanism when dealing with people.

"I see your tearful reunion with perfect Rhys is going well," he remarks.

I roll my eyes, falling back into the rocking chair beside him. "I like you much better when you aren't being sarcastic."

He tilts his head skyward, letting out a sigh. "Then there's no chance for me. Better grab my things and head back home."

"Stop this," I snap. "Say what you came here to say. We were in the middle of something."

"Right." He taps his knee. "Where were we?"

"I believe you were about to offer to be the father of my hypothetical children and pay for the entire delight."

"Children?" His eyebrows shoot up. "I thought you wanted just the one."

I shake my head. "Three. And I will need a surrogate to carry them. Which also costs a pretty penny. Still interested?"

I'm not seriously considering this, and neither is he. This is just one of his many games. I'm sure of it.

"I'm still interested," he says flatly. Dang him and his weird sense of humor.

I give him a lopsided smile. "We can go around in circles forever, but I wanna know why you're really here. With flowers."

Do you really want to ask me out? Am I really about to abandon everything I ran away from and say yes?

"I just told you," he says, slowly and with distinctive irritation. "I came here to ask you out, but also, if you wish, to give you babies. What's so hard to understand?"

"Well"—I let out an awkward laugh—"that usually exists only after you've had a few good years of the other. You're acting like you want to give me babies *now*."

"There's no better time than the present," he informs me gravely.

I cover my face with my hands, laughing hysterically, to the point of hiccups. "Arsène, do you mean for me to take this seriously? We've known each other properly for less than a year."

"Time is not a good indicator for anything. I'd known Grace since before she could tie her shoelaces properly, and she let me down. You can't convince me this isn't a good idea, because I've already made up my mind, and I never make bad investments."

I'm speechless, so I just stare at him, waiting for more. A few months ago, this man yelled at me that I was nothing but an employee of his, threatened me, then proceeded to destroy my contract publicly. When he came here the first time, he made no sign that indicated he wanted anything more than to wring my neck. Where is this all coming from? And am I really so lucky—or unlucky, depending on how you look at it—that the man I fell for fell for me too?

"This is just all so . . . sudden?" I manage, finally.

"For fuck's sake, Winnifred!" He stands up, flinging his arms in the air, exasperated. "Don't tell me this is coming out of left field. My need to be near you and next to you at all times had stopped being about Grace and started being about you very, *very* early on. Since you ran out of the New Amsterdam after knocking poor Cory to the ground."

"You acted like I was a peasant back there." I stare at him, confused.

"That's because to me, you were. So what? You were also the most infuriating, entertaining, sweet, fascinating creature I'd ever laid eyes on. Those two things are not mutually exclusive. It was never really about them. Grace and Paul—so help me God, I'm tired of saying their names over and over again. They were an excuse. Something to fall back on every time you questioned why I was in your sphere, in your line of sight, every time I wanted into your rehearsals and your apartment and your bed. It hasn't been about them since I walked into that theater and saw you." He stops, frowning now, mulling it over. "Maybe even since Italy. Who knows? Not me, and I don't care to find out. I'm completely consumed by you, and the last few months have been hell on earth trying to forget you."

"But Grace—"

"What I had for Grace doesn't even begin to scratch the surface of how I feel about you. You're the only woman who's ever made me feel worthy without the armor of estates, money, and pedigree. You don't care about any of those things. And it makes you special. You're the exact opposite of Grace."

My mind is running five hundred miles a minute. It's going to take me a month, maybe two, to digest this entire conversation. I don't even know where to begin.

"Then why did you insist on not kissing me at your apartment, the night you held me?" I finally find my voice, and it is choked. Tears prickle the backs of my eyeballs, never making their way out. "Why did you want to walk away the night we got into Paul's office?"

"Because it was too much." He starts pacing across my porch, murmuring, more to himself than to me. "I knew that if I had you, I would never let you go, and not letting you go wasn't an option, because you were still hopelessly in love with Paul. I didn't want to insert myself into another disastrous situation, of becoming obsessed with a woman who could never be mine. Once was enough. More than recommended, actually."

He stops. Stares at me helplessly. "I *am* Mars, and there might be life on it. There could be. Thanks to you. I burn for you, Winnifred. And I'm tired of living in the cold. Come back to New York. Make the place livable. For both of us. *Please.*"

I'm tempted. Oh, I'm so very tempted. But I'm still not sure if it's the right thing to do. To leave everything behind again and go back to the place where every awful memory of mine was created. And there's another part of me. A more apprehensive part that thinks of me as Nina. Chekhov's Nina. And if I'm Nina, he must be Trigorin. A master of turning love into an unhealthy obsession like he did with his fiancée. He would try to ruin me without even meaning to—and he'd succeed.

"What are you thinking about?" he asks urgently. I stand up, and he gathers me in his arms.

I close my eyes. "I want to believe every word that comes out of your mouth, because I've been in love with you from that moment in Italy when our eyes met and the world ceased to exist. But I'm afraid I'm another obsession. Another great idea that could turn into a lackluster reality for you. I don't want to change my entire life and move back to New York for another man. You may burn for me, but I'm terrified of getting burned."

When I open my eyes, his face is still tender and hopeful. I want to say yes. But ultimately, and especially after what Paul put me through when we were trying to get pregnant, I have to put myself first. Ask all the right questions. And I'm not sure what they are yet.

"I'm not going to let you down," he says quietly. "Try me."

"I need time." I'm proud of myself. Proud of my ability to put myself first for a change. Even if I'm frustrated with the idea of saying goodbye again.

This is the part where I expect him to close up on me. To become indifferent, aloof, but he surprises me by placing a kiss on my forehead—a gentle brush of a feather—before he steps away.

"I'll be waiting."

"I might never come back." I look up, searching his face for . . . something. I don't know what. But he is done convincing me. I can see this on his face. He said his piece, and now the ball's in my court.

He smiles, tucking a lock of my hair behind my ear, and kisses the tip of my nose. "I'll *still* be waiting."

"Don't I have a deadline?" I ask.

He shakes his head, grinning. "I feel strongly that you could do with some unconditional love, and that's exactly what I'm going to offer you, Winnifred."

CHAPTER THIRTY

ARSÈNE

The interesting thing about saying hello is that you have no idea how hard it'll be to say goodbye to that same person.

When I first met Winnifred under the unforgiving Mediterranean sun, I thought of her as somewhat of a toy. Now, as I sit on a plane to take me from Nashville back to New York, I realize that she was the endgame.

She has been everything from that very first moment, right there, in that restaurant, when she challenged me. When she ridiculed me right back. When she refused to fit into the stereotype I'd attached to her.

There's a good chance I will never see her again. I came here to say what I had to say, and now it is her decision to make.

All I'm left with is the hope that she'll remember what brought us together.

Because it was never them—it was us.

And while it is true that I am a conceited, manipulative, highly serpentine man, I am also a person of many angles.

And angles, as we know, are everything in life.

This is why the sunset on Mars appears to be blue.

CHAPTER
THIRTY-ONE

"Winnie and Arnie sitting in a tree. K-I-S-S-I-N . . ."

I punch my sister's arm before letting my head fall back between my arms at the kitchen table. Ma and Dad are still away, and Georgie is practically glowing, sitting beside me, slurping her iced coffee.

"Don't be so sad. This is a good thing." She flips through a glossy magazine on the table, her perfectly manicured nails halting each time she sees an ad for something she likes. "I never saw you like this with Paul. Everything about him was *so* vanilla." She raises her gaze to make sure she has my full attention. "You were kind of existing on autopilot. For a while, I wondered what Paul had done to my sister and her sass. But now I see that it's back. Who knew all you needed was a gorgeous, tall billionaire from the city who shows up at your doorstep with spontaneous love declarations?"

"I did love Paul," I protest.

"No, you loved the *idea* of Paul. You loved what he was offering you. The cute, happy family and white picket fence. And to be the wife of a man who is more than the son of a random rancher in Tennessee."

"That's very shallow," I point out. "And untrue."

"Because people usually start dating each other for altruistic, philosophical reasons?" She arches an eyebrow. "Please. People are attracted to others because of superficial things. To pretend otherwise is to insult both our intelligence. At least what you have with Arnie seems to be a little more earnest than that."

"It's Arsène."

"Arson?" She gasps. "I wouldn't go that far. I mean, he seems a little toxic, but not enough to raise alarm bells."

"Be serious." I take a sip of my coffee, engulfing the mug between my fingers to warm up. "I don't know if I can do this, Georgie. Go back to New York. Take a chance. After everything that's happened."

"Please, Jesus called. He needs his cross back." Georgie slams her magazine shut. "Can we please skip this part? We both know you're going. You'd be crazy not to go. You love that man."

"But he is offering me exactly what Paul did. And look how my previous relationship ended."

Of course, I relayed everything that happened to Georgie. All the bad stuff. The *Grace* stuff.

My sister stands up and rounds my chair. She places both her hands on my shoulders and digs her thumbs into my sore muscles in a massage. "Heartbreak is a terrible reason not to give love a second chance. It's like swearing off food because of food poisoning. Or . . . or . . . I don't know! Like avoiding ice cream because you don't like one flavor. Love has so much more to offer than heartbreak. It's hope. It's butterflies. It's wisdom. It's family and shelter. Peace and babies."

I clutch one of her hands over my shoulder, letting out a shaky breath.

"I may not be able to have children. He says he doesn't mind, but what if he does? What if he will, Georgie?"

She freezes for a moment. She's been circling this subject for a while now, trying to get more information. I, on my end, never gave her an answer. Too afraid I'd break down if I open the subject. Not anymore. Now it's all out in the open.

Georgie regroups. She clears her throat and returns to massaging my shoulders. "What if the sky falls? What if a meteor strikes us tomorrow? What if a war breaks out between us and Canada? I know, they're nice, but can we truly trust people who buy their milk in bags? I've seen somethin' about it on the news. It's a thing, Winnie. And it's real."

"Thanks for the detour." I look up at her, grinning.

"It's not just a detour, hon. I mean it. Maybe you won't be able to have kids. But that could be said about every single woman out there who isn't currently pregnant. And as far as I know, men don't ask for fertility proof from the doctor before popping the question. Life, by definition, is a gamble. You win some, you lose some. The important thing is—always lose with a victorious smile."

But I think it is more than that. In this game of life, the really important part is not who wins or who loses. It is that you and your partner have the same goal. The same endgame.

Ever since Arsène left yesterday, I couldn't sleep, couldn't eat, couldn't even breathe properly. All I did was think about him and his offer. An offer I cannot refuse, even if it means putting my heart on the line again.

"But . . . what do I do?" I rub my cheek. "Do I just show up at his place?"

"I mean . . ." Georgie pushes away from me and grabs her iced coffee. "A phone call would be anticlimactic, considering the circumstances. Especially as he's come here twice now. That's a Hugh Grant–level gesture right there."

"You don't even like Hugh Grant." I frown. "You once said he was an inarticulate fool."

"I like what he represents, okay?" Georgie rolls her eyes, sucking hard on her straw. "Now go pack a bag. This room ain't big enough for both of us."

My body stands up of its own accord, and I'm moving toward our bedroom, in a weird, unbreakable trance.

It is time to hit Arsène with a truth stick. Even if I'll have to admit said truth to myself first.

CHAPTER

THIRTY-TWO

WINNIE

New York is cool and splendid in a dozen shades of gray and blue as I cab it from LaGuardia Airport into the city.

Fall has conquered every inch of Manhattan. The trees are naked, tall, the branches curling into themselves, shriveling from the frost.

My first stop is my apartment. *My* apartment, not Paul's. I stand and stare at it for a few minutes, hands balled over my hips, taking inventory one last time.

Then I grab all the junk mail from my mailbox, open a trash bag, and throw everything inside.

Possessed by energy I haven't had in forever, I proceed to my fridge, throw it open, and yank out all Paul's yogurts. His pickle jar. His favorite smoothies. Moon cakes. All gone. I shove my sleeves up my elbows and scrub the fridge clean. The residue of expired food assaults my nostrils, sour and lingering. I don't stop until it's spotless, laughing soundlessly when I remember how I'd given up on using the fridge so I wouldn't have to deal with the stench of the food.

Then I move on to the rolled newspapers I kept for him.

He is not coming back. Even if he did, in another life, in another universe—he can buy his own darn newspaper. The only news flash he needs is this: he was a bastard who tried to kiss my sister and impregnated another woman while we were married.

All the papers go to recycling. I have to make three separate trips downstairs before they're all gone, but it's worth it.

Next, I throw Paul's office door open. All his files go into the shredder. His computer, his monitors, I pack up to be donated to a charity. I don't want any proof of the fact this man ever lived here. Because he didn't. Not really.

It takes me six hours to get the apartment in order and completely Paul-less. By the time I'm done, I'm exhausted. I drag myself into the shower and let the scorching water hit my skin. When I get out, I choose a nice dress and put some makeup on.

I'm just putting my lipstick back into my makeup bag when the doorbell rings. I smile at the mirror, knowing who it is, and walk briskly down the hallway. The place is spotless. Clean, tidy, and completely me. It smells of the cinnamon-and-vanilla candle I lit up earlier, a scent Paul never liked—cinnamon made him nauseous—and open the door.

Arya stands on the other side of it, holding Louie, who is not so tiny anymore.

I immediately reach to take him from her, and he gurgles happily, nestled in my arms. The weight of him is delicious, and I laugh when he shoves his chubby fingers into my mouth.

"Louie, keep your hands to yourself." Arya tugs her scarf free and flings it over my couch. "I have a feeling I'll need to say those words a lot, considering his daddy's success with the ladies before we got together."

"Come on in." I laugh, stepping aside so she can enter.

When she walks inside, I realize she isn't alone. Chrissy is here, too, marching with her signature fat-burning-tea tumbler and electric cigarette in hand.

"I thought you were in Los Angeles with your boyfriend." I snatch her into a quick hug before she escapes.

"Oh, I was." She waves me off, plopping onto the couch. "But then Arya told me you were coming back, and I couldn't help myself. Especially when I heard the *reason* for your arrival. Now, look at this place. It's almost as though Paul's never lived here!"

The three of us look around in amazement while Louie wiggles, trying to break free and roam the place.

"It was time," I say.

"I'm really proud of you." Arya gathers me into a squeeze. "For all you did today, and all you're about to do. Now, hand me my bundle of booger, please. I have something I need to give you."

I hand Louie back to her, albeit reluctantly, then open my palm between us as she fishes for the thing I asked for in her purse.

"Are you sure Christian is not going to mind? About you giving this to me, I mean?" I ask. It's a violation of privacy and possession.

Arya lets out a laugh. "Oh, he'll mind. I'll never hear the end of it. But can he really be mad at me for long? I don't think so. Besides, once he understands what's at stake, he'll be delighted. Trust me." She curls my fingers around the key. "The doorman's name is Alfred. If he gives you trouble, tell him to call me."

And just like that, I have the key to Arsène's apartment.

Now all I need is to unlock his heart.

Of course I wanted Arsène to be home when I arrived in New York. But as soon as I landed and called Arya to let her know I'd arrived, she told me that Arsène mentioned to Christian that he'd be in London until late tonight to sign off on an agreement selling Calypso Hall.

A pinch of sorrow squeezed at my belly. Calypso Hall is in need of some TLC, and it's true it wasn't always a thriving establishment, but it holds so much charm. There's beauty to it. Something I cannot put my finger on. And besides, it belonged to his mother. To Patrice. His very last piece of her. The *real* her.

But I do want to be here, waiting for him, when he arrives back from London. Mainly because I remember him once saying that no one's ever waited at home for him. He was always a lone star, moving in the dark, vast universe.

Using the key Arya gave me, I push the door to his apartment open. A rush of pleasure floods me. It smells just like him. That unique Arsène scent that makes my knees weak.

His apartment looks exactly the same way it did the last time I was here.

Glancing at my phone, I realize I have a few more hours to burn until he arrives. I decide to give myself a tour of the place. Arsène never did, and seeing as last time we parted ways he told me he wanted me, I find it hard to believe he'd take issue with it.

First, I go back to the guest room where he held me. The linen is pressed, and the room is neatly organized. Like I've never been there. I don't know what I was expecting . . . for the bed to be unmade, the way we'd left it? This is not Arsène's style. I amble through the hallway. Walk into the bathroom. Open the cabinets, my ears heating at my own brazenness. All he has there are Band-Aids, Tylenol, and some TUMS.

When I reach his bedroom, I halt. My hand is on the doorknob. There's an irrational part of me that's afraid I'm going to find him there with someone else. Why, I don't know. It is obvious he is not here. Arya told me he went to meet a pompous colleague of his who went to Andrew Dexter Academy with him.

But ever since Paul . . .

No. Screw Paul. You've moved on. You're not going to let what happened in the past dictate your future anymore.

I shove the door open. The second I do, all the oxygen leaves my lungs.

Because it is here.

Full size and hung on his wall. Where the TV should be. Right in front of his bed. And it's just as magnificent as I remember it to be.

The Seagull's poster.

The huge one that got magically "lost" all those months ago. With the close-up of my face.

It was Arsène who took it. Who *stole* it. Who then tampered with the cameras and took the damning footage of himself seizing the thing.

My face stares back at me. I look tranquil . . . maybe even a little dreamy.

But it can't be here. It can't be him. The poster was taken so early in our relationship—or whatever that was that started between us.

This is . . . how?

His words from the last time I saw him, on my porch, haunt me now.

My need to be near you and next to you at all times had stopped being about Grace and started being about you very, very early. Since you ran out of the New Amsterdam after knocking poor Cory to the ground.

He wasn't lying. He really did like me from the get-go.

I walk over to the poster and plaster one hand against my printed face. Something wet and weird caresses my cheek. I reach with my hand to wipe it, examining the tip of my finger to find a perfectly round, see-through, salty tear staring back at me.

I'm crying.

I'm crying!

I'm no longer cursed or numb or incapable of fully feeling.

The waterworks start right away. Loud, childish wails rip from my chest and through my mouth. I cry for the entire year that I couldn't.

Cry for Paul's death. For what he did to me. For Grace. For what she did to Arsène. For losing my role of Nina. For gaining perspective. For Rhys. For Arsène, for hiding for decades behind a wall of erudition and wit.

Most of all, I cry for myself. But shockingly, these are not tears of despair or self-pity, but of relief.

I feel courageous. Stronger than I've ever been. And so incredibly hopeful.

I've been through hell and walked through fire, only to come out the other side of it, scarred and bruised, but stronger than ever.

I burn for you, he said. And I'm ready to burn right back for him.

I fall into Arsène's bed and cry and cry and cry for hours.

Cry until I fall asleep in the comfort of the scent of the man I love.

CHAPTER THIRTY-THREE

ARSÈNE

My phone is blowing up when I'm in the Uber on my way back to my apartment from the airport.

Christian: Something happened when I was away.

Arsène: I'm not helping you bury any bodies.

Christian: You think I'd ask you for something like that via text message? You think I'm that dumb?

Arsène: Don't ask questions you're not prepared to hear the answer for. What happened?

Christian: Arya took the spare keys for your apartment.

Arsène: I'm flattered, but she is not my type.

Christian: Winnie asked her for them, YOU MORON.

I will my heart to stop beating like a sledgehammer, but to no avail. The thought that Winnifred is in my apartment right now makes my pulse go haywire. I don't even bother answering Christian. Just check the traffic app on my phone, which alerts me that, as usual, there's a traffic jam from hell on my street.

I tap my foot against the car's floor. Would it be an overreaction to bribe every single asshole in front of us to pull over and let us through?

When we get about five blocks from my apartment building, I tell the driver to stop and throw a wad of cash at him.

"You're gonna walk the rest of the way?" he asks, surprised. "A little dangerous in the middle of the night . . ."

But I'm already out, running like a maniac. When I get to my building, the door to the stairway is locked. I swear, kick a trash can, and call the elevator. The wait takes forever. So does the ride up to my apartment. Then I get inside, and my living room is completely empty. Winnifred-free.

I scan the kitchen and living area, then move swiftly to my bedroom, where I find her sprawled on my bed, fast asleep. The view of her like this, alone, takes my breath away.

Torn between my need to wake her up and talk to her and her need to sleep off her exhaustion, the latter wins, and I crawl into bed, wrap my arms around her, bury my nose in her strawberry hair.

There's no way I'm going to fall asleep. The adrenaline pumping in my veins alone can keep me awake well into next year. But just holding her is enough. After a few minutes of us lying still, I feel her stirring in my arms. A soft moan escapes her lips, and her hands circle around mine, pressing me harder against her.

"Hey, Mars?" she murmurs. "Tell me something interesting about the universe."

I close my eyes, smiling into her hair. "There's a planet made of diamonds. It is twice the size of planet Earth and is covered by graphite and diamonds."

And, if given a chance, I would give you a ring with a diamond even bigger. If you say yes.

But, of course, Bumpkin is not Grace. She doesn't care for expensive jewelry.

"I bet it's beautiful," she whispers. Shivers roll down my skin, and I kiss the side of her ear.

"Not as beautiful as you."

She laces her fingers through mine and drags my hand up her chest. Her heart is beating like a drum, each thump thrusting into my palm. *Mine.*

She is not wearing a bra, and her nipple pebbles through her dress. My thumb massages her nipple soothingly, and my mouth clasps over the curve of her neck and shoulder. My cock is engorged, aching for her. She rolls on top of me and straddles my hips, staring down at me with unabashed hunger, and I cannot believe I've ever fucked a woman who wasn't her. A person who didn't look at me the way she does now. Like I'm her entire world. Her moon, her stars, the Milky Way, and the galaxies around it.

"Missed you, Bumpkin." I let loose a vicious smile. She leans forward and shuts me up with a dirty kiss.

Blood roars in my veins. I unbuckle while she hikes up her dress. I tug her panties sideways and slide into her. She rides me, slow and tauntingly, our gaze never breaking.

"I thought you never allow women into your bed." She bites my neck and rolls her hips, meeting me halfway, like she knows my body like the palm of her hand.

"What did you want me to say?" I groan out, my pleasure so acute I can barely breathe. "Sorry, you can't get into my bedroom because I stole a giant poster of you from your workplace. PS, please don't file a restraining order against me?"

"Why'd you do that?"

"Become your stalker?" I thrust into her, staring deep into her eyes. I'm trying to concentrate on the conversation so I don't blow my load after five minutes. "It was premeditated, believe it or not."

She reaches to kiss me. "No. Take the poster."

"So I'd always feel close to you."

This pleases her, and she picks up the pace while I tug at the front of her dress, freeing those magnificent breasts. I pull her down by holding one button between my fingers, then suck on one of her nipples hungrily.

Her head drops to my shoulder. "Arsène."

"Winnie."

She stops. For a moment, I think something's happened. She straightens her back, though I'm still inside her. I feel my pulse in my balls. My cock would scream if it could.

"What?" I ask.

"You called me Winnie."

I smile. "It's your name."

"You never call me by my nickname. Other than that one time, you've only called me Winnifred or Bumpkin."

In one swift movement, I flip her over on her back, pinning her underneath me, doing all of this without withdrawing from her once. I kiss the tip of her nose.

"That's because everyone calls you that, and I always wanted you to remember me."

She strokes my cheek. "There wasn't one moment in time since Italy that I haven't remembered you."

I pound into her. The sound of skin slapping skin fills the air. It is brutal. It is hungry. It's nothing like I'm used to. We're in our own little bubble. I never want to leave.

She gasps, digging her nails into my back, like she is about to fall apart. I thrust into her, harder still, faster, almost manically. Because I have no guarantee that I will see her tomorrow. No one promised me this is hello and not a goodbye. We haven't spoken yet, and the sense of urgency is seizing each of my bones in a choke hold.

"I'm coming, I'm coming," she pants.

She arches beneath me, spasms around my cock, and suddenly, she feels hotter—much hotter—and my balls tighten as I come inside her.

When I collapse on top of her, we're both sweaty and wasted. Two bags of useless limbs. So human, so mortal, it is almost laughable that what we shared right now was divine. When I pull away a little to give her some space—crushing to death the woman I love is not on my agenda—she looks confused and childlike.

"You okay?" I ask.

She presses her lips together. "That really depends on how our next conversation is going to go."

❖ ❖ ❖

After we take a shower together, we dress to the sound of the city waking up. Winnifred leans against the poster I stole of her, her arms pressed behind the small of her back. She is staring at me as I get dressed. It's a small gesture, but I'm not used to being observed. I decide I like it.

"What if we can never have babies?" she blurts out into the room. The question echoes between the walls.

"Then we'll never have babies." I roll a sock up my foot. "Why must there be an *if* about it. Since when do babies determine the strength of a relationship, or lack of?"

"We may *never* be able to have biological babies." Her eyes are shining in the blue-pinkish hue of dawn, like two diamonds. She is thinking about Paul. She is thinking about the disappointment, the pain, the betrayal. She is worried about history repeating itself.

"You mean, we'll be able to spend our time traveling all over the world, making memories, living the high life, and fucking twenty-four seven? I'll try to bear the burden of such a scenario." I stand up, but I don't make a move toward her. Not yet.

"Oh, be serious." She stomps her foot on my granite floor.

"I *am* serious." I smirk. "I don't care if we never have children. Quote me on that."

"Then again, we might have lots of children. Three, maybe four!" she says heatedly. "I like babies. I *love* children. And if we can adopt, I'd definitely want to. How would you feel about that?"

"Exhausted, I assume." I dig my heels into the plush rug under the bed, making a point that nothing she says is going to make me run for the hills. "And excited. The house will always be full. I will never be bored. I do prefer children to full-size people, as a general rule. They've yet to surrender every part of their individuality in order to fit in, and they view the world through a fascinating prism."

What I don't say is that I'd love a do-over. A real family. A place of my own. That I think Winnifred will make an amazing mother—like Patrice—and that I want to see her have everything her heart desires.

She takes a deep breath. Closes her eyes. Her walls are breaking. I can feel them tumbling down, brick by brick.

"We both had such toxic relationships," she whispers, eyes still closed.

"Yes. And we've learned so much from them. This feels different. Grown up. Fully ripe. It feels like I dismantled something unsteady and built it back together, but better."

She opens her eyes and licks her lips. "I'm sorry I bailed on *The Seagull*. It was wrong of me—"

"I don't give half a shit about *The Seagull*," I cut her off. "It was never about the play. Never about your commitment to it. Always about us."

She digs her teeth into her lower lip, considering this. "Yeah. I guess so. You couldn't wait to get rid of Calypso Hall, could you? How was London, by the way?"

I smile. *This* is what she wants to talk about right now? Classic Winnie.

"Beautiful. Cold. Gray. The restaurant was fantastic." I pause for a moment. "But I couldn't do it. Calypso Hall is still mine."

She tilts her head sideways, staring at me funny. "It is?"

"Yes."

"Why?"

"Well . . ." I take a step toward her. Check the temperature. She is standing still, not inviting me to come closer but not withdrawing from me either. "I did pour five hundred thousand into renovations and a complete refurbishment just a few weeks ago. They're due to start working on it after *The Seagull* finishes."

She cups her mouth, her eyes flaring. "You didn't!" She stomps, so full of joy I can't help but tip my head back and laugh.

"Did too."

"But . . . why?" She shakes her head in disbelief.

"I was going to sell it to Archie Caldwell, an old friend of mine, if you can call him that. He wanted it for his wife, who is moving here and looking for a project to keep her entertained. Then I realized if everything goes according to my plan, maybe *I* will have a wife who would like to keep Calypso Hall for herself too. Besides, turns out I'm one sentimental little shit. My mother loved this theater, and . . . well, I loved her.

"Anyway, I didn't want to make any drastic business moves without consulting you first."

"Me?" She stubs her finger to her chest, raising her eyebrows.

"You." A smile spreads across my lips.

"Your business is yours, not mine." She shakes her head.

I laugh. "What's mine is yours—as long as you're mine. This is the deal. And I *never* make bad deals."

"Why did you fly out to London in the first place?" She frowns, confused.

I wave a hand in her direction. "Archie compared the loss of his wife's beloved dog to the death of Grace, so I wanted to dangle the carrot in his face before I told him personally he'd never have Calypso Hall."

"You're really terrible." She bites down on her lower lip.

I sigh. "I know. Love me, anyway?" I grin hopefully.

When she doesn't say anything, just stares, I walk toward her. "In case I haven't made myself clear thus far, I'm not Paul. I'm not interested in a prenup. Or in a baby machine. Or in a woman who makes cookies for my colleagues. I want a partner. An equal. I want you to be exactly who you are." I take another step, then another. Now I'm flush against her. Her body heat rolls into mine. She is pressed against her poster. The one I went to sleep in front of every night for months, imagining she was next to me. That we shared the same home. "And who you are is who I fell in love with," I finish.

She wraps her arms around my shoulders and rises on her toes to kiss me. I grunt into our kiss, wrapping my arms around her.

"I'm not going anywhere, Arsène Corbin. Whether you like it or not, I will always be your home. I will always wait for you, like the poster. I'm your family now."

I believe her.

EPILOGUE

WINNIE

"I am a seagull."

Only I do not symbolize destruction, the way Treplev demolished the seagull in Chekhov's play.

I represent freedom, and healing, and tranquility.

I once read somewhere that seagulls are one of only a few species on Earth that are able to drink saltwater. How amazing it must be. To defy nature like that.

The theater lights pound over my face hotly as I finish my monologue, Rahim by my side. My feet are firm on the stage, and I know that's where I belong.

And when I deliver my closing line, when the curtains are drawn, when the audience is on its feet, giving us a standing ovation, and I hold my colleagues' hands—my second *family's*, home away from home—I know I made the right choice. That staying in Mulberry Creek was never my calling.

"Can't believe you almost gave all of this up," Rahim whispers in my ear, as if reading my mind.

"Can't believe you didn't run after me to stop me." I squeeze his hand in mine.

He laughs. "There were moments I was tempted to."

Backstage, Ma, Dad, Lizzy, and Georgie are all waiting for me. Georgie jumps on me, knotting her legs around me in a sloth hug, as always. "Oh my God, you don't even suck a little bit. What's the opposite of embarrassed?"

"Proud?" I murmur, squashed to her chest.

"Yes!" she exclaims. "That's how I feel about you right now."

"Georgie!" Ma chides, peeling my sister off me as I laugh breathlessly. "What a terrible thing to say to your sister."

Momma gives me a fierce hug, and I tremble a little in her arms. Lizzy's and Dad's turns are next.

"Y'all can give it to me straight if I need to find a new day job," I say. I don't mean it, though. I could have the acting chops of an expired Twinkie, and I still wouldn't give up this dream of mine. Especially as Lucas was kind enough to give it back to me *before* he found out I'm about to be the owner of Calypso Hall.

I don't like you one bit, Winnie, and I want you to know that. But no one does Nina better than you.

As it turned out, I learned how to like myself in the process, because now my hands are going to be full. I'm also opening a theater class in Brooklyn, free of charge, for at-risk youth.

"You did amazing, honey," Dad says.

"So good I cried three times!" Lizzy bellows.

"You always cry," Georgie points out, side-eyeing her. "You literally cried when they ran out of your favorite peanut butter at the grocery store."

I'm about to turn around and look for the one person I long to see now, but Chrissy and Arya—the latter holding little Louie in her arms—charge toward me from the distance like possessed rugby players.

"It's so good to have you back!" Arya kisses my cheeks.

"*Literally*," Chrissy adds, plucking Louie from Arya's arms and cooing at him. "I thought Lucas was going to commit murder if he didn't find a new, suitable Nina. You know he used to call me five times a day asking if I could bring you back? At one point he suggested we should *sedate* you."

"I'm here, and I'm getting my butt kicked for ditching him." I laugh, stealing a sleepy Louie from her hands, breathing the sweet toddler in.

Lucas has been making me stick around after shows for a daily minitalk, just to assure him I'm not going anywhere. He also changed *The Seagull*'s poster so that the entire cast is featured before me. That's fair. He shouldn't have given me a second chance after what happened in the first place.

"Damn straight. I might forgive you for what you did, but I'll never forget." Lucas materializes out of nowhere, draping an arm over my shoulder.

Craning my neck, I try to see through the forest of people surrounding me.

"Looking for someone?" Chrissy teases. "You look distracted, Win."

She knows exactly who I'm trying to find.

"Where is he? Is he late?" I demand, willing my heart not to beat so fast and hard just at the *thought* of him.

"Never." The coarse, dark voice I know and love rasps behind me. He creeps up to me, kissing my shoulder blade, then bends down and kisses Louie's cheek while he is in my arms. We are the picture of a perfect family.

Arsène and I managed to freeze a few of our embryos but decided to wait until after our wedding to try to have children. We don't have a wedding date just yet, but he did propose, with a beautiful ring that belonged to his late mother. It is an honor to be wearing Patrice's ring, and it will be a greater honor to make this magnificent woman's son happy as his wife.

And if the embryos won't do? Well, there are more ways to create a family, and I'm willing to explore all of them.

My head falls across my fiancé's chest, and he bends down, capturing my mouth with his in a kiss.

"Aw. Gross." I hear Riggs, Arsène's friend, making gagging sounds. "There are literal children here."

"You're not *that* young anymore," Christian, Arya's husband, deadpans. He approaches me, taking Louie from my hands. "You know, just in case your little hello is going to turn into something less than PG-13 friendly."

I turn around to look at my future husband.

"Tell me something out of this world." My lips move over the skin in the hollow of his neck.

"Planets can float through space for eternity without a parent star. They just drift through the galaxy. Astronomers believe they got 'kicked' out of their family system at some point. They're like rebels with a backpack and fifty bucks to their name, but somehow, they survive."

"Well, you won't have to drift anymore." I kiss his chin, his cheek, his nose. "You have a home planet now. You have me."

◆ ◆ ◆

ARSÈNE

"It's not safe," I clip out through clenched jaws. This may very well be the understatement of the century. Winnie and I are standing on the top of the roof of the Corbin mansion. The very same one I sold to Archie Caldwell as a consolation prize for not getting Calypso Hall. I'm glad to get rid of this concrete box of bad memories. Bonus points: the juju in this place is so bad it's not even like I'm doing him a favor.

"Humor me!" Winnie steadies herself on the edge of the rooftop, stretching her arms horizontally.

"It's a little hard when every bone in my body tells me to pounce on you and yank you back to safety," I murmur bitterly. "Just get down from there. We can still make it to the six o'clock show if we leave now."

"I don't want to go to the movies." Winnie makes an adorable face. The one that disarms me to submission. "I want to play a game of tight-rope one last time before you evacuate this place. For old times' sake."

"The old times sucked," I remind her.

"Well, let's make one great memory here before we leave."

I see what she is trying to do, and I appreciate it, I do, but if she hurts herself, I will goddamn lose it.

"Are you timing me?" Winnie whips her head around, watching to see if I'm taking the time. The woman is nuts. Fortunately, she is *my* nutcase.

I'm contemplating my next move when an idea pops into my head.

"I'll time you. But I want to go first."

She tsks. "Ladies first."

I look around myself. "No ladies I can see from here. Let's set the rules: if you win, if you finish before me, I'll give you whatever you want."

She hesitates, then relents. "Fine."

She makes her way across the ledge and props herself against the chimney, then pops her phone out of her pocket. "Ready? I'm timing you."

Placing myself at the center of the edge, I swing my arms in the air, stare ahead, and take a breath. "Ready when you are."

"Go."

I take a lazy step forward. Then, after a few seconds, another one. I'm going to finish walking this tightrope in ten minutes if I can, just to make sure she doesn't rush it. This one, I can't afford to lose.

"Are you kidding me right now?" Winnie laughs behind my back, delighted. "I thought you said you guys were competitive! You're moving at a turtle's pace."

"Time is relative, Bumpkin."

"Don't Bumpkin me! Are you deliberately being slow?"

"Is that how you know me?" I bark out. "I never play to lose."

"Hmm," is all she says, when I'm not even a quarter through my journey to the other chimney. She will have a lifetime to cross her way to safety. A whole goddamn hour, if that's what she needs.

Because there is one thing Winnifred doesn't know about me. Doesn't need to know.

And that is that I will always let her win.

The End

ACKNOWLEDGMENTS

It's true, what they say. The anxiety attached to not forgetting anyone while writing the acknowledgments section never gets easier. This is the part where I try my best. Bear with me.

First of all, to my support group, for everything: Tijuana, Vanessa, Marta, Yamina, Sarah, Jan, Pang, Ratula, Ava, Parker, Amelie, Gel, Nina, Ivy, and Kelsey. Thank you, thank you, and thank you. I am so forever grateful to have you in my life.

To my family, for having my back and for being so understanding.

Huge thanks to the Montlake team for their amazing support and attention to detail. Anh Schluep, Lindsey Faber, Stephanie Chou, Alicia Lea, and Heather Buzila. Thank you so much.

And to my agent, Kimberly Brower, for taking the time and the effort to make this series shine. I really appreciate it from the bottom of my heart.

To the talented cover designer, Caroline Teagle Johnson.

Last but not least, to the readers, bloggers, and TikTokers who make my dreams come true. I thank my lucky stars every day for you.

Before you leave, here is an excerpt of another book of mine, *The Kiss Thief.*

PROLOGUE

What sucked the most was that I, Francesca Rossi, had my entire future locked inside an unremarkable old wooden box.

Since the day I'd been made aware of it—at six years old—I knew that whatever waited for me inside was going to either kill or save me. So it was no wonder that yesterday at dawn, when the sun kissed the sky, I decided to rush fate and open it.

I wasn't supposed to know where my mother kept the key.

I wasn't supposed to know where my father kept the box.

But the thing about sitting at home all day and grooming yourself to death so you could meet your parents' next-to-impossible standards? You have time—in spades.

"Hold still, Francesca, or I'll prick you with the needle," Veronica whined underneath me.

My eyes ran across the yellow note for the hundredth time as my mother's stylist helped me get into my dress as if I was an invalid. I inked the words to memory, locking them in a drawer in my brain no one else had access to.

Excitement blasted through my veins like a jazzy tune, my eyes zinging with determination in the mirror in front of me. I folded the piece of paper with shaky fingers and shoved it into the cleavage under my unlaced corset.

I started pacing in the room again, too animated to stand still, making Mama's hairdresser and stylist bark at me as they chased me around the dressing room comically.

I am Groucho Marx in Duck Soup. *Catch me if you can.*

Veronica tugged at the end of my corset, pulling me back to the mirror as if I were on a leash.

"Hey, ouch." I winced.

"Stand still, I said!"

It was not uncommon for my parents' employees to treat me like a glorified, well-bred poodle. Not that it mattered. I was going to kiss Angelo Bandini tonight. More specifically—I was going to let *him* kiss *me.*

I'd be lying if I said I hadn't thought about kissing Angelo every night since I returned a year ago from the Swiss boarding school my parents threw me in. At nineteen, Arthur and Sofia Rossi had officially decided to introduce me to the Chicagoan society and let me have my pick of a future husband from the hundreds of eligible Italian-American men who were affiliated with The Outfit. Tonight was going to kick-start a chain of events and social calls, but I already knew whom I wanted to marry.

Papa and Mama had informed me that college wasn't in the cards for me. I needed to attend to the task of finding the perfect husband, seeing as I was an only child and the sole heir to the Rossi businesses. Being the first woman in my family to ever earn a degree had been a dream of mine, but I was nowhere near dumb enough to defy them. Our maid, Clara, often said, "You don't need to meet a husband, Frankie. You need to meet your parents' expectations."

She wasn't wrong. I was born into a gilded cage. It was spacious, but locked, nonetheless. Trying to escape it was risking death. I didn't like being a prisoner, but I imagined I'd like it much less than being six feet under. And so I'd never even dared to peek through the bars of my prison and see what was on the other side.

My father, Arthur Rossi, was the head of The Outfit.

The title sounded painfully merciless for a man who'd braided my hair, taught me how to play the piano, and even shed a fierce tear at my London recital when I played the piano in front of an audience of thousands.

Angelo—you guessed it—was the perfect husband in the eyes of my parents. Attractive, well-heeled, and thoroughly moneyed. His family owned every second building on University Village, and most of the properties were used by my father for his many illicit projects.

I'd known Angelo since birth. We watched each other grow the way flowers blossom. Slowly, yet fast at the same time. During luxurious summer vacations and under the strict supervision of our relatives, Made Men—men who had been formally induced as full members of the mafia—and bodyguards.

Angelo had four siblings, two dogs, and a smile that would melt the Italian ice cream in your palm. His father ran the accounting firm that worked with my family, and we both took the same annual Sicilian vacations in Syracuse.

Over the years, I'd watched as Angelo's soft blond curls darkened and were tamed with a trim. How his glittering, ocean-blue eyes became less playful and broodier, hardened by the things his father no doubt had shown and taught him. How his voice had deepened, his Italian accent sharpened, and he began to fill his slender boy-frame with muscles and height and confidence. He became more mysterious and less impulsive, spoke less often, but when he did, his words liquefied my insides.

Falling in love was so tragic. No wonder it made people so sad.

And while I looked at Angelo as if he could melt ice cream, I was the only girl who melted from his constant frown whenever he looked at me.

It made me sick to think that when I went back to my all-girls' Catholic school, he'd gone back to Chicago to hang out and talk and *kiss* other girls. But he'd always made me feel like I was The Girl. He sneaked flowers into my hair, let me sip some of his wine when no one was looking, and laughed with his eyes whenever I spoke. When his younger brothers taunted me, he flicked their ears and warned them off. And every summer, he found a way to steal a moment with me and kiss the tip of my nose.

"Francesca Rossi, you're even prettier than you were last summer."

"You always say that."

"And I always mean it. I'm not in the habit of wasting words."

"Tell me something important, then."

"You, my goddess, will one day be my wife."

I tended to every memory from each summer like it was a sacred garden, guarded it with fenced affection, and watered it until it grew to a fairy-tale-like recollection.

More than anything, I remembered how, each summer, I'd hold my breath until he snuck into my room, or the shop I'd visit, or the tree I'd read a book under. How he began to prolong our "moments" as the years ticked by and we entered adolescence, watching me with open amusement as I tried—and failed—to act like one of the boys when I was so painfully and brutally a girl.

I tucked the note deeper into my bra just as Veronica dug her meaty fingers into my ivory flesh, gathering the corset behind me from both ends and tightening it around my waist.

"To be nineteen and gorgeous again," she bellowed rather dramatically. The silky cream strings strained against one another, and I gasped. Only the royal crust of the Italian Outfit still used stylists and maids to get ready for an event. But as far as my parents were concerned—we were the Windsors. "Remember the days, Alma?"

The hairdresser snorted, pinning my bangs sideways as she completed my wavy chignon updo. "Honey, get off your high horse. You were pretty like a Hallmark card when you were nineteen. Francesca, here, is *The Creation of Adam*. Not the same league. Not even the same ball game."

I felt my skin flare with embarrassment. I had a sense that people enjoyed what they saw when they looked at me, but I was mortified by the idea of beauty. It was powerful yet slippery. A beautifully wrapped gift I was bound to lose one day. I didn't want to open it or ravish in its perks. It would only make parting ways with it more difficult.

The only person I wanted to notice my appearance tonight at the Art Institute of Chicago masquerade was Angelo. The theme of the gala was Gods and Goddesses through the Greek and Roman mythologies. I knew most women would show up as Aphrodite or Venus. Maybe Hera or Rhea, if originality struck them. Not me. I was Nemesis, the goddess of retribution. Angelo had always called me a deity, and tonight, I was going to justify my pet name by showing up as the most powerful goddess of them all.

It may have been silly in the 21st century to want to get married at nineteen in an arranged marriage, but in The Outfit, we all bowed to tradition. Ours happened to belong firmly in the 1800s.

"What was in the note?" Veronica clipped a set of velvety black wings to my back after sliding my dress over my body. It was a strapless gown the color of the clear summer sky with magnificent organza blue scallops. The tulle trailed two feet behind me, pooling like an ocean at my maids' feet. "You know, the one you stuck in your corset for safekeeping." She snickered, sliding golden feather-wing earrings into my ears.

"That"—I smiled dramatically, meeting her gaze in the mirror in front of us, my hand fluttering over my chest where the note rested—"is the beginning of the rest of my life."

ABOUT THE AUTHOR

L.J. Shen is a *USA Today*, *Washington Post*, and Amazon number one best-selling author of contemporary, new adult, and YA romance titles. She likes to write about unapologetic alpha males and the women who bring them to their knees. Her books have been sold in twenty countries and have appeared on some of their bestseller lists. She lives in Florida with her husband, three sons, pets, and eccentric fashion choices and enjoys good wine, bad reality TV shows, and catching sunrays with her lazy cat.